No Man's Land

Arne Weinz

Table of Contents

Copyright

Published by Defiance Press & Publishing, LLC

Bulk orders of this book may be obtained by contacting Defiance Press & Publishing, LLC. www.defiancepress.com.

Defiance Press & Publishing, LLC

281-581-9300

info@defiancepress.com

Previous books by Arne Weinz:

"Perfect Storm" (Part 1 of the Europe Series), Global Village, 2019
"Den snabbaste vägen", Ekerlids, 2013

To Sorina

Möller's Reflection

The mirror's reflection revealed
more than years of brooding.
He saw his face, deformed
by punch after punch,
like a ring wreck
who had lost
every round
throughout his life.

Prologue

The collapse of the welfare system and the economic insolvency of one-third of Sweden's 290 municipalities were deeply alarming. However, it was the escalating crime, marked by frequent shootings and explosions, that finally made Swedes realize their society was cracking and falling apart—though this awakening came far too late.

Not until 2030, when Arabic was elevated to an official language and the Swedish cross flag was removed, did most of the Swedish population grasp what was happening before their eyes—they were losing their own country.

In a desperate bid to curb the violence, politicians opened the doors to family immigration, believing that bringing in imported wives would calm the aggressive immigrant men. The result was a massive increase in both male and female immigrants. The influx of Muslims became unstoppable, and those who understood the situation knew that a civil war was inevitable.

On the night of July 17, 2032, Sweden was plunged into war when the Muslim Brotherhood landed a total of ten thousand elite soldiers in Stockholm, Gothenburg, and Luleå. Simultaneously, hundreds of thousands of battle-ready young men, so-called *God's Warriors,* and *Holy Warriors,* were unleashed across the country. This surprise outbreak of war caused chaos within the completely unprepared Swedish Armed Forces, while Sweden's political leadership was paralyzed as most leading politicians were murdered in their homes.

The war could be entirely blamed on the politicians who naively not only allowed but actively encouraged the mass immigration of Muslims, which quickly destabilized the country and drained its economic resources.

In the background, globalists rigged and financed mass immigration, having realized that Sweden was wide open to a military attack and the destruction of the Swedish nation-state.

Sweden was unique because a single-family controlled half of the media and most of the book publishing. The rest of the media, led by state television, had been infiltrated and, for decades, preached the same message—the alluring illusion of a multicultural society—which tricked Swedes into willingly giving away their country to people who hated and despised them.

The message from the wealthy northern European countries was heeded primarily in the Middle East and Africa. Sweden seemed to be a sanctuary for the world's poor Muslims. To leave no room for doubt, the generous benefits system was advertised in ten languages on embassy websites.

In Sweden, one could live a life of plenty without effort, with rumors of sex offered openly and freely by beautiful, blonde women without even requiring marriage.

From 2014 to 2025, approximately eight thousand Muslims immigrated every month. From 2026 until the outbreak of war in 2032, immigration grew uncontrollably to more than double that number. Very few of these immigrants, nearly ninety percent of whom were young men, came from war zones.

Hundreds of thousands of young men, lacking social control from older relatives and without families to support, became armies of criminal violators who took control of the streets and public squares. But Swedish women – except for older so-called "batik witches" who preferred young toy boys from Afghanistan – were not so easily accessible. On the contrary, they were usually dismissive, except for those who were lured by free drugs and willingly offered their bodies once they had become drug dependent.

The number of rapes skyrocketed, ending the freedom of Swedish women once and for all. Groups of immigrants who robbed, assaulted, degraded, and urinated on their victims made it so that Swedish men could no longer move freely either.

In many schools, the social situation resembled that of heavy prisons, where gang affiliation is a survival strategy and ethnic belonging determines gang membership. Swedish students generally tried to stay out of the way of the dominant and dangerous immigrant gangs, aiming to get through school unharmed. They knew that at any time during their free time, they could encounter gangs from school, so most avoided going outside.

Home entertainment, such as movies and video games, had to suffice during the long winter evenings. Socializing with friends was managed through social media until the outbreak of war in July 2032, when both the Internet and mobile phones were knocked out. New challenges awaited. The fantastical battlefields of computers suddenly materialized and became part of the new reality of civil war.

Led by the universal genius and Military Commander Ahmed Ben Barka, the Muslims quickly took control of significant parts of Sweden. However, in some areas, spontaneously formed free Swedish armies mounted resistance, arming themselves by plundering military armories.

The Swedish Armed Forces were severely battered at the war's outset but still managed to put up some resistance with their limited resources. Since the 1950s, Sweden's military capability had rested on a strong air force. However, the Swedish Air Force was knocked out on the first morning of the war due to successful attacks on the three virtually undefended air bases.

Sweden's artillery, stationed at the regiment A9 in Boden, was destroyed by flooding that caused the water levels in the town of Boden to rise by forty feet after the Muslims blew up the central power plant dams in the mighty Luleå Rivers.

The Swedish Navy avoided more severe damage, except for the critical bases in Berga and Karlskrona, which were bombed to smithereens by Russian bombers. Most of the navy's ships docked at Finnish ports, where they remained for political reasons until the armistice was achieved in the New Year of 2028.

In terms of ground forces, Sweden had remarkably few resources at the outbreak of war, as the country's political leadership had for decades de-prioritized infantry in terms of volume and equipment. The number of trained ground soldiers was far too small to combat the enemy effectively, but those who were present fought bravely in cooperation with the free forces.

The Russian-led liberation of Stockholm on December 26, 2032, gave the Swedes new hope and control over Sweden north of the Göta Canal. Since the armistice in the New Year of 2033, the country has been divided south of the Göta Canal into a Muslim occupation zone in the west and a Russian zone in the east—with the European Highway 4 as the border.

Sweden, or more precisely, the Swedish zone north of the Göta Canal, had since the fall of 2032 been governed by the National Council, where the former Chief of Defence, Daniel Gyllenstierna, took control as Reich Chancellor. The Swedish exile government formed in Helsinki in the fall of 2032 became obsolete and disappeared from the scene for good when its leader, Margot Wallfors, was murdered by an unknown assailant. Instead, the newly crowned King Carl Philip Bernadotte, with the regal name Carl VII Philip, became a national symbol under which the Swedes could unite and find inspiration.

As the war in Sweden continued, Western Europe was shaken by marching Muslims. What happened in Sweden was just the beginning of a more extensive process. The most severely affected was Germany, which was on the brink of open civil war.

Chapter 1 – No Man's Land

Walpurgis Night 2014

The social democracy was embedded in Jöns Möller's DNA. He was a true social democrat and had always assumed he would be that for the rest of his life. But that was before circumstances and his strict moral code forced him out of the party.

Möller was a relentless truth-teller who never allowed issues to be swept under the rug. He had no respect for tactical maneuvering, which was also why his political career ended abruptly at that meeting in Malmö City Hall on Walpurgis Night in 2014. Möller wasn't for compromising. If he wasn't valued for who he was, so be it. That meeting led to a break with social democracy—though he wasn't even sure whether social democracy severed ties with him or vice versa.

The Möller family had long been an integral part of the vibrant and ever-growing organism, also known as the city of Malmö. Back in the day, most members of the Möller family lived in the part of town called Lugnet. The men worked at Kockums Mekaniska, the proud shipyard headquartered in Malmö. They worked in the foundry or the large workshop, with ten-hour workdays, six days a week. Before they married, the women worked as maids for wealthy families in the city's patrician apartments and palatial villas in the exclusive suburb of Limhamn.

When the low, single-story clay brick houses were condemned due to poor sanitary conditions, Möller's parents moved from Lugnet to a small apartment in another part of town called Sorgenfri. A few years later, they relocated to a two-room flat near Davidhallstorg. Here, Möller grew up with his two sisters, knowing every nook and cranny of the area around the square.

Möller's strong connection to social democracy was reinforced by his ability to boast of his distant relation to Per Albin Hansson, who came from Kulladal, just a few miles from Lugnet. Per Albin Hansson, often referred to simply as Per Albin, was the leader of the Social Democratic Party for nineteen years and served as Sweden's prime minister for fourteen years. However, his connection to Per Albin was relatively distant.

Gustav Möller, on the other hand—the minister of social affairs who lost the power struggle to succeed Per Albin to Tage Erlander in 1946—was Jöns Möller's great-grandfather. What Jöns Möller was less inclined to discuss was that there was at least one – closer related –

Möller, who had veered off the straight path. His cousin, Thorstein Möller, was the Swedish leader of the Swedish Hells Angels and a well-known and feared figure throughout Malmö. Möller recalled how, on that Walpurgis Night nineteen years ago, he entered his childhood friend Anders Skenfors' new office at Malmö City Hall. As fifteen-year-olds, both had joined the Swedish Social Democratic Youth League, SSU, which was the obvious choice for a Möller, and Skenfors had followed his friend out of habit.

Just as the two childhood friends settled around the small conference table, the security guard from the reception called to inform them that Morgan Olofsson and Mona Wahlbin had arrived. As Skenfors took the elevator to greet his visitors, Möller looked around Skenfors' new office. The four-module space, with room for a substantial desk and a conference table with six chairs, indicated that his friend had risen significantly in Malmö's social democratic hierarchy.

On the wall, Skenfors had a series of twelve framed black-and-white photographs from a visit by the former Swedish Prime Minister and Social Democrat Olof Palme—commonly known as "OP." On a pedestal beneath the photographs burned a white pillar candle. The thick wax candle stood on a round plate atop a piece of granite. Möller immediately recognized that the gray granite piece was a miniature of Olof Palme's gravestone. Just like the original, Palme's signature was engraved in the center of the stone.

Möller often took the short walk from the party headquarters on Sveavägen 68 in Stockholm to Adolf Fredrik's Cemetery, where the revered and esteemed icon rested. He doubted that the disreputable addict, Christer Pettersson, could have suddenly decided to murder Sweden's Prime Minister Olof Palme. Given the mishandling of the murder investigation, it was easy to suspect it had been deliberately sabotaged. Perhaps the murder was a conspiracy involving Palme haters in high societal positions, of which there were many. Regardless of who the murderer was, the Social Democratic Party, even twenty-nine years after Palme's death, remained in the shadow of the radical reformer.

Möller surmised that the photographs on Skenfors' wall were from a 1970s election campaign. Palme appeared youthful, vibrant, and joyous, almost glowing with an otherworldly aura. He exuded confidence unique to true aristocrats, never apologizing for his provocative, occasionally offensive, and often unjust comments. Those who challenged Palme soon learned that stepping aside was the wisest course.

The young aristocrat had charisma like a Hollywood star. Judging by the pictures, OP had an intense inner life, manifesting in expressions and poses that included every part of his body. Möller had never seen a speaker so adept at switching between bombastic speeches and seductive charm. Back and forth, countless times.

Even Palme's feet seemed to express his feelings. Two photographs zoomed in on his shiny black shoes in various positions. Like the Rat Catcher of Hamelin, he was a natural speaker who captivated his audience. As prime minister, he achieved great things with his persuasive charm. He seemed capable of making a statue smile and nodded in agreement—especially when he brought sacks of gold from Swedish taxpayers on his trips to impoverished countries worldwide.

The man who founded the Social Democratic Workers' Party in Malmö in 1889 was a tailor's apprentice named August Palm. Palm and Palme, Möller thought: the names were strikingly similar. Still, it was impossible to find two people born under more different circumstances— the proletarian upstart versus the aristocratic rich man. The poor boy who began working at ten, having grown up without a father, stood in stark contrast to the privileged youth sent to an elite private school in Sigtuna, near Stockholm, where even the king was a student. Yet, despite their different backgrounds, Palme and Palm possessed a remarkable gift for oratory and shared a profound calling to champion the cause of the poor and oppressed."

"Yes, you know, Jöns, OP is my hero... yes, really so," Skenfors blurted in his almost demonstratively coarse Skåne dialect as he entered the room with party leader Mona Wahlbin and Höganäs native Morgan Olofsson. "I worship him so much. I've been contemplating setting up a little altar here under the pictures. I can never get enough of him, and it would just feel great to kneel here before Olof."

Möller looked at Skenfors' face to make sure he was serious, which seemed to be the case. Of course, OP was one of the movement's icons, but still. He glanced at Mona Wahlbin, who was a well-known Palme devotee. She seemed pleased.

"Well, Morgan, don't just stand there. Please, take a seat," Skenfors said, gesturing sweepingly toward the conference chairs.

Morgan Olofsson, barely reaching above Skenfors' navel, stood in stark contrast to his colleague. While Skenfors' dark, voluminous hair highlighted Olofsson's thinning blond locks and more petite frame, their physical differences were inconsequential. Despite their contrasting appearances, they forged a solid and enduring partnership, navigating successes and challenges together.

Behind their backs, the jesters from their own and rival parties dubbed them "The Lighthouse" and "The Trailer." Yet The Trailer steered The Lighthouse, driven by a clear and unyielding ambition that set him apart.

Morgan Olofsson came from a humble background, just like Skenfors and Möller. All three had fathers who worked as wage laborers in small industries and construction companies and mothers who worked at the bottom of the office hierarchy within municipalities and county councils. They felt a strong sense of solidarity through their shared experiences growing up in the working class of Skåne.

The four people in the room knew each other from all the summer SSU camps at the Bommersvik conference site, where they had crossed paths several times during their teenage years. Morgan Olofsson stood out a bit, as he had a degree in Political Science from Lund University. Olofsson was plotting a political career at the national level, but he wasn't keen on sharing that with any local party colleagues. He had no desire to be seen as a traitor.

Mona Wahlbin was also a product of the SSU. Still, she had the added distinction of having her father serve as a policy advisor to Ingvar Carlsson, who became prime minister after the assassination of Olof Palme in 1986. The Wahlbins were one of the many family dynasties in the movement, where high positions seemed to be inherited. Joining the

SSU early was a reliable career path, often leading to a lifelong seat at the table where the decisions were made. "Who you know is more important than what you know," as Mona Wahlbin used to say.

Wahlbin was just an unsophisticated Stockholm girl, a tart who spoke and dressed like any kindergarten teacher. Yet, she had risen to the top. Her down-to-earth style was the key to her success in an era that favored emotional and populist media statements over knowledge and education. She had a keen sense of what was timely, was street-smart, and quick-witted. Above all, she knew how to leverage her status as a woman in an era that celebrated feminism in all its forms, both extreme and moderate.

Mona had many mentors in the party—benevolent father figures who had lifted her from one level to the next. When Mona flashed her sweet smile, batted her long eyelashes, and spoke like their teenage daughters, she made the old, powerful men's eyes well up with emotion. It was a crazy time. The media gave left-wing feminists a platform to express virtually any absurdity.

The left-liberal press and state television had long provided a stage for unabashed and unchecked misogyny. On these platforms, left-wing women openly disparaged white, middle-aged men, blaming them for all the ills and dangers of the world. Male politicians, aware that criticizing the rampant feminism could spell political and media disaster, endured in silence, nervously observing the escalating tide of extreme norm criticism. No one dared oppose the Social Democratic Women's Association, which had declared it was time for a female prime minister.

The result of all these converging forces and trends was that what should have been unthinkable had happened: Mona Wahlbin had been elected party leader and chair of the party's actual power center—the Executive Committee. It was practically a given that the Social Democrats would soon regain governmental power, which meant that Wahlbin would become Sweden's first female prime minister.

On Walpurgis Night 2014, the four social democrats were gathered in Malmö City Hall to fine-tune the first of May speech that Wahlbin would give at Malmö Folkets Park. The structure and a few catchy anti-conservative clichés and "take-from-the-rich-and-give-to-the-poor" formulations were already in place in the draft from Wahlbin's speechwriter, which had been shared with the meeting participants in advance.

However, the conversation had primarily turned to a topic that definitely would not be addressed in Wahlbin's speech: the issue of how the ever-increasing Muslim presence was affecting the lives of Malmö residents.

"I firmly believe in a multicultural society," said Wahlbin. "The party has invested all its credibility in this issue, so we can't back from this now."

"Yes, that idea is the foundation of everything we do here in Malmö," Skenfors agreed, nodding towards Mona. "Malmö's future lies in multiculturalism."

"But I see with my own eyes what's happening, so to speak, on the ground," Möller countered. "In practice, it does not play out so well. Muslims are building their parallel structures. They're building their mosques, opening halal food stores, and sitting in cafés smoking water pipes. Moreover, they're contributing to most of the crime here in Malmö."

"That sounds like pure racism," interjected Morgan Olofsson. "And that's something our party doesn't want to be associated with. That's for the Sweden Democrats to handle. I agree with Mona. The party has invested its credibility in multiculturalism, and we cannot waver on this. I think, contrary to what you say, Jöns, that we should accept many more Muslim immigrants, both here in Malmö and across the country."

"Yes, but there must be some limit on the number. Malmö needs people who work, follow the laws, and pay their taxes punctually."

"That sounds like xenophobia," Wahlbin snapped irritably. "One might think you represent another party, and you know which one I mean."

"There must always be room for humanism," said Morgan Olofsson, looking pleadingly at Möller and with his innocent, light blue eyes at Wahlbin. "Many of those who come to seek our protection have had tough lives. Sweden should continue to be a moral and humanitarian superpower."

Morgan Olofsson had a way of looking like a cute, cuddly puppy, which could disarm just about anyone. Morgan came across perfectly on

TV, and the party needed people who spoke about humanism and compassion to justify mass immigration.

Mona Wahlbin had started preparing for her time as prime minister, and in her dreams, she was already distributing ministerial posts. She needed people who could think in structures and foresee things before they happened. She was astute enough not to rate her analytical skills overly—she had picked up that some party members occasionally snickered, "Mona always has bad luck when she thinks."

But she trusted her political instincts and manipulative abilities. Thinking and analyzing could be done by others. Her role was that of communicator—and power player. She needed people like Morgan Olofsson.

"Many of them truly need our help—they come from difficult circumstances. They're fleeing from war and persecution. Many are homosexuals risking the death penalty in their home countries," Olofsson continued, fully aware of what the powerful Wahlbin wanted to hear.

"It's our humanitarian principles, according to the UN Declaration of Human Rights, that set us apart from the Sweden Democrats," said Wahlbin. "Tomorrow, the main theme of my speech will be equality for all people. That and anti-racism."

Möller sighed deeply and took a new breath. He felt himself starting to lose his composure.

"That's just lofty, politically correct mumbo-jumbo with no bearing on the ground level. I see and hear what's happening every day around me."

"Exactly what is happening?" Skenfors asked sharply. "Tell us so we know!"

"It's shootings, murders, and bombings—things even you should have noticed. Our kids are getting robbed down to their underwear and beaten up, and they're afraid to go to school. Our girls are being raped by immigrant gangs and beaten up on top of that—that's what's happening here in Malmö. My little girl told me she's been called a whore so often that she doesn't even react to it anymore. Is this how it should be in Skåne, do you think?"

Möller took a breath and continued his verbal and emotional outburst before anyone could interrupt him.

"Teachers are being beaten by their students. Immigrant gangs are breaking into stores and taking what they want without paying. Daily."

Mona Wahlbin leaned back and stared coldly at Möller before speaking.

"The Sweden Democrats are Nazis, and we must constantly remind people of this so their racist ideas don't gain traction among ordinary people. Multiculturalism, anti-racism, and more anti-racism—that's our message to the voters. And feminism, of course."

"It's not racism to emphasize the importance of law and order. It's not racism to point out economic realities. We need to stop accusing all critics of racism."

"As a good social democrat, you must support our views, Jöns. Otherwise, I suggest you start looking for another party to join."

"Me? Not a good social democrat? Now I'm getting furious," Möller roared. "My family has been social democrats ever since my great-great-grandfather founded this party, together with August Palm. My great-grandfather's brother was Gustav Möller, the social affairs minister under Per Albin. But now it feels like the party is just pandering to Muslims to get their votes."

"A Muslim vote is as good as any other."

"But it can't be right to feed anti-democratic and anti-Swedish forces just to get their votes. Social democrats should uphold a higher moral standard than that."

"That's pure Islamophobia, and that's your opinion, Jöns," said Morgan Olofsson, turning to Mona before continuing. "That's not how the rest of us experience the collaboration. I recently spoke at the Muslim Federation's annual meeting and received cheers and applause. I think they are wonderful people. Very wonderful. I see them as cultural enrichers."

"Saudi Arabia, Kuwait, and Qatar have set up special funds for investments in Sweden, and we need to ensure that as much as possible goes to Malmö," continued Wahlbin. "If we support their organizations with taxpayer money and give them land for their mosques, they will invest large sums here."

"We'll also get a couple of hundred million for the campaign through intermediaries. That's good money to help us win the election."

Möller shook his head and sighed.

"Don't you understand that they're just exploiting us? We're nothing but useful idiots for the Muslims."

"That's not the case at all," Wahlbin countered. "We've had a very close collaboration for over a decade, and it's long-term. The Muslim population is increasing, and with their votes, we can secure government power for the long term."

"But what about the financial consequences? Malmö City is running a deficit of several billion per year, and the shortfall is due to the costs of handling all the immigrants. More immigrants will only lead to larger deficits, and we won't be able to manage that."

"Stop, stop, stop," Skenfors interjected. "Hold on! It seems like you're not familiar with the municipal tax equalization system. The system automatically covers the deficit in Malmö City, so it's not a problem."

"Yes, but someone still must cover the costs that come into our account. It can't be right to let others finance us in Malmö. Good social democrats take responsibility!"

"We're taking full responsibility," Skenfors replied. "Malmö-Lund is going to become a multicultural million-city, which is in the interest of all of Sweden. In the long run, we'll surpass the capital in both population and economy. Örestad will become the hub around which Sweden revolves."

"But the expansion will increase the deficit by billions! We'll become even more dependent on Stockholm. Who coined the phrase, 'Every wasted tax crown is theft from the people'? It was Gustav Möller, and I'm in his tradition! Who's going to cover the deficits?"

"Swedish taxpayers will," said Morgan Olofsson. "Malmö's expansion is a national interest."

"There's plenty of money," Mona said. "social democracy is about taking from the rich and giving to the poor. We must never forget that."

"And, by the way, Jöns," Olofsson continued, "while you're bragging about your esteemed relatives, you might also mention your cousin, Thorstein Möller, the leader of the Swedish Hells Angels."

"We're only distant relatives and have nothing to do with each other," Möller snapped, clenched. "Morgan, I think you should refrain from such insinuating comments."

A tense silence filled the room before Anders Skenfors took the initiative to redirect the discussion.

"So, what we're doing now is building the infrastructure needed for Malmö's expansion. We're constructing cultural centers, sports arenas, train tunnels, road bridges, sewage plants, cable tunnels, and everything else necessary. We're connecting Malmö-Lund with the Nordic capital, Copenhagen. The bridge is already there. We'll build a tunnel linking Helsingborg and Helsingør. Together, we're creating Örestad, a dynamic job market with five million inhabitants. After London and Paris, the area will become Europe's third most powerful economic hubs."

"And the best part is that the people from Stockholm will pay for it," Morgan Olofsson said with a sly smile. "The bigger Malmö's deficit gets, the more they'll have to pay."

"Every immigrant is worth their weight in gold to us in Malmö," Skenfors agreed contentedly.

Skenfors turned to Mona Wahlbin and smiled ingratiatingly at her. "What does the chief from Stockholm say? Are we on the right track?"

"Yes. Malmö's expansion is a national interest, and this country has plenty of money. It's all about priorities. As Olof always used to say, 'We must not set different groups against each other.' Those are sage words, and I constantly remind myself of them. We must never pit the interests of immigrants against those of Swedes."

"For my part, I think it sounds like utter madness," Möller said emphatically. "It seems like the party has lost its way. A system that gives unlimited money to the municipality that mismanages itself the most is not sustainable in the long run."

"Oh, we will sort this thing with the gold. You heard what Morgan said. The people from Stockholm will foot the bill for us in Malmö."

"It's not just about money. Mass immigration of Muslims is a national danger that keeps me awake at night."

"Oh, what now," Skenfors snorted, waving his arms irritably. "You're starting to sound completely paranoid."

"Oh-what-now-what-now," Möller retorted, mimicking Skenfors' carefree attitude. "Jöns, what exactly are you trying to say?" Skenfors asked. "I'm starting to get a bit concerned about how you express yourself."

"I think it's pretty clear. Our country has taken in far too many uneducated and illiterate immigrants from foreign cultures who will never have a chance to get jobs – if they even want to. They're a drag on the entire societal structure."

"It's all about creating conditions for integration," said Morgan Olofsson. "The immigrants will become very profitable for Sweden. Very, very profitable. In the long term."

"I don't even think you believe that yourself. They'll need pensions, too, without contributing to the pension system. But what worries me most is the Muslim expansion. They're here to conquer and take control of our country. You've even received PMs from SÄPO with some of the hate preachers' speeches."

"That's just pathetic Islamophobia," Skenfors exclaimed. "Jöns, you're as paranoid as the fools at the Security Police. And, by the way, what makes you think you have more right to be here than the Muslims? Let me remind you that Sweden is a secular country with no state religion."

"What do you mean? We're from Skåne, and Skåne belongs to us, the people from Skåne!"

"You're off track again," said Morgan Olofsson, shaking his head. "Skåne doesn't belong to us any more than anyone else on this planet. And Christianity has no special status. Christianity is not superior to Islam in any way."

Mona Wahlbin looked dissatisfied and sighed loudly to signal that enough was enough. She felt the discussion was going off the rails and made a failed attempt to smooth things over with a philosophical comment she'd picked up from her mentor. She pointed to the photographs on the wall.

"When European colonists came to America and began fencing off large areas of land, Indian Chief Seattle gave a long speech to the whites. He said: 'No one can own the land we walk on, just as no one can own the air we breathe. The earth belongs to all people.'"

"Wasn't that beautifully said? Olof shared that anecdote when we discussed the labor funds."

The three combatants continued to argue with each other, ignoring Chief Seattle's philosophical musings.

"Jöns, just because you were born here in Sweden doesn't mean you have more rights to the country than the immigrants," Skenfors said sharply.

"So, if I understand things correctly, Sweden is a country that no one owns," Möller said, scrutinizing the others' reactions. "And, logically, no one feels compelled to defend it."

No one responded to Möller's observation. He stood up and gave a short speech before leaving his fellow party members.

"I urge you all to consider what you're doing seriously. Really. Sweden should be a country of law and order and well-managed finances. Order and tidiness have always been hallmarks of social democracy."

Möller breathed while the other three silently looked at him with disapproving expressions.

"Mass immigration of Muslims cannot possibly be in the interest of the Swedish people. And you know it, but you're doing it anyway. You're inviting the enemy, even though you know they plan to take over Sweden. I will do whatever I can to defend our country. Against the Muslims. I'm prepared to fight for what I know is right."

"You might as well leave," Wahlbin said coldly as Möller headed for the door. "The party no longer needs your services." Fuming with rage, no longer a social democrat but a newly born patriot, Möller left Malmö City Hall. The next day, he scheduled a meeting with an acquaintance who worked as a personnel officer in the Swedish Armed Forces out in Toftängen. Soon after, he was on his way to the regiment P7 in Revingehed. And that's how it all began.

Chapter 2 – Deep Freeze

Walpurgis Night 2009

"So, we almost need to apologize for our party comrade's behavior," Skenfors said after Möller slammed the door behind him. "I just can't understand what's gotten into him. He sounded like the worst kind of Sweden democrat."

"He is no longer a fit for the party," Morgan Olofsson said. "I think we should expel him before he resigns himself. It would make a strong statement."

"Good suggestion," Mona Wahlbin agreed. "Do it at the local level as soon as possible. There won't be any problems with the party leadership if he tries to resist. I'll make sure of that. Does he have any skeletons in his closet?"

"Yes, Mona, there's probably an entire battalion of skeletons," said Morgan Olofsson, glancing at Skenfors. "Möller has always had a bit of a thing for women if you know what I mean."

"Ah, that doesn't surprise me. Not with that man," Wahlbin said, intrigued. "Do you know any details?"

"There are rumors that he's violated the sex purchase law. At least in Copenhagen, where he's said to have been at one of those Gentlemen's Clubs, you know."

"Oh, that's quite serious. Violating the sex purchase law is about the worst thing you can imagine."

"It's probably the lowest thing one can do," Skenfors said, agreeing with Wahlbin. "It's like spitting on girls who are exploited and abused daily. Buying sex is supporting human trafficking."

"Mmm, it's a terrible, despicable crime," Wahlbin said. "Is there anything else?"

"Yes, there's also the alcohol issue, and I can back that up with receipts," Skenfors said. "If I remember correctly, it was Möller who signed the bill from the last meeting of the Malmö Labor Council. About thirty to forty people of us were celebrating, so the alcohol was more than fourteen thousand kronor."

"That sounds like something we can use," Wahlbin said.

"There are more receipts in the finance department. I'll ask a journalist friend at Kvällsposten to request all representation bills from the past five years. Möller has signed quite a few of them."

"Sex and alcohol are a lethal cocktail," Wahlbin said, satisfied. "Email me the information with as many details as possible, and I'll make sure it gets out to the media after the weekend," Wahlbin said.

It was a momentous meeting with far-reaching consequences for the three Skåne residents. Morgan Olofsson's career took off, and he soared to the position of Minister of Justice, while Anders Skenfors solidified his status as a leading Malmö politician.

Möller, on the other hand, left the party to reevaluate his life. His departure cost was a relentless media frenzy focusing on alleged scandalous events in Copenhagen. Since only two people had attended that porn club twenty-two years ago, Möller knew the source had to be Skenfors.

He had long repressed that too-wet night from his youth and relegated the events to the cemetery of expired youthful transgressions, but now it was resurfacing like a foul-smelling sausage for public display.

But that wasn't all. To Möller's dismay, the scandal was fueled by supposedly well-informed sources claiming that leading social democrats had long reacted negatively to Möller's racist comments. The tabloids reported that Möller had been exposed as an online troll, spreading his immigrant hatred in right-wing extremist forums on Facebook and Flashback. It was reported that Jöns Möller had deep ties to the criminal underworld, where his cousin played a leading role as a Hells Angels leader.

Jöns Möller was as ruined as a person could be. Not only had he been cast into the cold – they had thrown him into a freezer and locked away the key.

His closest friends barely wanted to talk to him anymore, and his children were bullied at school. He was desperate but realized it would only worsen if he tried defending himself. He gritted his teeth and remained silent. It was a matter of taking cover and waiting for the storm to pass, but he couldn't help but get worked up over the comments from his former party mates in the media, especially the epilogue from his childhood friend Anders Skenfors:

"Jöns and I have been together since we joined SSU as fifteen-year-olds. Unfortunately, a once-sound person has lost his moral compass. I suspect it's due to his drinking habits. I hope Jöns will get help for his problems."

Möller came to see the rest of his life as penance for his previous contribution to what he now viewed as Sweden's downfall. He felt he was in debt, and his only way to repay it was to fight for Sweden's freedom and independence.

Chapter 3 – An Unexpected Visit

December 9, 2032

It was as if the media were controlled by a single, invisible hand—one that loathed Swedish identity. Anything contrary to the average Swede's intuitive beliefs was celebrated to undermine the Swedish self-image. Even the biblical truth that humanity has two sexes was not spared—gender transitions were rebranded as gender correction as if it were a matter of fixing something God had done wrong.

To coerce the Swedes into submission, they were frightened by fabricated external threats, where belief in the greenhouse effect had morphed into something akin to a world religion. Consequently, those who questioned the pseudoscientific doom prophets were labeled 'climate deniers'—a term that evoked the old epithet of godless heretics, who were famously burned at the stake during the Catholic Church's inquisitions.

Then came the coronavirus, a boon for those who wished to divert Swedish attention from the real threats.

Coverage of the Holocaust was incessantly broadcast on TV and in newspapers, subtly suggesting that anyone who did not buy into the multicultural illusion was a Nazi. Some writers even managed to twist it to indicate that the Swedes themselves were responsible for the Holocaust.

Journalists had taken on the role of opinion enforcers in the service of the rulers. The Swedes were expected to shut up and silently accept the Islamization and dissolution of their society. The zeitgeist, culture, the Swedish people, authorities, organizations, and large corporations—were all striving to achieve maximum political correctness.

Pelle Nestander was the first to see the profit potential in the immense power generated by media propaganda, which was fundamentally about stripping Swedes of their right to independent thought. The market screamed for help positioning itself politically and communicating the correct values, especially within government agencies, county councils, left-leaning municipalities, and universities.

To broaden the market to the private sector, Nestander claimed that seventy percent of the Swedes wanted companies to engage more in societal debates—a claim entirely fabricated but eagerly noted by corporate leaders who had secured their positions by demonstrating suitable political correctness. Statements on climate, multiculturalism, feminism, and LGBTQ issues became a means of self-promotion for further advancement, with the media all too willing to play along.

By exclusively hiring leftist and LGBTQ activists, topped with Muslim and Black racial alibis, Pelle ensured that the employees of his political correctness firm, Nestander PR & Influence Inc., headquartered at hipster central on Södermalmstorg, radiated the correct values. It was no coincidence that Pelle Nestander coined the term "shared values," which was used to eliminate dissent within organizations nationwide.

With a background from the non-governmental peace movement organization, The Swedish Peace and Arbitration Society, he had gained notoriety by reporting the Swedish arms producer Bofors for arms smuggling. Pelle was tailor-made to lead the operation and serve as the face of political correctness. His involvement with another non-governmental organization, the Fairness Agency, which unearthed and promoted executive candidates with immigrant backgrounds, only bolstered his reputation.

Pelle had also won the Swedish "Lobbyist of the Year" award at an advertising gala and was named "Swedish Master of Dagens Nyheter Debate" by national television itself. Pelle had a creative and winning strike, and his agency was certainly not lacking in linguistic creativity when it came to bending reality to fit their desired narrative.

Expressions like "guys guessing" and "green-darkening" were coined at Nestander, alongside established buzzwords like "mansplaining" and "whiteness norms." However, the proper stroke of genius was the demand for a "shared values" framework, despite some perceptive critics noting that this concept could easily have been lifted from Mao's Chinese Cultural Revolution or Pol Pot's reign of terror in Cambodia.

Another masterstroke from the founder was the newsletter "Weekly Climate News," which often received positive media attention. The agency made a concerted effort to be the first to uncover alleged climate catastrophes in other continents. Muhammed al-Hassan, who headed the "Nestander Climate and Sustainability" unit and hosted a personal environmental podcast, was the perfect editor for the newsletter. The almost monopolistic media empire Bonniers' climate site, "Actual Sustainability," had given al-Hassan an extra boost by naming him one of the "101 Most Influential in Swedish Sustainability," and al-Hassan reciprocated by constantly referencing and linking to "Actual Sustainability."

Nestander was the PR agency—or rather, the "PC agency, PC meaning Politically Correct"—that everyone needed to navigate the demands of the new era. Nestander PR & Influence Inc. was a success created by its driven and experienced founder, who, with a hundred percent calculated cynicism, crafted a concept designed to satisfy every imaginable PC zealot's wet dream of doing good for the world.

The founder had yet to communicate that the "PC" agency Nestander had been sold to new owners as early as 2020 when a Saudi fund secretly acquired one hundred percent of the shares. The purchase price was highly generous, structured to be paid out over eight years with annual payments into the founder's bank account in Doha, intended to keep the "PC genius," Nestander, motivated to continue leading the firm.

The Muslim Brotherhood needed its PR base in Sweden, and the PC agency Nestander was perfect for their purposes. Nestander promoted and cemented the belief in a multicultural society, which was merely a rebranding of an Islamized society governed by Sharia law. The Saudi ownership fund was secretly controlled by the Muslim Brotherhood, which had earmarked Sweden as the first European country to be conquered.

But it wasn't just the PC agency Nestander preaching multiculturalism, gender theory, and climate transition. Many of the South Stockholm-based media activists had been receiving various types of fees from Muslim organizations for decades, many of which were ultimately funded by Swedish taxpayers.

All major media outlets had hired specialized climate journalists whose job was to spread disaster scenarios—how else would they justify their salaries? The supposed climate rampage was the external enemy needed to divert attention from the real threat.

One chilly December evening, Pelle Nestander suddenly faced a minor dilemma when the doorbell rang at his spacious seven-room apartment on the street of Bastugatan, just above Ivar Los Park on

Södermalm in Stockholm. The stylish and tastefully decorated apartment, filled with art and antiques, was two units of apartments merged into one.

When Pelle's neighbor was arrested and executed at Medborgarplatsen Square during the Muslim invasion of Sweden, Pelle seized the opportunity to acquire the vacant apartment. He secured the place for himself with a generous bribe to the co-op chairman rather than letting it pass to the rightful heirs. Thanks to his close connections with the ruling Muslims, no one dared to object, and Pelle now enjoyed living like a king in his splendid new and palace-like home.

Pelle, who had just settled in to savor some crackers topped with hummus seasoned with sumac and cumin before enjoying a climate-neutral, vegan dinner with his wife, wasn't thrilled about an unexpected visitor interrupting his attempt to unwind after a grueling day at the agency. Who could it be, arriving unannounced? Such surprises were rare these days and felt rather unsettling.

With some trepidation, he tiptoed to the front door and looked at the small screen that served as his electronic peephole. Standing outside was an unfamiliar man with glasses, a large beard, and a black hood pulled down to his eyes. For a moment, Pelle considered pretending he wasn't home, but curiosity got the better of him, and the heavy security door offered adequate protection.

"Who's there?" he asked cautiously through the closed door.

"It's Benno. Just a little disguised if you don't recognize me."

Thoughts raced through Pelle's mind. Could it be his old childhood friend, Benno Ronkanen, whom he hadn't seen in months? He had heard that Benno had suddenly disappeared and was likely imprisoned or executed. It couldn't be anyone else.

He unlocked the white wrought-iron gate, pulled it aside, and opened the massive security door.

"Can I come in?" Benno asked as he stepped over the threshold and gave Pelle a somewhat awkward, masculine hug.

"Come on in!" Pelle chirped. "You can hang up your coat here."

They settled into the comfortable armchairs by the panoramic window in front of what was usually a magnificent view. But in the December darkness, nothing of the bombed-out and blackout city was visible, even if one bothered to peek behind the black drape covering the panoramic window. Even City Hall was indistinguishable. Pelle's apartment was sparsely lit, with a few oil lamps. A small gas heater hummed in one corner of the living room, ensuring Pelle's home was always warm and cozy.

"Here you go. Would you like some crackers with hummus?" Pelle gestured to the table. "It's perfect, especially with cumin."

"No, damn it. I don't eat that kind of crap if you'll excuse me. I'm allergic to everything that's Arabic."

The rude response took Pelle aback, but he quickly composed himself. He knew Benno tended to be blunt and direct in a rather un-Swedish manner. But then again, he also had a Finnish background.

"Okay, I understand. You have every reason not to love Arabs. But if you're hungry, we can offer you mushroom burgers with pita bread and ayvar yogurt, which Maja prepares for dinner."

Benno nodded silently and glanced toward the kitchen entrance. He could hear Maja working on the meal. It felt good that they could talk uninterrupted.

"Thanks, that sounds good. I love mushrooms."

"Unfortunately, I can't offer you a cocktail, as you can imagine, but we can smoke instead if you want. Like the old times, he-he—what memories we share, Benno!"

"Okay. A little drink wouldn't go amiss, but it is what it is. You might be wondering where I've been?"

"Least to say! The last I heard, you were making a splash as a sausage maker, and then you just went silent. I thought the Muslim security service had picked you up somewhere."

"Remember that feminist chick, Cilla Melin, who accused me of rape?"

"Of course. It was hard to miss that, ha-ha. You were on the front page every day for weeks. I felt for you, you know."

"That was appreciated, but you didn't reach out."

"Uh... I think I tried a couple of times. There was so much to do at the agency, so that's all I could manage. Unfortunately. I should have sought you out."

Pelle sighed deeply with a troubled and guilty expression. He had had wrinkles on his forehead for a long time, and now they were more profound than ever.

"In adversity, a friend is tested, they say, and I, of all people, know that all too well. Everyone loves a winner. And the opposite. You become like a plague when everything falls apart. No one reached out a hand," Benno said bitterly.

Benno leaned forward and looked steadily at his old childhood friend in the eyes. He had removed the fake glasses with the yellow-tinted lenses and placed them on the white marble table.

He and Pelle had essentially grown up together. They had children of the same age who still met occasionally. They had often socialized in the same circles in Söder and shared some professional networks in advertising and PR.

Pelle noticed that Benno seemed to have aged ten years since they last saw each other before the scandal and the rape accusations.

"You might get a chance to redeem yourself now. I need your help, Pelle. Now you can show if our lifelong friendship has meant anything to you."

"Of course, I'll help—if it's possible for me. Just tell me what I can do for you."

"To make a long story short, I'm innocent of the rape charge, though I haven't lived like an angel, as you know. But rape – I'm not inclined that way."

"I've truly never believed you're a rapist. I've never seen you commit violence against anyone, not even in school when there were brawls."

"After I lost all my contracts, I had to find another source of income, and I decided to start making sausages. It became a success."

"I heard about that, and I even had some of your sausages at one of our old favorite joints—now all closed, by the way—super good sausage! But why did you stop with the sausage business?"

"Well, it turned out that the entire Muslim council at Al Zayed Mosque was feasting on my sausages, and they got a bit less happy when lab tests showed that the sausages were made of wild boar meat."

"Oh, damn, that's not good!"

"No, you could say that without exaggerating. The sausage factory was blown up, and I had a death sentence hanging over me. Likely topped with the worst torture before they beheaded me. That's why I had to move to the Swedish side."

"Oh, dear, but why have you come back here?"

"Have you seen my boys lately? They weigh several pounds less now than when the war started. You can count their ribs. I need to find a source of income so they don't end up stunted. And, you know what I can do professionally."

Benno fell silent and watched Pelle intently, who now had even deeper wrinkles on his forehead than just moments before. The silence felt ominous as Pelle pondered what to say next. "I can probably contribute some money. And food for the boys. You can already take some canned goods and dry supplies tonight. We've stocked up a bit for safety's sake—like everyone else who could. But I can't hire you at the firm, considering what you just said. We mostly work for Muslims. If I hire you, I might lose my head, too. I'm sorry, Benno, but...I can't do it."

Benno pulled out a driver's license and a passport from his inner pocket, holding them up in front of Pelle's strained face.

"You're talking to Fredrik Myllivirta now. With a new social security number and everything."

"Well, I'll be damn! Where did you manage to get that?"

"There are printing houses and everything needed on the Swedish side. All infiltrators are provided with fake identities that are virtually foolproof."

Pelle thought intently, feeling Benno's scrutinizing gaze like a burning laser on his face. He couldn't bear to meet Benno's eyes, so he grabbed Benno's passport and driver's license, examining them thoughtfully as he spoke.

"It's not going to work. Everyone at the office knows who you are. Some have probably met you in person. They'll recognize you even if you're in disguise."

"Would they turn me in then?"

"Somehow, it will get out. Plus, I have a few Muslims employed at headquarters who I'm not entirely sure about. They're closely connected with Saudi Arabia and Qatar and with a lot of Muslims here in Sweden."

Pelle remembered well that the secret owner of the company had instructed him to hire them. They were the owner's eyes and ears in the business, even though he was still the boss for now. That was how the Muslim Brotherhood wanted it.

"Benno, there might still be a way I can help you."

"Fredrik, you mean Fredrik Myllivirta."

"Yes, that's right. Fredrik Myllivirta. I can offer you a PR consultant position at the Malmö office, where no one knows you personally. They're about to appoint a new site manager, and it would be appropriate for you, as Fredrik Myllivirta, to meet them first."

"Malmö? That's quite a distance."

"But Malmö is in the Muslim zone, so it's not unusual, and there are effective transport options for those who have the favor of the Muslims. I'll ask the incoming manager in Malmö to draft an employment contract for you. I won't put my signature anywhere, and I won't know your employment, understand?"

"Okay, we'll go with that. Thanks, Pelle, I'll never forget this!"

"No problem. I'm just glad to be able to help. But you should be aware that you'll be doing PR for the Muslims down there."

"I'd do PR for the devil if it meant my boys could get a good meal. Who is the new site manager in Malmö? Is it someone I know?"

"Honestly, I don't know."

"You're kidding! You've managed the company down to the last detail all this time."

"I'll let you in on a secret. You're the first to know, and you must promise me to keep quiet until it becomes official, which will be a couple of weeks after New Year's."

"Now, you've piqued my curiosity. What's happening?"

"Nestander has new owners, and I'm leaving the company. I'm taking my family and leaving the country as soon as possible. To Doha."

"Doha? Qatar, then! Haven't you had enough of Arabs?"

"We've probably all had enough, but I must handle a little business in Doha. After that, we'll move on. I'm thinking of getting residency in Florida."

"Lucky you, who wouldn't want that? What's happening with the apartment?"

"It'll be taken over by the Muslim becoming the new boss. Otherwise, you could have had it. I'm not taking a single thing with me from Sweden. I have enough money to get by."

"But what happens to the agency if Stockholm becomes Swedish again?"

"Nothing at all. We've been operating as usual since the Muslims took Stockholm, and the agency will continue to do so regardless."

"There are rumors that the Muslims are planning to leave Stockholm. Have you heard anything?"

"There are always new rumors circulating. My advice is to head to Malmö and get started there. If Stockholm becomes Swedish again, you'll have to find your way back somehow. And then you'll have a job at the agency."

"Okay, that's what I'll do."

Pelle reached for the antique, massive English mahogany desk and pulled out the bottom drawer. With a big smile, he retrieved a pre-rolled joint and handed it to Benno.

"Make sure to bring your family to Florida so we can have some company on Miami Beach," Pelle said cordially. "Let's smoke the peace pipe now—you get the honor of lighting it," he continued, pointing to the lighter, which was shaped like a seven-inch-high, gold-plated soldier standing at attention on the white marble slab.

Benno guessed that the lighter was also an English antique, and he was right. He tilted the soldier's hinged head backward, causing a gas flame to ignite from the hole in its severed neck. Benno couldn't help but think about what might happen to his neck if the Muslims got hold of him.

He took a few deep puffs from the joint, drawing the smoke deeply into his lungs, before passing it to Pelle.

Chapter 4 – Dessert with Obstacles

December 17, 2032

Benno Ronkanen had been plagued by one misfortune after another, and it seemed like his bad luck would never end. First, he lost his prestigious and well-paid position as the country's leading columnist due to accusations of rape from leftist feminist Cilla Melin. Then he lost his successful sausage business, "Ronkanen's Söderkorv" – Ronkanen's South Sausage, because of the war and the Muslim overlords' aversion to pork. And now, as he tried to crawl up from the mud the third time, everything had gone awry again. Benno could hardly believe his ears. It felt like he was suffocating. He gasped for air, shaking his head as he stared at the floor. This was too much!

"Should I get you a glass of water?" the receptionist offered kindly, with her broad Skåne accent. "I have some Tylenol if you need it. Or do you need a doctor?"

"I'm fine," Benno managed to reply. "Just a little asthma attack, which I get from time to time. I'll spray a bit in my nose, and it'll pass soon."

"Alright, I was starting to get a bit worried about you. Sit here and rest for a while. I'll wait until you tell me before I call Cilla."

Benno was at Nestander's Malmö office to meet his new boss, who had just started her new position. They were supposed to sign the employment contract as per the instructions from the agency's head, Pelle Nestander. But now everything seemed to be going disastrously wrong. He was falling apart when the receptionist mentioned that he would be meeting the new boss, who, as it turned out, was also a Stockholm native named Cilla Melin.

Cilla Melin, of all people!

It had been over twenty years since they had last met, that fateful evening and night when everything was supposed to have happened. The things that didn't happen, at least not as he remembered. They were both so high and drunk that who could know so many years later? They had had sex, as evidenced by waking up naked in the same bed, but even that Benno didn't remember with certainty.

Benno tried to calm himself down and gather his thoughts. He was now going by the name Fredrik Myllyvirta, and his bushy beard and large fake glasses with yellow-tinted lenses hid his face reasonably well. It has been over twenty years, and people can change significantly during that time. He had lost nearly thirty pounds since his decadent days of drug and alcohol abuse, during which he let his employer's credit card finance his unhealthy barhopping. His body was lean, as it should have been in his youth, though he had been quite overweight. The lean, mostly alcohol-free wartime diet had done wonders for his health.

With a bit of luck, she wouldn't recognize him. Besides, he would be working out at the Muslim clients' office and closely with their leader, Ahmed Ben Barka, who had realized that the ruling Muslims needed to improve their image. Long-term success in ruling the Swedes couldn't rely solely on violence; if they were to convert them, PR and advertising for Allah's good cause would be essential.

Benno put on his cap and pulled the brim down a bit. As a PR guru, I find it perfectly fine to look eccentric. That was the whole point. He decided to play the role of the reclusive artistic genius, saying as little as possible—contrary to his true personality.

"Hello, you must be Fredrik, I assume?" Cilla Melin said as she suddenly appeared in the reception.

Benno stood up and extended his hand. "Yes, I'm Fredrik."

"Welcome to Malmö! I'm almost as new to Skåne as you are—I started here last Monday. I've never even been to Malmö before. Let's head to the meeting room."

Benno followed his new boss down the corridor. At least she hadn't recognized him yet, and he could barely remember her. She had dyed her long, straight hair red with heavy makeup, with a foundation layer on her cheeks, topped with a bit of blush and thick, bright red lipstick that was almost provocative.

Cilla reminded him of a sex doll in a store window that he had smirked at with his colleagues the last time he was in San Francisco. He recalled that the doll was described as "petite" and came with a biography saying she was a little geisha whore named Kikko from the Kabukicho district in Tokyo, where Benno himself had once roamed. Many Japanese women are pretty short and slight and can indeed be described as "petite."

Kikko's hair had, as far as Benno could remember, the same shade as Cilla's. He also remembered that geisha-clad girls were confirmed, found in clubs throughout Shinjuku, but it was only in Kabukicho that they openly sold their services. Many of them had dyed their hair unnatural colors and painted their faces white, making them look like doll-like fairy-tale figures, at least in the eyes of drunk men. Perhaps this self-chosen objectification appealed to both parties—a momentary escape from reality, something not entirely accurate.

To his surprise, Benno also remembered encountering a Swedish geisha and overhearing others speaking Russian. Japanese men highly sought-after true blondes. They seemed willing to pay almost anything and had plenty of money back then.

They settled into the tiny meeting room, where a middle-aged, glasses-wearing woman with light brown hair was already waiting.

"I brought Jennifer Brynson, our HR manager, here in Malmö since we're supposed to sign the employment contract. Jennifer, why don't you start? Fredrik and I will take over once you finish your part."

Benno walked around the table and carefully extended his hand to greet Jennifer.

"Hi Jennifer, I'm Fredrik Myllyvirta."

He tried to adopt a slight Finnish accent, fearing that Cilla might recognize his voice. HR manager Jennifer took Benno's hand and greeted him without standing up, merely stretching a bit on her chair as a small gesture.

"Ah, Fredrik, you've come down here from Stockholm?"

"Yes, that's correct."

"Are you flying?" the HR manager asked abruptly, her lips clamped shut as she scrutinized Benno intently, waiting for his answer.

The perplexing question took aback Benno, and he wasn't sure how to handle the heavy silence. Jennifer Brynson's question was her standard icebreaker during interviews, meant to throw the interviewee off balance. Ideally, the question wasn't about how one arrived at the interview but about broader sustainability and environmental consciousness issues. Most people were bewildered by the blunt and unexpected opener and began nervously discussing which modes of transport were the most eco-friendly under the HR manager's critical gaze.

Flygskam, or "Flight Shame," was one of the buzzwords invented at Nestander's politically correct agency. Jennifer had coined the term herself and took pride in it. As the agency liked to say internally, the power of words could change the world.

"Flying?" Benno asked thoughtfully. "You mean in general? I traveled to Malmö by train and car, around the Russian occupation zone. I always take the train when possible," Benno lied, as he usually flew to save time.

Moreover, Benno liked powerful cars from the old days, especially those with American V8 engines. Still, he realized that Jennifer, the HR manager, probably didn't share his passion for growling, gas-guzzling monsters.

"Okay, I understand. I don't have any more questions, so I'll leave you to it. Just sign the documents."

After demonstrating her authority, HR manager Brynson left the room, creating a moment of silence that made Benno nervous. He could feel his heart pounding. Had Cilla suspected something? What would happen if he were discovered?

Cilla looked curiously at the all-black-clad, soft-spoken man across from her, huddled behind his lowered cap brim and yellow-tinted glasses. He looked like an absolute muppet, but there was something about him that intrigued her nonetheless. His reserved demeanor was oddly endearing, and there was no doubt he had a sharp intellect, considering Pelle Nestander had selected him for the most critical position in the company. His lean, youthful physique was also striking. Perhaps even handsome behind the curtain. Intriguing!

"You know, Fredrik, we should sign the contract right now. Unfortunately, I've been called to another important meeting—typical, just before you arrived."

"It's okay. We can talk more later."

"Yes, we'll have time. We could have dinner tonight to get to know each other better."

Benno was sweating profusely and desperately tried to devise a suitable excuse to escape, but he was so stressed that his mind went blank.

"Well, that sounds great!"

"You're booked at the Clarion Congress, where I'll stay. How does eight o'clock at their Japanese restaurant sound?"

"That works for me. See you there."

"Perfect. I've got to run now. See you tonight!"

When Benno arrived at eight o'clock, the traditional washi-paper door was open. He took a few steps into the high-end restaurant, glancing just in time to see Cilla's back disappearing around a partition toward their reserved table. The long red hair was unmistakable.

In the hours before, in his room, Benno had been devising a fitting life story to present to Cilla and perfecting his newly adopted Finnish accent. He had chosen a Tempura Symphony with fried vegetables and seafood. Even in Malmö, it was still possible to find good dining options at restaurants favored by the Muslim elites. Japanese food was not off-limits.

"Do you speak Finnish, then?" Cilla asked curiously.

"Yes, I speak fairly good Finnish, but not fluently."

Cilla smiled with delight. She had appropriately dressed in a white, Japanese-inspired silk blouse with floral patterns, which suited her perfectly. The blouse was sheer, and Benno could faintly see her black A-cup bra through the fabric. She paired the blouse with tight black pants that accentuated her slender figure. She looked genuinely charming, even more so than he remembered.

"Ha-ha-ha, that sounds interesting," she chuckled.

They had a pleasant time, and Benno started to relax, even though he remained cautious. He tried to say as little as possible without being rude, letting Cilla take the lead, which she seemed to appreciate. She was in high spirits and chattered away.

"This is good. But it would be nice to have a few drinks, too," she sighed.

"Hmm, I'm not really into alcohol," Benno lied, though he was tempted to lighten his mood.

"What does little Fredrik like, then? There are other things, you know."

"Such as?"

"Well, it's no secret that the whole advertising industry is full of coke if you know what I mean."

"Hmm, do you have something?"

Cilla fell silent, regarding him with a bit of shock at his direct question. Benno regretted asking it, as he had planned to retreat to his room as soon as possible.

"So, if I had something, you wouldn't say no?" she continued with an enigmatic smile.

"Maybe not. I don't see anything wrong if it's done in moderation. It's good for creativity, positive energy, you know."

"Exactly. I have some in the room. I feel like I'm in a prison here and can't even go out after work—one needs to have some fun."

"I'm not sure," Benno replied, eager to lift his heavy mood. It had been a tumultuous day. "This is a business meeting, and you're my boss."

"Nestander PR & Influence AB has just decided you should take some coke with your boss, Melin. Consider it our dessert."

Cilla signaled the waiter and asked him to charge the bill to the room, which appeared to be standard practice since he didn't ask for the room number.

Soon, they were in Cilla's suite. She carefully tapped a small pile of volatile white powder from her tiny box onto the glossy black desk mat. Using the hotel key card, she divided the powder into two equal piles and shaped them into two narrow, parallel lines on the mat.

"Here you go, Mr. Myllyvirta," she said coolly, handing Benno a small, silver-colored metal tube.

Benno knelt and snorted the powder greedily through his right nostril, and then Cilla did the same.

"Ahhhhh," Cilla exclaimed. "So freaking nice."

In seconds, she wrapped her arms around Benno's neck and kissed him passionately, as if she hadn't been near a man in a long time. Benno hesitated, tilting his head back to defend himself and extricate himself from the awkward situation. He needed to get out of there as quickly as possible.

Cilla removed his cap, dropped it on the floor, and gently removed his yellow-tinted glasses. He felt her hand between his legs, and as the stimulating effect of the cocaine began to kick in, he suddenly decided to give in. Whatever it may be.

He unbuttoned her silk blouse, revealing her pert, girlish breasts, and pulled her close again.

"You look so beautiful, little Kikko," Benno whispered in her ear, gently caressing her breasts with his right hand.

"What do you mean, Kikko?" Cilla said indignantly, pushing him away. "I don't want to be compared to your past lovers."

"Oh, I was just joking a bit. Kikko—or Akiko, as she was called—was a Japanese girl who was an exchange student at school," he lied. "She was a real angel, and you're just as beautiful, even more so!"

Cilla seemed to accept this and began unbuttoning his shirt, which he shrugged off while she knelt and undid his belt. Everything seemed promising to Benno, but suddenly, the atmosphere changed drastically.

"What the hell is this!" Cilla screamed with an utterly wild voice, standing up abruptly. "I've seen that tattoo before!"

She pointed at Benno's abdomen, on the right side of his navel, where he had a portrait of Freddie Mercury tattooed.

"I knew something wasn't right, I knew it, but I just couldn't figure out what! You're Benno Ronkanen and no one else! How the hell could you do this to me? I mean, what kind of person are you?"

She was furious, flailing her arms while screaming in a high-pitched voice. Benno stood there passively, not knowing what to do. Then she suddenly calmed down and curled her lips downward, giving her an extra malicious look.

"And you're never showing your face at Nestander again, understand? You're fired."

"It wasn't supposed to turn out like this," Benno said quietly. "I couldn't have known you'd be my boss."

"I don't care. You're done at Nestander, anyway. Just get out of here as soon as possible."

"If you reveal my identity, the Muslims will kill me."

"I'm giving you a chance to leave before I say anything, even though you don't deserve it."

"I must keep this job to support my family, so leaving isn't an option. And you probably want to keep your job and your position with the Muslims, don't you?"

"What do you mean?"

"It says on the website that you have a degree in Business Administration from the Stockholm School of Economics, topped with a degree in Behavioral Science from Stockholm University. But I know you only have a two-year high school education in social studies. Have you forgotten that you told me you forged your school grades for me, that time I didn't rape you?"

Cilla was stunned, and her entire demeanor seemed to shrink before she gathered herself again.

"Well, damn. My whole career rests on those grades. But I did take a few university courses, so it's not all fake. But you must never reveal anything, or I'm done in the industry."

"You can't take university courses with just a two-year high school education. I won't say anything if I get to keep the job. Let's share our secrets. We don't have anything against each other—hell, we were about to sleep together just now. We had a good time at dinner, too."

She looked at him calmly and shook her head while buttoning up her blouse.

"Fredrik, we'll see each other at the office around nine tomorrow morning."

"Sounds good. I'm heading to bed now."

"Good night."

Benno turned to leave but then turned back to Cilla.

"One question, though: Why did you accuse me of rape after more than ten years?"

"Well… I felt that things had happened that I wasn't a part of."

"Can you be more specific? I have no idea."

"There were several things. I felt violated and exploited. And then #metoo happened, and I saw a chance to get back at you."

"And maybe a chance to promote yourself, get some PR, and build your brand?" Benno said sarcastically. "While the vultures tore my life apart."

"I didn't intend for it to go this far. But I don't believe that it's my fault. You've made your enemies."

"But those other feminists you got involved with—that wasn't fair."

"They were the ones who convinced me to go public when I told them about our evening together. And there was no going back once the genie was out of the bottle."

"No, then it became a matter of prestige and morality. Don't you want to apologize for ruining my life?" Benno said, looking deeply into Cilla's eyes.

She hesitated and remained silent for a few seconds.

"Yes, I apologize for how things turned out. But it wasn't how I planned it."

"Okay, let's drop it and move on. It is what it is, and we have our lives to live."

"Good night, and sleep well, Fredrik. It's going to be an intense day tomorrow."

"Sleep well yourself."

She gave him a brief conciliatory hug to close their conversation.

Should he still try to make a move? No, that wasn't going to work. Their relationship was complicated enough as it was. Fortunately, he would work at the Muslims' general headquarters, so they hardly needed to see each other.

Benno couldn't see how their already complicated relationship could become more complicated.

Chapter 5 – The New Head of Security

January 16, 2033

The formidable figure seated across from Ahmed Ben Barka, at the other side of the desk, was every bit as extraordinary as Ahmed's secretary had described, compelling him to take the time to meet.

The man fixed Ahmed with a calm and steady gaze, and nothing in his body language or expression suggested that he felt uneasy or even subordinate despite sitting across from the esteemed, almost mythical leader of the Muslims.

Most people with an audience with Ahmed Ben Barka would shrink a few sizes once in his presence, feeling the weight of Ahmed's razor-sharp intellect and intuitive ability to grasp complex issues. Those subjected to Ahmed's scrutinizing gaze usually found themselves intellectually outmatched. They often focused more on navigating the meeting without making too much of a fool rather than presenting their intended message to his superior intelligence.

But not this powerful athlete. His demeanor was unwavering, yet without compromising the necessary respect that must be shown to the highest leader.

Zlatko Muslimovic responded to each question with clarity and precision, though he spoke only as much as needed. His English, while not perfect, was sufficient for the task at hand. It was apparent that Muslimovic lacked formal education, but his street smarts and sharp intellect were unmistakably evident.

Zlatko Muslimovic had to employ every ounce of his persuasive skill to secure a meeting with Ahmed's secretary. His sole message was clear: he was eager to work for the Muslims in any capacity. He left it to his future employers to determine the most suitable role for him. Muslimovic expressed his unwavering commitment to be one hundred percent loyal to whatever task he was assigned.

After the interview with Ahmed's secretary, a background check revealed some interesting but not entirely straightforward information.

The thirty-nine-year-old Muslimovic's biography could be divided into three phases. The first phase was his impoverished upbringing in the

Malmö suburb of Rosengård, isolated from Swedish society, with poor and somewhat drifting parents and friends from the Balkans, the Middle East, and Africa—a childhood in a criminal environment.

His father was a Serbian Muslim from Herzegovina, while his mother was from Montenegro, also Serbian. His parents divorced when he was nine years old. By then, the young Zlatko was given the choice of which parent he wanted to live with, and he chose his father.

The second phase of Muslimovic's biography was his career as a soccer player. At eleven, the talent scouts from Malmö FF had earmarked him for the famous soccer club. What he did with the ball was almost magical, showcasing a ball skill MFF's elite players wished they had. The fact that Zlatko was also unusually tall and physically strong—being Serbian, of course—was naturally an advantage.

It was an understatement to say that Zlatko was born with a competitive spirit. He would become almost unhinged when his team lost, sometimes physically confronting his teammates, pressing them against the wall in the locker room, and staring them down for their underperformance. Some experienced Zlatko's drive firsthand, receiving a so-called Danish headbutt when the back of their heads were pressed against the wall.

After a few such incidents, the parents of the other players banded together and demanded that Zlatko be expelled from MFF. However, he was a unique gem that every coach dreams of handling at some point, so he stayed despite the known fact that he continued his criminal activities in his spare time. Zlatko was more dedicated to training than the others, meticulously preparing and perfecting his skills. He was a perfectionist to the core. Even in maintaining his physical fitness, he stood out positively from his Swedish teammates: he was a teetotaler, reacting to his father's less successful life, which mainly revolved around the cheapest strong beer and homemade Slivovitz.

To further enhance his physical capacity and agility, Zlatko trained in taekwondo, where he was naturally the top talent in Malmö. He was a born fighter who truly enjoyed mano-a-mano combat, even in the rare instances when he found himself on the receiving end of a beating. However, a concern was his difficulty finding sparring partners, as there was always a shortage of heavyweights.

On one occasion, during a sparring session with Swedish heavyweight boxing champion Håkan Krock, the training session escalated into a full-blown fight in the ring. Rumor had it that Krock was very grateful when intervening trainers and martial artists broke up the fight in time, while Zlatko was eager to go the distance. Krock later declined Muslimovic's invitation for an actual boxing match, even though Muslimovic was primarily a taekwondo practitioner, not a boxer.

There was never any doubt that Zlatko was in charge, both on the field and in the locker room. Zlatko was the star around whom everything else revolved. The MFF coaching staff was unanimous in their belief that Zlatko Muslimovic was the most remarkable talent they had ever seen—and they had seen many, as most of them had been elite players.

But just when Muslimovic, at the age of seventeen, had secured a spot in MFF's starting lineup and was called up for his first national team gathering, everything suddenly came to an end. Zlatko crashed a stolen racing bike during a police chase, shattering both of his knees. He managed to evade the police, but at a high cost. After multiple surgeries and a couple of years of rehabilitation, he had somewhat recovered, but his knees could never withstand the demands of elite-level football. His career was over, and half of Malmö mourned the lost prodigy, who had been destined to become a world-class player.

The third phase of Zlatko Muslimovic's life began when soccer faded from his world and continued until January 16, 2033, when he met with the Muslim commander, Ahmed Ben Barka, to embark on the fourth phase of his life. For the past twenty years, Zlatko had poured his immense strength and energy into the underworld, gradually rising to what resembled the godfather of Malmö. Muslimovic led an organization that controlled a significant portion of the drug trade in Malmö and engaged in sophisticated financial crimes, including VAT fraud, tax evasion, and well-organized corporate raids. Remarkably, Muslimovic had managed to evade the law, never being convicted of a single crime despite committing hundreds. His record included numerous assault cases, some quite severe. Yet, understandably, no one dared to report him.

Even more astonishing was his ability to avoid attempted murder. One explanation was that Zlatko had successfully balanced power in Malmö's underworld with Sweden's Leader of Hells Angels, Thorstein

Möller, who had connections and influence among police and politicians, especially within the social democrats who governed Malmö. Thorstein Möller, from the renowned social democratic political family, was a wise and well-organized leader focusing on money and profits, only employing the Hells Angels brand of violence when necessary.

However, over time, the positions of Malmö's two mafia kings grew increasingly precarious. With each passing month, they seemed to bring a new wave of trigger-happy lunatics from the Middle East and Africa. These young men shot indiscriminately at anything and anyone over the slightest provocation, disrupting and destroying the operations of the former gangster kings, who saw their empires eroding and shrinking toward oblivion. The newcomers detonated thermite bombs and powerful Polish-made bangers at any time if their money for protection was not promptly delivered, which led to increased police activity—not ideal for Zlatko's business.

Frustrated and deeply weary of his criminal life, Zlatko contemplated retiring from his role as a crime lord before it was too late. He had no desire to be gunned down by a Kalashnikov wielded by some deranged kid eager to make a name for himself in his new homeland. These youngsters didn't grasp the importance of operating with discretion and prudence to stay under the radar of authorities and media. Long-term planning brought results, not sensational coups or, especially, unnecessary murders. But the young thugs destroyed everything—absolutely everything—without restraint. Zlatko remembered all too well how his uncle Dragan Joksovic had met his end: a bullet to the temple at Solvalla Horse Racetrack in Stockholm.

"We have a pretty good understanding of who you are and what you've been involved in," Ahmed said. "And my impression confirms our assessment. You're clearly of interest to us. I believe you could become a significant asset."

"I'm glad to hear that," Zlatko replied. "I've never been on a job interview, but everything feels right. I want to work for our common cause and find a new direction for my life—one with purpose and goals."

"You've come to the right place. The head of our security force has been vacant for a while, and I believe you're a perfect fit for the role, so I'd like to give you a chance."

"That sounds exciting. What happened to the previous holder of the position?"

"Uhh... he was executed for making a serious mistake."

"What did he do wrong?"

"He failed to properly oversee the security at Stockholm Castle when we were there last year, which resulted in an attack that wiped out most of our staff."

"That sounds like unforgivable negligence. I heard rumors about the attack. I'm a perfectionist and would never be careless with something like that."

"We're aware of that, and it's one of the reasons we believe you're suited for the role of leading our security force, which consists of eighty *God Warriors*."

"Great. What are the other reasons?"

"That you're intelligent and possess the leadership qualities needed to manage eighty energetic and troublesome *God Warriors*. Many have backgrounds like yours, so you'll likely find common ground with them."

"Thank you; those are flattering compliments."

"You'll report to my right hand, General Mahmoud Khalil, who will oversee your progress. I need to attend to other matters, if you don't mind. However, I'll receive reports on your performance, and I'm confident we'll meet again. For a man like you, there are many opportunities."

Zlatko stood and extended his hand to thank him while Ahmed greeted him from his seated position.

"*Allahu Akbar!*"

"*Allahu Akbar!*"

Ahmed reflected on his recruit for a moment. He saw a man with immense resources who could be entrusted with greater responsibilities over time—a man with great potential. Suddenly, Ahmed realized he hadn't addressed whether Muslimovic was a devout Muslim. The background, the name, the appearance, the large beard, and the Muslim and Arabic references all suggested he was genuinely devout, which led Ahmed to overlook asking the question. For now, the matter would remain unresolved, as it seemed Muslimovic had all the right pieces in place.

It would later become apparent that Ahmed should have dug deeper into this question.

Chapter 6 – PR Plans

March 2, 2033

Ahmed Ben Barka didn't like the look of the so-called PR genius sent their way by their advisor, Pelle Nestander, but he accepted that this was just another quirk of the strange Swedes. Even their political leaders often looked like drifters, and Ahmed could never entirely understand how the Swedes would voluntarily elect such people to power.

Unlike in other countries where wealthy businessmen were admired — the richer you were, the greater the admiration— and could ascend to political power, the Swedes seemed to shy away from solid and intelligent figures. The media, at least, appeared to distrust anyone who displayed such qualities, and the Swedes seemed to trust their media more than most other people.

Perhaps the decadence of the Swedes had to do with PR and indoctrination, Ahmed mused. It was a testament to how decades of Muslim-funded indoctrination had taken its toll. They had also been bolstered by globalist media's relentless erosion of Swedish identity and their brown-smearing campaigns against anyone brave enough to question what was happening openly.

The fifty or so journalists and PR consultants secretly paid by the Muslim Brotherhood had done a commendable job spreading the illusion of a multicultural paradise, starkly contrasting with the reality of a Muslim monoculture.

It was the Swedes' preference for politically correct mediocrity, their fear of standing out from the group— essentially, their cowardice—that allowed the invasion to happen. What was politically correct was dictated by journalists, who were generally far left and perpetually preached diversity from their narrow perspective.

The other members of the Muslim General Staff frowned and murmured in discontent as the chosen PR genius introduced himself. However, Ahmed was wise enough not to judge the man across the table by his appearance and attire. True, the man dressed entirely in black looked like an immoral Swedish vagrant, but Ahmed knew enough about Swedish media to understand that this was often their typical appearance.

It was as if they took pride in looking like impoverished vagrants, even though they usually earned substantial sums of money. Behind the yellow-tinted glasses and deep-set cap, Ahmed sensed a sharp intellect and considerable capability.

Ahmed ensured that Fredrik Myllyvirta was given an office beside his own. The two would cooperate to overcome the Swedish public's instinctive resistance to the Prophet's message. Myllyvirta's PR plan, which he first presented to Ahmed in private, stretched three years into the future and was divided into various phases.

"The Swedish translation of the Quran was done by a professor named Zettersteen in 1917," Benno explained. "The translation, made directly from the Arabic original, is considered high quality, but the language is so outdated that modern Swedes find it difficult to relate. Therefore, I suggest we develop a new, linguistically modern translation as soon as possible."

"I'm aware of this issue. When can it be completed?"

"Plenty of people are fluent in Arabic and Swedish, so it should take a few months. I can have a printed Swedish Quran ready by summer."

"You have my approval to proceed. We'll probably need to print three to four million copies. By the way, where will our holy text be printed?"

"I plan to have a printing company called Magma handle the entire process once the manuscript is ready. I have an old acquaintance I trust who works there."

"Magma? Do you mean Peter Nordman? He's been on our payroll for many years, earning his keep more than most. But does Magma have the financial capability to do this? The company only has an annual turnover of around thirty million crowns. How will Magma manage to print so many Qurans?"

Benno stared at Ahmed, taken aback by Ahmed's well-known photographic memory. It felt surreal. Benno couldn't have known that Ahmed had obtained information about Nordman's personal preferences, leading him to look closely at Magma. Ahmed now saw new possibilities in a close collaboration with Magma.

"Ah, you know Peter Nordman. How has he been instrumental?"

"Magma has published several books that have been valuable to us, but that's not all. Peter Nordman, in cooperation with the chairman of the Swedish Publicist Association— that Jewish guy, Robert Schwansberg— has managed to stop and censor several books we don't like."

"Okay, fine. Then, we'll go with Magma as the publisher. But why does Schwansberg handle your errands?"

"It's no surprise at all. He's also on our payroll."

Benno felt confused. It seemed that almost all of Sweden's journalists and writers were on the Muslim Brotherhood's payroll. He wondered if the entire dominant media family was bought. Benno took a deep breath and continued.

"But there's a small issue we need to discuss. The holy book might seem a bit intimidating to the Swedes and could be counterproductive. There are about thirty to forty passages in the book where the infidels are to be seized, mutilated, and killed in various ways. To win the Swedes' trust, I suggest we omit these sections."

"So, you propose we tamper with the sacred words that come directly from Allah?"

Ahmed fixed Benno with a hard stare, his brow furrowed. Benno felt he was walking on thin ice and needed to tread carefully.

"No, absolutely not. We won't change a comma, of course. We'll omit a few minor parts that might be seen as frightening. As you know, I've studied the texts and believe anything beneficial to the cause is permissible."

"Yes, that's correct. It's always allowed to deceive the infidels if it benefits Islam. Even in everyday situations, infidels should be tricked and deceived. We're always playing a game against them, but they don't get it."

Ahmed paused, looking thoughtful before continuing aloud:

"The Quran is Allah's pure and unaltered word. It is one hundred percent untouchable. I must think this over and discuss it with the imams. Proceed with the translation project, but hold off on printing."

"Our PR plan includes having all Swedes speaking Arabic within three years. Therefore, we need to start an extensive educational program. All school instruction will be in Arabic, and all adult Swedes must attend Quran schools in the evening. Swedes will read the Quran in its original language within three years—and then we'll burn all Swedish Qurans, as they are not entirely complete. The Swedish language will disappear entirely anyway."

"Okay. I can probably accept this, as it's a temporary measure. But we should never mention that this Swedish Quran is incomplete. These are susceptible issues for serious Muslims. And the Swedish Qurans must be burned, along with all other Swedish texts."

Benno felt satisfied as his PR plan seemed to be approved with minimal changes. He had secured his position and his survival. He despised Islam down to his very core and hated himself for what he was doing, but necessity had no laws. When the time was right, he would find a way back to Stockholm, which Swedish hands had recently retaken. The problem was that he was under round-the-clock surveillance by the Muslim General Staff's guard, indicating that he had not fully won the Muslims' trust—at least not yet. He would bide his time and seize the opportunity when it arose. He felt confident that, eventually, a weakness would appear, and he would strike swiftly.

But until that day, it was crucial to play the game to the fullest. He had re-converted to Islam and donned a floor-length kaftan. The cap was replaced with a ridiculous, crocheted topi, which he hated most. It was exactly like the white topi he had worn during the Muslims' occupation of Stockholm. He looked like a damn fool. Again.

"I have taken the liberty of adding something to the PR plan. It involves shifting the perspective by increasing the Muslims' understanding of the Swedes."

"Yes, that might not hurt, even though the Swedes should be converting and adapting to us. How do you propose to do this?"

"I believe humor is the right medicine for achieving this. Humor can transcend ethnic and cultural boundaries and subtly introduce the message without the audience realizing it. Humor can be used as very effective propaganda."

"That sounds interesting, but how?"

"I've already approached two well-known figures – two well-known stand-up comedians who have made a living mocking Swedes and Swedishness for many years. Considering their success with Swedish audiences, you can imagine how a Muslim audience would react."

"So, who are these two people?"

"One is a Swede named Henrik Skyffel. The other is a Swedish Kurd named Özgür Gegin, known by the stage name Özz Nöjen. Skyffel has the right touch for Swedish humor, while Özz understands the Muslim audience. They've already started working on a talk show together, where Özz plays the wise and strong Muslim, while Skyffel takes on the role of the Swedish fool."

"Yes, that's right. Muslims must always be the strongest ones. In our culture, we don't have a tradition of mocking ourselves, as you Swedes love to do. Anyone who mocks Muslims will certainly be beaten to death by the audience."

"Özz Nöjen's participation guarantees that no mistakes will be made."

"If they do make mistakes, it's their fault. It can be dangerous to play with fire. I know both of them, as I've seen their names on the Muslim Brotherhood's payroll lists. But I haven't met them yet."

"My idea is for them to tour in front of a Muslim audience as court jesters. Even the *God Warriors* in the field will appreciate the show."

"I'm sure they will, and they need entertainment to relieve the pressure."

"Trust me—these guys will have the entire audience doubled with laughter. I almost died laughing when I read one of their sketches where Skyffel is dressed as a large dog, led on a leash by Özz. In another skit, Skyffel will be dressed as a pig."

"Ha-ha-ha, it sounds like you're on the right track. Promise me that the first show will be for the General Staff—then we can invite some prominent guests."

"It will be a great honor for both myself and Skyffel and Özz."

Chapter 7 – Muslim Attack Plans

April 1, 2033

The divinely favored Supreme Commander of the Muslims, Ahmed Ben Barka, observed with barely concealed distaste as his right-hand man, General Mahmoud Khalil, struggled to open the plastic wrapping around the coveted sesame honey cakes. Eventually, Mahmoud's efforts were rewarded with success. He looked up, allowing his unshaven, strained face to break into a wide smile that exposed his discolored, brown teeth. Ahmed could smell his rancid breath from across the table despite the six-foot-wide expanse that separated them. Mahmoud immediately shoved a honey cake into his mouth, biting it in half, and continued his report, alternating between chewing and sucking on the crumbs.

"Our intelligence clearly shows that the Swedes are preparing a major offensive, but I'd guess it will be at least another week before it happens," Mahmoud said, shoving the other half of the honey cake into his mouth. "Our infiltrators report that additional reinforcements are heading to the little town of Tomelilla, where the main force is spread out in smaller units around the town."

Ahmed hoped the crumbs flying from Mahmoud's mouth wouldn't reach him sitting across the table. He instinctively leaned back to avoid getting hit in the face. His loyal aide, Master Chef Hassan, fortunately, had more freshly pressed shirts ready if needed.

"Yes, sooner or later, the offensive will come. The infidels have been unexpectedly passive since the Russians entered Sweden," Ahmed said. "The Swedes haven't had the resources to challenge them, but now it seems the parties have reached some agreement. The Russians are in the process of packing up, and we can see they are leaving the occupied zone while Swedish forces are moving in."

"It would be exciting to know what this agreement entails!" Mahmoud replied. "Will we be fighting the Russians as well?"

Mahmoud suddenly inhaled a crumb of the honey cake into his airway, coughing and scattering crumbs and saliva across the table. He quickly wiped the table with a few swipes of his hand and forearm, then cleaned his hand by rubbing it against his pants. The others observed the spectacle in fascinated silence, with uncomfortable smiles.

"I'm betting the Russians will let the Swedes handle the groundwork, but they will support the Swedes with at least weapon supplies and intelligence," Ahmed said. "In the worst case, they might provide air support for the Swedes. If that happens, we could face problems."

"But the Russians must have gained something from this agreement; otherwise, they wouldn't have given up the occupation zone. The question is, what?" Mahmoud asked.

"I believe the Swedes have agreed to abandon their claims to the islands of Gotland and Öland for good in exchange for returning the rest of the country. Russians inhabit the islands, and the months are ticking by. For the Russians living there, the islands are already their home and the only home they have. Soon, the islands will also be considered Russian by the international community. Additionally, the Russians will retain the two bases on the east coast and the base in southern Halland."

"Yes, that seems logical. The Russians' interest is to control the Baltic Sea and the outlet to the Atlantic. They're not particularly interested in Sweden itself."

"Yes, an occupation of Sweden would be too challenging against the major powers, and the Russians don't want to challenge them unnecessarily," Ahmed concluded dryly. "We must not sit idly by and wait for the Swedes to attack. The best defense is a good offense! Therefore, in the spirit of the Prophet, we will surprise the enemy with an attack when they least expect it. *Inshallah!*"

"I agree with you, Ahmed, and I will soon present my plan for attack," Colonel Shahram Gaidan said, nodding slightly as he spoke. "We should launch the attack as soon as possible before the Swedes have had time to organize properly. There is some disorder as the Russians leave the area before the Swedes fully establish themselves."

Colonel Gaidan was one of eight highly experienced military officers flown in from the Middle East after most of the Muslim General Staff was eliminated by the successful assassination at Stockholm Palace, carried out by the two Swedish special forces operatives, Max Adlerswärd and Ina Sjöstrand.

Another attack on the General Staff was not to be allowed. With the new Head of Security, Zlatko Muslimovic, the security measures have been ramped up several notches. Muslimovic was meticulous and uncompromising by nature. He would also control all factors if responsible for the staff's security. Now, it wasn't just the meetings that were closely monitored. Every movement by staff members was accompanied by soldiers from the security team, who also served as their bodyguards. Staff members frequently changed their sleeping quarters, selected by Muslimovic, and constantly guarded by the security team.

"Mahmoud, how's our new star, Muslimovic, doing?" Ahmed asked curiously.

"He's amazing! Our security is at a level I've never seen before. What happened at Stockholm Palace would never have happened if Zlatko had been in charge," Mahmoud replied.

"Yes, I realized that immediately when I met him," Ahmed said, not without a hint of self-satisfaction.

"You should meet Ivan, whom Zlatko has brought in as his deputy. They're childhood friends. He's just as ruthless as Zlatko, though smaller and different."

"Is he also Serbian?"

"No, he's a Macedonian Albanian. From Sarena Dzamija. You know, where the world-famous ornate mosque is located."

"Yes, I've been inside that mosque. But are you sure he's a devout Muslim?"

"Yes! Albanians in North Macedonia have been devout Muslims for five hundred years, no problem. They are stricter Muslims than anywhere else in the world, except perhaps the Chechens, but no one believes that because they are Europeans."

"But Muslims don't usually go by the name Ivan."

"It's just what he's called. His real name is Zuber Ivanisevic. You can be completely at ease."

"Okay, it seems to be in order. Just wanted to check. But he should change his last name."

Ahmed's concerns about the Muslim conviction were because he hadn't fully assured himself of this when he hired Zlatko Muslimovic as head of security. There was a seed of unease within him, a vague sense that Muslimovic might not be a committed Muslim, but he was willing to accept Mahmoud's explicit assurances for the time being.

Mahmoud couldn't know that the new deputy head of security, Ivan, was actually from Skopje, the capital of Macedonia, an ethnic Serb long active in the Macedonian Orthodox Church in Northern Rosengård. Ivan, like all Orthodox Christians in the Balkans, harbored a deep-seated hatred for anything related to Islam for historical reasons, and they had ample cause for it. There were significant tensions between the Christian Macedonian and Albanian Muslim populations, which had led to several armed conflicts, the latest in 2001 when Albanian-Muslim rebels took up arms once again.

Conflicts had flared up intermittently for hundreds of years, and there was no reason to believe they would ever cease. The most recent civil war in 2001 led to the Ohrid Agreement, essentially a ceasefire rather than genuine peace until the next war. The wounds from the Balkan wars of the 1990s were still unhealed. No wounds between religious groups in the Balkans ever seemed to heal. Historical grievances dating back hundreds of years were often cited to justify the wars, and the storehouse of grievances grew with each new conflict.

Ivan expected more wars in the eternal conflict between Islam and Christianity, but things were calm back in North Macedonia. The conflict had, much to Ivan's dismay, followed him to Sweden, where he had moved to work hard and earn money, but also because the country was politically stable, without ethnic-religious conflicts. But that was then. Sweden had now become the Balkans of the North, with all its problems, which Ivan was heartily tired of. In particular, he resented a specific event that directly affected his beautiful – now former – church in northern Rosengård. The construction of the massive Umm al-Muminin Khadijah Mosque on the church's neighboring lot, inaugurated in 2017, made his church look like a small shed belonging to the mosque complex. When the war broke out on July 17, 2032, one of the first acts of war in Malmö was the vandalism and subsequent bombing of the Macedonian Orthodox Church by *God's Warriors*, who went on a rampage against Malmö's Christian population—none of this surprised Ivan. Since then, he had been constantly contemplating how to blow up the Umm al-Muminin Khadijah Mosque in revenge.

Colonel Shahram Gaidan replaced the highly experienced Syrian General Mohamed, who had been the foremost expert on urban combat for the Muslims before he was eliminated in the attack on the Muslims' staff meeting at Stockholm Palace. Although General Mohamed's expertise was highly valued, the level of proficiency rose even higher with Colonel Gaidan's arrival. His efforts during the Battle of Fallujah in 2004, during the Iraq War, garnered his attention and earned him the Golden Eagle, the highest award for field operations. Now fifty- eight years old, he spoke with the gravitas that only genuine combat experience can bestow. At the same time, the Golden Eagle's outstretched wings gleamed on his right breast pocket, further enhancing his authority. The Eagle was made of almost one troy ounce of pure gold and was every Iraqi soldier's dream to display at home as a highly admired national hero. Yet, few had been awarded, making it an unattainable dream for most.

"Looks like the Swedes are also mounting a serious effort east of Ystad," Mahmoud observed. "They've already brought in an estimated twelve thousand infantry soldiers and hundreds of armored vehicles that they're taking over from the Russians. More soldiers are joining all the time. According to our intelligence, they're currently repainting the vehicles. The Russian symbols are being painted over with brushes and replaced with Swedish decals."

"Some of these vehicles are equipped with automatic cannons, the same kind they use on their attack helicopters. Nasty stuff that we need to watch out for," Colonel Gaidan interjected.

"That's precisely why we need to strike swiftly and ruthlessly," Ahmed said. "They shouldn't be allowed to organize themselves at their leisure. When do we launch the attack?"

Colonel Shahram Gaidan stood up next to the map of southwestern Skåne, projected onto the white wall. Before he began his address, he pointed to today's Quranic verses on a wall screen.

"That's right, Ahmed. The infidels know that our *jihad* warriors never waver—until Allah calls them. Their unwavering faith and boundless cruelty are our greatest assets. The infidels tremble with fear when we approach them, just as they always have since the days of the great conquerors."

Colonel Gaidan paused dramatically before emphatically declaring, "In the spirit of the Prophet, I say: We shall show no mercy."

He paused again, gesturing meaningfully for the audience to respond, which they did obediently. "We shall show no mercy," the others echoed in unison.

Gaidan looked satisfied. He extended his arm, pointing to the screen, and read the first Quranic verse aloud and clearly with his powerful voice.

4:93 "Seize them and kill them wherever you find them, for over the infidels we have been given open authority."

Gaidan retrieved a red plastic ballpoint pen from his pocket and pointed to the screen.

"I think the true words of God from our sacred scripture's seventh *Surah* are especially fitting for today," he said. He read the second Quranic verse with the full force of his authority:

7:3 "How many cities have We destroyed? And Our power overwhelmed them by night."

Gaidan placed his red pen on the map, at Ystad, before continuing.

"We will commence the attack at dawn on Thursday, which is in four days, with a feint via the European Highway 65 towards Ystad. Ystad will be shelled with heavy artillery from the guns east of Skurup while we advance our troops along the E65. Even though it's a feint, we will take the opportunity to lay Ystad to waste, as the town is considered historically significant by the Swedes."

"Sounds like music to my ears!" Mahmoud grinned. "All that Swedish, pathetic, lowly trash will be leveled to the ground!"

"But as you know, our main force is positioned along National Highway eleven, between Sjöbo and Tomelilla, where we have discreetly assembled over fifty thousand soldiers, troop transport vehicles, civilian buses and trucks, armored vehicles, our remaining eight Abrams tanks, and eighty lighter tanks," Colonel Gaidan continued.

"Good, excellent!" Ahmed exclaimed. "I didn't think we'd be ready so soon. But how do you plan to use the main force?"

"A smaller portion of the force, about twelve thousand soldiers supported by lighter tanks and artillery, will make a flanking maneuver north of the infidels' forces in Tomelilla, via Hedeberga, and then south to

Lunnarp. This way, we block the infidels' retreat both north and east, and they will be forced to retreat since they are not yet in combat formation."

Colonel Gaidan traced his red pen over the map as he spoke.

"And now for the best part," Colonel Gaidan continued. "We will advance with the main force through a nature reserve, a valley called Fyledalen, which the infidels will never expect due to the small roads. There's only a road named Fyledalsvägen that follows the small Fyle River here," Gaidan said, sweeping his pen over the map once more. "It will be cramped on Fyledalsvägen, but there are no natural obstacles, and according to our calculations, it should proceed smoothly. It's only about twelve miles. Most troops will be transported in regular buses and trucks; we do not expect artillery fire."

"How do we know that?" General Mahmoud inquired.

"There isn't a single Swedish soldier visible in the valley, and we already have our reconnaissance troops in place, discreetly positioned in the terrain with coverage of the entire valley."

Gaidan looked at Mahmoud, who nodded silently in acknowledgment of the satisfactory answer before Gaidan continued.

"We will pass through the valley and occupy the small villages of Benestad, Övraby, and Bollerup before the infidels can get there, as they will be engaged in battle when the smaller part of our force attacks from the north," Colonel Gaidan said.

"Then we've got them cornered!" Ahmed declared with a satisfied smile.

"Once we've eradicated their forces in the little town of Tomelilla, we'll push south with all our forces towards the village of Köpingebro and then to the sea at Nybrostrand to trap their forces in the town of Ystad. At the same time, we will launch a heavy assault from the west against Ystad, where we initially started the feint attack."

"They have nowhere to go; they're completely trapped," noted Prince Saud, the Saudi intelligence chief. The staff members often referred to him as Prince Saud, as his full, elaborate name was a bit cumbersome.

Prince Saud had extensive experience from the war in Yemen and from many years as the head of Saudi Arabia's feared and intensely despised religious security service, the Mutawa, which was notorious for intervening in people's private lives. At the same time, Prince Saud was the head of Saudi Arabia's paramilitary forces, which numbered up to seventy-five thousand men, making him a person with significant experience.

Prince Saud was indeed a prince, though only one of about fifteen thousand genuine princes, excluding illegitimate offspring.

"The cowardly Swedes will surrender once they realize they're trapped!" Mahmoud said, laughing crudely. "What do we do with them afterward?"

"Those who surrender will be allowed to give up, but we will shoot them all as soon as they have capitulated," Ahmed said with an impassive expression. "As we agreed just now," Colonel Gaidan confirmed. "We will show no mercy."

"Those who are trapped but still refuse to surrender will be wiped out by artillery. We don't have the resources to feed the enemy, and the cowards who surrender don't deserve to live," Ahmed concluded.

A spontaneous applause broke out among the fourteen officers, who chuckled contentedly as they envisioned the upcoming victory. "The plan is excellent!" Ahmed summarized. "I don't think we can fail. Once we have completely crushed them, they won't have much defense left. Then, we'll take over the entire Russian zone as our first step. After that, we'll return to Stockholm – *Makat Almukarama* will be ours again. I truly want to realize our grand plans for this beautiful place and turn it into a Mecca for Muslims across Europe."

Applause and cheers erupted at a volume that suggested many more people than were in the room. The men patted each other on the back, laughed, and did high-fives in an American manner.

Hassan, who had discreetly stayed in the background, waited for the celebratory noise to die before stepping forward to the conference table, maintaining his usual dignified and friendly demeanor.

"If it suits the gentlemen, Saudi lamb stew, the national dish, *Kabsa*, will be served in the dining room in ten minutes," Hassan said with a smile towards Prince Saud. "Even the dessert today is a Saudi specialty, but exactly what it is will be a little surprise for you," Hassan added with a smile before leaving the room to put the final touches on the

Muhallabia. At the same time, the high-ranking gentlemen enjoyed their *Kabsa* with freshly baked pita bread.

Hassan was not one to leave anything to chance, whether it came to food or other matters. In the West, he had been called a perfectionist. Or a detail-oriented stickler, depending on who was speaking.

Chapter 8 – Evacuation

April 4–5, 2033

"You have about fifteen hours to evacuate the valley," said Russia's Ambassador to Sweden, Iosif Vissarionovich, fixing his gray-blue eyes on Gyllenstierna. "That should be more than enough time."

"It's not a problem getting our troops out of the way, but it might be more challenging with the civilian population," Gyllenstierna replied. "We appreciate you giving us this information and your willingness to help, but I'd like to know exactly what you plan to do."

"You'll have to make do with the information I've given you," Vissarionovich said, his tone slightly aggressive. He paused briefly before continuing. "But if I were you, I'd take this information seriously and do exactly as I say. Our intelligence indicates that the Muslims will start moving their troops into the valley of Fyledalen at 4.30 a.m. tomorrow, and we're confident in our sources. We've intercepted their command communications, and everything they say is corroborated by what we observe from our reconnaissance satellites."

"But I still don't understand," Gyllenstierna persisted. "They'll be moving along the road of Fyledalsvägen if your information about the attack through the valley is correct. Why do we need to evacuate the entire valley? It should be enough to evacuate the farms along the road if you're planning to bomb the Muslims' troops to bits."

"The information I've received from my superiors is what I've just shared with you. I don't have all the details on what will happen, but my conclusion from what's been said is that anyone in the valley is at high risk of being caught in the crossfire."

Ambassador Vissarionovich stood up and extended his surprisingly pale, slender right hand across the table.

"That's all for today. The rest is up to you now."

Gyllenstierna shook the Russian's hand firmly and held on, urgently asking his final questions. He was not pleased with the Russian's demeanor, which was more reminiscent of a Hell's Angels enforcer than a traditional ambassador. There were no "honest and straightforward words," as diplomats put it when arguments arose, but instead threats, insults, and demands. Still, mutual respect had slowly developed between them after numerous lengthy meetings throughout the winter. They were both critical of each other. Gyllenstierna's impressive work capacity and structural thinking impressed Vissarionovich, just as Gyllenstierna was impressed by the Russian's ability to distill complex situations into a few easily understandable statements. The Russian would have made an excellent instructor at the Karlberg Military Academy, perhaps in military geopolitics, Gyllenstierna mused.

"One might think you're planning to use tactical nuclear weapons, but surely you're not going that far?" Gyllenstierna said. "The column moving along Fylevägen road should be a suitable target for missile and automatic cannon attacks. Or conventional bombs—you have plenty of combat aircraft stationed on Gotland and Öland. I see no reason to go any further."

"Military decisions are not mine to make. What happens will become clear in less than fifteen hours," the ambassador concluded, glancing at his wristwatch. "To be honest, I'm as curious as you are."

Gyllenstierna accompanied Vissarionovich to the door, opened it, and thanked the ambassador with a friendly smile. Vissarionovich was rather unpleasant, but it had proven that he had significant influence over Russian activities in Sweden, so it was wise to maintain the relationship. Gyllenstierna was a consummate relationship builder, never burning bridges unnecessarily.

After Vissarionovich left the room, Gyllenstierna stood in place for nearly a minute, contemplating what had been said with a vacant, inward-looking gaze. He needed someone who could get the job done quickly before it was too late and knew more about swiftly clearing areas than Björn Väster of the National Order Council, the master of deportations.

Within a few minutes, Väster entered, dressed in his usual black uniform, which seemed a bit overloaded with ornate gold details, at least to Gyllenstierna. Gyllenstierna thought the uniform resembled the flamboyant outfits often worn by African dictators, always holding marshal's staffs, but Väster seemed proud of having the most ostentatious uniform of all. He had designed it himself, and modesty was not Väster's strong suit.

"Björn, something very urgent and important has come up, and I need you to handle it immediately without asking why. Okay?"

"Sure, what can I do for you?" Väster replied, eager and attentive.

"Great, I knew you were the best person for this job," Gyllenstierna flattered him. "The entire area known as Fyledalen needs to be completely evacuated," Gyllenstierna said, sweeping over the map he had just used in discussions with the Russian ambassador. "It's a fairly narrow valley, thirteen miles long."

"Got it. That shouldn't be a problem. How many people live in Fyledalen?" Väster asked.

"Not sure, probably a few hundred. Scattered across farms and cottages. As far as I know, there's no town."

"What's the timeline?"

"The area needs to be cleared by midnight."

"Midnight? You must be joking!" Väster exclaimed, glancing at his watch, which was crammed with various dials and gauges. "That gives me eight and a half hours."

"Aim for midnight if you can. If not, you and all our personnel must leave the area by 3 a.m. Absolutely."

"Well, there's no time to waste. I need to get started right away," Väster said, his tone slightly stressed but still filled with his usual positive energy.

"You have access to all the resources available here. I suggest using your team, which is experienced in evacuating civilians. You know where the trucks and buses are. About fifteen to twenty should do the trick. Ideally, drop the people off in Ystad, with resources and housing. I'll make sure someone oversees reception there."

"I'll get back to you with a report once we're done, which will be by 3.30 a.m. at the latest," Väster said, already pulling out his radio and heading out of the room with brisk steps.

Thank God for people like Björn Väster, Gyllenstierna thought as he settled into his office chair. For once, he was not getting much done that afternoon and evening, as he couldn't stop thinking about what the Russians were planning. What on earth were they up to in Fyledalen? No matter how he twisted and turned the situation, he couldn't figure out what to expect. He realized it must be something truly extraordinary.

An hour and forty minutes later, a convoy of twenty-two buses and four trucks rolled out from the base near Tomelilla, heading towards Fyledalen. True to form, Väster wanted to oversee the operation personally, and he had already activated two of the timing functions on his advanced watch, which was more of a sophisticated little computer than a mere timepiece.

Björn Väster wasn't entirely satisfied as he glanced at his watch. It had taken too long to get the vehicles ready, which weren't even fueled when he finally got control. There had also been some issues with the organization, as there weren't enough maps to distribute and mark. It was old-fashioned paper maps now that all civilian technology had failed. To make matters worse, the printer ran out of toner, causing an additional twelve and a half minutes delay.

The camp's organization was still not up to speed, something he would have to point out to Brännström, who was in charge. It certainly wouldn't have looked like this if he had been responsible.

But now they were on their way, and within twenty minutes, the forced evacuation of the valley would begin. Väster had ordered that civilians who resisted should be restrained with plastic zip ties and, if necessary, carried into the buses. Those who ran off to the forest would be left to their fate. There was no time for searches in the terrain, which likely concealed enemy reconnaissance troops. However, most people would probably obediently get on the buses. While Swedes were generally accustomed to obeying authority figures, Väster had learned that the people of Skåne were stubborn and always distrusted their superiors, mainly if they spoke with a Stockholm accent. He was from the "whining belt," born in Lindesberg, and even his accent seemed to irritate the people in Skåne just as much as Stockholm's did. He had come to believe that his accent was provocative for many Swedes, not just the Skåne people, and he was right in that assumption.

The first four farms went smoothly. His team from the National Task Force, reinforced with a couple of trigger-happy Icelanders from the Lagerbäck Battalion, knocked on doors and explained that the enemy— Muslims—was approaching and that the valley needed to be evacuated immediately for the safety of the residents. To increase motivation, they lied that the enemy had just carried out mass executions in Sjöbo.

The fifth evacuation target was a modest, small cabin up the slope on the forest's edge. As they approached the house and drove onto the yard, they noticed it resembled a junkyard. A few old diesel and gasoline cars that had seen better days decades ago stood rusting right in front of the house. An old red tractor from the early days of agricultural mechanization was parked in front of the entrance. The tracks in the mud suggested the tractor was still in use, though Väster wondered how the owner managed to get diesel for it.

After Väster's two men had knocked on the door and waited almost a minute, the house owner suddenly appeared behind them, holding an old Husqvarna shotgun with barrels side by side, raised threateningly.

"What the hell are you doing here?" the man growled in such a thick and gruff Skåne accent that they could barely understand him. "Get lost! You have no business here on my property."

Väster observed the scene from his seat inside the bus, right by the driver's position. He thought the burly, overweight man looked like a parody of a Skåne peasant. He was dressed in ugly, worn-out Chinese jeans that he'd probably picked up for twenty-five crowns at the cheap mall Gekås in Ullared, without a belt, sagging so low that the top of his butt crack was visible at the waistband. The jeans were so dirty they seemed to stand on their own. He looked like he had just come from working in the manure pit, and it was unlikely he wore deodorant. The overly tight T-shirt, which had once been white, was pulled up to reveal the lower part of his pale, bloated stomach. On his feet were a pair of worn and unevenly shaped clogs, inexplicably called "wooden shoes" by Swedes, despite not being made of wood. His head was topped with a dirty, green, white free cap that read "Swedish Farmers Association."

The epitome of a country bumpkin, Väster thought, such specimens probably only existed in Skåne and in surprisingly large numbers. The country bumpkins back home in the "whining belt" were of a different sort. They always smelled of oil because all their energy and time were spent repairing and refurbishing old American cars, which they then cruised endlessly around the streets of small towns, never seeming to tire of it. Their jeans often bore traces of fingers, as they had a habit of wiping their greasy hands on their pants. This bumpkin's jeans, however, were uniformly filthy.

"We're here for your safety," said the one who had knocked on the door. "The Muslims are coming, and they're killing all civilians."

"What Muslims?" the bumpkin asked aggressively. "If any damn raghead shows up here, he'll taste my shotgun, you get it?"

The man's red eyes and pink face, with sparse gray stubble, made him resemble a pig. The purple blood vessels forming an exemplary network on his swollen, misshapen nose revealed that his drinking habits would have made any alcohol counselor frown. The moonshine still was probably bubbling away somewhere in the hovel. It was the kind of drunkard that had led to the valley being nicknamed "Fylledalen" – Drunk Valley by the locals.

Perhaps a Muslim occupation might save him from cirrhosis of the liver if it wasn't already too late, Väster thought. A complete dry-out of the region would probably be good for his health. But, given his pig-like appearance, he might run into trouble with the Muslims for that very reason.

The man's thick, slurred Skåne accent made Swedes from the north demand subtitles when Skåne people appeared on TV.

"You don't think you can come here and tell me what to do, do you?" the man said. "I've worked and paid taxes my whole life. A real damn hellhole, you should know. I worked at the chicken slaughterhouse all those years without anyone ever thanking me. I should get a medal from the king."

Had any of his escorts understood his muddled speech, they would have realized that "the faith" meant "the feather," which was the local slang term—or at least his slang—for the giant chicken slaughterhouse outside Kristianstad. In reality, he had only worked at the slaughterhouse for three and a half years before his commuting ended abruptly due to a police checkpoint in the village of Brösarp, which resulted in two months in jail and a revoked driver's license.

After that, there was no more wage work and no driver's license, but he had scraped by all his life with a basic income from social services and black-market sales of homegrown new potatoes, homemade moonshine bottled in light blue bottles with crinkled glass, neatly labeled as "Fyle Absolut Pure Vodka," and a constant dozen or so growing piglets. He fed the pigs with his grown potatoes and corn until they could be sold as prime fattened pigs to consumers with deep pockets, yielding premium pork neck, delicious chops, meticulously trimmed pork tenderloin, and farm-smoked bacon.

Tourists from Stockholm gladly paid exorbitant prices for organic pork from Österlen farms, with red meat, unlike the white and tasteless, often Danish, antibiotic-laden chops sold in supermarkets for a fraction of the farm prices. The Stockholmers got the organic pork they wanted, for no one could deny that his pig production was at least small-scale like in the old days, even if the pigs were fed crops that he sprayed heavily, but it didn't affect the taste, so what did it matter?

Like many others in the countryside, he had become a skilled survivalist out of necessity, a born genius with constantly new ideas on how to "bring in a little extra cash" on top of the primary social benefits. They could have built up a substantial operation without him and his partner, who consumed much of the moonshine production. But as it turned out, alcohol always took priority over everything else.

Sometimes, he missed his job at the slaughterhouse, which involved gassing the newly arrived chickens. The mere thirty-five-week-old birds were subjected to a proper dose of carbon dioxide smoke before being hung upside down, their feet pierced by conveyor hooks, and transported away in a long line, spaced a few inches apart, for their final fate in the slaughterhouse. There, their heads were literally torn off, mechanically, before their plucked, scalded, and cleaned two-pound-heavy bodies left the factory, neatly packaged on a white foam tray, vacuum-sealed, and adorned with a generously extended expiration date.

Occasionally, one of the arriving chickens' cardboard boxes would get dented or torn by the forklift, causing some birds to fall out. He referred to these as "stray piles of crap" because they were usually dirty and just caused problems. He disliked them, if possible, even more than the regular arrivals. After a brief inspection of their condition, he would decide whether they would get a turn on the conveyor or end up in the waste grinder. Annoyingly, he had to keep statistics on the number that ended up in the grinder.

At the slaughterhouse, he used to daydream during his monotonous shifts, pretending that the new arrivals were some of the hundreds of thousands of fake refugees who had invaded Skåne and destroyed everything he valued. They were all counterfeit refugees, that was for sure. Not that he read newspapers, but he knew well enough that they hadn't fled from wars and persecution as they claimed. Just the fact that they threw away their passports was suspicious. No, these incoming slackers had come only to have good Swedes—like him—support them for life. He hated them with all his heart. Above all, the massive influx of refugees had forced social services to cut his monthly benefits, as even social services' resources were not inexhaustible. Everything that had gone wrong in his crooked life was the fault of the invaders. In his fantasies, he turned his little reception unit into his very own Bergen-Belsen—a refugee slaughterhouse instead of a chicken slaughterhouse—where he was the absolute commander with the right to decide life and death. He often ordered roll calls for the twenty thousand new arrivals, with his booming voice echoing through the empty hall.

"Attention! *Achtung*! Hurry up! *Schnell*!" After being subjected to harsh German commands, the new arrivals were treated to massive German military marches played at top volume. The swirling drumfire and heavy, thunderous bass drumbeats, booming like cannon fire, accompanied by the rhythmic chanting of the bass drummers, reverberated through half the factory.

The new arrivals enjoyed singing along to lyrical battle songs from the nine-teen-thirties, often his absolute favorite, "*Die Fahne hoch*" by Horst Wessel. He had played it so many times that he could sing along to the entire text, even though he only understood a few words.

"Die Fahne hoch!
Die Reihen fest geschlossen! S.A. marschiert
Mit ruhig festem Schritt ..."

On special occasions like Hitler's birthday and death day, Wagner's pompous and fateful operas would blast through the airwaves instead. Wagner's music sets the mood, and he sometimes stands at attention while enjoying the music.

However, the new arrivals needed help to appreciate the fine music. They had already been gassed to unconsciousness with carbon dioxide in the large, open industrial hall where they had spent their short lives as "free-range chickens." The "free-range" label was a stretch, as it hardly applied during their last weeks when they had grown so large they had to step on each other.

The chickens arrived at the slaughterhouse in large boxes, each containing ninety-nine unfortunate brothers, after a final and often rather long truck ride. They were all roosters, sorted out by the only ones in the world who can sex newly hatched chicks—the Japanese—because roosters build muscle mass faster than hens. Thus, they had become accustomed to traveling from the start of their short lives.

Upon arrival at the slaughterhouse, they weighed just over three pounds, including feathers, heads, innards, and feet. The fresh air they encountered during transport made most of them perk up a bit and perhaps even move around a little, which is why the drunkard from Fyledalen took pleasure in gassing the roosters again in his own little Bergen-Belsen. He smiled broadly every time he turned on the gas valve.

"Savor the gas, ha-ha-ha!"

Chicken from supermarkets was something he would never put in his mouth. The chickens that roamed freely and pecked at feed peas on his small farm in Fyledalen, although well-sprayed peas— "got to keep the pests away!"—were something entirely different, and they didn't taste fishy. They were sold as organic chickens, as evidenced by their darker meat, and were extremely tasty, fetching two hundred crowns each from foolish tourists from Stockholm. Most of them were hens, unlike the tasteless roosters from the supermarkets.

When the man arrived at the bus, Björn Väster hurriedly opened the ventilation window. At the same time, the man's unapologetic partner was brought into the bus, screaming obscenities and curses. She didn't look more pleasant than her partner or sound any more enjoyable, but at least she had splurged on hydrogen peroxide to bleach her graying hair. And she was no less drunk, rather the opposite. But at least she had made a small beauty investment compared to her unkempt partner.

"Drive, damn it, we've done our part!" Väster urged the driver, ensuring the ventilation window was open as wide as possible.

The bus rolled off toward Ystad, where a hastily set up camp awaited in some barns outside the bombed-out town. The Muslim forces' artillery bombardment had left a few buildings unscathed in the small city.

Shortly after 2 a.m., Väster delivered his verbal report to Gyllenstierna and Brännström. Väster reported that the valley was emptied of people, except for a few small cottages they hadn't had time to clear.

"It's probably around twenty to thirty people, at most," Väster said.

"Excellent job, as always," Gyllenstierna remarked.

Väster savored the praise from Sweden's Chancellor and left the room for some much-needed sleep.

"Just let us know if you need more evacuations or anything else," Väster said while leaving the room.

Väster had no idea why the valley needed to be emptied, and he wasn't the type to dwell on such matters. It would soon become clear anyway, and Väster wasn't one to waste energy on unnecessary concerns. Why worry about things you can't control? It was pure logic.

Once Väster left the room, Gyllenstierna and Brännström remained, pondering what the Russians might be planning for the now-empty area.

"They wouldn't be deploying tactical nukes unnecessarily, would they?" Gyllenstierna asked. "They could stop the Muslims with conventional weapons, so let's hope that's what it is."

"What's odd is that Vissarionovich was so adamant that the entire valley had to be evacuated. That wouldn't have been necessary for a standard airstrike on a convoy," Brännström replied.

"I have a feeling the Russians are going to test some new weapon tomorrow, but I have no idea what it could be."

"I've had the same thought," Brännström said. "There have been reports over the years about the development of vacuum bombs—or FAEs, to use the correct term— which is short for Fuel Air Explosives – continuing in utmost secrecy. Even though there has been little talk about FAEs recently, I suspect that's what it might be. What else could it be? It's not conventional weapons, and I consider nuclear weapons entirely out of the question at this point."

"Yes, you might be right. I had almost forgotten that those thermobaric bombs even existed. It could be just as you suspect."

"In a couple of hours, we'll have the answer," Brännström concluded. "I'll try to get an hour of sleep before the attack."

"Same here. See you at 4.15 a.m. then."

"Sounds good. Good night."

Chapter 9 – From Swaziland to Fyledalen: A Historical Overview

The world's oldest mine is the Ngwenya Mine, located in the Bomvubu Mountains in northwestern Swaziland, better known by its popular name, the "Lion Cave." Here, the ancestors of the local San people began mining "bloodstone ore," or hematite, more than 40,000 years ago. This red ore was extracted to produce red ochre, an excellent pigment when powdered. The ochre was mixed with water and used for rock paintings and cave wall art, which can still be seen and admired today. About 1,500 years ago, the hematite in the Lion Cave began to be mined for iron by migrating Bantus who knew how to melt iron ore. Hematite is also commonly found in Sweden, and its pigment is the basis for Falu Red Paint, which is why all old houses in Sweden are red.

Mining is a hazardous endeavor, and it's not just collapses and cave-ins that claim lives. Throughout history, countless people have perished in treacherous mine explosions caused by explosive gases—known as mine gases—that seep out of the rock and slowly fill the mine shafts until a spark ignites the gas. There are hundreds of documented mine explosions with tragic outcomes, and even today, media reports on mining disasters are standard, often occurring on continents other than Europe. Such explosions can be avoided with modern measurement equipment, ventilation technology, and unions advocating for workplace safety.

Long ago, measurement instruments were unavailable, so other methods had to be used. Caged canaries were early warning systems in Cornwall's hundreds of tin mines. When the canary fell off its perch, it was time to halt work and quickly evacuate to the surface.

Another well-known hazard in mines is dust explosions. These are particularly problematic in coal mines, where fine coal dust fills the shafts and can explode similarly to a gas cloud. Dust explosions occur due to the rapid combustion of small particles, creating effects like gas explosions.

If the dust concentration is high enough, dust explosions can happen with combustible material. Unprovoked explosions have occurred with coal, flour, sugar, and wood.

The trail from the horrific event in the valley Fyledalen on April 5, 2033, can be traced back to the Lion Cave in Swaziland. At that time, forty thousand years ago, the first mine explosions likely occurred, laying the groundwork for developing what are now called thermobaric bombs.

The leap to considering how to harness the forces of mine explosions for military or civilian use is not far. In particular, dust explosions in coal mines had attracted the attention of German weapons developers. The force is immense, and the components are almost free.

In the 1920s, German weapon engineers within the Luftwaffe and Wehrmacht began developing the Taifun weapon. The Taifun was based on coal dust and concentrated oxygen, which was pumped into the air and ignited. The first and possibly only use of the Taifun during World War II was in 1944, in an attack on Russian bunkers in the port city of Sevastopol on the Black Sea. The effect was a disappointment for the Germans. They had previously planned to use Taifun B in the V1 – the world's first cruise missile – but those plans never materialized.

Taifun B was an advanced version of the Taifun, based on kerosene, coal dust, and aluminum powder, which were dispersed and detonated over targets, such as infantry soldiers and armored vehicles, using rockets. Taifun B was intended to thwart the Allied invasion on D-Day, June 6, 1944, but Allied air forces bombed out the weapon systems before they could be used.

The weapon's field effectiveness remained uncertain. A significant drawback was that these artificial dust explosions required calm weather, as wind would disperse the particles, preventing detonation.

After World War II, these thermobaric bombs largely faded from memory, except among American intelligence agencies, which eagerly absorbed information from Germany's highly innovative and visionary weapon engineers. Germany remained the world's leading scientific nation at the war's end but was soon surpassed by the U.S., notably through the mass import of German scientists.

Taifun and Taifun B were early examples of what are now known as thermobaric bombs, although the term was not coined then. The concept involves dispersing a fuel as an aerosol in the air, which is then ignited and reacts with the oxygen in the atmosphere. Thermobaric bombs, or Fuel-Air Explosives (FAEs), have a higher energy content than conventional bombs because the oxygen in the air is used to oxidize the fuel. In contrast, conventional bombs must contain oxidizers to explode.

Unlike conventional bombs, thermobaric bombs produce a powerful blast wave without shrapnel. An FAE typically contains two explosive charges: a small charge that disperses the fuel into an aerosol and a second small charge that ignites the aerosol. Modern FAEs operate through both heat and pressure. The heat wave is created by adding "metallic dust," which burns at high temperatures, usually magnesium or aluminum.

Thermobaric weapons are particularly effective against enemies in enclosed spaces, a fact explored by Russian and American researchers during the Cold War in the fifties and sixties. The aerosol created and dispersed in the air infiltrates bunkers and fortifications before detonating. The explosion and heat wave affect both the outside and inside of the shelter, making it impossible to defend against.

During the later stages of the Vietnam War, from 1955 to 1975, the U.S. used thermobaric bombs. The Americans have carefully perpetuated the myth that FAEs were only used to clear jungle landing zones for helicopters to land and evacuate or deploy troops, but the reality was different.

When the Americans terror-bombed the civilian population in Hanoi during Operation Rolling Thunder and Operation Linebacker from May to October 1972, the Vietnamese responded swiftly. Hanoi is located in one of the world's most fertile agricultural regions, with several feet of soil that is easy to dig. The Vietnamese built tens of thousands of small bunkers by digging holes in the ground along the streets of Hanoi and Haiphong—the port city of Hanoi. Concrete pipes were placed in the holes to form the walls of the bunkers. Steel roofs, resembling giant lids, weighed around twenty to twenty-two pounds and could be locked from the inside.

When air raid alarms sounded, the streets were quickly emptied as people dove into these small bunkers, which provided exceptional protection. It generally required a direct hit to kill those inside. This was a setback for the Americans, who were dissatisfied with the number of casualties. However, they found a solution implemented during Operation Linebacker II, 1972, better known as the Christmas Bombings of Hanoi and Haiphong. The Christmas Bombings were carried out with a massive deployment of B-52 bombers, which are still in service with the U.S. Air Force. The operation was comparable to the most extensive bombing raids on Germany in the final stages of World War II.

The Americans had discovered the bunkers' weak point. Since the bombing lasted for hours, the Vietnamese needed an air supply, so the "lid" was equipped with air vents. The aerosol from the thermobaric bombs entered through these vents and exploded the bunkers from within. The U.S. used conventional bombs to reduce the cities to ruins, complemented by FAEs to kill the people in the bunkers. It was a deadly concoction so effective that the U.S. decided to cease its use due to international protests led by Swedish Prime Minister Olof Palme.

The development of thermobaric bombs continued in utmost secrecy. On August 6, 1982, during the Lebanese-Israeli War, the Israeli Air Force dropped a single American-made FAE as a pure field test against an eight-story residential building. The explosion destroyed the building and killed around three hundred people, most of whom were outside the building.

During the Afghan War from 1979 to 1989, the Russians deployed an unknown number of FAEs of various sizes. The bombs were primarily used to target Afghan fighters hiding in extensive cave systems, but in many cases, they were also weapon tests under field conditions. Afghanistan served as the Russians' testing ground for new weapons, just as Vietnam had been for the Americans.

In August 1999, the Russian Air Force dropped a large FAE during an operation in Dagestan, part of the Second Chechen War. The bomb was released over the village of Tando, where a large number of Chechen soldiers had assembled. Several hundred Chechens were killed, and the town was completely obliterated, leaving barely a trace on the surface.

Throughout the rest of the war, the Chechens fled in all directions in panic whenever a Russian aircraft appeared, demonstrating the profound psychological impact of these doomsday weapons. To our knowledge, no more FAEs were deployed during the Chechen War.

In 2003, the U.S. detonated the largest FAE to date, which the publicity-savvy Americans dubbed the Mother of All Bombs (MOAB). The MOAB was the most powerful bomb ever detonated, aside from nuclear weapons. It used BBH-6—a TNT, hexogen (RDX), and aluminum powder mixture.

The ever-record-hungry Russians, as usual, sought to outdo the Americans in raw power. On September 11, 2007, they detonated a bomb named the "Father of All Bombs" as a nod to the Americans' MOAB. The bomb was parachuted from a TU-160 strategic bomber. Weighing 7.1 tons and yielding forty tons of TNT, its blast area was estimated to be twenty times larger than that of the MOAB, and its temperature was believed to be more than double. The exact explosive mixture used by the Russians remains a secret. Still, it is known that their formula achieved four to five times the explosive power per weight due to advanced nanotechnology with particles as small as a few atomic sizes. The aerosol of nanoparticles dispersed is effectively considered a gas, at least in terms of its effects upon detonation.

FAEs resemble atomic bombs. When the bomb detonates, it creates a nuclear-like flash, followed by a supersonic (faster than the speed of sound) shockwave. This shockwave is significantly weaker than conventional explosives, resulting in a lower impact on buildings, vehicles, and bunkers. However, the shockwave from an FAE lasts much longer and is devastating for living beings. The shockwave is followed by a heatwave with temperatures so high that it melts the surrounding soil.

A unique effect of FAEs is the low-pressure wave that follows the shock front and heat wave. Some claim that the subsequent zone of extreme low pressure has the most devastating impact on humans, which has led to FAEs also being referred to as vacuum bombs. Witnesses report that the low pressure has ripped victims' eyes from their sockets and even pulled their lungs from their bodies due to the vacuum effect, though these claims seem to be strong exaggerations.

What truly makes thermobaric bombs unique is that the pressure wave does not bend around obstacles or repel when encountering them. The aerosol penetrates every crack and shelter before detonating. Therefore, seeking refuge in bunkers, ditches, and trenches is futile, as these offer good protection against pressure waves from conventional explosives. Lying flat in a two-three feet-deep ditch can protect one from most of the pressure wave's force from traditional explosives, as well as the bomb's shrapnel. Only a nearby crater could kill someone seeking refuge. But against FAEs, there is no way to protect oneself, making them more terrifying than conventional bombs.

It would soon become clear to all parties involved in the Swedish war that the technological development of thermobaric bombs had not stalled since the Russians detonated the "Father of All Bombs" in 2007.

Chapter 10 – Thermobaric Barbarism

April 5, 2033

The offensive began as scheduled. At 4.30 a.m., the Muslim troops moved out from their positions along National Highway 11 between the small towns of Sjöbo and Tomelilla. A smaller portion of the force, about eight thousand soldiers supported by light tanks and medium artillery, would conduct a flanking maneuver north of the infidels' forces in Tomelilla via the village of Hedeberga and head south to the neighboring town of Lunnarp.

With just over thirty-one thousand soldiers and armored vehicles, the main force followed National Highway 11. It turned south onto the Tomelillavägen road, just past the village of Rödinge, while the eleven thousand infantry remained in reserve at their posts. After about a mile, at 4.52 a.m., the advance guard began to penetrate the valley of Fyledalen along Fyledalsvägen road. It was still quite dark, but dawn was breaking in the east. It promised a beautiful day, with a high-pressure system over southern Sweden. The weather was perfect.

The Muslim leadership believed they had been observed by Swedish reconnaissance troops in the field as early as their 4.30 a.m. departure. Reports from these scouts had likely reached the Swedish command, prompting the immediate deployment of all available forces. The Swedes likely occupied defensive positions along National Highway 11 to block their advance. Perhaps they had even assigned a smaller force to enter Fyledalen from the south to block Fyledalsvägen road. If so, fighting would soon break out. Still, the Muslim leadership anticipated overcoming the resistance relatively quickly with artillery bombardment, followed by four Abrams tanks leading the way, supported by lighter armored vehicles and infantry.

"That's exactly what I would have done if I were the infidels' commander, Brännström, I believe he's called," said Colonel Shahram Gaidan to the other officers as they sat around the rectangular oak conference table in the temporary headquarters housed in a farmstead outside Sjöbo.

Neither Colonel Gaidan nor anyone else on the Muslim command staff knew that contrary to all conventional military logic, the Swedish troops in Tomelilla had, at the behest of Russian Ambassador Vissarionovich, left Tomelilla during the night to establish new positions in the village of Smedstorp, ten miles to the east. They also didn't know that the entire Fyledalen valley had been emptied of its inhabitants the previous afternoon and evening by the loyal forces of the National Order Council Väster. The valley was deserted except for a few insignificant cottages on the valley's outskirts, up the slopes, which Väster's troops had not yet managed to clear. These cottages were home to thirty-four people, most of whom were retirees.

By 5.30 a.m., the Muslim advance guard had reached the end of the valley without encountering any gunfire or incidents whatsoever. It seemed almost too good to be true. But where were the Swedes? Retreating? Living up to their usual reluctance for open combat? "Cowards," muttered the Muslim soldiers.

What was strange was that the valley was completely deserted, which puzzled the advance guard's leadership. It didn't matter since the Muslim soldiers had orders to spare the civilian population. But if the residents of the valley had somehow known that the Muslim offensive was starting today and would take this unexpected route through the nature reserve, then it meant that the Swedish military leaders had the same information. But where was the Swedish defense? Why hadn't they attempted to block the only narrow road available, which all military logic suggested was the only sensible course of action? Something was amiss, causing some concern among the Muslim army leaders. Were they walking into a trap? Would they soon be surrounded by Swedish troops with no chance of retreat?

The advance guard temporarily halted to wait for contact with the main force, which was spread out in a twelve-mile-long column of armored vehicles, buses full of soldiers, and trucks carrying alternating supplies and soldiers along Fyledalsvägen. The force was now in the somewhat hundred-foot-deep valley, only a couple hundred feet wide at its narrowest points. The leadership of the advance guard sat down in the already lush grass to enjoy a cigarette while silently admiring the beautiful surroundings, as there was nothing particular to discuss.

The weather was perfect. The sky was clear blue and entirely still. Despite it being only late April, nature was in a pre-summer state. The fields were entirely green, and most flowers and leaves on the trees were in full bloom. There was a faint smell of manure, as expected around fields where crops had just begun their growth period in earnest. They remained two to three months before the arduous and hectic harvest season began. The fertile Skåne landscape's strong growth potential was palpable with every breath. The thick, lime-rich soil didn't require irrigation to yield its bounty. Sweden's granary, or perhaps more accurately, a lavishly swelling storeroom of wheat, cabbage, lettuce, oilseeds, and various beets—particularly sugar beets—as well as potatoes, beans, peas, corn, strawberries, apples, and pears. Even apricots had started cultivating in the most sheltered southern locations, though only for personal use, thanks to the warmer climate. Grapes, mostly green varieties, were increasingly grown on the southern slopes, thanks to the warm summers. Skåne seemed poised to become a prominent wine exporter in the longer term, but within the Muslim territories, that prospect would soon end regardless of climate developments.

The leadership trio of the Muslim advance guard had all grown up in Malmö, mainly in the suburb of Rosengård, and had rarely had cause to leave their urban domains for visits to the countryside. Their knowledge of Skåne's flora and fauna was minimal, as was their interest in it. They hadn't even heard of Fyledalen.

Yet even the least trained eyes could not miss the rich wildlife in the reserve while they scanned intensively for enemy soldiers presumed to be hiding in the terrain. Their binoculars revealed a variety of deer, wild boars, foxes, hares, and rabbits everywhere. Above them, numerous buzzards circled, along with hawks, kites, golden eagles, and larks high in the sky. If they had been more informed, they would have also known about the giant bats that flew around the valley at night, hunting insects.

"I had no idea there were so many animals in Sweden," Captain Ibrāhîm said thoughtfully to the other two in the leadership team. "Strangely, we never bothered to come here; it's beautiful! It's called Fyledalen, I believe. We should get out to the countryside more often, to relax. Like meditate and think properly."

"Yeah, it's lovely here, though I dislike the pigs. Have you been to the Kullaberg peninsula, by the way? It's pretty nice too. When we were there during last Ramadan ..."

He paused in the middle of his sentence and pointed at the sky before continuing, "What kind of planes are those? They don't look like fighter jets, anyway."

"Good thing, too, since we don't have any air defense, just a few automatic cannons. They look like transport planes. Five of them in a row. Flying quite low, maybe only a couple of thousand feet."

They raised their binoculars and scanned intensely at the first plane approaching.

"Wow, those look like Russian planes. What's going on?"

As the plane approached, they could see the five-pointed red star, often called the Heineken star, as it was the same symbol as the famous brewery.

"It IS the Russians. But we're not at war with them, so what are they doing here?" he asked with rising concern. "Maybe they're going to supply the Swedes with materials."

Captain Ibrãhîm agilely climbed onto the roof of their armored vehicle and fired a short burst into the air with his submachine gun to attract the attention of the fifty soldiers in the advance guard.

"Hostile aircraft, take cover in the ditches!"

The road was cleared in moments, and the deep ditches on either side were filled with soldiers scanning the sky.

The first plane was already overhead, but to their relief, it continued across the valley without dropping any bombs. The second plane soon passed, followed by the third and fourth, flying directly above them at regular intervals, emitting a low, persistent hum from the sky but not releasing bombs. The Muslims' hearts pounded in their chests; their breath held in tense anticipation.

When the fifth and final plane was directly overhead, something released, and a parachute quickly unfurled. The parachute carried a large container that glistened in the sunlight and slowly descended straight toward them. They could see that the fourth plane had also released a similar container further away from their position in the ditch.

"Fire the autocannons quickly! Take down whatever that is!"

Before the autocannons could engage, the soldiers began shooting at the container with their assault rifles, but it was still too high to hit. Now that the autocannons had acquired the target, a loud explosion was heard, and ten smaller bomb pods ejected from the large container, descending evenly toward them with parachutes much smaller than the one carrying the large container. It looked like a giant dandelion puff, but the seeds descending toward them were not harmless.

"Cluster bombs, damn it! Shoot, we must bring them down before it's too late!"

The dull thudding of the autocannons shattered two of the bomb pods into pieces before their eyes at about four hundred feet high. Likely, several hundred rounds from the AK47s also hit their targets before the subsequent explosion set off all remaining bomb pods simultaneously through a remote detonation mechanism. Debris and shrapnel rained down, and suddenly, there was nothing left to shoot at, causing the gunfire to cease. Silence fell as everyone stared at the now-empty sky, where a mist slowly spread over them.

"What's happening? I don't understand anything!" Captain Ibrâhîm yelled, panic rising.

One of the soldiers stood up from the ditch, speaking resignedly but loudly, "Same thing that happened in Dagestan during the Chechen War. In a few minutes, we're all dead, and there's nothing we can do about it."

The soldier dropped to all fours, facing what he believed was the direction of Mecca, and began to mumble a final prayer for mercy to Allah fervently.

The soldiers huddled desperately in the ditch, trying to protect themselves from an unknown threat. The last sensation they had was a faint smell of aviation fuel before the entire Fyledal valley exploded in an intense flash that, from above, looked like a ten-mile-long fire streak right in the middle of the Skåne farmland.

The supersonic pressure wave caused vehicles to slowly drift away as if an invisible, gentle hand moved them into the ditches. The cars seemed to float and drift away in a ghostly slow motion that continued for several seconds, unlike a typical explosion where everything was hurled violently but briefly.

Then came the heat wave, with temperatures in the thousands of degrees, instantly igniting everything flammable. The subsequent vacuum wave affected no living creatures in Fyledal, as no life was left. Not a single one of the thirty-one thousand soldiers survived. The fields and forests were littered with lifeless, burned bodies of mammals and birds. The small animals dwelling in caves and dens were dead, their homes having exploded from within. Not even a single insect remained.

The fertile soil of Fyledal had been burned away, turning into a gray, sterile, dust-like layer several inches thick, which weapons engineers working on bomb development referred to as moon soil.

It was a successful test of FAE cluster bombs, conducted for the first time under field conditions, in actual combat, and under ideal circumstances, which the Russian military leadership had long sought. The narrow valley's hundred-foot-high walls created a semi-enclosed, windless space that optimally dispersed the deadly, explosive aerosol, leading to maximum blast effectiveness.

Now, Russian weapons engineers and scientists have material to study for months. The development of thermobaric bombs had reached another milestone. FAEs in the form of cluster bombs undoubtedly belonged to the arsenals of the future.

Chapter 11 – A Confidential Conversation

April 6, 2033

"Gyllenstierna was right, as usual, I have to say. He has a keen intuition. So, it was thermobaric bombs," Gyllenstierna said to intelligence chief Alfred Baksi.

"It's inconceivable that the Russians are so barbaric as to use these kinds of weapons," Baksi said. "Do they have no limits at all?"

"It doesn't seem so. Human life has never meant much to them. This is a weapons test under field conditions, but more than that, they want to show the world what doomsday weapons they have in their arsenal."

"I didn't think they needed to show off more after detonating the Tsar Bomba on Novaya Zemlya in 1961 – the largest hydrogen bomb ever detonated. Since then, the U.S. hasn't seriously considered going to war with the Russians, which is understandable."

"A full-scale war would mean the end of humanity, and everyone knows that."

"The Tsar Bomba released so much energy that it melted the mountains and flowed out, making the entire area resemble a giant ice rink. The message to Washington was that they could turn every American city into an ice rink."

"So, why are the Russians doing this now?" Baksi asked.

"They probably want to assert that they are still a significant player in the geopolitical game despite Russia being an economic dwarf compared to the U.S., China, and India. In the end, only military power grants political power. The economy primarily exists to create military resources. The EU constantly talked about soft power and how they could wield influence through mere economic means, but look at the result of the EU's soft power. Civil wars across Western Europe."

"Yes, but that's because globalists and Arab oil money bought off the leading EU politicians to allow uncontrolled mass immigration from Muslim countries. The civil wars didn't have to happen. Everything was rigged, a devilish, evil plan to crush Europe's nation-states once and for all – and unfortunately, they succeeded," Baksi responded.

"Yes, besides the fact that our enemies paid the human traffickers to handle the boat traffic and asylum fraudsters were given loaded prepaid cards by the Open Society Foundation to make their way to Sweden, it was rigged," Gyllenstierna said. "Very, very tragic and very, very evil."

"And with instructions and manuals on how to abuse asylum legislation. The first step was to sell or discard passports and provide false identities. There was no way the authorities could investigate millions of fabricated stories, and of course, Soros and his followers knew this."

"That bastard," Baksi said resignedly. "He made billions by exploiting the Swedish krona with the help of Rothschild. I think it was during the early nineties' economic crisis."

Gyllenstierna stood up and went to the coffee machine for a refill. At the same time, Baksi remained seated in silence, his grim thoughts stubbornly returning to the horrific massacre in the Fyledal valley. Gyllenstierna returned to his chair and fixed his gaze on Baksi, leaning forward to come closer. It seemed as though he could read Baksi's thoughts.

"So many fine Muslim boys turned into charred remains in a single blast," Gyllenstierna said, sighing deeply.

"Yes, war is terrible, but this was worse than anything I ever thought I'd witness," Baksi replied. "Horrific."

"Sometimes I think about the summers our family always spent back home in Turkey," Gyllenstierna said. "The sense of community and warmth among the people in the small mountain villages."

"Compassion and joy. There's something in Islam that's very good and creates a sense of community—a shared value that's there but hard to grasp," Gyllenstierna said.

"Mmm…, I also have fond memories of family gatherings here in Sweden, not to mention the Kurdish association parties, where we danced our traditional ring dances and laughed heartily. It was a genuine community. We Kurds have a special friendship among men that doesn't exist in Sweden. We were often several hundred Kurds, which was a lot of fun. I was only two years old when we came to Sweden, so I don't remember anything from Turkey. And, for political reasons, no one in our family has been able to return there either."

"Sadly, all the wonderful things we had are lost—our cultural heritage. We Turks will never truly become Swedes. It hurts my heart to think about all the Muslim mothers, fathers, and siblings who will soon be told that their beloved son or brother is no longer here on earth."

"Daniel, don't forget our enemy was affected, not us!" Baksi said unexpectedly sharply. "Not one of our boys was harmed, and I'm very grateful for that."

"Yes, I realize that too. I'm glad it wasn't our Swedish boys and girls who were affected. But still, it feels somehow like it was us who suffered. No matter how hard I try, I can't shake that feeling. Swedes are Swedes. Muslims are Muslims."

"You must!" Baksi insisted. "We can't be at war with ourselves. There should be no doubt about where our loyalties lie. Imagine the disaster if the others in the National Council heard this discussion. What would they think of you?" Baksi asked, scrutinizing his superior's reaction.

What neither Gyllenstierna nor Baksi knew, even though the heads of the different security organizations SÄPO, MUST, and FRA reported directly to Baksi, was that SÄPO secretly bugged the room they were in. This was done on the orders of its Commander, Bianca Popovic, one of the eight members of the National Council that governed Sweden. Bianca Popovic believed she had the right and the duty to eavesdrop on the highest leadership, citing national security concerns.

Bianca Popovic did not know that the NRSS bugged her office, the National Council's Special Security Service, which effectively served as Gyllenstierna's private security force. Though only four months old, the NRSS had quickly achieved a high level of competence thanks to the recruitment of renowned intelligence professionals. The NRSS was a small, efficient, and enthusiastic organization in its early stages, still unburdened by the bureaucracy that had dulled the edge of other intelligence agencies.

It seemed particularly odd that someone within the NRSS, a certain Ken Persson, had taken it upon himself to personally monitor and surveil Chancellor Gyllenstierna, which had a historical explanation.

Everyone seemed to be spying on everyone, believing they acted in Sweden's best interest. However, what constituted Sweden's highest interest appeared open to interpretation by intelligence leaders and sometimes even by individual members of the security services, who acted on their own accord beyond their directives.

"You're right, of course," Gyllenstierna replied hesitantly as if weighing each word carefully before speaking. "There must be no doubt about our loyalties, but we are still Muslims, both you and I. Deep down, we are both indeed that. Muslims. I am a Muslim, and I know that applies to you as well, Ali. You can't just wash off a thousand years of cultural layers like that."

"That interpretation is yours, Daniel. I'm blue and yellow. Whether I'm truly Swedish doesn't matter to me; I'm blue and yellow one hundred percent!" My family fled from Islam, and Islam is not something I want here either."

"I understand," said Gyllenstierna, clearly on the defensive. "I am also blue and yellow! But I will always be a Muslim in my heart. Also."

"Isn't it for freedom that we fight?" Baksi asked. "Freedom to say and think what we want and to do what we want with our lives. I love the free Sweden we had before the politicians destroyed everything, and that's the society I want to restore. Call it the 'People's Home,' the 'Welfare State,' 'Good Old Sweden,' or whatever you like. But people should be able to feel safe on the streets and in their homes. People should be able to say and write exactly what they want without being censored or punished, even if what's said doesn't please those in power. The land must be built with laws! That was written in the old Swedish provincial laws from the thirteenth century. Swedes have freedom in their blood, so it's puzzling what made them voluntarily give it up."

"It's due to Marxist-feminist indoctrination that starts in preschool before a Swede has even begun to speak. The lie of equal value for all people is drilled into Swedes' minds so thoroughly that they never manage to free themselves from it," Gyllenstierna said. "Then the lies are reinforced throughout their upbringing and later in adulthood, through leftist media and regime TV channels."

"There's an awful lot that has gone wrong here in Sweden," Gyllenstierna said. "Muslims are right about one thing: Sweden has become perhaps the most decadent country in the West, which says a lot. As chancellor, I must correct this as much as possible."

"It's an incredibly long journey spanning an entire generation. New children must be born and grow up free from Marxist indoctrination. It's a huge task ahead of us. Still, first, we need to win the war and free Sweden from the Muslim invaders," Baksi said provocatively, watching Gyllenstierna's expression to see if he could discern anything behind his words.

"Yes, the war must be won at all costs," Gyllenstierna acknowledged. "But if it's to mean anything, we need to build an entirely new society, not on the rotten foundation the politicians left behind. The old foundation must be completely eradicated. But I'll leave the war to you in the military leadership: you, Brännström, and the others. I see my role more as a nation-builder and head of our foreign affairs now."

"You can count on us to conduct the war for you to the best of our abilities. But you need to handle the Russians; that's not something we in the military leadership can do."

"I'll handle the Russians, and the Chinese too, who are starting to become a bit too pushy, in my opinion," Gyllenstierna said, rising to signal the end of the conversation. "I have things to attend to now. I'll see you next week when the National Council meets."

"See you then!" Baksi concluded.

After Gyllenstierna left the room, Baksi sat for a few minutes, reflecting on their conversation. What Gyllenstierna had just said matched Baksi's observations and those of the intelligence agencies too closely. Gyllenstierna seemed concerned about the kind of society they were creating and, at worst, about who he was truly loyal to.

Bianca Popovic had reported to her superior Baksi that Gyllenstierna had a copy of the Quran and a couple of books about hadiths in Turkish in his office. What could that mean? The law banning the possession of the Quran had been one of the first new laws passed by the National Council, and it applied to all Swedes, including the Chancellor himself. But perhaps they were just reference copies. Gyllenstierna kept monitoring that Muslim groups didn't use illegal Quranic quotes. That was indeed the case. It had to be the case.

Chapter 12 – Valley of the Shadow of Death

April 7, 2033

The evacuated residents of the valley of Fyledal could not be prevented from returning to their homes, nor was there any reason to try to stop them. From the Swedish leadership's perspective, it was better that the people of Fyledal left the camps outside Ystad and disappeared for good, as their departure also meant the end of their responsibility for their welfare. A shortage of daily necessities was already needed to keep the army's boys and girls somewhat content. The civilian population was left to fend for themselves as best they could.

Two days after the catastrophe in the valley, about fifty of the Fyledal residents had returned. They had managed to bribe their way onto one of the military's confiscated civilian buses. Still, they got only a couple of miles into the valley before the road was blocked by burned-out armored vehicles that could not be cleared with manpower alone. The passengers left the bus and began walking, each heading toward their home. The high pressure had started to wane, and now the light breezes stirred up gray, flour-like dust that swirled just above the ground. Everything was eerie and silent, with no bird chirp to be heard and no background hum from insects. This was no ordinary walk through the old homeland.

"Damn, is this what it looks like? Let's hope it doesn't look like this all over the valley," one said.

"Now I understand why they evacuated us; we should be grateful. Otherwise, we'd all have met an early cremation."

"It looks like a lunar landscape. It can only be from atomic bombs."

"In that case, everything is radioactive and deadly, but I don't care. You'll find out if you start glowing in the dark."

The young priestess of the congregation took the initiative. She stood in the middle of the road in front of a group of desperate and anxious people, who resembled zombies accidentally ejected onto the moon from a crashed spacecraft. No one cried or lamented; everyone stared blankly ahead with expressionless, slack faces. No one said anything either as she raised her right arm and got the group to stop.

"Though I walk through the valley of the shadow of death, I will fear no evil, for you are with me; your rod and your staff comfort me. Let us pray together!"

She clasped her hands and knelt, but no one followed her example.

"Should we thank God for turning our entire homeland to ashes? No, I won't do that. Not a chance!"

The priestess did not let herself be provoked and continued reciting Psalm twenty-three.

"The Lord is my shepherd; I shall not want.

He made me lie down in green pastures and leadeth me beside the still waters.

He restoreth my soul: he leadeth me in the paths of righteousness for his name's sake."

"Damn, don't you dare keep pushing this nonsense! Not in this situation! If God exists, He has completely forsaken us."

"We seek God's grace and comfort in our darkest hour," the priestess replied quietly.

"Ah, keep your mouth shut. There's no damn God who can help us now. But the devil seems very present and has been very active here."

The group continued their grim march through the desolate landscape. Everywhere along the road lay thousands of charred bodies of dead Muslim soldiers. Decay had not yet begun. Only a faint, sickly sweet odor reached the travelers, strong enough for most of them to pinch their nostrils to avoid the worst stench. Usually, thousands of flies would have buzzed around the bodies and started crawling in to lay eggs in nostrils, mouths, and eye sockets, whose eyes had been blown out by the feared vacuum forces following the pressure and heat waves. Yet not a single insect was in sight.

Hundreds of burned-out armored vehicles and remains of other civilian vehicles lay overturned around and on the road. They looked strangely intact, except they were so thoroughly charred that the paint had melted, leaving them with a ghostly, soot-gray appearance.

The group grew smaller as people took side roads heading toward what had once been their farms. Many lost their way as the total devastation erased familiar landmarks like large buildings and trees, leaving only burnt skeletons behind. All the wood had burned. The beautiful timber-framed houses' beams had collapsed along with the clay walls they supported. Very few houses still had their frames standing. All that remained of the trees were branchless, sooty stumps rarely more than a couple of feet high.

Even life in the small local river of Fyleån had mainly been wiped out as the water in the shallow stream had boiled away. Only in the bottoms of a few deep pools had some creatures survived, including the little Mussel reintroduced to the stream fifteen years earlier, something that would have pleased the region's environmentalists if they had known. Unfortunately, its crucial symbiotic fish partner, the Bullhead, had not survived, but there was hope for its return with fresh water flowing in from the north.

By leaving the main road, they managed to avoid the dead human bodies. Instead, they encountered the sooty remains of horses, cows, sheep, and pigs scattered like random piles of soot in what had once been enclosed and lush pastures. Some scorched brick buildings, built from locally fired clay bricks that could withstand almost any temperature, remained here and there. In cases where the brick houses had metal roofs, some soot-covered metal was still visible. Homes with tile roofs generally collapsed as beams, rafters, and trusses turned to ash, eventually falling under the weight. Houses with traditional thatched roofs had caught fire first. Of most houses, all that remained were the foundations—rectangular slabs of solid, hewn stone.

Finally, the drunkard couple, forcibly evacuated on Björn Väster's bus, arrived at what had once been their modest dwelling. But where was his father's farm? Nothing was left behind the row of maples, and not much remained of the maples. It was empty, burned, ravaged, and barren. The rock slab was bare where the barn once stood, and now only the memory was left.

"There's nothing left here, not even a little mouse. So, why the hell should I still be here?" exclaimed the male drunkard, instinctively searching for some way to end his misery but without success. His double-barreled shotgun had been confiscated and was now to be found somewhere in Ystad. And even if there had been any suitable branches to hang from, there wouldn't have been any rope.

Suddenly, they noticed a movement a few feet ahead. A severely burned little rabbit dragged itself slowly toward them, carving a small path through the ash-like dust. They could follow the rabbit's tracks back at least a hundred feet. It had likely huddled deep in a burrow several feet underground, protected by winding tunnels, and thus escaped the deadly aerosol that had seeped into every crevice. The rabbit stopped before them and looked up with its large, glossy eyes in its scorched and burned face as if pleading for help. The response was a few decisive stomps from a rubber boot with an unusually coarse tread and steel toe, branded "Drottningfågel" with a stylized rooster head with an exaggerated comb on the outer sides of the shoes.

"It was better to take him away from his misery," he said apologetically to his partner, which wasn't necessary as she stood utterly stunned, lost in her world, with tears streaming down her cheeks. "But, who can help us now?"

Chapter 13 – The Procession for Oath of Allegiance

Spring 2033

It was no surprise that the National Council assigned the most challenging tasks to Björn Väster of the National Order Council, aside from the war itself: the ethnic cleansing of residential areas and the deportation of undesirable citizens. The National Council named this undocumented operation the *"Edkrävartåget"* – "Procession for Oath of Allegiance." Gyllenstierna coined the name from Swedish history, carrying a fitting, symbolic significance. He proudly explained to the others in the council,

"Edkrävartåget" was carried out on the orders of King Karl XI by my ancestor Johan Göransson Gyllenstierna during the winter and spring following the New Year of 1677, when we Swedes famously defeated the Danes at the Battle of Lund on December 4, 1676. My ancestor Johan had a crucial role as the leader of the infantry center. He performed with great distinction and was richly rewarded for his bravery and resourcefulness amidst the whistling of bullets when the Danish cavalry came crashing down with all its might."

The other council members stared in stunned silence, exchanging glances of bewilderment and embarrassment. It sounded like the chancellor was convinced his ancestor Gyllenstierna had carried out the task. But everyone knew well that Gyllenstierna was just a name taken from a long-extinct noble family and that the chancellor himself hailed from Turkey with the surname Öztürk.

"It's not just anyone who can stand firm in such a situation," the chancellor continued, "but Johan Göransson Gyllenstierna was no ordinary man—he was, I would say, very courageous. My ancestor Johan later became close to King Karl. They became excellent friends. Since then, my family has always been close to the Swedish royal court."

Gyllenstierna puffed up a bit more and, visibly proud, delivered yet another piece of news.

"At The House of Nobilities – we Gyllenstiernas are represented by shield number twenty-nine. The beautiful dove-blue shield adorned with a golden, seven-pointed star reflects the brilliant genius of my forefathers. The seven-pointed star, the Septagram, symbolizes supernatural intelligence in classical astrology. The star's metallic tincture was modified during the fifteenth century, turning from silver to gold, when our family was elevated to baronial status."

The council members were shocked, unsure of how to deal with the madness being spewed by their leader. Most took Gyllenstierna's exposition as proof that he hadn't just lost his grip—he was stark raving mad. It was an unabashed historical falsification, evidently part of the chancellor's efforts to build a cult of personality around himself. With ancestors who had played significant roles in Swedish history, he automatically garnered a stronger position as the natural leader of the Swedish people while shedding all his natural associations with Islam. Agents from the National Council, who had overheard hundreds of loud discussions in taverns, had noted that many Swedes deeply mistrusted the chancellor, using expressions like "that damn Muslim" when discussing Sweden's leadership and the war against the Muslim occupiers. The Swedish people, however, adored their Supreme Commander, Anton Brännström from Luleå, whose loyalty and Swedishness were beyond question. This could not continue.

The other council members had worriedly noted that Gyllenstierna had posters of his portrait all over the country, reminiscent of the portraits of leaders in Saudi Arabia everywhere in the oil-rich country's cities. There was no doubt about who was Sweden's leader: Chancellor Gyllenstierna, whose noble lineage now traced back to the powerful Oxenstiernas and the Bonde family, who had played decisive roles in Swedish history. Thanks to his family connections traced back to Albrecht von Mecklenburg, he could also claim royal ancestry. Daniel Gyllenstierna was no ordinary man, according to his history description.

It was becoming increasingly apparent that the self-styled chancellor sought to present himself as a modern-day version of Chancellor Axel Oxenstierna, who, through four decades of relentless reform and organization, gave Sweden the most efficient government in the world in the middle of the seventeenth century, which was the crucial groundwork for Sweden to solidify and expand its position as a European power despite its small population and underdeveloped economy.

Whether or not he was an Oxenstierna, members of the National Council were concerned about the growing cult of personality surrounding Gyllenstierna. What was particularly alarming was that Gyllenstierna seemed to believe his fabrications. There was something off about their chancellor, and they all began to question whether he was genuinely sane. But they did not dare discuss it, even in private, knowing that the trap door could suddenly be opened under anyone. No one could be sure who might report such discussions to the Chancellor, with devastating consequences.

Once, however, the usually reserved and cautious Admiral Palmquist had dared to refer to Gyllenstierna as "our own Kim Jong-un," which elicited a burst of restrained amusement from those present. No one dared laugh out loud for fear of the National Council's agents, but smiles were impossible to suppress. Long before the war, Sweden had often been dubbed Europe's "new DDR" due to the regime's censorship and surveillance of its citizens, reminiscent of East Germany's Stasi. But now, it felt as though Sweden was moving even further away from democracy, with a tyrannical and bloodthirsty dictator claiming to control every detail personally. Sweden was on its way to becoming a European version of North Korea.

"My ancestor Johan Göransson Gyllenstierna traveled through the parishes of Blekinge and northern Skåne, demanding oaths of loyalty to the Swedish king in what came to be known as the *Edkrävartåget*," Gyllenstierna continued. "Those who refused or broke their oaths were immediately executed. Väster's mission is to carry out a nationwide Procession for Oath of Allegiance to all the areas inhabited by Muslims, using our new anti-Islamic laws as the foundation."

Björn Väster of the National Order Council was not neglecting his duties. He was the consummate executor—a dream for any employer, the National Council. Väster was goal-oriented, loyal, and meticulous, if not obsessive, inventive in overcoming obstacles, and everything was done with the "Väster urgency" that had become well-known. Everything was essential and urgent, down to the smallest detail, and it had to be done quickly. In every organization he worked for, he always received the assignments when something large and urgent needed to be accomplished.

A monumental task lay ahead for Väster when the ceasefire was declared on Christmas Eve, 2032. While some NoGo zones had been cleared during the ongoing war, nearly three hundred and fifty areas remained largely intact. Väster was tasked with carrying out the clean-up that the Swedish state should have done years earlier: apprehending and deporting terrorists, war criminals, Muslim extremists recruiting terrorists, undocumented individuals, criminals, and illegal immigrants who remained at large despite having been sentenced to deportation years earlier.

But Väster was also set to undertake something that the Swedish state had never done—namely, to arrest and deport all Muslims who refused to sign the conditional contract offered by the new regime as an alternative to lifelong exile from the country. The Muslims would be required to swear an oath renouncing everything related to Islam, including personal aspects like dress style, haircuts, and shaving. Those who refused to take the oath or broke it would be immediately detained and expelled from the country as swiftly as possible.

The National Council had enacted new laws criminalizing and labeling Islam as terrorism. Anyone expressing sympathy for Islam would be considered and treated as an instigator of terrorist acts. The demolition of mosques was well underway, with most being blown up with dynamite to make way for other buildings. Mosques remained only in the still-intact NoGo zones, but Väster's troops would soon address that. Muslim associations were banned, as was the possession of the Quran.

The laws extended to forbidding all Muslim symbols, including veils and traditional Muslim clothing and headwear for men. *Halal* slaughter, circumcision, and the celebration of Muslim holidays were prohibited, as were all beards longer than one inch. The contract stipulated immediate deportation for anyone who refused to sign it or who violated the signed contract.

Islam was to be eradicated once and for all, and Väster saw his task as a grand and historic mission to restore Swedish society with security, law, and order. Sweden would be a Western society grounded in Christian values and Nordic history. It would be a land of free enterprise, competition, and complete personal freedom—with Islam as a clear exception.

Väster estimated that most NoGo zones housed between five thousand and forty thousand people. In these areas, the Swedish state had relinquished its monopoly on violence starting around the year 2010 and had progressively since then lost control. The police lacked both the mandate and equipment to handle stone throwers and gunfire, and their diplomatic attempts—offering lemonade and cinnamon buns and engaging with Muslim children in bouncy castles—were met with contempt and seen for what they were: weakness.

Väster's and the National Council's responsibility was to clean up the mess of the Swedish politicians' total failure. The first step was, of course, to halt all Muslim immigration. The outbreak of war immediately stopped all legal immigration, but people from Muslim countries continued to pour into the country as long as border control was ineffective. Väster ensured that all airports, ports, and road checkpoints were operated around the clock by police, supported by the Home Guard and local citizen militias under the National Task Force, effectively bringing nearly all immigration to Sweden to a halt. Asylum immigration was non-existent since the National Council's first decision was to terminate all international agreements concerning asylum legislation. As far as they were concerned, organizations like the UN and the EU could go to hell, not to mention directly harmful charitable organizations like Amnesty International and the Open Society Foundation. One of the National Council's first decisions was to shut down the Swedish aid agency SIDA entirely and permanently. Sweden would no longer feed corrupt regimes on other continents.

The next task was to gain control over all Muslim residential areas, which could only be done by force. Those deported had to leave the country as quickly as possible so that the justice system could function as before, as well as bailiffs, social insurance offices, employment agencies, pharmacies, medical clinics, and schools. Regular stores should be free of Muslim products. Police presence would be massive and permanent after the cleanup until it could be reduced without adverse effects. Muslim residential areas would be wholly de-Islamized and transformed into normally functioning Swedish neighborhoods. However, in the future, they would likely be inhabited by former Muslims who had abandoned their faith and traditions.

The work was grueling and laborious, week after week, month after month. Areas were surrounded, and everyone within was checked as soldiers from the National Intervention Force, supported by heavily armed units from Brigade Viking—Lagerbäck Brigade—who went from house to house, from apartment to apartment.

Those who could not identify themselves were immediately detained and put on buses for transport to detention camps awaiting deportation. Those not in the database with signed contracts were allowed to sign under duress, after which the contracts were sent for registration. Those who resisted or acted aggressively or mockingly were shot on the spot.

All those given a chance to remain in Sweden were photographed, fingerprinted, and had a buccal swab for DNA to be registered in a national database. They were aware that the slightest contract violation would result in lifelong deportation.

According to Väster's calculations, deportations of undesirable citizens in the area controlled by the Swedes, including the Russian occupation zone that had been returned, would be completed by Christmas 2033. Väster planned to deport at least two hundred thousand to three hundred thousand undesirable Muslims, possibly up to half a million. The part of the country under Swedish control would be free of Islam from 2034 onward and forever.

The cleanup of the Muslim residential areas was a significant task but still manageable and far more straightforward than carrying out the deportations themselves. Five large passenger ferries had been converted into floating prisons and served as holding camps until it was time to set sail for a suitable destination. The ships could house up to eight thousand prisoners, crew, guards, and support staff. There was no alternative to ship transport, as air transport was far too expensive. Land transport was not an option because Sweden's neighboring countries were unwilling to allow the deportees to pass through. Additionally, ongoing wars in Western Europe made land transport extremely unsafe.

Thanks to Väster's near-genius organizational skills, the ferries could travel back and forth to their Middle East and Africa destinations. A special agreement had been established with local warlords controlling the extensive area along the African Mediterranean coast, formerly known as Libya. In exchange for targeted Swedish aid of five billion US dollars per year and promises of future deliveries of Swedish weapons, the warlords agreed to assist with the unloading of prisoners and ensure they were transported by bus to their African home countries.

Since the agreement stipulated that a portion of the funds would be paid out after prisoner transports were completed, most prisoners eventually reached their home countries. However, some prisoners remained in Libyan camps and were forcibly recruited as soldiers, enslaved people, or sex workers, among them thousands of Afghans and Pakistanis who, lacking alternatives, were dumped in Libya. Väster considered his task complete upon the disembarkation of the prisoners. Their fates were unknown, but that was no concern of official Sweden.

The goal was to win the war to liberate southern and western Sweden and to repeat the purging and deportation actions as soon as possible. Most indications suggested that another couple hundred thousand Muslims would be deported once the rest of Sweden was freed.

Chapter 14 – The Elusive Shadow from Tyringe

"Kontoret för särskild inhämtning" (KSI) – "The Special Collection Office" – is a covert intelligence agency under the Swedish Military Intelligence and Security Service (MUST). Unlike its parent organization, MUST–KSI is a closed organization (meaning it is officially non-existent). As a logical consequence of its non-existence, no information about the KSI has ever been released. Employees within the KSI hold other jobs as cover, often within the military, but they can also be employed in other state-run, confidential operations.

The structure of open (known) and closed (unknown) security services is a logical outcome of the need for secrecy to ensure success while sometimes also requiring open interactions with society and the public. Even the Security Police (SÄPO) has a closed division, about which very little is known.

When Gyllenstierna left his post as Chief of Defence four months earlier to lead the newly formed National Council as chancellor, he took the opportunity to establish his private security service, *Nationella Rådets Speciella Säkerhetstjänst* (NRSS) – the National Council's Special Security Service. The task of setting up the NRSS was assigned to Ken Persson, a well-known and skilled operator within the leadership of MUST, who Gyllenstierna personally selected. The two had interacted numerous times when MUST had information or other matters to discuss with the country's Supreme Commander. Gyllenstierna was greatly impressed by Persson and trusted him implicitly.

Even Gyllenstierna did not know that Persson belonged to MUST's secret division, the KSI, and had long been tasked with monitoring the Supreme Commander's professional and private activities.

Contrary to popular belief, all senior politicians and military leaders are constantly monitored by one or more entities, and no one has a complete overview of who is doing what. This is a logical result of having multiple independent security services, some of which have secret divisions. Even the heads of these security services are rarely monitored by their agencies. The system of multiple security services, which monitor each other in addition to their primary functions, is seen as a safeguard against coups and treason.

There was an imbalance in the information that Chancellor Gyllenstierna and NRSS Chief Persson had about each other, which was unknown to Gyllenstierna. He felt he knew enough about Ken Persson. It was common among intelligence and military leaders not to discuss personal lives unnecessarily. However, Persson knew everything about Gyllenstierna: the circles he mingled with privately, the friends of his ex-wife, the media he read, the names of his occasional lovers, who were alarmingly often Russian, and even the names of his two Siamese cats and their preferred type of Whiskas cat food the furry ladies preferred.

Everything Gyllenstierna knew about Persson was that his name was Ken Persson and that he was from the village of Tyringe, which matched Persson's Skåne accent. However, Persson wasn't even from Tyringe. If Gyllenstierna had had more knowledge of Skåne dialects and a keener ear for language, he might have detected a faint French accent clumsily disguised as a Skåne accent. Whenever Ken Persson was confronted by other Skåne people about his dialect not being from Tyringe, he would evade the issue by saying that his family had lived in various places in Skåne and that he had also attended a Belgian school for a few years, during the time his stepfather had been a less successful footballer in KV Mechelen's B team—an outright fabrication. He had never been to Belgium except for a brief visit to Brussels.

The first name, Ken, was inspired by the name of a well-known American doll that six-year-old girls usually adore, which has a female counterpart named Barbie. His last name was also a nod to the ironic, as he was named after the French word "*personne,*" which means "nobody" in French. Ken Persson was indeed nobody, nothing more than an elusive shadow made up of a few disconnected pieces of fake information. Even his social security number was fabricated, though the number necessary for living in Sweden was genuinely registered with the Swedish Tax Agency and other authorities.

Only two people knew who Ken Persson was, and both were members of the National Council, where Gyllenstierna served as chancellor and chairman. The first was Bertil Wiklund, the head of MUST, who met Ken Persson while working at the FRA and personally selected him for the KSI. The second was Rudolf Enbom, head of the FRA, who had personally recruited Ken Persson as a young man while serving as a conscript cryptographer in the signal corps.

The rumors and consistent reports about Persson's ability to crack the toughest encryptions and his generally high intelligence were too strong for Enbom to ignore, and so it was. To complete the story, Persson's parents were deceased, and he had no other family or childhood friends.

Only one person except the two intelligence chiefs and Persson himself knew who Ken Persson was, and all three parties wanted it to remain that way. Ken Persson was the perfect spy in every sense, and he reveled in his shadowy life as a constant undercover operative. He had no desire for real life, no need to share his experiences and memories with others. The heads of the FRA and MUST, Rudolf Enbom and Bertil Wiklund, created Ken Persson's CV. Ken Persson barely knew who he was himself, and he wanted it to stay that way. He thrived as the head of the NRSS, acting as the spider in the web, reporting directly to Chancellor Gyllenstierna and surveilling him.

Ken Persson knew more about what was happening behind the scenes than his former bosses at the FRA and MUST—at least, that's what he believed. He was not one to relinquish his informational advantage unnecessarily, as this very advantage gave him satisfaction.

He had not yet discussed his observations and suspicions about Chancellor Gyllenstierna with anyone else, but the situation was becoming problematic and perhaps urgent. The logical step would be to cautiously approach the matter with Baksi, who had the three other intelligence agencies reporting to him. However, he could not make vague claims and insinuations about the country's highest official without concrete evidence, and he had not yet obtained such proof. The issue was sensitive, especially since Gyllenstierna and Baksi had been friends for many years. Both were also Muslims or at least had Muslim backgrounds, which could be relevant.

Persson understood Gyllenstierna had been imprisoned and had many of his critics and potential challengers eliminated during the spring. Ken Persson needed to be more experienced and strategic to expose himself to such risks. He would have to keep a low profile until he had

unequivocal evidence, and how he would proceed then was a question for
later.

Chapter 15 – Offensive

April 20, 2033

If the Swedish high command believed they could relax after the Russian thermobaric bombs had annihilated the Muslim forces in the valley of Fyledalen, they were gravely mistaken.

Instead of halting their offensive, as the Swedes had expected, the Muslims reinforced their positions with massive contingents from the garrisons in the small towns of Skurup and Svedala. Meanwhile, the advance guard moved into the ruins of the bombed-out town of Ystad, which was virtually deserted as residents had fled east to escape the heavy artillery bombardments. The town—or rather, the ruins of the devastated city—was still ablaze. There was no reason to linger on the spot. The advance party pressed on eastward along National Highway 9, along the coast, where they quickly had to take cover when they came under fire from Swedish automatic cannons and heavy machine guns.

At the same time, National Highway 9 was being filled from behind with hundreds of armored vehicles and tens of thousands of battle-hardened Muslim soldiers. The Swedes were taken aback by the intensity and ferocity of the attack and quickly realized they were not yet prepared to face such a strong enemy, having only just entered the former Russian occupation zone a few days earlier. The buildup of Swedish combat forces had barely begun, and this was the situation that the Muslim leaders exploited: Military leaders Colonel Shahram Gaidan and General Mahmoud Khalil, along with their Supreme Commander and strategic leader Ahmed Ben Barka. With his nearly infallible intuition, Ahmed sensed the Swedes' vulnerable position. He convinced his military leaders to go on the offensive rather than retreat and fortify their defenses as the two military leaders had initially planned.

"We'll break their morale before they've even launched their offensive," Ahmed noted dryly. "The Swedes are cowards, and their soldiers lack the will to sacrifice."

"Without the Russians, they are nothing," said Colonel Gaidan. "We'll drive them into the sea before they realize the war has started again."

Swedish Army Chief Gunhild Svartenbrandt, now a Major General, ordered a rapid retreat without consulting her superior, Chief of Defense Anton Brännström. Since Brännström had previously been Army Chief, it was customary for him to have the final say on all matters concerning ground combat forces. However, the situation was urgent.

Svartenbrandt did her utmost to organize an orderly retreat northeast along National Highway 11 to join forces with the main contingent now stationed around the village of Smedstorp. The plan was to establish an impenetrable defensive line with the combined forces where Highway 9 and 11 intersected, just east of the town of Östra Tomarp. A mass panic retreat had to be avoided at all costs, as it would mean abandoning valuable war materials and resulting in significantly more significant losses. If they failed to slow the Muslim advance, there would be no time to establish the planned defensive line.

Major General Svartenbrandt, using her camera-equipped drones, was closely monitoring the alarmingly rapid Muslim advance. The first defensive line, hastily established east of Ystad, was breached within hours. The Muslim advance guard had now reached the village of Nybostrand, where National Highway 9 veers off to the northeast.

To her surprise, Svartenbrandt noted that a smaller segment of the Muslim force—estimated at around three hundred soldiers in trucks—was veering south towards the village of Kåseberga. What could they possibly want there? There was nothing of strategic value at that location. It seemed unlikely that a flanking maneuver along the coast would benefit the Muslims; rather, it would waste valuable time. Svartenbrandt couldn't know that the Muslims' Supreme Commander, Ahmed Ben Barka, viewed the megalithic stone monument called Ale Stenar as a strategic target. Ahmed's declared aim was to destroy all Swedish cultural monuments to deprive the Swedes of their brief and meager history, which was a crucial step in the Islamization of Sweden.

During the eight-month occupation of the western part of Skåne, the Muslims' special demolition brigades had been active. Hundreds of historical buildings and monuments had been blown up, burned, and removed. The remains were usually covered with fill to prevent permanent restoration. All churches in the Muslim-occupied zone had been obliterated.

The demolition of Lund Cathedral had been staged as an elaborate event, with food and treats distributed to starving Swedes who could not resist the much-needed supplies. They had been forced to applaud and cheer at gunpoint while the nine-hundred-year-old and two-hundred-foot-tall structure collapsed into a heap of stone and debris. As they consumed the distributed food, the Swedes watched the cleanup process and saw the cathedral's remains being loaded onto trucks to fill elsewhere.

Just four hours after the demolition of Lund Cathedral, Ahmed Ben Barka performed the ribbon-cutting ceremony. It took the first shovel full of dirt to construct what would become Skåne's largest mosque, located precisely on the cathedral's former site. The well-known imam Abd al Haqq Bielat, who had been an imam in Luleå before being forced to flee, delivered a lengthy and inspiring speech welcoming a couple thousand newly converted Swedes who had embraced Islam as their faith and guiding principle.

Now it was time for the Muslims' special demolition brigade to obliterate the Ale Stenar, which consisted of fifty-seven narrow, upright granite and gneiss blocks, each weighing around five tons. The stones were arranged on a hilltop near the village of Kåseberga, with a beautiful view of the Baltic Sea, in a two hundred-feet-long and fifty-foot-wide oval shape that outlined the silhouette of a mighty ship. The effort required to carve, haul, and erect the stones during the Vendel period, one thousand five hundred years earlier, was thousands of times greater than the relatively simple task of dismantling and transporting them using excavators and winch-equipped trucks. It was a well-planned operation that went essentially according to plan. The blocks were transported by truck to Ystad Harbor, where they were unloaded onto a barge.

Less than two days after the Muslims had driven their vehicles up the hill where the ship-setting had stood for one thousand five hundred years, the stones now rested on the bottom of the Baltic Sea, over three hundred feet deep, one mile south of Ystad, where they would remain forever. The heap of elongated boulders quickly became an attractive habitat for sea creatures, who appreciated the shelter provided by the cave-like spaces formed by the blocks lying on the seabed like a gigantic pick-up sticks game.

The main Muslim force continued to advance slowly along National Highway 9 under sporadic fire from the retreating Swedes. From time to time, the main force had to pause, allowing parts of the troops to make flanking maneuvers to clear out Swedish units that had entrenched themselves where the terrain was favorable for defense. However, the Swedes' tactic was to delay the advance to facilitate an orderly retreat, leaving no equipment to benefit the Muslims.

When the Muslims reached the locality of Hammenhög, a detachment from the special demolition brigade veered off towards the medieval-era castle named Glimmingehus, which was situated two miles to the east. Soon, the demolition soldiers arrived and positioned themselves in front of the moat, looking up at the eighty-five-foot-high fortress. With the defenders firing from the castle, using the drawbridge to cross the moat would be impossible, but Glimmingehus had long since outlived its role as a military stronghold. The fortress was to be destroyed and erased from history, along with the three adjoining buildings that formed a square inside the moat. Posthumously, King Karl XI of Sweden would fulfill his wish—the castle was to be demolished. During the Skåne War of 1676, the King had sought to prevent the Danish enemy from capturing and utilizing the fortress for military purposes. Now, a different enemy faced the castle, one who did not know King Karl XI but desired precisely what the king wanted. They unknowingly assisted the Swedish king in achieving his goal 357 years after his failed demolition attempt.

It took twenty minutes to plant explosives on the castle's four floors. The adjoining buildings were already on fire, and the blaze spread rapidly, fueled by the fresh winds sweeping across the plain. The demolition soldiers left the castle area via the drawbridge and took cover behind some stone walls a couple of hundred feet away. The powerful explosion hurled carefully carved sandstone and quartzite building blocks across the moat, and the structure collapsed into a cloud of dust and scattered stones.

The efficient demolition brigade wasted no time. Less than an hour after the explosion had obliterated the five-hundred-year-old building, bulldozers began leveling the remaining stone heap and the ruins of the burnt-out buildings in the moat, which were then covered with a two-feet thick layer of the plain's rich topsoil. Ahmed Ben Barka's explicit orders were to raze the entire area, leaving no trace behind, and this was accomplished. Now, the once mighty Glimmingehus existed only in people's memories and thousands of photographs, drawings, and paintings—things even Ahmed Ben Barka could not destroy.

When the Muslim force reached the Tommarpså River, they encountered a halt. The bridge at National Highway 9, along with all nearby bridges over the river, had been destroyed by Swedish engineering soldiers. The Muslim troops, subjected to intense fire from the Swedes, decided to retreat a short distance to set up camp for the night. Meanwhile, the Swedes continued to build their defensive line, which proved so formidable that the Muslims could not advance despite five days of intense fighting. The Tommarpså River remained the frontline for the coming weeks until the Swedish major offensive began across Skåne.

After the Muslim demolition brigade had completed leveling Glimmingehus, they turned their attention to the next target: the rock carvings known as the Brage Stenar, located less than six miles from Glimmingehus. The Brage Stenar had to wait until the following day, as it was time to prepare for the night's rest.

The energetic and highly motivated demolition soldiers rose with the dawn to continue spreading the Prophet's teachings. They began their task an hour after sunrise. The well-known sun wheel and other images depicting ships and people were meticulously eradicated using portable rock drills. The technique had evolved and refined since the hundreds of artistically more decadent carvings at Tanumshede in Bohuslän had met the same fate a few months earlier.

The Muslims were not satisfied with merely erasing the rock carvings. Since they were already on site, using the drills to create new, more fitting messages was natural. The machines' clattering quickly followed the lines drawn on the rocks with thick markers, depicting mosques with minarets, the classic crescent moon with a star, and a few short verses from the Quran in Arabic. Creating these new carvings took only a few hours, and the results were far superior to what the Bronze Age people had achieved. The Muslim carvings were around four inches deep and designed to last for eternity. The giant carving displayed the Islamic declaration of faith, the Shahada, "*La ilaha il Allah. Muhammed rasul Allah,"* which translates to "There is no god but Allah, and Muhammad is His Messenger."

This simple message covered a few square feet. Finally, the Shahada was framed with beautiful Arabic-style swirls. As a finishing touch and the artist's signature, the emblem of the Muslim Brotherhood, consisting of two crossed swords, was engraved.

The demolition brigade's next target was the rock carvings in Järrestad, which, to the Muslims' dismay, were on the wrong side of the Swedes' impenetrable defensive line. The carvings in Järrestad would remain a greeting from those who inhabited southeastern Skåne thousands of years earlier. The Muslims' new greetings on the Brage Stenar, created for eternity, would not last as long as the Muslims had hoped. Volunteer Swedish workers managed to erase all traces of the Muslims' messages within less than a year of their creation. The original carvings were then restored using photographs.

Chapter 16 – The Warning

May 1, 2033

On a beautiful spring day, as Benno was heading to the kiosk by the office to buy his lunch kebab, something unexpected happened. The two guards who monitored him around the clock and followed him everywhere stealthily approached from behind and grabbed him by each arm.

"You're coming with us. The boss wants to see you."

Benno's heart skipped a beat, and panic surged through him. It was over! They had seen through his false identity. He could hardly imagine the suffering he would endure before being executed.

They ushered him into the backseat of an old Land Rover and shut the door. One of the guards sat beside him in the back while the other drove them to the building Kronprinsen, where the chief of the general staff's security force had his office.

Benno had heard of the feared Zlatko Muslimovic, and he felt sweat bead on his forehead as he breathed heavily with terror.

"Sit down," said the imposing Muslimovic sternly, pointing to the chair in front of his desk. "You two wait outside," he added, addressing the guards.

Muslimovic leaned back comfortably in his chair, hands clasped behind his head, and stretched his long legs out in front of him.

"Do you understand why you're here?" Muslimovic asked gruffly.

"Eh...no, not really. Could it be about that *fatwa*, perhaps?"

It was widely known that Iran's Supreme Leader, Ali Khamenei, had issued a *fatwa* against Fredrik Myllivirta, which meant that all Shia Muslims had a duty to kill him. The mullahs could not accept that anyone, especially a nonbeliever, had violated Allah's sacred word by omitting parts of the Swedish Quran.

The Swedish Quran hadn't even been printed yet, but one of the translators had apparently already distributed the manuscript. Thanks to the fact that the occupying Muslims were Sunni, the *fatwa* had not yet been enforced.

However, Sweden also had plenty of Shia Muslims, most of whom had Iranian roots. Benno realized that his days were numbered. At least Fredrik Myllivirta's days were numbered. He had to escape and obtain another new identity before it was too late.

"No, it's not about the *fatwa*. My job is to protect you from the vile renegades," Muslimovic said with a sarcastic smile.

"I appreciate that."

"It's something entirely different. Who are you?"

"Now, I don't quite understand. It's well-known who I am and that I work closely with Ahmed Ben Barka," Benno tried, hoping that the name of the esteemed Muslim leader would offer him protection.

Muslimovic stared at him scrutinizingly and shook his head slightly. "You're not Fredrik Myllivirta. One of the guys in the security forces worked in Stockholm until the Muslims left the city when the Swedes returned last Christmas. He's certain he escorted you to the Swedish Exhibition Center in Stockholm last summer. He also says it became known that you managed to get to the Swedish side from there."

Now, it was Benno's turn to shake his head. He sighed with raised eyebrows and a questioning look.

"I haven't heard anything about that. It must be a misunderstanding."

Benno felt sweat pouring down his back under his white kaftan.

"You don't need to be afraid. You're here because I want to help you, Benno Ronkanen."

Benno felt utterly confused but sensed a faint glimmer of hope. There was no point in denying it any longer. They knew everything.

"Okay, it's true. I am indeed Benno Ronkanen. But now I'm working for you, and I am loyal. I've converted to Islam. Everything that happened was just a tragic misunderstanding, not my fault. I can explain everything."

Muslimovic's stern face broke into a big smile, and he burst into loud laughter. "Ha-ha-ha, that's the funniest thing I've heard in a long time! The entire Muslim council feasted on pork, ha-ha-ha. It couldn't get any better!"

Muslimovic laughed uncontrollably and leaned forward before suddenly becoming severe again. "You need to get out of here, and you understand why. On Friday at 7 a.m., you will be picked up by car outside the Clarion Congress, where you're staying."

Benno's confusion deepened. He didn't understand anything. Why would the chief of security help him? He feared the worst. Perhaps he would be taken to the execution site in the park of Tjyvaparken.

"Okay, but where will I be taken?"

"I can't say any more. Just ensure you exit the entrance exactly at 7 a.m. on Friday."

"But the guards?"

"I'll make sure no guards are there."

"I'll be there exactly at 7 a.m."

"One more thing: Keep your mouth shut about this! If you leak a single word, I will personally kill you, understand?"

Benno swallowed and nodded silently, watching Muslimovic press the send button on the communication radio.

"Okay, you can come and pick him up now. Take him back to the general staff."

Chapter 17 – Staff Meeting

May 3, 2033

Without better options, the Swedish staff had set up camp in the historic mansion Kockska Gården in the village of Simrishamn, which otherwise served as a hotel. The old half-timbered building was far from ideal for conferences and meetings, but it was a good choice since Simrishamn remained under Swedish control. This allowed for continuous operations without sudden relocations. The hotel's modest dining room was the only option for larger meetings.

Observant locals in Simrishamn noticed something unusual upstream from the little river of Tommarpsån. The sluggish waterway, which typically flowed more than usual during early summer, carried vast amounts of debris that collected around its mouth in the Baltic Sea, right by Simrishamn's harbor. These activities, which resulted in the increased debris, were a minor inconvenience for the Swedish staff, as the front line, where National Highway 9 crosses the Tommarpsån, was now only a few miles away—well within range of Muslim artillery. Despite the staff's efforts to avoid drawing unnecessary attention, the movement of armored vehicles and ordinary cars with uniformed passengers was impossible to miss, observed around the clock by the local population.

They hoped that the staff's exact location would not reach the Muslim artillery's gunners and that they would manage to leave before the artillery zeroed in on the target. There were no shelters available in the old town center.

There was also the risk that Simrishamn could meet the same fate as Ystad—namely, being devastated by prolonged, indiscriminate bombardment with heavy artillery. Fortunately, the Muslims had launched so many shells at Ystad that they were temporarily running low, though the Swedish staff was unaware of this.

Every street in Simrishamn was meticulously monitored around the clock to thwart potential attackers and infiltrators who might use laser pointers to direct artillery fire directly onto the target from the first shot. Intrusive, young, and not discreet, soldiers questioned anyone moving about the streets. Those who didn't respond in flawless Skåne accent were subjected to extra scrutiny and often placed with their hands against a wall while they were searched. There was always the constant risk of suicide bombers everywhere and anywhere in the country.

The meeting was led by Sweden's Chief of Defense, Anton Brännström, the former army chief. The former Chief of Defense, Daniel Gyllenstierna, who had promoted himself to Chancellor of the Realm four months earlier, had abandoned military duties to focus on political issues and negotiations with foreign powers, usually the Russians and Chinese.

"It looks like the situation has stabilized, at least for now. The Muslims have stalled at the small river of Tommarpsån, and we're blasting them to pieces every time they attempt to establish a foothold. The river isn't wide enough for tracked vehicles to cross at its shallowest point, but it's still large enough to stop most vehicles. Even though the water flow is shallow, the riverbanks are about ten feet high, steep, muddy, and fairly difficult to breach."

"Anyone trying to drive straight across the river is taking an extreme risk," noted Army Chief General Svartenbrandt. "If they get stuck in the mud, they become a sitting duck and turn into scrap within less than half a minute. I wouldn't take that risk."

"I think they've given up their attempts for now and are probably contemplating their next move," said Ali Baksi, the Swedish liaison officer responsible for communications since the outbreak of war, among other things. "Everything suggests they need some time to recover."

Baksi, who had the heads of the SÄPO, MUST, and FRA reporting to him, always had the most information.

"They likely need to rest and regroup to keep things relatively calm. Meanwhile, we can consolidate and continuously bring reinforcements. Time is on our side."

"Absolutely. The massacre in Fyledalen marks a definitive turning point in the war. The Muslims lost their chance to maintain the initiative there. This attack on southeastern Skåne seems like an act of desperation. We will... win... this war... unless something unforeseen... occurs," Brännström said with solid conviction, speaking slowly in his characteristic Luleå accent. It was as if he pondered each word before speaking, adding weight to his statements. His words were not casually tossed out; they were considered carefully, especially when he tried to talk in that reassuring, steady Norrbotten manner. Unshakeable and calm in all situations.

"That's what we'll do," Baksi agreed. "Provided we can maintain control of the sea, so the Muslims can't bring in reinforcements."

"As long as the Russians enforce the no-fly zone, no reinforcements will make it through," said Navy Chief Fridolf Palmquist. "No reinforcements will come by sea, that I can guarantee."

"We trust you know what you're doing, Fridolf," Brännström said. "But now I'm considering whether we should let the *Snapphane guerilla fighters* strike the Muslims from behind, giving them something else to worry about while we consolidate our forces," Brännström proposed. "Instead of getting much-needed rest and reorganization, they'll face a new and unexpected enemy that suddenly appears and attacks from the rear."

Brännström had chosen to let the free Swedish forces continue operating independently. He was well aware that the free troops had won the "Kebab War"— or the Battle of Botkyrka—using only their resources and had played a crucial role in the liberation of the Norrbotten coastal region. Brännström's strategy was to allow the free forces to continue their operations independently but under the requirement that they adhere to and follow his directives when needed and to inform him before launching significant operations. The advantage of the free forces was that they managed their own armament and supply logistics, relieving the strained and limited resources of the regular army. And the question was whether they would have accepted anything other than continuing their independent operations.

Snapphanarna, the name given to the free guerilla fighters in Skåne, was led by a former commander from one of the six battalions at the Southern Skåne Regiment at Revingehed, often referred to as P7. His name was Jöns Möller, and he was destined to play a crucial role in the Swedish liberation war. Möller was a die-hard Malmö native and had never considered leaving his hometown, not even when it was overwhelmed by Muslims to the point where Swedes became a minority. The greatest pride for Möller was the city's successful soccer team, with their sky-blue jerseys. He had worn the sky-blue jersey and played for "Iff-iff," as they were nicknamed, though his talent only reached the B team, with a few appearances in the A squad.

Nevertheless, he had played a few matches alongside soccer genius Zlatko Muslimovic, and that was something to remember and tell his children, even though the soccer genius had unfortunately been injured at a very young age. Sadly, he had recently received reports that Zlatko was now working for the Muslims in Malmö. It was painful to hear but perhaps inevitable. The name alone said it all.

The so-called *Friskyttarna* – "The Free Rangers" – was another small group of guerilla fighters with a few hundred combatants. They were led by a civilian who had worked as a project manager on constructing Malmö's uniquely designed skyscraper, the Turning Torso. Despite his civilian background, he was well-versed in weaponry, being an avid competitive shooter. His name was Jeppe Hofman-Bang, and as both his first and last names suggested, he was of Danish origin, traceable back to before 1658, when the Swedes took over Skåne, Halland, and Blekinge. Jeppe's guerilla fighters often joked about his surname, "Bang," which they felt suited their leader ideally. To top it off, Jeppe's wife, one of the fighting guerilla warriors, was named Gun, frequently amusing the other fighters. "Gun Bang" was undeniably a memorable name, especially in the English-speaking world.

While *Snapphanarna* often conducted more significant attacks, sometimes synchronized with the regular army, the Free Rangers were quintessential guerilla soldiers who focused on sabotage, intelligence gathering, and pinprick operations against smaller Muslim units. Another difference was that Jeppe Hofman-Bang had completely ignored invitations to collaborate with the regular army. Jeppe had no objections to the military itself, except that it was Swedish, but he believed his operations were best carried out without interference from the defense staff.

Anton Brännström, Sweden's Chief of Defence, had come to terms with the situation and could only hope that the Free Rangers would inflict maximum damage on the Muslims without his oversight. As long as the Free Rangers did not attack the Swedes, they were allowed to operate, and it would require significant resources to stop them if possible. Brännström realized it was wise to utilize all available resources in the war against the Muslims.

Brännström had received information from Ken Persson, the head of NRSS (National Council's Special Security Service), that Gyllenstierna had been secretly holding private prayers, performing Muslim rituals, and prostrating toward Mecca with his forehead on the ground. If Persson hadn't been able to show films of these prayer sessions, Brännström would hardly have believed it, but the evidence was unequivocal. Religion was private; perhaps Gyllenstierna had been a devout Muslim while still a good and loyal Swede. However, Gyllenstierna, as Chancellor, had signed laws prohibiting the practice of Islam.

Brännström didn't know how to interpret the situation, but he knew his own life was at risk if he confronted Gyllenstierna with what he knew. Brännström knew that the list of people eliminated by NRSS was becoming quite long, even though NRSS, under its secret head, Ken Persson, whose name even Brännström didn't know, officially did not engage in assassination. He had no desire to find himself on that list. All those on the list of the dead who mysteriously disappeared had one thing in common—they had fallen out of favor with Gyllenstierna, who increasingly resembled a classic blood-soaked dictator with paranoid tendencies. Dictators who handle problems with excessive brutality often have cause for their paranoia. When one murders others indiscriminately, one becomes a target for revenge-seeking assassins, and that was the position Gyllenstierna found himself in, fully aware of it.

No one was left to oppose Gyllenstierna when he proposed new plans and ideas. Everyone knew that negative criticism of Gyllenstierna's suggestions always came with a price. Gyllenstierna was making a classic mistake, a severe weakening, by surrounding himself solely with yay-sayers.

It was safest to withhold strategic military information from Gyllenstierna as much as possible. Not that Brännström seriously believed his old friend and colleague would be a security risk, but it was better to be safe than sorry.

And what about Baksi, who also had Muslim roots? Could he be trusted? There was no information suggesting that Baksi practiced Islam in any way. However, could any devout Muslim ever indeed be utterly free from their faith? Baksi had claimed to be a 'believer' when he was younger. Brännström had never seen an example of someone altogether abandoning their faith, though some Muslims had converted to Christianity for opportunistic reasons in societies where it offered advantages. Brännström was genuinely confident of Baksi's loyalty, but still, something nagged at him.

Chapter 18 – Operation Mina

May 5, 2033

The grand holiday *Eid al-Adha* always takes place on the tenth day of the Muslim lunar month of *Dhul-Hijjah*. *Eid al-Adha* is celebrated because it follows the completion of the *Hajj* pilgrimage to Mecca on the previous day, known as *Arafah* Day, which is devoted to prayer and fasting.

The *Hajj* concludes in a valley near Mina, three miles from Mecca. The day before, pilgrims had completed the mandatory seven circuits around the *Kaaba*, Islam's holiest site. In the valley outside Mina, Muslims perform the ritual of stoning the devil by throwing twenty-one stones each at three of the eighty-foot-high stone pillars explicitly erected for this purpose.

Eid al-Adha is intricately linked to the prophet Ibrahim, known as Abraham, in Jewish and Christian traditions. Muslims regard Ibrahim as their patriarch, which gives them a sense of kinship with Jews and Christians and leads them to share fragments of their faith. However, as is often the case, familiarity breeds contempt. The supposed brethren are regarded as infidels, to be driven out and killed unless they convert to Islam.

Eid al-Adha is mainly associated with a trial in Ibrahim's life when God commanded him to sacrifice his son, Ishmael. Ibrahim's family completely trusted God, so Ibrahim told Ishmael about the dream. Ishmael reluctantly agreed to his father's plan to fulfill God's command. Together, they went to the place of sacrifice, where Ibrahim prepared to offer his beloved son—while Ishmael prepared himself to die. The devil tried to tempt Ibrahim to cease, but he remained steadfast in his unwavering faith.

Ibrahim saw his son alive for what he thought would be the last time. But as the knife approached Ishmael's neck, God stayed in Ibrahim's hand, showing that his sacrifice had already been fulfilled, as Ibrahim had proven his faith despite the devil's temptations. God commanded Ibrahim to substitute Ishmael with a sheep, which would be offered instead.

The story's moral is that God provides a way out of all difficulties for those who fear Him. Those who trust in God need nothing else. God is the greatest and the source of all joy and comfort.

After the rigorous fast of *Arafah* Day, the feast of *Eid al-Adha* is eagerly anticipated, as the devout Muslims' empty stomachs are to be filled with delicacies. During *Eid al-Adha*, families are required to sacrifice an animal. Usually, a goat or sheep is sacrificed, but cattle and camels are also acceptable. However, they are much more expensive and, therefore, rarely used.

It is not acceptable to sacrifice a damaged or starved animal. The sacrificial animal must be of prime quality and at least one year old. The prime meat is to be shared with the poor, which also occurred in Malmö during *Eid al-Adha* on May 5, 2033, but it was only for Muslims. During *Eid al-Adha*, no Muslim should go hungry. Since camels, cattle, and goats were scarce in Malmö, almost only sheep were sacrificed, with a few goats as a supplement.

Halal slaughter involves cutting the animal's throat, which allows the still-living animal to drain its blood. Typically, the animal's legs are first bound, rendering it defenseless, before it is brought down with a powerful hockey tackle by the *halal* slaughterer, who then performs a neck strike and uses a sharp knife to cut the throat. The specific choreography of the slaughter, which Muslims consider beautiful, is, however, frightening to modern urban dwellers.

There are various local customs. Sometimes, the slaughterer rests a knee on the animal after it has been knocked down while the throat is cut. In some areas of the Muslim world, animals are hung by their hind legs. After a minute or so, the animal loses consciousness due to blood loss. Regardless of the method, one thing is common throughout the Muslim world: During *Eid al-Adha*, blood flows down the streets everywhere and in every community.

The shedding of blood during *Eid al-Adha* is considered to build character for young boys, who are to be raised as fearless and sacrificial warriors of God, steadfast in the face of bloodshed and suffering.

The Swedes in Malmö, starving for months, looked on with envy as sheep and goats were grilled over open fires in the streets and squares. The wonderful smell of grilled meat, which most Swedes hadn't experienced in over a year, led many to spontaneously convert by loudly proclaiming the magical words, "There is no god but Allah, and Muhammad is His Messenger," just to join the feast—and they were invited. Once you're a Muslim, even if just for a minute, the simple confession of faith is something like an "Open Sesame" for non-Muslims in Muslim communities. However, anyone who pretends to be Muslim and then does not follow Islamic laws or even practices another religion is immediately killed.

Eyes watched the Swedes' daily activities in every neighborhood. Those who had participated in the barbecue would do well to dress in traditional Muslim attire from now on—women fully covered, men with beards—and attend Friday prayers.

Slowly but surely, the many foreign and peculiar rituals began to feel more and more natural. The Muslims, once feared, started to feel like friends who could be relied upon for advice and help with various concerns. It felt comforting and safe to be welcomed into the warmth of Islam.

Eid al-Adha is a day of celebration and joy when people are expected to reconcile with one another, especially with their parents and other family members, neighbors, and friends. During the *Eid* prayer at the mosque, both men, women, and children are expected to be dressed in their finest clothes, and this was indeed the case that day at Scandinavia's largest mosque, Umm al-Muminin Khadijah Mosque, at the road Danska vägen in Northern Rosengård.

The Umm al-Muminin Khadijah Mosque was inaugurated in 2017. The funding primarily came from the Qatari authority, "The Ministry of Awqaf and Islamic Affairs." Still, the Kuwaiti state and some local Swedish organizations and businessmen also contributed to the raised one hundred and forty million kronor.

The inauguration was conducted by Qatari Minister Khalid Shaheen Al Ghanim, who was among many high-ranking Muslims present, alongside Malmö's social democratic Councilor Frida Trollmyr, who at the time did not see any issues with Qatar, as well as Kuwait and Saudi Arabia, having the extreme Sunni Muslim orientation of Wahhabism as their state religion.

Trollmyr's brief comment after the inauguration was, "Hopefully, this cultural center will bring joy to many Malmö residents." Frida Trollmyr was correct that many Muslims in Malmö were pleased with the impressive complex, which could accommodate nearly two thousand worshippers. The neighboring property, the Macedonian Orthodox Church, looked like a miniature.

But the joy was not universal. When war broke out on July 17, 2032, the Macedonian Orthodox Church was bombed by Muslims. The cemetery was desecrated, and the contaminated soil, including partially decayed bodies and old bone fragments, was removed and dumped in the old limestone quarry in Limhamn. It was replaced with seventy thousand cubic feet of halal soil from neighboring Söderslätt to convert the site into a Muslim burial ground.

Since its inauguration, the Scandinavian Sunni Muslim community, Wakf, has managed the mosque. Initially claiming to be entirely independent of Qatar, Wakf was, from the beginning, Wahhabism's sharpest spearhead in Sweden.

On May 5, 2033, at 6.55 a.m., the Umm al-Muminin Khadijah Mosque was packed to capacity as the first-morning prayer of *Eid al-Adha* was about to begin. The crowd was so large that Eid prayers were scheduled every hour until 11 a.m. to ensure that all devout Muslims would have a chance to participate.

As the devout Muslims gathered for the important *Eid* prayer, an old black Pontiac Trans Sport approached the road Industrigatan, then turned right onto Danska vägen toward the mosque. When the SUV turned onto the whole parking lot in front of the mosque twenty seconds later, the four security guards stationed at the entrance, under the orders of Security Chief Muslimovic, reached for the AK-47s slung over their shoulders. They knew that the black SUV wouldn't get any farther, as the concrete block barrier at the end of the parking lot would stop any potential car bombers, so they felt no immediate stress.

No Swede would think of trying anything here, as there was no chance of escaping. They were deep within the Muslim zone, so security around the mosque was not overly concerned, and the security responsibility lay entirely with the highly trusted Muslimovic.

The few security concerns raised by Muslimovic's superiors were met with the standard response from the ever-smiling and self-assured Muslimovic: "I'm handling it, and you know you can always count on me. Just relax and enjoy life. I'll be on-site and keep an eye on everything."

Muslimovic had dispatched most of the security team to Kronprinsen, where the staff would hold a smaller *Eid* ceremony in the basement. Muslimovic claimed there was a threat related to the Kronprinsen meeting, justifying the presence of forty *God Warriors* for security. The rest of the security team was out on various assignments around Malmö, on Muslimovic's orders.

The SUV stopped in front of the concrete blocks while the four guards at the mosque entrance aimed their automatic rifles at it, just for precaution and to demonstrate their vigilance. They knew their strict and demanding boss, Zlatko Muslimovic, was watching them from his discreet position in the bushes on the neighboring property near the Muslim preschool.

No one but the four guards noticed the two men who stood quite visibly among the bushes, but the arriving worshippers' gazes were drawn, as if by an invisible force, towards the large mosque they were headed to. Muslimovic was flanked by his right-hand man, Deputy Security Chief Ivan, who was not a boss to be taken lightly.

It was best to stay alert. The guards expected high-ranking Muslims to leave the car and hurry into the mosque before the *Eid* prayer began. Once the prayer started, the gates would close, and it was the guards' duty to turn away latecomers, regardless of rank, to prevent any disturbance during the prayer.

The first prayer at 7 a.m. was reserved exclusively for the highest and most significant Muslims. The prestige of being among the chosen few meant that many thousands wanted to attend the earliest *Eid* prayer, but there was only room for two thousand people, so most had to settle for later prayers.

A distinguished crowd had gathered for the first prayer session, now going down on all fours on the exclusive marble floor under the large dome. Among them were military personnel, politicians, businessmen, artists, and the religious elite. Many were long-distance guests, mainly from the Muslim-occupied zone in western Sweden. Still, there were also Muslims from Denmark, Germany, the Netherlands, and a handful from the Gulf states—the actual leaders of the Wakf community running the mosque.

Standing at the pulpit—the *minbar*—was Imam Hassan Haddad, chairman of the Swedish Imam Council, and thus the highest-ranking imam in Sweden, comparable to the church's archbishop.

As Haddad looked out over the two thousand men already down on all fours, their foreheads touching the floor, the heels of their bare feet resembled a forest of luscious mushrooms waiting to be harvested amid a sea of white-clad backs and buttocks. Everyone was dressed in white on this sacred day, as is proper. The murmur subsided, and silence fell despite the excellent acoustics under the giant dome amplifying even the slightest sound. No one speaks as loudly and clearly in daily life as Arabs, but no one can be as silent as they are when gathering for prayer.

Meanwhile, Benno Ronkanen exited through the main entrance of the Clarion Congress, where a dark Audi was waiting. The driver waved to Benno, who opened the door and sat on the passenger side. He was taken aback to see that the driver was none other than Thorstein Möller, who had long been the Sweden leader of Hells Angels.

"Hello," Benno said, receiving only a glance and a slight nod.

The car moved off silently. Benno had yet to learn where they were going but felt this was not the time to ask questions. All he could hope for was that Muslimovic meant him well. Thorstein Möller was not someone Benno usually wanted to deal with.

Imam Hassan Haddad raised his right hand, with his thumb folded in and the four fingers pointing upward—the Rabia sign, which is the symbol of the Muslim Brotherhood—while he began the *Eid* prayer with a powerful and steady voice.

"I seek refuge with God from the accursed Satan. In the name of God, the Most Merciful, the Most Compassionate."

Two guards remained in front of the entrance, still holding their AK-47s at the ready, while the other two went to check the black SUV, which was still idling with no one getting out.

Suddenly, Zlatko Muslimovic and his right-hand man, Ivan, opened fire on the guards with their Kalashnikovs from their hiding place in the dense foliage. The four guards fell immediately, dead before they hit the ground. At the same time, the SUV doors opened, and four men dressed in black, armed with enormous and powerful automatic weapons and heavy backpacks full of ammunition belts, stepped out and spread out, two on each side of the vehicle.

Like everyone else in the mosque, Imam Hassan Haddad heard the gunfire with some concern and hesitated about what to do. After a few seconds of contemplation, he concluded that he could do nothing about it, so he decided to believe that the security guards were merely dealing with a problem and that everything was probably already over. Haddad prepared to continue the prayer in front of the still-silent congregation, some of whom had curiously lifted their foreheads from the floor to see what their imam would do about the gunfire. Haddad signaled with a broad but slow and dignified gesture for them to return their foreheads to the floor, which was immediately obeyed.

Just as Imam Hassan Haddad drew a breath to proceed with the second verse of the prayer, Zlatko Muslimovic pressed the remote detonator that completed the electrical circuit. This caused the explosive charge to detonate, igniting a hundred pounds of Dynamex hidden in a box under the *minbar*. The explosion was so powerful that it blew out the eardrums of everyone in the prayer room, which was not surprising given that the blast was heard up to several miles away.

Thanks to everyone in the prayer room being hunched on their knees with their faces to the floor, only a few hundred in the front rows, the most prominent visitors, were instantly killed by the shockwave. Those closest to the pulpit were torn apart by the blast, with their body parts thrown into the air like a red confetti shower of dismembered arms, legs, hands, feet, heads, and broken torsos wrapped in an aerosol of blood droplets that landed on the rear rows or slammed hard against the walls. Many of those who survived the shockwave further back were crushed and maimed instead by hundreds of tons of concrete debris that fell upon their hunched backs when the entire dome shattered into a thousand pieces, seeking a way out and collapsing in a cloud of smoke and dust that made it impossible to see even the hand in front of one's face.

Seconds after the explosion, people began pouring out of all exits in the massive mosque complex. Among those who had been in the prayer room, only those furthest from the explosion could stagger and crawl out of the smoking inferno, wrapped in their bloodied, sheet-like, once-white kaftans. But hundreds of others who had been in the office area and other rooms were now running to escape the building, fearing more bombs.

Zlatko Muslimovic waited for fifteen seconds, which felt like an eternity, to ensure most people had exited the building before ordering the attack group's four machine gunners, positioned on either side of the SUV, to open fire. They used the Swedish Army's lightweight, single-man machine gun, the KSP 90C, with thirteen rounds per second firing rate. Together, the four KSPs unleashed fifty-two rounds per second.

The intense firepower caused long lines and large groups of fleeing people to fall simultaneously as if struck by an invisible scythe repeatedly sweeping across the courtyard. The machine gunners were strategically placed in a semicircle to cover the escape routes without risking hitting each other.

As a final measure, after nearly forty seconds of peppering the area with over two thousand shots from the machine guns, and when no upright people remained in sight, the gunners ran to all open doors. They threw a couple of grenades into each doorway. The eighteen remaining grenades were scattered among the fallen bodies on the mosque grounds to kill as many as possible who had only been injured by the gunfire or who had managed to throw themselves down before being hit.

The order from the attack group leader, Muslimovic, was relentless. As many men as possible were to be killed. Women and children were to be spared, if possible. Still, it was impossible to avoid hitting them with the 5.56 and forty-five-millimeter ammunition, which made no distinction between who was who, and neither did the grenades. While the shooting continued, Muslimovic and his associate rushed to the SUV, where Muslimovic took the driver's seat. They hadn't bothered to shoot further after killing the guards, as the firepower from their automatic rifles was negligible compared to the force of the four comrades' KSP 90Cs.

The machine gunners jumped into the SUV, having completed their task, with their heavy weapons in hand, so large they barely fit in the car, but leaving their now-empty backpacks behind at the scene. Muslimovic took a left at the exit, accelerated on Danska vägen, and then took the first right onto the minor road of Scheelegatan, the last anyone would ever see of the black SUV.

Muslimovic slowed to average speed, aware that no guards with vehicles were nearby since he had dispatched them to entirely different parts of Malmö. At the transport company Mortens Buss & Taxi, Muslimovic cautiously drove through the already open gate, which immediately closed behind them. At this early hour, the streets were virtually empty, and no one noticed anything unusual. Since it was mostly Swedes on the move heading to their jobs, they wouldn't mention anything to the Muslims, even if they had observed something.

Mortens Buss & Taxi was a relatively new establishment, essentially just a sign. In reality, the location served as the headquarters for the Hells Angels in southern Sweden. However, the organization realized it was safest to keep a low profile after the Muslims took over Malmö. The solution was a discreet sign change and a suspension of most activities. Everyone knew that motorcycle clubs—except for a few exclusively immigrant clubs—had members who were Swedish patriots. The motorcycle clubs were part of the hard core of the National Guard, led by Ernst Höök, who had himself been a motorcycle club president.

At Mortens Buss & Taxi, Zlatko's former adversary, Hells Angels leader Thorstein Möller, was waiting with Benno Ronkanen and a team of four who immediately went into action. The windows were plastic-wrapped and taped before the paint sprayer was turned on. Chrome trim and other details had already been covered with black tape, as had the areas in the trunk and engine compartment that weren't to be painted.

Six minutes later, a white SUV stood before them. The rims had been replaced with the original ones. The license plate had been swapped out, and the fake 'Chrysler' emblem had been replaced with the original 'Pontiac' one.

Within ten minutes, a white 1999 Pontiac Trans Sport rolled out into the sparse traffic, driven by Muslimovic himself. Despite its age, it had unusually fresh paint, though it looked pretty dirty after being doused with a few buckets of muddy water. A brand with Arabic text on the lower left corner of the windshield indicated that the vehicle belonged to the security team. Muslimovic rolled down the window and showed his well-known face as they passed through two fixed roadblocks with barriers. The checkpoints were on high alert, instructed to stop and search all dark SUVs, but they likely wouldn't have stopped the feared security chief Muslimovic anyway.

The Pontiac was eventually parked on the lowest level of the Emporia parking garage, after which the license plate was swapped out again, and the security team's sticker was removed. It remained there for three weeks before it was adequately investigated and linked to the attack at the Umm al-Muminin Khadijah Mosque. Still, by then, all six attackers were already in the Swedish zone.

Some surviving witnesses had seen a black Chrysler SUV. One witness could also recall that the license plate number was MFF 999. The letters amusingly spelled the name of the city's famous soccer club, making it easier for her to remember, and the numbers were even more accessible.

The black Chrysler SUV seemed to have vanished without a trace, and it took investigators a few days to realize that it must have been their highly esteemed and trusted Security Chief, Zlatko Muslimovic, who had carried out the devastating attack, triggering a frantic hunt for him and his accomplices. But the Muslims were too late.

The disaster at the Umm al-Muminin Khadijah Mosque caused profound dismay throughout the Muslim world. Most of the Muslim community's Swedish-based elite had been wiped out, including the distinguished Skåne guests, among them Anders Skenfors, Ilmar Repaluu, Gudrun Schyman, and Per Gahrton. The attack led to significant difficulties concerning the war and the management of civil society. Fortunately for the Muslims, their general staff had decided to hold their *Eid* prayer in a smaller gathering, led by their imam, at Kronprinsen, where the staff had their office.

The Muslims' revenge on the Swedes was brutal, unleashing a wave of terror never before seen in the entire Muslim-occupied zone, especially in Malmö. Zlatko Muslimovic's sensationally successful attack astonished and delighted the Swedish war leadership, who had been entirely unaware of the plans. This operation was of a scale that would significantly influence the war's outcome, in which the Swedes had already begun to gain the upper hand.

The Swedish command center celebrated the event with champagne confiscated from a nearby wine cellar. The atmosphere was exuberant, and they poured Dom Perignon from Magnum bottles.

"I think damn well we should erect a statue of Zlatko Muslimovic in Malmö after the war," Anton Brännström exclaimed cheerfully, toasting once more to the Skåne superhero. "Or, maybe it's more fitting in Stockholm?"

"Well, that might be a good idea," Gyllenstierna replied, though not very convincingly. "We'll see how that turns out later."

Another person celebrating the attack was Benno Ronkanen, who was comfortably reclining in the passenger seat of a Volvo V90, passing Norrköping on its way home to Stockholm. Soon, he would be reunited with his family. Perhaps he could even continue as a PR consultant for Nestander under his real identity?

His life had been a real rollercoaster, and now he hoped for a peaceful existence under stable circumstances, but it seemed that wasn't his fate. His psyche also appeared to be a rollercoaster, though he thought somewhat gloomily despite being free. He briefly wondered if that was just his nature or if he was merely a victim of unfortunate circumstances.

Chapter 19 – A Forced Partnership

May 6, 2033

The Russian embassy in Marieberg, in Stockholm, remained completely unscathed during the war and the Muslim occupation of the fall of 2032, even though the nearby newspaper buildings, belonging to morning papers Dagens Nyheter and Svenska Dagbladet, were turned into ruins on the very first day of the conflict. This was no coincidence, as the media outlets were prime targets for the Muslims.

However, an embassy is considered the territory of its owner, and an attack on the Russian embassy would be a direct assault on Russia itself. This move would hardly benefit the Muslim occupiers. Thus, the building was left untouched. The many long and famous antennas on the embassy's roof remained intact. Communications across the Baltic Sea continued as usual even though Sweden's overall communications had virtually ceased, with the military being the only exception.

Gyllenstierna had been summoned to a "strategic meeting" by the Russian Ambassador to Sweden, Iosif Vissarionovich, and arrived well ahead of time. He was well-prepared, as he always was for essential meetings. As additional preparation, he spent several hours discussing Russia's intentions with the General Staff Advisor and expert on Russia's intentions in Sweden, Katerina Kutepova-Andersson. As chief of defense, he had known her for many years and had frequently attended her lectures on European geopolitics.

Gyllenstierna felt reassured regarding the Russians' territorial ambitions. Kutepova-Andersson was convinced that Moscow had already secured what it needed for the future. She also suggested that Russia could help Sweden win the war—if Sweden complied with Moscow's demands.

Compliance was something he could likely offer Moscow. However, the last point Kutepova-Andersson had made, just as they were wrapping up the meeting, deeply troubled him. She had mentioned that the Russians would almost certainly have opinions on who should form Sweden's highest leadership in the future—something that included him, even though Kutepova-Andersson had tactfully avoided being specific.

The armchair he had been assigned was comfortable, but after waiting for forty minutes, he began to feel a growing irritation. After all, Gyllenstierna was the chancellor of the realm and, by protocol, of significantly higher rank than a mere ambassador, even if it was a representative of a powerful neighboring country. Gyllenstierna suspected that his delay was not a coincidence but part of a power play, an apparent attempt to show who was in charge, regardless of the formal rank.

When Gyllenstierna was finally shown into the room, he was pleasantly surprised and very much taken aback. He was pleasantly surprised to see Sergei Larionov, the friendly, burly man, extending his large hand to him. Russia's well-known and somewhat legendary foreign minister, whom he had met a few times and perceived as influential and having a significant impact on President Putin's foreign policy. Despite radiating power and immense presence, Larionov was flexible, constructive, and, in general, a genuinely pleasant individual—an exception to the usual demeanor of Russian power brokers at that level.

Larionov was a big and warm personality who never needed to play any role other than his own. He was known for his exceptional intelligence and for reading people as quickly as others read newspapers. His powerful charm was why he almost always persuaded others to adopt his views.

At least the meeting was at the right level, even if it should have been with President Putin himself. Putin had never visited Sweden during his years as president and was unlikely to do so. Gyllenstierna's surprise stemmed from seeing a familiar face enter the room through another door. The man was Alfred Baksi, Gyllenstierna's longtime friend and confidant. Baksi looked just as surprised and greeted Gyllenstierna with a nod, raising his eyebrows slightly to express his astonishment and curiosity about what was happening.

However, Baksi was not surprised to see Gyllenstierna's familiar face. Baksi had been summoned half an hour earlier and had been thoroughly interrogated by the two Russians about Gyllenstierna's "Muslim inclinations," as they put it, though how they knew about this was unclear. Baksi had answered cautiously, careful not to cast any suspicion on his good friend and boss, whom he owed so much. He had said it was purely a private need for spirituality and vouched that

Gyllenstierna was unwavering in his commitment to fight for Swedish core values of freedom, equality, and democracy. In Baksi's view, the Russians' numerous questions and overly meticulous probing of his answers were why Gyllenstierna had to wait for the meeting so long.

Baksi wondered to himself how the Russians could know details about Gyllenstierna that even he did not, after so many years of close cooperation and friendship.

The four men, all impeccably dressed in exclusive blue suits, placed in armchairs around a small round marble table in the corner of the spacious room. An oval conference table with seating for thirty dominated the center of the room. Above the marble table hung a heavy crystal chandelier, sparkling in its grandeur.

The room smelled of stale smoke. On the long wall hung a large painting of Russia's President Vladimir Putin, dressed in a blue suit and matching blue tie, ceremoniously greeting former U.S. President George W. Bush at their first meeting in Ljubljana, Slovenia, in 2001. The painting's placement was of particular significance as it had previously been occupied by Soviet leaders who left the heaviest marks: Lenin, Stalin, Khrushchev, Brezhnev, and Gorbachev. Malenkov, Andropov, and Chernenko had never been featured on the wall, as their tenures as Soviet leaders were too brief.

Putin was said to particularly appreciate this painting, executed from a photograph, because he appeared average-sized next to George W. Bush, who was also not particularly tall. It was worse when Putin met China's President Xi Jinping, especially when he met Germany's former Chancellor Helmut Kohl, a true giant. No matter how the photographers angled their cameras, President Putin appeared relatively small next to Kohl, and it was even worse when they were seated side by side. Not even cropped images with just their heads could fit together, as Kohl's hat size was eight sizes larger than Putin's.

They were seated in a mixed arrangement around the table, not with Swedes on one side and Russians on the other. Such a seating arrangement typically indicated that the host sought consensus. In formal negotiations, the parties usually sat across from each other.

Foreign Minister Sergei Larionov opened the meeting as the blonde, plump, and somewhat heavily made-up secretary, in a slightly tight and low-cut dress that accentuated her ample charms, filled the crystal glasses with water from the beautiful decanter. After Baksi's interrogation, Larionov skipped the formalities, as they already knew each other. Straightforwardness, without frills, was the Russian style, and many appreciated the simplicity and directness that laid a solid foundation for efficiency and decisive action.

Gyllenstierna observed that the usually obstinate and aggressive Ambassador, Iosif Vissaronovich, had shrunk into a submissive and attentive boy beside his superior, Larionov. When Sergei Larionov entered a room, he filled it with his presence. It was inevitable that he would always become the center of gravity at any gathering he attended. The only exceptions were meetings where his boss, Putin, was present. In those instances, Larionov always let his superior take the lead. Those were the only times Larionov took on the role of the attentive boy.

"Today, we would like to present a plan for strategic cooperation between our two countries. A plan that is highly advantageous from a Swedish perspective. Russia wants to build a close political and military alliance with Sweden. We want to consider Sweden a reliable friend and close ally—for all time." Larionov deliberately paused and reached for the cigarette pack on the table. "But to get there, we must both forget historical grievances. The well-known Swedish hatred of Russians must not be a hindrance."

"That sounds interesting and exciting," Gyllenstierna replied. "We are certainly not bogged down by historical grudges. We are open to doing anything that benefits Sweden, especially given the current situation. We don't have many options—at least not many good ones."

Foreign Minister Larionov pulled a massive, gold-plated lighter from his right suit pocket as he spoke.

"Russia wants to ensure that Sweden wins the war against the Muslim occupiers, but that you do it with your resources; at least, it should appear that way. Our little show in Fyledalen is to be considered an exception. It was a field test and a demonstration for the world, which is closely watching what happens in Sweden. Now, both the Chinese, Americans, Indians, and Muslims worldwide know what we have in our arsenal, and I don't think any of them are eager to get acquainted with this dreadful doomsday weapon."

Larionov fitted a small silver tip onto his cigarette, placed it between his lips, clicked the lighter, and took a deep drag. He leaned back in his chair and exhaled the smoke with pleasure while adjusting his highly polished black shoes slightly. As Gyllenstierna drew in a breath to comment, Larionov raised his right hand to indicate he intended to continue his explanation. "Starting May tenth, Russia will declare a no-fly zone covering the entire Muslim-occupied zone, which means the western parts of Svealand and Götaland, including Swedish territorial waters. Anything that flies in the no-fly zone without permission will be intercepted by Russian fighter jets from our squadron at *Ostrovnaya Strana*—what you call Öland—and shot down without warning. At the same time, while we declare the no-fly zone, we will grant the Swedish Navy—whose main bases in Berga and Karlskrona were unfortunately bombed to pieces during the early, chaotic days of the war—free access to our large naval base in *Iznosheny* on eastern *Khoroshaya Strana*, which is what you refer to as the base in Slite on the eastern coast of Gotland. Russia will offer services and repairs, free fuel, and provisioning."

Gyllenstierna and Baksi exchanged glances while Larionov took a few sips of water to prepare for the next part of his long speech. This sounded promising! Except for the fact that they didn't like that the Russians had already replaced all Swedish place names on the islands of Öland and Gotland with Russian ones. But they would have to get used to it.

"We know you have plenty of ammunition, as your navy has hardly been involved in hostilities, except for the Swedish submarine that managed to sink the American sub intruding into Russian territory off *Khoroshaya Strana*. Your Naval Chief, Palmquist, skillfully did that. But he also sank our anti-submarine ship, entirely unnecessarily, and in Russian territorial waters, too! Russia would appreciate it if you looked for a new naval chief, as this Palmquist could not be part of any maritime cooperation between our countries. He risks serious consequences if he ever encounters the comrades of those who were killed in the Russian Navy."

Just as Gyllenstierna was about to comment on the events off the eastern coast of Gotland, Larionov raised his hand again to signal that he wanted to continue his discourse. Larionov took another deep drag on his cigarette before speaking again.

"For the time being, we will refrain from requesting the extradition of Palmquist out of respect for the fact that he was following orders from above. My boss, President Putin, initially wanted Palmquist deported, but I managed to prevent that. I believe Palmquist is a skilled individual with qualities that would be valuable in the Russian Navy. He can remain the naval chief, but he should be removed from the National Council before President Putin changes his mind about the extradition. Just as a piece of advice."

Gyllenstierna and Baksi exchanged another glance without commenting on the Swedish naval chief's issue while Larionov took a deep breath to continue his explanation.

"With *Iznosheny* as a base, your navy can undoubtedly establish an iron barrier, both on and beneath the sea surface, preventing any reinforcement or weapons supply to the Muslim occupation zone. Once our base in Russian Halland—Russkaya Kholland—is completed, it will also be open to Swedish vessels, at least until you reclaim your ports on the West Coast. And possibly indefinitely if we move forward and develop the partnership into a political union. How does that sound?"

"That sounds interesting," Gyllenstierna replied. "As you know, we no longer have an air force, so the no-fly zone is something we truly appreciate. However, discussing a political union—which in practice would mean Sweden becoming a Russian republic or perhaps another form of Russian federation subject—seems inappropriate if we are to gain the support and approval of the Swedish people and, more importantly, the military. If we become too challenging, we risk coups, popular uprisings, and possibly even civil war among the Swedes. That would benefit no one but our Muslim enemy."

Larionov's impassive stone face showed no reaction or acknowledgment of Gyllenstierna's objection regarding a potential political union.

"When that time comes, Russia is very interested in helping you build up your combat aviation to the highest level, but that's a few years away. In the coming years, Russia will assist in rebuilding your electricity production. Russia can construct several gas power plants within a few months, which can then be operated with Russian gas at very favorable prices. It's easy to connect to the Nordstream 1 pipeline in the Baltic Sea, which runs just outside *Khoroshaya Strana*. This pipeline has supplied gas and played a crucial political role as it passed through what was formerly Swedish territorial waters. Without Nordstream, we wouldn't be discussing a partnership here. Unfortunately, the Americans blew up Nordstream 2, but number one fully operates."

"The energy issue is also very urgent to resolve. People are freezing in their homes, and many froze to death last winter. Since restoring hydropower takes so long, we are interested in Russian gas."

Larionov decisively flicked the cigarette into the marble ashtray.

"But everything in life is about give and take. You are probably wondering why Russia is making such a generous offer to Sweden despite your irritatingly anti-Russian stance throughout history. It boils down to two simple things that won't cost Sweden any resources."

The room fell silent as the Swedes anxiously awaited the downside of the Russians' offer, which seemed like the kind of proposal one could not refuse.

"'First of all, we want the Swedish National Defense Radio Establishment – FRA – to cease cooperating with the United States, which has essentially abandoned Europe. Times have changed. FRA's antennas should be redirected westward, southward, and northward instead of spying on your friendly neighbor. Russia wants FRA to be integrated with our global information network,'" Larionov said, glancing at Baksi, the head of the three most well-known Swedish intelligence services.

Baksi leaned slightly forward, indicating he was about to respond while pondering what to say. FRA had always been akin to a branch of the NSA, the U.S. National Security Agency, specializing in signal intelligence. Most of its technical equipment was American or based on American components. It was easier to imagine that FRA would function with American involvement.

"If Russia and Sweden are in partnership, there's no need for intelligence operations aimed at Russia. However, FRA is closely tied to that and has cooperated closely with the U.S. In concrete terms, FRA has been ninety-five percent focused on signal intelligence, first against the

Soviet Union and later against Russia. Many of our employees have personal connections with Americans in the NSA and would likely have difficulty shifting allegiances. I believe the logical course is to completely dismantle FRA and build a new organization—whatever it will be called —with new technical resources and mostly new personnel."

"Yes, exactly, that's precisely how Russia views it. It's hard to teach old dogs new tricks."

"I think the intelligence aspect is manageable," Gyllenstierna agreed. "But what is the second thing Russia expects?"

"That you exclude the Chinese from any form of cooperation. You're even discussing giving them concessions to operate your ports, which is highly concerning to us. The Chinese have promised to build coal power plants, but you'll get gas power plants from us instead."

Gyllenstierna and Baksi exchanged looks once more. Both were relieved that the Russian demands did not involve more Swedish territory, which had been their expectation. Instead, they were offered solutions to their most pressing problems: the war and energy supply. Sweden could essentially be restored if the war could be won, with only the islands Öland, Gotland, and a small enclave lost on the west coast in southern Halland. Given Björn Väster's efficiency regarding deportations, they might even look forward to a better Sweden than before the war.

They knew this was an offer they could not afford to refuse. Another issue was how the Russians could understand what had been discussed with the Chinese under the strictest secrecy. Sharing information with Russia's security services might be a good idea.

"We don't like the Chinese's intrusive interest in Sweden anyway, so we can easily and gladly accommodate this last request. The Chinese have stolen incredible amounts of patents and industrial secrets from Sweden over the years. They also see Sweden as a platform for their interests in the Arctic, where we Swedes believe they have no place. Spontaneously, we consider Russia's total offer highly interesting, and it could serve Sweden well."

"Good, that's what I expected," Larionov said. "The agreement is prepared, in both Swedish and Russian, with a hundred and sixty-four-page document with all the necessary details, and you can take it with you now, which Iosif will handle. We expect your response within sixty-four hours and hope to sign an official partnership by next week. We're already preparing the PR machinery, and it might be wise for us to synchronize this. The world must know this is a genuine and well-balanced partnership, formed entirely voluntarily."

"We will immediately analyze the agreement. There are certain details to consider, but we agree on the main points. We'll start working on our side of the PR effort right away."

Ambassador Vissarionovich rose at Larionov's signal and opened the door to the liquor cabinet in the large wall unit. Soon, a bottle of Russo-Baltique, the world's most expensive vodka, and four disturbingly large, high-stemmed glasses were placed on the table. The glasses were filled to the brim.

"In Russian tradition, we don't toast with Champagne. We prefer to toast with vodka—the water of life—to celebrate our new and friendly relationship, which will bring a bright future to both our countries. *Davayte tost za nashe zdorov'ye*—let's toast to our health."

"*Na zdorovje*"

"*Na zdorovje!*"

The Swedes followed their Russian hosts' custom and drained their glasses.

"By the way, you can call me Sergej," Larionov said generously. "Now that we are good friends."

"We are Daniel and Alfred," Gyllenstierna replied on their behalf.

Ambassador Vissarionovich promptly filled the glasses again, causing the Swedes to exchange worried glances. There was no way they could keep up with the Russians, mainly since their Muslim backgrounds had not accustomed them to even standard Swedish drinking. They had heard too many stories about Swedes in Moscow drinking themselves into oblivion, which seemed to amuse the Russians. It was rumored that Larionov could down an entire liter of vodka without it showing.

"Let's toast to Nordstream 1!"

"*Na zdorovje!*"

"I bring a small message from our great President, Vladimir Putin. Vladimir is so excited about the new opportunities in our cooperation with Sweden, which will change the course of history, that he wants to invite both of you to his residence in La Zagaleta on the Spanish Sun coast for a private party. You should know that this is the highest honor, reserved only for a few of his most cherished friends."

"That sounds quite flattering," Baksi responded, feeling his eyes grow misty and his cheeks flush from a large amount of vodka—probably seven or eight ounces in just two quick sweeps—that his body wasn't used to.

"What kind of party is it, and who are the other guests?" Gyllenstierna inquired, struggling to maintain his composure. He already felt his tongue was failing him, causing him to slur his words.

"Vladimir calls them bunga-bunga parties. The guests and what exactly happens there are among the most tightly guarded Russian state secrets, but I have a standing invitation to the bunga-bunga parties, so I'm in the know but will, of course, not utter a word. Iosif will provide you with a formal invitation as soon as our strategic partnership agreement is signed."

Russia's ambassador to Sweden, Iosif Vissarionovich, looked somewhat crestfallen. Unlike the other three in the room, he knew he would never be invited to the infamous and sought-after bunga-bunga parties. He felt bitter about his arrogant boss, the foreign minister, but dutifully poured the rest of the bottle into the glasses despite the Swedes' attempts to refuse. Not wanting to appear impolite, they raised their glasses for a final toast, this time clinking all four glasses together.

"*Na zdorovje!*"

"*Na zdorovje!*"

The meeting was over, and it was time for the two Swedes to wobbly make their way home. The last thing they saw as they left the room was Foreign Minister Sergej Larionov retrieving another bottle of Russo-Baltique from the liquor cabinet and, with a pleased smile on his face, settling back at the round table and reaching for his cigarette pack. The party had only just begun, but the Swedes were grateful to leave before they became unconscious and completely enshrouded in cigarette smoke.

Gyllenstierna, for his part, was relieved to still hold his position as Swedish chancellor. He might even be able to establish a personal relationship with Putin, which boded well for the future.

Chapter 20 – Allahu Akbar

May 6, 2033

The morning shower took longer than usual that day. *Salat* required purity, which wasn't an issue for Gyllenstierna, who always maintained good personal hygiene naturally and without the religious mandate. He shaved his armpits, gently trickling the warm water over him, even though it had only been four days since the last shave. He carefully removed his pubic hair, which had grown slightly longer than he usually allowed. After each stroke with the double-bladed razor, he let the water wash away the black strands from the blade. The process took time, as Allah had blessed him with abundant body hair.

Once all the pubic hair was gone, he leaned forward, holding the razor in his right hand, with the shower water streaming over his shoulders and back. With his left hand, he parted his buttocks so he could gently shave the inside of his cleft. Then, he transferred the razor to his left hand and finished the task.

It was a bit bothersome for Gyllenstierna, who had always been meticulous about hygiene, that he had such heavy hair growth in unwanted areas. On his head, however, he was starting to thin out, which his barber had noted with some concern. As the vain, handsome man he had always been, he felt anxious about his future as a balding man. He thought he would have to consider a hair transplant when his scalp became too noticeable. But the first thing he would do when the war was over would be to undergo a laser treatment that would make shaving his cleft unnecessary once and for all. Maybe he should treat himself to anal bleaching at the same time, he thought as he stepped out of the shower.

Gyllenstierna carefully brushed his teeth and spent a few minutes on nail care. He filed his toenails, which was unusual for men. Sometimes, he felt a bit envious of women who could paint and strengthen their nails, making them shine beautifully. He would have liked to paint his nails, at least on his hands, but he wasn't the type for that, so he had to make do. He was a real man, just a little more refined.

He dried himself meticulously with a freshly washed towel and unfolded his newly laundered and pressed clothes, which his aide had neatly arranged in the wardrobe. He put on his underwear and the dark gray uniform pants, leaving the shirt and socks on the chair. He would meet Allah in just his undershirt this morning.

To finish, he sprayed a little Jean Paul Gaultier perfume on his fingertips and gently applied it to his cheeks. Finally, a slight, delicate spritz on his chest and abdomen, as if preparing for a sensual seduction of a new woman. But it wasn't a woman he was meeting now. It was Allah who awaited him.

He had drawn a discreet cross on the wall indicating the direction of the Kaaba, the sacred Mecca building. There was no risk of facing the wrong direction when he began his Sabah, the first of the five prayer times he would try to fit in between meetings and other duties.

To perform his ritual washing – the *Abdest* – he had placed a small plastic basin with warm water within reach on the desk. He began by mumbling the Muslim phrase, *Bismillah*. Then he performed the ritual washing of his hands up to the wrists and rinsed his mouth and nose three times each, despite being freshly showered. He continued by washing his arms from the hands up to the elbows three times, first the right arm and then the left. After he had wiped his face, the front of his head, the inside of his ears, and the back of his ears with his wet hands, he moved on to his neck, which was wiped with the back of his damp hands. Everything had to be done with the perfection that characterized everything Gyllenstierna undertook.

While performing his ritual purification, Gyllenstierna silently recited the *Kalimat ash-shahada* to himself. He concluded by washing his feet, first on the right and then on the left. After the ablution, he dried his face and hands with a white washcloth, leaving his feet air-dried.

Once he had finished his purification, he placed both hands near his ears and pronounced the *niyya*—the intention of worship. Gyllenstierna used Turkish mixed with a few expressions in the original Arabic. It bothered him that he didn't speak Arabic, but he planned to address it soon. Turkey's President and autocratic dictator, Recep Tayyip Erdogan, had recently decided to reinstate the Arabic script, so the trend was clear. Arabic was on the rise again, and every devout Muslim had a duty to at least try to learn the language as best as possible.

142

He wasn't entirely sure if he performed all the essential steps correctly, as his parents had been relatively secular. Only on special occasions had they taken him and his brothers to the mosque, where he and his brothers had merely imitated the more knowledgeable Muslims without truly understanding what was happening. His parents hadn't emphasized teaching the children all the rituals, so he had learned them from reading over the past few months.

Gyllenstierna stood perfectly still with his gaze lowered, hands clasped, the right hand over the left. His right index and middle fingers were extended, while his thumb, ring finger, and little finger gripped the left hand. His legs were positioned with the recommended three-finger gap between them.

"I perform the morning prayer to seek God's pleasure," Gyllenstierna said to himself and then in Arabic. "*Allahu Akbar* – God is the greatest."

It was time for *Rak'a*. He fixed his gaze on the prayer mat, placed his left hand on his chest, and gently put his right hand on top. He couldn't thoroughly shake off the distracting thought about whether Allah would appreciate his forthcoming anal bleaching, but he quickly pushed it aside and refocused on his religious duty.

"You are honored, O God, and You are praised. Your name is blessed, Your majesty exalted, and no God exists but You. I seek refuge with God from Satan, the outcast. In the name of God, the Merciful, the Compassionate."

With his back straight and hands still on his chest, he continued with *al-Fatiha.*

"All praise and thanks are due to God, Lord of the worlds. The Merciful, the Compassionate. Master of the Day of Judgment. You alone, we worship, and You alone, we ask for help. Guide us on the straight path of those who have received Your grace, not those who have brought down Your anger or gone astray."

He bowed deeply, still standing, his hands on his knees, and looking down at his toes.

"All glory is to my Lord, the Greatest."

As he straightened up, he said, "God hears the one who praises Him." After standing upright again, still with his hands on his knees, he said, "My Lord, praised are You! *Allahu Akbar.*"

He then went down on all fours, with his forehead touching the ground, head between his outstretched arms and fingers. His gaze was directed downward along his nose. The soles of his feet were straight, while the ritual required that his toes be curled. He then sat back on his knees and performed another bow to the ground. He rose to a standing position from this position to perform the second *Rak'a*, just like the first, and then the third and final *Rak'a*.

As he lay with his forehead pressed to the floor during his third *Rak'a*, he suddenly heard a key inserted into the lock and the door creaking open. He sprang up into a standing position, facing the door, and saw the back of a cleaning lady backing into the room, pushing her cleaning cart. She turned the cart around and froze when she saw the room wasn't empty.

"Oh, I'm so sorry. I was told you were away. I deeply apologize."

Gyllenstierna, who had been interrupted in an almost meditative state, was momentarily at a loss for words as he watched the dark-blonde woman maneuver the cart back through the door. She turned around with a small smile and glanced at the plastic basin on the desk.

"I'm so sorry for interrupting your *Sabah*. I'm from Bosnia. *Allahu Akbar.*"

Gyllenstierna stood there, utterly perplexed, for half a minute, contemplating what it would mean if others knew how deeply his Muslim faith had taken root. He concluded that the Bosnian cleaning lady was hardly a cause for concern and returned to his interrupted *Salat*. He decided he had completed his three *Rak'as* and continued with his prayer.

"All glory is to my Lord, the Most High. *Allahu Akbar.*"

He straightened up again but remained kneeling, gazing downward along his nose.

"Oh God, forgive me, be merciful to me, guide me, provide for me, and protect me. *Allahu Akbar.*"

He then placed his forehead back on the ground.

"All glory is to my Lord, the Most High. All my prayers, worship, and deeds are for God. May God's peace, blessings, and mercy be upon

144

the Prophet. May God's peace be upon us and His righteous servants. I witness that there is nothing worthy of worship except God and that Muhammad is His Prophet. Oh God, bless Muhammad and his family as You blessed Abraham and his family. I seek refuge with God from the punishment of the grave and the fire of Hell. I seek refuge with God from the trials of life and death, the Antichrist, and his trials."

He rose again.

"*Allahu Akbar.*"

Gyllenstierna's *Sabah* – the morning prayer – was complete, and he thanked Allah one last time before sinking into the armchair and reclining with his eyes closed. He relaxed. His body felt relaxed and comfortable, almost like after a liberating orgasm. This was genuinely restorative, perhaps akin to yoga, he thought.

The war trials had to be processed somehow, and Gyllenstierna had found his method in the Muslim rituals. There was a liberating sense of surrendering to Allah's will and mechanically performing the rituals. The length and complexity of the rituals helped keep his thoughts tightly controlled. He remembered and coordinated all the movements correctly while reciting long prayers required alertness and concentration. It was more accessible in the mosque, where one could drift into other thoughts and follow the movements of others.

War could not be viewed calmly and objectively, even though everyone tried. Even for those working in the staff and spared from the worst slaughter, it was impossible to keep the war at bay. War insidiously crept under their skin, infiltrated their minds, and poisoned their thoughts, no matter how hard they fought to remain mentally healthy. None of them were truly well anymore, Gyllenstierna thought as he dozed off in his armchair.

They were all in urgent need of both psychologists and therapists— someone who could help them deal with their dark and terrifying thoughts, which ultimately risked breaking down even the strongest minds.

When darkness and terror take control, the human body is flooded with adrenaline, often accompanied by suppressed aggression. Sooner or later, the lid blew off, and the perceived helplessness turned into mindless violence against a real or imagined enemy or completely irrational outbursts at colleagues or anyone unfortunate enough to be in the wrong place at the wrong time.

War was a sinister force that no one could protect themselves from, and it was even worse for the frontline soldiers who had to witness bodies being blown apart right beside them. Soldiers took their last breaths with glassy eyes, leaving their surviving comrades behind in hell while they found peace. War was an absolute hell on earth, Gyllenstierna thought before dozing off for a short while, compensating for the lost sleep—an absolute hell.

But he had begun to entertain a small thought about how he might escape the Swedish war. Soon, he hoped, he would be free of his endlessly heavy burden. That was how it was supposed to be, and nothing could stop him from dreaming of a brighter future. He deserved it, his final thought, before falling into a deep and dreamless sleep.

Chapter 21 – Thieves' Park

Fall 2032

The war changed everything. Massive population relocations began shortly after it broke out on July 17, 2032. The affluent areas near the Øresund, southwest of Malmö, were emptied of Swedes, and Muslim families were given access to the exclusive villas and spacious, modern apartments. The affluent residential areas Limhamn, Bellevue, Västervång, Fridhem, and Bunkeflostrand were transformed into strictly Muslim enclaves, as were Kronprinsen, the Old Town, and Värnhem.

Instead, the Swedes were moved into the dilapidated, grimy, high-rise complexes in Rosengård, Hyllie, and Fosie. Two or three Swedish families often had to share a single apartment, which reeked of mold and should have been renovated twenty or thirty years ago. Here, for the first time, the Swedes could get familiar with some other tenants who only came out at night: cockroaches and bedbugs were found everywhere in the run-down buildings. There were millions of them.

It wasn't without a sense of satisfaction that the sneering *God Warriors* wished the Swedes a "Good Luck" in their new homes as they shoved them off the buses they had just been herded onto.

"You'll probably like it here, ha-ha-ha. You thought it was good enough for us, so it should be good enough for you, too. After all, you Swede-whores aren't racists, ha-ha-ha."

"Enjoy your time in Rosengård! As for me, I'll be living with my wives and children in your nice house in Bellevue. It's just a shame you have such poor taste, but we'll decorate it the way good Muslims would."

"A beautiful sea view, free from infidels. The only Swedes we'll see in Limhamn will be cleaners and service staff. Oh, and your whore women who come to visit from time to time, ha-ha-ha."

The Swedes suddenly found themselves in ghettos they had only seen on TV. Each Swede was allowed to bring just one suitcase of clothes. It was essential not to pack the items in too-exclusive travel suitcases, as the *God Warriors* often would open them up and dump the contents on the ground. They would hand over a garbage bag to pack the items if they felt generous. The Swedes weren't allowed to bring furniture, as the apartments they were moving into were already furnished.

A woman in her fifties found her twenty-seven-year-old IKEA furniture in the apartment her family was assigned. During a previous separation, she had temporarily stored the furniture in a common area and had marked the sofa, armchair, coffee table, and bed by signing her name on the underside. It was not a happy reunion.

The former Muslim immigrant ghetto Rosengård was now entirely Swedish. The Muslims disapproved of racial mixing, and the only integration they would consider was if the Swedes converted to Islam and adopted the Muslim way of life. But even those Swedes who did convert were treated as second-class citizens, subordinate to their Muslim masters. Pale, blue-eyed bastards weren't considered a high rank, no matter how much they fawned over their new overlords. They also had thin, patchy beards, which were seen as a sign of lacking masculinity.

The reason the Muslims did not execute the Swedes who refused to convert was because they needed slave laborers to support them and servants to look after them. Sex workers, primarily women but also gay and transsexual men, were also highly desirable for that purpose.

Thousands of Skåne girls aged up to nine were put in Koranic schools and in Muslim kindergartens, where they were to be taught the Muslim way of life until they were old enough to get married. In Muslim culture, men's right to sexual satisfaction always takes precedence. Many girls were enslaved and got married as early as six years old. But no girl was to be used for conjugal pleasures before she reached the age of nine, for so the Prophet had said.

It was essential to find suitable wives, as there was such a surplus of Muslim men. The war had made it challenging to import child brides from the home countries. Swedish little girls were better than none, even if they were whinier than the girls from their home countries. They weren't used to being beaten, but they soon learned never to question anything and do as they were told."

Before the war broke out, the wealthy residents of Malmö—almost exclusively Swedes—were concentrated in wealthy residential areas like Limhamn, Bellevue, Västervång, Fridhem, and Bunkeflostrand. In these neighborhoods, the prices of villas often exceeded ten million kronor, and occasionally, especially desirable properties sold for twice that amount. Other affluent Malmö residents lived in condominiums in the Old Town and Västra Hamnen—particularly in the famous and exclusive high-rise Turning Torso that overlooked the Öresund strait.

Despite the evident economic and ethnic segregation, Malmö's politicians had always stubbornly insisted that their city was more integrated than their much-despised rival, Stockholm, but that wasn't entirely true.

In Stockholm, the poorest people live in the concrete suburbs built under the former "Million Apartment Program," which are geographically peripheric and isolated from the city's central parts. The lower your income, the farther you live from the city center. The proportion of Swedes decreases with distance from the inner city, while the proportion of poor immigrants increases.

Greater Stockholm is surrounded and intersected by fjords, straits, and inlets, making the geographical distance to the poorest suburbs significant. Segregation and its divides are starkly visible, as there's no natural, daily mingling of people on the streets.

Malmö, on the other hand, is built on flat land and has a significantly smaller population, so the poorest areas are much closer to the city center, which gave a false sense of integration. The city center is reachable with a short bike ride or a walk of just one or two miles from the especially 'vulnerable areas'—using bureaucratic Swedish—like Rosengård, Hyllie, and Fosie. But just because people of different ethnicities walk the same streets doesn't mean they're integrated. In practice, Malmö was already strictly divided into Swedish and Muslim areas before the war, and they rarely had anything to do with each other. They didn't even shop at the same stores as Muslims had their own.

Then there's Seved, officially named Södra Sofielund, which is centrally located. Seved became notorious when hooded youths took over the area in the 2010s and began harassing the Swedes, who, unsurprisingly, moved out. It only took a few years to turn the area into a strictly Muslim enclave.

If you wanted to buy drugs in Malmö, all you had to do was go to Seved, where the trade was carried out openly after the Muslims took over. The large boulders placed to make it difficult for drug buyers in cars ended up creating perfect escape routes for the criminals, who laughed and flipped off the police as they sped away on their mopeds.

Kirseberg is a district in northern Malmö spanning three square miles. The name comes from the Danish word for cherry, "kirsebær," which usually evokes pleasant associations, but in Malmö, the opposite is true.

Even though the area is just a few miles from the Old Town, Kirseberg has never been considered an integrated part of Malmö. This is partly because Kirseberg has a long-standing reputation as a notorious neighborhood that the "real" residents of Malmö—who proudly refer to themselves as Malmöites—prefer to avoid. The people living there have been somewhat disdainfully called *"Backabor"* – "Inhabitants of Backa" for centuries, a name derived from the small hills in the otherwise completely flat landscape of Malmö.

The slight elevation compared to the rest of Malmö led to the construction of a large water tower on one of the hills in 1879, which resulted in the main street of Kirseberg being named Vattenverksvägen, or Waterworks Road. In 1915, the water tower was converted into emergency housing for the poorest families in all of Malmö.

In Kirseberg, rental apartments stand alongside traditional, low-built Skåne-style houses constructed when rural residents moved closer to the city in the early 1900s. Today, Kirseberg is seen as well-preserved—or perhaps modest—since it escaped the demolition frenzies of previous decades. Not even the Swedish Civil War caused much damage to the area. Kirseberg seems to be immune to most things.

On Kirseberg—oddly enough, it's important not to say "in" Kirseberg but "on" Kirseberg—about sixteen thousand residents of Backa lived before the outbreak of the war. Surveys showed that the residents didn't particularly appreciate their surroundings, as they ranked highest in perceived insecurity in their neighborhood. This might have had something to do with the extensive drug trade and the many addicts living in the area. Drug users who found Seved too closely watched by the police would instead head to Kirseberg for their purchases. After the relocations following the outbreak of war, Kirseberg became inhabited solely by Swedes, indicating that even the Muslims didn't find the area appealing.

Kirseberg boasts several large parks, giving the area an almost rural feel. The largest of these is the long, narrow Bulltofta Park, which was created on the runway of the former airport. The smallest park, located closest to the city center near the water tower, is officially named "*Garnisonsplanteringen,*" but it's commonly called "Thieves' Park" – "*Tjyvaparken.*" Around four thousand people are buried in and around the park. It's the resting place for poor soldiers and their families from the Malmö Garrison, as well as prisoners who died in the now-closed Kirseberg Prison and Malmöhus Fortress. Persistent rumors claim that young boys occasionally dig up skulls and use them as soccer balls.

Kirseberg Prison was used as a temporary sleeping quarter during the refugee crisis in 2015. At the top of the hill in Thieves' Park, there was one of Malmö's old execution sites. Here, several women were burned at the stake after being convicted of witchcraft in the local court. During the Danish era, witches were burned alive at the stake. When the Swedes occupied the city, they switched to the Swedish standard method, which involved beheading the witches before throwing them onto the fire.

In 1997, a memorial stone was erected in Thieves' Park, which, surprisingly, has remained standing, to honor the innocent women with an inscription that the Muslims didn't adhere to:

"This stone honors all those who, for various reasons, were excluded from the community of their time and encourage future generations to reflect."

No reflection or remorse could be seen in the executioners, who now hanged and beheaded the people of Malmö at an alarming rate. In the months following the outbreak of the war, thousands of Swedes were executed. Initially, the Muslims targeted the same groups they always do when they seize power. In the first weeks, prominent Swedes who had collaborated with the Muslims and helped them rise to power were executed. This included politicians, media personnel, police officers, and leaders of public institutions—practically all with left-leaning views. The reason large crowds of ordinary people were herded to the execution sites was to ensure they understood what happens to those who don't fall in line and submit.

Thieves' Park, located almost in the center of the city, now drew even larger crowds than during the era of witch burnings when public executions were a twisted and perverse form of popular entertainment. Even if the people of Malmö managed to avoid the executions in person, they couldn't escape the message. The events were broadcast on TV from the execution sites for hours each day, ensuring that the gruesome spectacle reached everyone.

After the first wave of executions of prominent people, which included a couple of thousand Malmöites, the turn came for the remainder of the undesirable. In the *Umma* – the congregation of the faithful – which Muhammad began to build in Medina in 622, there is no place for everyone.

In the second wave, more than a thousand Malmöites were executed, such as Jews, active Christians, artists, and trans and homosexuals who too clearly deviated from the norm. Homosexuals, who are discreet about their orientation, are tolerated because many Muslim men appreciate sex with men, even if they are not born with that orientation. It is a cultural issue throughout the Muslim world and, most often, at odds with Christian doctrine. This is also the explanation for why the first wave of Muslims who came to Sweden were also so appreciated by Swedish LGBTQ people.

In standard Arabic, *Umma* means people, community, or nation, but is usually used in religious contexts as a designation for all Muslims regardless of nationality. The Umma has room for all races and skin colors, and it provides active practice of Islam. Islam is not a fundamentally racist ideology, but since there are hardly any Muslims in groups such as whites and Chinese, it is not possible in practice to distinguish what is outright racism and what is just a logical consequence of the view of infidels. There is a racially conditioned hatred and contempt, especially against whites, within the Muslim world, which the Malmöites became fully aware of.

A few months after the Muslim takeover, a calm began to settle in Malmö, or *Jazirat Alkham*, as the city was renamed. *Jazirat Alkham* was translated from Swedish to Arabic – The Island of Ore. The Malmöites had learned that the town was now called ‫ماخلا قريزج‬., which should be read from right to left. The word Malmö was not allowed to appear on signs or in any writing at all. Swedes who pronounced the city's old name were punished with fifty lashes. The same was true for Swedes who pronounced the word Skåne, which was now called شبه الجزيرة الخطرة, and was written as *Shbh aljazirat alkhatira* in Latin letters.

All conceivable opposition was crushed after the terrible terror of the first months, and the Malmöites gradually began to find their roles as slave laborers and servants in the Muslim caliphate. The number of executions had decreased to just a few per day, mainly to keep the fear of the Malmöites alive.

It was the usual beheadings, hangings, and dejected trances that, in demonstrative shows, were pushed from tall buildings, blindfolded, and handcuffed. There were hardly any Malmöites who watched any longer, and even fewer could get involved emotionally. Executions and floggings were the new normal and were all about not being one of them.

Zlatko Muslimovic's bombing of the Umm al-Muminin Khadijah Mosque changed everything. Ahmed Ben Barka decided that the prominent Muslims who had been killed would be avenged in a ratio of 25:1. Since 1,846 Muslims were killed at the Umm al-Muminin Khadijah mosque, it meant that 46,150 Swedish Malmöites would now have to pay with their lives. The official message was that every fourth ethnic Swede would be killed.

The Muslims left it to the Swedish families to choose who would be sacrificed. The rationale behind this procedure was that it was expected that the elders would be sacrificed – voluntarily – to ease the burden of old people who were no longer useful. Ahmed Ben Barka's fiendish calculation was correct, but only around seventeen thousand old men could be executed before the city was back in the hands of the Swedes.

Most of the executioners in Thieves' Park were Swedes, who were assigned the task of testing whether their alleged and newly awakened Muslim beliefs were severe. Those who failed in the faith were to be put on the scaffold themselves after first receiving one hundred lashes. No one failed in the faith.

Some Swedes voluntarily applied for the job to gain a good standing among Muslims. Merit as an executioner made one well-suited for future tasks, and merit was considered life insurance.

In and around Thieves' Park, about twenty iron posts had been driven into the ground, with signs with appropriate Quranic quotations written in both Arabic and Swedish:

3:3 "Those who deny the signs of God, surely a severe punishment awaits them: yes, God is mighty and ready for vengeance."

5:37 "Their reward shall be only that they be killed or crucified, or that their hands and feet be cut off crosswise."

7:132 "And, so We took revenge on them and drowned them in the sea because they took Our signs as lies and were indifferent to them."

8:7 "God wants to confirm the truth with his words and exterminate the unbelievers to the last man."

There was no doubt that what happened in Thieves' Park was proper. Those who arrested and executed the infidels had all the moral and – in their opinion – even legal support they could imagine. The Quran is the basis of Sharia law, and no single comma in the holy scripture can ever be questioned. The massacre and mass extermination of Swedes was the unmistakable will of Allah. The executioners were God's representatives on earth, as were the imams who directed the show. And who could ever question the commands of the one God?

But it happened often that the Swedish executioners, in silence, failed in their new faith and pondered over that text on the memorial stone.

"This stone honors all those people who, for various reasons, were excluded from the community of their time and invites the future to reflect."

Chapter 22 - The Viking King

June 1, 2033

Coordinating operations with the free armies in Skåne would have been beneficial. After all, they shared the same goal: liberating Skåne from the Muslim occupation. Establishing cooperation shouldn't have been impossible.

Despite Möller's warnings, Brännström wanted to try negotiating with the phlegmatic leader of the Swedish para-military group, the "Free Rangers," Jeppe Hofman-Bang. Brännström was adamant, and in the end, Möller reluctantly agreed and reached out to Hofman-Bang to arrange a meeting, though he would not participate himself.

Brännström's first idea was to send the diplomatic Alfred Baksi as a representative of the Swedish military. Baksi was known for convincing and winning over even the most resistant people. But when Möller heard about the idea, he strongly opposed it.

"Look, Jeppe is a bit peculiar. To be blunt, he doesn't like foreigners, and unfortunately, Ali doesn't have the right look. If Jeppe suspects that Ali is a Muslim, things could get ugly—Jeppe might even get violent. If there is any chance, it must be a "true" Swede, but not someone from Stockholm. He hates them perhaps even more than foreigners."

Brännström decided to attend the meeting himself. He was a "true" Swede and, as a Norrbotten and northern Sweden native, walked free from the stigmatizing Stockholm label—or so he believed. As the Swedish supreme commander, he should, in theory, command respect, even from someone as generally disrespectful as Jeppe Hofman-Bang. After all, they were on the same side.

A promising sign was that Brännström didn't need to wear a blindfold, usually required when outsiders were brought to the Free Rangers headquarters. This indicated some level of trust—a good start. The problem was that Hofman-Bang viewed all Swedes from the northern provinces as foreigners. The counties Skåne, Blekinge, Halland, and Bohuslän, in southern Sweden, had been under occupation since 1658, and the occupying power was Sweden. In Hofman-Bang's eyes, that fake nation wasn't even real. Not even the name "Sweden" was real. The

Swedes had been brainwashed into believing that the name of their false country was derived from "*Svea* Rike" – Svea Kingdom – but that was just historical falsification, like everything else regarding the low-level Swedes.

There had never been a people called the "*Svear*." It was all fake—all those battles against the local "*Göta*" kings, who had never existed. The name "*Roslagen*" *is* supposedly related to rowing boats and ship laws—tales of sacrificial feasts in Uppsala and fantasies about the Viking island of Birka.

There had never been any Swedish Vikings. The Swedish-Finnish Viking Rurik, who had been chosen as the ruler of the Rus kingdom in Kyiv, was a Danish Viking named Rørik, also the king of *Frisia*. Even less so, no fake Swedish Vikings had sailed down Russian rivers. The real Danish Vikings from Gotland, Bornholm, and Skåne had navigated the rivers down to both the Black and Caspian Seas and traded with Persia. The runic inscription on the wall of the Blue Mosque in Istanbul had been made by Danish Vikings who, via the Mediterranean, reached what they called Miklagård, which is today Istanbul.

The fabricated name "Sweden" could be traced back to Danish, the original and authentic Nordic language. The people named *Götar on both sides of the lake Vättern*, on the other hand, had existed. They had once been under the Danish king, and Jeppe still considered them genuine Danes, whose language had unfortunately been corrupted under Swedish occupation—but languages can be restored.

Denmark was the original and only legitimate nation in the North, and the people who now called themselves Swedes had been Danish subjects, and they would one day be so again. Hofman-Bang knew that the once mighty Danish realm would one day be restored when all of Scandinavia would reunite under a true Viking king—someone like himself. The North also included all the islands in the North Atlantic: Iceland, Greenland, the Faroe Islands, the Shetland Islands, and the Hebrides. And, of course, Norway, the Danish province they had lost through that cowardly attack from the fake so-called Swedish nation to the north.

Even the majority of England, under Danish rule, when it was known as the *Danelaw a thousand years ago*, would become Danish again. However, being a realist, Hofman-Bang considered that the United Kingdom might need a bigger bite in the first phase of re-establishing the Greater Danish Viking Kingdom. *Frisia*, for the moment, a part of the Netherlands, on the other hand, was just a morsel.

Unfortunately, the reincorporation of Newfoundland was likely far off in the future. It would take quite some time before the Danes became powerful enough to challenge the Canadians and Americans, but Jeppe knew that day would come. But it was essential to remain realistic about the time all these wars would take.

Hofman-Bang's headquarters was a small cabin near the site of Höjehall, up on the ridge of Söderåsen in northwestern Skåne. Brännström was astonished by the steep climb, not at all what he had imagined Skåne to be like. But then again, the cabin was located near Skåne's highest point, seven hundred feet above sea level. The narrow road through the beech forest, barely letting in daylight, finally led to the Free Rangers headquarters. The cabin was well hidden in the dense beech forest and almost impossible to spot from the air. A well-chosen headquarters, thought Brännström, as his eyes scanned the little there was to see.

At the entrance hung a small square cross flag that Brännström had never seen before, in colors of yellow, red, white, and blue. He had expected the Skåne flag, which he knew was red with a yellow cross—a combination of the Danish and Swedish flags. However, the flag at the entrance incorporated elements of all the colors found in the Nordic flags. Hofman-Bang seemed to be a Nordic patriot, which Brännström found hopeful. They should be able to find common ground to work from.

A young man with a three-day beard and an automatic rifle AK5 casually slung over his shoulder opened the door to the back seat where Brännström was sitting. The driver was instructed to wait in the car.

"Welcome," he said in a deliberately thick Skåne dialect. "The boss is waiting for you in the office."

There was no doubt that this was Skåne country. In the doorway, Brännström was greeted by a blonde woman who introduced herself as Gun, the boss's wife. The hallway walls were adorned with several small paintings, flags, photographs, and other items, most of which had Norse motifs. The largest painting was a map of the Nordic region, its margins decorated with the Odal rune and Tyr rune, which Brännström recognized. He could also identify the Celtic cross and the mythical black sun, thanks to his interest in ancient history, but beyond that, he was stumped. Except, of course, for the square four-inch-sized swastika wrought in iron. It was the first time Brännström had seen a swastika displayed in an entrance, and he found it both repulsive and puzzling. Was Hofman-Bang a Nazi? No one had mentioned anything about that. Or maybe he was a patriotic nerd who liked potent symbols and provoking people. He would soon find out.

Gun opened the door to the office, and there sat the Nordic Viking King, Jeppe Hofman-Bang, in a high-backed armchair that resembled a throne. He didn't rise from his seat. Brännström's eyes were drawn to the clenched fist carved in marble, pointed firmly toward the ceiling, resting on a small side table next to the throne. Somehow, he associated the symbol with right-wing extremist and nationalist movements, though he wasn't entirely sure.

"Welcome," Hofman-Bang said curtly. "I hear you have something to tell me."

Hofman-Bang wasn't one to waste time on pleasantries. No coffee was offered either, but maybe that was just a Swedish tradition, Brännström thought. He was in Skåne country now and would have to adapt to the local customs. He took a seat in one of the chairs arranged opposite the throne. Gun also sat down. Brännström noticed a silver Thor's hammer hanging from her tight necklace.

"Thank you. I wanted to meet with you to discuss how to coordinate our military efforts for maximum effect. It would be of benefit for all of us."

"There's something important you don't understand, my friend," Hofman-Bang replied in a superior and condescending tone. "The Swedes are our sworn enemies; we can't fight alongside them. No way."

"OK. But I didn't say we necessarily have to fight together. I'm talking about coordinating our operations. It would be unfortunate if our forces ended up clashing with each other, and I've received reports of a couple of incidents where it came close," Brännström said.

"Well, unfortunate or fortunate, who knows? It depends on who wins," Hofman-Bang replied.

"As the supreme commander of the Swedish Armed Forces, I have significant resources at my disposal that could be useful to you."

"Thanks for the offer, but no thanks. We can manage on our own, as we always have. Without the Swedes. And that make-believe country you claim to represent doesn't even exist."

Brännström raised his eyebrows and stared in astonishment for a few seconds. What was this man talking about?

"I'm not entirely sure what you mean, but Sweden exists, even though our country is under threat right now."

"What you call Sweden is just a fabrication. Your entire so-called history in this make-believe land of Sweden is a forgery, starting with your so-called King, Gustav Vasa—the one who rebelled against the rightful King, Christian the Good, who held power over Stockholm. Your historical falsification began early in Peder Swart's Gustav Vasa chronicle. Just because Christian the Good is called Christian, the Tyrant is proof enough."

Brännström realized that the meeting was ending before it had even begun, but he decided to attempt diplomacy, having tried to come all this way.

"Yes, it might be true that our historians have romanticized the past a bit, but Sweden certainly has a history. While studying at the military academy in Karlberg, I used to bike around Vallentuna and the Sigtuna area. Hundreds of runestones are almost lined up there, attesting to the Vikings' presence in the region. We share history with the other Nordic countries and should base our cooperation on that shared heritage."

"Have you not realized that those are forgeries? Your so-called nationalists manufactured those stones in the eighteen hundreds. The Götar and the Gotlanders stole the few that were genuine. Some were even stolen from Denmark."

Brännström decided to make one last attempt.

"Be that as it may, I'd like us to establish a connection to coordinate our operations to achieve maximum effectiveness. Are you not interested in that?"

"No, not in the slightest. We don't take orders from make-believe people. And by the way, what do you mean by saying you share history with the other Nordic countries? There's only one Nordic kingdom,

Denmark, and Copenhagen is its capital. Stockholm, by the way—it's just an overgrown village."

Brännström felt it was hopeless. He sat silently, staring blankly ahead as Hofman-Bang prepared to continue his rant.

"And those backwoods you come from, what do you call it, Norrland? What do we have to do with that? Those wildernesses don't interest us more than they were interesting for our great Viking Kings Sven Tveskägg or Harald Bluetooth. I bet people there still walk around with clubs slung over their shoulders."

Brännström stood without a word and headed out to the waiting car, escorted by the Viking wife, Gun. Sure, Möller had warned him, but he couldn't have imagined that people like Hofman-Bang existed. He began to understand why cooperation with the Skåne forces had often been strained during his time as army chief and why so few Skåne officers chose to further their education at Karlberg War Academy in Stockholm. But luckily, there were many kinds of Skåne residents, not least people like Jöns Möller.

"I'm sorry, Jeppe has days like this sometimes," Gun said as a parting remark. "I could talk to him tomorrow."

"I think we'll leave things as they are," Brännström replied, smiling politely.

Just over an hour later, he was back at general staff headquarters, where Möller was anxiously waiting to hear the outcome of the meeting.

"Jeppe Hofman-Bang is not playing with a full deck," Brännström said, shaking his head in frustration as he poured two generous whiskeys.

"Well, it's a bit of both, I'd say," Möller replied, accepting the offered glass. "You've got a dose of Danish-Skåne nationalism, I understand. But remember, I did warn you. Jeppe is incredibly talented and historically knowledgeable, but when it comes to Skåne nationalism, he's stuck in a juvenile mindset."

"That's the least you can say. He reminds me of a rebellious sixteen-year-old locked in a stubborn phase, responding to everything cynically and aggressively."

"Unfortunately, that's about right. It's best to let Jeppe do his own thing. As long as he's working with Skåne residents and Danes, it goes smoothly—provided they accept that Jeppe is the Viking king. But it's hard to comprehend how someone so intelligent and well-read can be so damn narrow-minded."

"To our coming victory," Brännström said, raising his glass.

"To Sweden and Skåne," Möller replied. "That beautiful and cherished land we Skåne residents love dearly and are ready to die for."

Chapter 23 – What Happens in La Zagaleta

July 29, 2033

Daniel Gyllenstierna and Alfred Baksi had served at the highest levels of the Swedish Armed Forces for many years, but they had never flown first class. The travel regulations for Swedish civil servants didn't allow it, and "Mother Svea" certainly didn't pay them high enough salaries to afford expensive first-class tickets for family vacations. So, they were usually crammed into what cabin crew disdainfully referred to as "M-Class" – Monkey Class – the tightly packed low-cost seats in economy.

But it was first class this time, simply because they were special guests of Russia's President, Vladimir Putin. Another state was footing the bill with more generous travel regulations: the Russian state. The flight was comfortable in the spacious, plush seats, with fine food served on light beige porcelain with gold trim and perhaps a few too many glasses of champagne from beautiful crystal glasses. They almost wished the flight could have been more extended when, after just over four hours, they landed at Málaga-Costa del Sol Airport under the blue skies of the Spanish Sun Coast. Along with the other first-class passengers, the two Swedes were quickly escorted to the exit and off the plane before the chaos in M-Class began. The small group was ushered through the VIP entrance, bypassing customs and other checks.

"If only flying could be this pleasant every time," Baksi said to his boss.

"Yeah, that would be something. Now, let's enjoy the warmth—I can't remember the last time I had a vacation day."

Suddenly, they spotted a uniformed man with a matching cap on his head, holding a white cardboard sign with the names Gyllenstierna and Baksi printed in thick black letters. They noticed theirs was the only sign with neatly printed names; the others were hastily scribbled with a marker.

"This looks promising," Baksi said. "Looks like Putin's arranged with a limo. We're getting seriously spoiled today, so let's enjoy it while we can."

"It'll take almost an hour. The place is up in the mountains. You take the exit off the highway a bit past Marbella."

"I checked the map. The palace is in a little village called La Zagaleta. It's where the ultra-rich have their estates. You know, oil sheiks, Jewish bankers, African presidents, Chinese party officials, and IT billionaires. Quite the mix."

"And Russian oligarchs, of course."

"Yes, of course. Our generous host has managed to be president and oligarch simultaneously for decades, possibly making him the richest person in the world."

"Yeah, heh-heh, Putin's certainly doing alright. What are fleeting internet billions compared to real and lasting assets like oil fields, gas reserves, gold mines, and world-leading weapons manufacturers?"

The uniformed man took their bags, which had somehow arrived before them, one in each hand.

"Welcome to Costa del Sol. Please, follow me."

It turned out that the limousine was a helicopter of the Russian Kamov brand.

"Not bad, not bad," Gyllenstierna chuckled as the helicopter door opened before them. "We're taking the chopper straight to La Zagaleta, ha-ha."

"This is shaping up nicely. I don't think I've ever been this VIP, not even when we've gone all out at the arms fairs."

Had they known that the Kamov helicopter was just one of fifteen in Putin's private air fleet, which also included forty-three aircraft, including two Dassault Falcon jets, an Airbus, and an Ilyushin Il-96, they might have thought they could have flown in a private plane from Sweden.

But the two Swedes were far from the most important guests invited to Putin's private "bunga-bunga party." A dozen powerful men were aboard the sleek white Dassault Falcon long-range 900LX Trijet that had departed from Moscow an hour before their flight from Kastrup and was now coming in for landing. They watched the sleek aircraft from inside the helicopter where they sat, strapped in with seat belts and headsets on, as the long rotor blade above their heads began to spin, and the faint whine of the engine shifted to a higher pitch. Just as they lifted off, they could see that the not-so-large flag on the plane's tail fin was Russia's horizontal tricolor in white, blue, and red.

The Kamov helicopter covered the twenty-five miles over the rugged, arid mountain landscape in less than fifteen minutes. Below, they could see steep peaks and deep valleys, almost entirely uninhabited except for the occasional houses. A forest of antennas and radar dishes stood on a few peaks, primarily military. Other mountain tops were home to monastic orders, whose only connection to the outside world for centuries had been the narrow, winding roads that snaked around the peaks. Before the advent of modern technology, these winding roads were traveled only by donkeys carrying supplies and solemn, ascetic individuals seeking answers to life's mysteries in the presence of the god they believed they could draw closer to by meditating in solitude on the mountaintops.

"We're flying over former Muslim territory," Gyllenstierna observed.

"Yeah, that's right," Baksi replied. "I think the Spaniards call the Muslim occupiers the Moors."

"Occupiers or not, the Moors brought a golden age to Spain. They contributed knowledge, technology, science, and new crops. Did you know that Andalusia comes from the Arabic name *Al-Andalus*?"

"I had no idea, but history is fascinating."

"Especially Muslim history. There was a time when our ancestors practically ruled the world. We have every reason to be proud of our cultural heritage."

"Of course. To the extent that it's our heritage. I'm Swedish, you know. I'd rather eat meatballs than falafel."

"Then, you don't have much of a cultural heritage to be proud of. By the way, meatballs aren't even Swedish—they come from our own country, Turkey. Look down. We're flying over *Alhaurín*! Do you know what that means?"

"No, but I'm guessing it's Arabic too."

"It means 'Allah's garden.' The Muslims built a mighty fortress right on top of the mountain. But the Spaniards later destroyed it."

"You're well-read!"

"I did some reading before we came. I've become almost obsessed with Muslim history. There's just so much, so much amazing stuff to absorb. The more I read, the more fascinated I become. You know, they were far superior to the Europeans. In every way."

"Hmm, that's interesting, but history isn't my thing. Look, it seems like we're coming in for a landing."

There wouldn't be much time for contemplation at Putin's bunga bunga party in his La Zagaleta palace. Very different, fast-paced, and far less spiritually oriented activities awaited the two Swedes. Like a giant dragonfly, the helicopter descended majestically onto one of the three helipads. The palace's location, perched atop a hill with an utterly flat summit, was impressive. The high position ensured that no one had to worry about prying eyes. Even if someone got curious, the vast estate was surrounded by twenty-foot walls. The few who had tried flying their drones over the property saw them shot down within seconds and, minutes later, found themselves being roughly shoved into a van and driven to a bare interrogation room, where a stern and relentless interrogator would spend five to six hours extracting every bit of information. These days, no one dared to fly drones in the area, as the rumors had spread far and wide.

The palace was guarded by eight Spetsnaz soldiers dressed in black, discreetly keeping out of sight of the guests with their heavy weaponry. They faced pay deductions if they showed themselves to the guests. The palace was also equipped with an anti-missile defense system for added security. You never know who might seize the opportunity to take out so many powerful men at once, and these men had plenty of enemies at every level—both personal and political, not least in Ukraine.

Instinctively ducking, though unnecessarily since the rotor blades were spinning five feet above their heads, Gyllenstierna and Baksi left the helipad and were greeted by yet another uniformed attendant. As they looked around, they were surprised to see that the entire plateau, which made up the estate, was covered in an intensely green, lush, and dense lawn, like a gigantic golf green, despite the surrounding dry and barren landscape. It was clear that the water bill was no small matter in this arid semi-desert where water is a precious resource. But that was hardly a concern for the wealthiest person in the world.

"At 7 p.m., President Putin will greet you on the grand terrace at the main entrance. After that, a buffet dinner will be served, and as you've already been informed, the dress code is casual, but long pants are required. If you have ties with you, please leave them in your rooms. Until then, feel free to enjoy the activities. Stroll around the pool area and have a drink at one of the bars, or maybe get a quick workout in one of the gyms. Or why not take the chance to rest for a few hours? The party will go on late into the night. The refrigerators are stocked with food, but if you miss out on anything, press the service button, and the staff will be with you in less than a minute. I hope you have a wonderful stay here at *Zhemchuzhina Ispanii*—The Pearl of Spain."

Despite its grand name, the palace was never called anything other than the "Putin House" by those who knew about it, which was everyone, even though the official owner was supposed to be a secret.

They were shown to their spacious rooms—or rather, suites—that measured well over a thousand square feet. The suites were intentionally positioned at opposite ends of the main building to ensure privacy. The view from the private terraces was breathtaking, even magical, with sparse palm groves on the slopes leading down to the sea, occasionally interrupted by picturesque villages and a couple of famous golf courses. Far in the distance, you could make out the Mediterranean, but at this time, the sky blended with the sea in the dense sun haze created by the sun's intense rays, causing water vapor to rise from the ocean. The shoreline became more distinct when night fell, as the string of lights along the coastal road became visible. In the evening, you could pick out the small towns along the coast, like San Pedro de Alcántara and Puerto Banús, which lay right in the center of the view. You could even faintly make out the lights from the city of Estepona, far to the west.

While Gyllenstierna took a much-needed nap before dinner, Baksi took the opportunity to explore the vast estate. Although the main building was only two stories, plus a basement, it was still monstrously large for a private residence. He estimated the living space to be around eighty thousand square feet.

Everywhere, the floors were made of exclusive marble with beautiful inlays depicting exotic animals—big cats, giraffes, zebras, elephants, chameleons, and butterflies in every imaginable color. The spaces were open, but seating areas of various sizes were scattered throughout. Along the walls, small niches were designed for intimate conversations, and here and there, alcoves accommodated small groups of people.

The ceilings were intricate works of art, with paintings, stucco, and wood carvings. On the walls hung paintings by famous Russian artists, a few of which Baksi recognized despite his limited knowledge of art history. Some walls were adorned with golden icons featuring the somewhat monotonous and ever-present motif of the Virgin Mary with the infant Jesus.

On several tables, Baksi noticed Fabergé eggs. Some opened, but most closed to showcase the gold and precious jewels to their fullest extent. Each was uniquely designed, enameled in different colors, and adorned with carefully selected gemstones.

Baksi thought he recognized one of the eggs from a photo he'd seen just before the war broke out when it had been sold at Christie's in London for fifteen million pounds—and now it was here. He briefly wondered what would happen if he pocketed one of the eggs, though it wouldn't be easy given their size, including the base and crown. But the thought vanished as quickly as it came.

The palace was a true Renaissance marvel, worthy of the Sun King, but in a modern style. With its costly antiques, the ostentatious luxury was on par with anything a Romanov had ever owned. However, the tsar's Winter Palace in St. Petersburg was at least thirty times larger.

The pool area was mostly deserted; it was far too hot in the sun. Occasionally, a servant hurried by on the way to some eager guest. A couple of slightly overweight men in their late middle age, wearing dark sunglasses, thick gold chains on their hairy wrists, polo shirts, white shorts, and plastic flip-flops, sat in the shade at a small round café table, smoking cigarettes and engaged in what was an important—and secret— conversation. They leaned close to each other and spoke in low voices, almost whispering, but Baksi could still make out that the language was Russian, Ukrainian, or possibly Polish.

He sensed a bit of irritation behind one man's stony expression and his small, discreet gestures that seemed eager and passionate. One of the men suddenly glared at Baksi and fell silent, prompting Baksi to move out of earshot. Maybe big deals were being made, he thought. Maybe deals that weren't meant for daylight. Instinctively, he felt it was safest not to know anything about their business.

The area included three smaller buildings housing the security staff and service personnel. There were no small villas, but they didn't look imposing compared to the main building.

Gyllenstierna and Baksi arrived on the terrace at the main entrance well ahead, ensuring they wouldn't miss President Putin's welcome speech. It was the first time they would meet such an influential person in real life, and they didn't want to miss the opportunity. Besides, it would be highly impolite, given that they were personal guests of the president.

They looked around at the other guests, estimating about sixty of them. All were men in middle or late middle age, not a single woman among them. Most men appeared to be in good shape—people who cared for themselves and their health, with only a few overweight exceptions. Only they looked somewhat worn and haggard. War affects even those in command posts, though in a different way than those on the battlefield. From their position on the terrace, they could see that the dinner buffet had been set up around the pool area, but white cloths still covered the food.

A minute after the scheduled time, a spry, small, balding man stepped up to the podium with light steps and looked out over the audience. It was Russia's famous and feared president, now celebrating his eighty-first birthday with a proper party. He seemed to be in a genuinely good mood.

The president began happily with a few brief sentences in Russian, which immediately led to cheers, applause, and a standing ovation. Gyllenstierna, who had trained at the Army Language School in Uppsala many years earlier, understood most of what was said and whispered a quick translation to Baksi. "He's turning eighty-one today; that's why they're cheering. I had no idea! Good thing we brought the gifts."

Then Putin switched to English to welcome the non-Russian-speaking guests.

"We extend an exceptional welcome to our non-Russian-speaking guests with a warm round of applause."

They looked around and saw that almost everyone was clapping. Only a handful of guests were not part of the Russian-speaking crowd.

"We're about to enjoy the evening and the delicious food prepared by the pool area. But before the festivities begin, I want to remind you of just two—only two—rules for tonight," said the president, holding up his index and middle fingers in a V-sign. He grasped his raised index finger with his left hand.

"One: What happens in La Zagaleta stays in La Zagaleta." He folded down his index finger and moved his grasp to his middle finger. "Two: It is forbidden to tip our escorts..." He paused and chuckled slightly at his Freudian slip, "...ehh, I mean our service staff, of course. All employees are very well paid by the Russian state... ehh, by me, I mean, of course." Another slip. Maybe age was beginning to play tricks on him after all.

"It's open seating tonight, so feel free to mingle and get to know those you find... pleasant to converse with. After dinner, there will be dance music by the pool, and I assure you, dance partners won't be in short supply. There will also be some entertainment and shows in between. Before we head down to the dinner buffet, as the good gentlemen we all are, let's allow the ladies we've invited tonight to start serving themselves. Before we indulge," he concluded with a sly smile.

Suddenly, the pool area was filled with beautiful women appearing out of nowhere. At least twice as many as the men were present. The women strutted confidently on their high heels, dressed in exclusive outfits—short dresses and skirts, tops, and blouses that revealed more than they concealed, with styled hair and carefully applied makeup. There seemed to be someone for every taste—different ethnicities, figures, and ages. Most women appeared to be in their thirties, but some didn't look older than teenagers. They were somewhat balanced out by a few more mature women for those men who might prefer a "granny." The women boldly helped themselves to caviar and Russian champagne while the men looked on, clearly appreciating the view of the evening's festivities.

"Oh, I think I'm gonna go bananas!" Gyllenstierna exclaimed enthusiastically. "Haven't been spoiled like this since the war started." "Looks like Putin's got dessert covered for us,"

Yeah, you bet. I think I'll go for a double! With sugar on top."

"I hate to rain on your parade," Baksi said, knowing his boss's weakness for women of all kinds, "but you have to assume everything you do is being filmed. We're dealing with Russians. How many Swedes have been caught in their honey traps? Don't do anything you'll regret—consider it good advice from someone who's headed three intelligence services. Look, but don't touch is the rule tonight. A shame, though, I must admit."

"Filmed or not, what difference does it make? As you know, I've been happily divorced for years, and as a single man, I can do whatever I want, right?"

"Think carefully, Daniel—are you prepared to let the world see what you do in the bedroom?"

"Honestly, I don't think it bothers me one bit. Why should I be ashamed of having sex with a beautiful woman? It's more unnatural not to when the opportunity arises. And what about you?"

"I'm married, and I love my wife. I respect my marriage and don't want to end up in any films."

"Well, you can live in celibacy all you want," Gyllenstierna grinned, "while I live it up. Maybe you'll get a gold star from God somewhere as a reward? A true Gyllenstierna—or Goldstar, as they used to call me at EU defense meetings, ha-ha!"

The extravagant buffet left nothing to be desired. The theme was seafood, but there was no risk that the meat lovers would go to bed hungry either. The guests initially flocked around the large, well-stocked bowls of caviar labeled Beluga, Sevruga, and Royal Oscietra.

The Swedes observed as many of the men shoveled large amounts of caviar into their mouths with spoons, without any accompaniments, while the women cautiously sampled, ever mindful of the calories.

"So, which one is the best?" Baksi wondered. "I've never had Russian caviar. My civil servant salary has never quite stretched to such luxuries."

"No idea. I've only had caviar once, and that was at restaurant Operakällaren in Stockholm when I celebrated my ex-wife's fortieth birthday. I think it was Beluga. It's so damn expensive it's ridiculous. Isn't Sturgeon on the endangered list, by the way?"

"Has been for a long time, but this crowd doesn't seem to care about such details."

Time flies when you're having fun, and fun was exactly what they were having. The two Swedes found it a bit unusual, not to mention flattering, to be constantly approached—if not outright hit on—by beautiful women, who only seemed to grow more attractive as the drinks kept flowing. The women were charming, engaging in light-hearted conversation about this and that, helping the men relax and enjoy the evening. After countless nights worrying about the trials of war, it felt like they had entered paradise.

Shortly after midnight, President Putin suddenly appeared by their side, accompanied by Foreign Minister Sergei Larionov, whom the two Swedes recognized from their meeting at the Russian Embassy in Stockholm. Larionov placed his large hand lightly on the president's shoulder, guiding him gently toward the two Swedes.

"I hope you're making the most of your time here," the president said, smiling warmly as he extended his hand in greeting. "This isn't like Sweden. Here, everything is allowed, so make the most of it."

"We will, thank you. And happy birthday, Mr. President."

Suddenly, he was gone. That was all they saw of the president and the foreign minister, whose activities for the rest of the evening remained unknown to everyone else. Perhaps the president was too old to enjoy himself with a woman—or several indeed—but then again, there were small bowls of individually wrapped blue Viagra pills scattered around. Just in case anyone, despite all the visual stimulation, needed a little boost in their male performance with a King Blue or two.

Gyllenstierna had eventually ended up in a small alcove upstairs, where he was getting cozy with a stunning Brazilian mulatto in her thirties with large, beautiful, natural breasts. Baksi happened to see them as they walked hand-in-hand toward Gyllenstierna's suite, but he thought it best to pretend he hadn't noticed.

Despite his good intentions, he began feeling an overwhelming desire for company in his room. He could even feel a slight tightening in his pants, and his whole body, almost desperately, cried out for a woman's touch. Baksi's lower instincts were starting to take control despite the upper part of his mind struggling in vain to resist. What he didn't know was that his drinks had been laced with both cocaine and amphetamines, effectively breaking down his mental barriers. He half-heartedly negotiated with himself, though deep down, he knew his lower instincts were the more vital negotiating partner and had practically already won.

Gyllenstierna was probably right after all: What was there to be ashamed of in having regular sex? Who could hold that over him in these times? He resolutely went to the pool area and conversed with a slim blonde from Ukraine who seemed up for just about anything. Her pink leather skirt was so tiny it almost looked like a wide belt.

The color matched her Hermès bracelet and lipstick. He started wondering if she was wearing any underwear under that little leather skirt and discreetly placed his hand on her slender knee under the table, letting it slowly move upward. A thong. Smooth. Soft, flawless skin. The Ukrainian made no move to push his hand away; instead, she brazenly suggested they invite a friend from Vietnam, who suddenly appeared beside them, and so it was decided. The Vietnamese woman was petite, probably under five feet without stiletto heels, and hardly over ninety pounds. She flashed a dazzling smile and looked at Baksi appreciatively. Baksi smiled back and hoped she was at least close to eighteen years old.

Gyllenstierna lay on his back in bed, simply enjoying the moment as his stunning lover slowly and sensually traced her fingertips, lips, and tongue over his entire body. She lightly scratched his skin with her long, perfectly painted nails, sending pleasurable shivers through his body. This was better than he could ever remember experiencing. What a delight! Despite her relatively young age, she seemed to know exactly how to push all the right buttons. A natural-born sex goddess—he even considered, in his aroused and slightly intoxicated state, that he might suggest they get married. This was paradise, and maybe one could live in paradise every day.

Suddenly, she pulled out a black blindfold from the bedside drawer. She gently lifted Gyllenstierna's head and slipped it over his eyes.

"Promise not to peek, hi-hi-hi."

Gyllenstierna complied willingly. It felt good to let things happen, even though it was a bit unusual for him, given his usual role as an active, high-energy stallion. Age and experience allowed him to relax and savor the pleasure for longer. He couldn't see his beautiful lover now striking different poses in the air with a riding crop in her hand. She lifted his arm slightly.

"Turn around now, baby."

Gyllenstierna rolled onto his stomach and soon felt something lightly tickling his buttocks, unaware that it was the whip. Then he felt a slight pressure against his anus with something that was a dildo, a strap-on that his lover had put on. He gently pushed the dildo away with his hand, indicating that this wasn't his thing.

"Sorry, many men like this very much, you know."

She turned him back onto his back. He still had the blindfold on, but he could feel her straddle him and kneel over his face. He was just about to indulge when he noticed she smelled clean and fresh. She gently placed her index and middle fingertips over his lips, and he opened his mouth, sucking lightly on her fingers. The nail polish tasted a bit chemical.

"Good boy. Keep your mouth open now, baby, and you'll get a nice surprise."

He followed her instructions, but suddenly, completely unexpectedly, he felt a warm spray over his face and into his mouth, prompting him to rip off the blindfold, shove his partner aside, and leap to his feet in one swift sequence of movements.

"What the fucking hell are you doing" he shouted loudly and just managed to stop himself in the movement when he was about to hit her with a punch. "Fucking bitch!"

She quickly gathered her clothes.

"I'm sorry, it's nothing personal. You are nice, but I get maximum payment for this."

Gyllenstierna stared blankly at her, still in shock, unable to get a word out.

"I need this money to save for my daughter's education. I wish her a better life than I have. A decent life without caviar and champagne. Please forgive me."

Before leaving the room, she turned to the Gyllenstierna again with a strained and slightly guilty smile.

" Take a shower now. In twenty minutes, two lovely ladies will visit you for absolute pleasure. You can choose one or both. They will do anything you want. And no tricks, I promise."

Gyllenstierna quickly headed to the bathroom and let the lukewarm water wash over him, cleansing him. He brushed his teeth three times longer than usual. What happened was a shock, which made him go completely soft immediately. In a moment of clarity, he realized that he had, quite unwillingly, made his film debut—how would the Russians use the footage?

The warm water began to revive his spirits. He, too, had consumed a few spiked drinks, and he could feel his pulse pounding in the lower regions. What the hell, what's done is done; it can't get any worse now, he thought resignedly. He put on the thick, white bathrobe and settled into an armchair with a stiff Talisker malt whisky from the minibar, waiting for the knock on the door that came precisely on time.

True to his habit, he diluted the whisky with a quarter of water to enhance the flavor. He sipped the whisky slowly and noticed that someone had come into the room and replaced the entire king-size bed with a different model while he was in the shower.

He detected a faint scent of perfume, which the considerate staff had sprayed into the room. Someone—his host, no doubt—wanted to patch things up and lift his spirits. It was time to start again; he didn't want to miss this chance. It had been so long since the last time. To set the mood, he led his visitors into the other bedroom.

Gyllenstierna and Baksi stayed another day, resting in the Pearl of Spain, Zhemchuzhina Ispanii. The service and food remained extraordinary, so they tried to enjoy themselves as best they could, considering what had happened. Neither Putin nor Larionov made any further appearances, and most guests had already left.

Neither of them felt like discussing the previous night's events. When evening came, Gyllenstierna, unashamedly, ordered a Lingam massage through room service, while Baksi, after some indecision, chose to go to bed alone in honor of his marriage.

Baksi had trouble falling asleep, so he got up again just before midnight and wandered around the nearly empty estate. It was a pleasant, warm evening, and he sat down on a stone wall that retained the day's heat, pondering to himself as he gazed at the stars, which shone much brighter than they did at home. What had they gotten into, and what would the Russians do with the information? He wondered, not without anxiety. As someone who had headed three intelligence services, he should have known better than to come here in the first place. They should have stayed home."

Suddenly, the calm was broken by a giggling woman's voice coming from above.

"Tihi-hi-hi, uuuuu crazy," the voice laughed, clearly belonging to an Asian woman, judging by the distinctive accent—probably Thai.

"You want it, tihi-hi," she giggled again. "Claaazy-uuuu."

Baksi looked up and realized he had inadvertently seated himself below Gyllenstierna's terrace, which had wide-open sliding doors. It seemed likely that the chancellor had popped a few of those King Blues, Baksi thought as he returned to his room. Gyllenstierna was undoubtedly a very energetic man, but still...

Baksi brought up the awkward subject when they were settled into the comfortable airplane seats, ready to take off for Copenhagen.

"So, how did it go with that gorgeous mulatta?"

"It wasn't too bad," Gyllenstierna replied neutrally. "Not bad at all," he repeated, just to be sure, but without being particularly enthusiastic.

"Aha, and nothing unusual happened?" Baksi asked, studying Gyllenstierna's expression.

"No, not that I'm aware of," Gyllenstierna lied, though he wondered if he was now starring in some film somewhere. There had undoubtedly been a lot of bunga bunga.

"Well, some strange things happened in my room, for sure. I brought two gorgeous girls back with me. When I was lying on my stomach getting a massage, I noticed a naked guy standing behind me, aiming his junk at my ass. I wonder what my wife would say about those pictures?" Baksi sighed deeply. "How the hell did I fall for that? I should know better!"

"You, with your vow of celibacy," Gyllenstierna laughed harshly. "But let's just leave the bunga bunga party behind us. Like Putin said: What happens in La Zagaleta, stays in La Zagaleta."

He didn't want to hear any more details about what had happened in Baksi's room, and he sincerely hoped that whatever had happened to both of them would remain in La Zagaleta forever.

The plane began to take off, and the loud engine noise forced them to pause the conversation until the plane reached cruising altitude and the engines throttled down.

"I think I need a triple whisky right about now," Gyllenstierna said, his thoughts unwillingly drifting back to the unwanted golden shower he'd received during the party. A Golden Shower, as he'd heard it called in the U.S. A Golden Shower on Mr. Goldstar, he thought ironically. Not something befitting a head of state—or anyone else, for that matter. "Then I'm going to try to sleep."

"Sounds good to me, too," Baksi said, leaning his head back, closing his eyes, and trying to push away the creeping anxiety that had taken hold of his entire body.

The feeling was worse than anything he'd experienced during the war. And now, he was returning to that wretched war again. A huge whisky would hit the spot. He downed it in two quick gulps and leaned his head back again, hoping to catch some sleep. And forget.

Chapter 24 – Kreuzberger nächte sind lang

August 7, 2033

Baksi knocked on the door to Gyllenstierna's office and pushed it open without waiting for a response. Gyllenstierna was leaning back in his chair, hands clasped behind his neck, eyes half-closed. He seemed deeply lost in thought. He looked more exhausted than usual, with pronounced dark circles under his eyes. His hair was tangled, uncut, and unwashed, and his wrinkled uniform should have been sent to the cleaners long ago. This was far from the ever-fresh, friendly, and alert Swedish chief of defense he had been before the outbreak of the war.

In just a year, Gyllenstierna had undergone an almost complete personality transformation. Nowadays, he was a prickly, authoritarian leader, seemingly ready to drop the trapdoor on anyone at any time, with no regard for past loyalties—or the future. Those who get blood on their hands also make unforgiving enemies, who neither forget nor forgive, a reality that Gyllenstierna didn't even consider—if he was thinking anything.

Baksi thought Gyllenstierna had made too many powerful enemies to survive in the long run. Sure, the Swedes are a subdued people, he mused, but not so subdued that they would tolerate a leader who orders executions at the slightest suspicion of wavering loyalty. Behind his back, Gyllenstierna had started to be compared to North Korea's leading psychopath, the chubby dictator who inherited his title and called himself the supreme commander.

War doesn't only claim victims on the battlefield, Baksi thought, somewhat sympathetically, about his old, good friend and boss. He could only hope that Gyllenstierna would recover, but Gyllenstierna just kept staring deeper into his Turkish raki bottles, becoming more unpredictable each week. Was he even in good health? Baksi had suggested that Gyllenstierna should take a few weeks to rest, but the idea hadn't gone over well. Two weeks of absence could expose him to the risk of a coup.

Gyllenstierna's growing paranoia made it seem like he no longer trusted anyone—not even his confidant and closest friend, Baksi. And Gyllenstierna's faltering trust wasn't entirely unfounded. In Baksi's eyes,

Gyllenstierna was no longer fit to be the country's top leader, but he hadn't yet dared to discuss this with anyone. The wrong words to the wrong person could have unpleasant consequences.

As the head of MUST and SÄPO, Baksi received regular updates on the mood among the top officials. More and more signals indicated that dissatisfaction with Gyllenstierna's leadership was not just brewing—it had firmly taken root, something apparent to everyone except Gyllenstierna himself. He ruled through terror and fear. People were frequently hauled in for questioning by NRSS agents, and some were never seen again. Baksi was one of the few who knew that the most troublesome individuals were being dumped alive from helicopters far out into the Baltic Sea. NRSS Chief Commander Ken Persson had borrowed the idea from Argentina. This elegant method avoided the need for graves and prevented families from demanding their loved ones' bodies be exhumed and autopsied. It also eliminated execution sites, along with the rumors that would inevitably follow: no murder investigations, no manhunts.

A disappearance is something entirely different from a murder. Just a little push—goodbye, and swim peacefully—and all was well—end of story. If a body happened to wash ashore in the wrong place, it would still look like an unfortunate drowning accident. Unless, of course, you noticed the plastic zip tie binding the hands behind the corpse's back, but that was usually cut off before the family got a chance to identify the body, which was rare anyway.

Baksi had reluctantly and almost subconsciously begun to entertain how Gyllenstierna could be removed from power and who might replace him as chancellor. It was a coup, really, but only for the good of Sweden, not because he craved power personally. Certainly not for that reason.

However, the coup would need to avoid sparking a civil war among the Swedes, which would be disastrous. Baksi eventually concluded that he was the most suitable candidate to take over the ultimate leadership, given his role as the unifying force within the intelligence services and his close relationship with Gyllenstierna, with all that entailed. No one could match Baksi regarding access to information and personal connections within Sweden's various power centers. He was the natural successor.

But the question was how Brännström would react to the idea. Baksi knew that Brännström enjoyed the most support within the top ranks under the National Council. Brännström was running the war and doing it so well that it was impossible not to respect his competence and efforts, making him very popular within military circles and among the Swedish public.

Yet, in Baksi's eyes, Brännström was just a soldier with little interest in broader political issues or the social structure of the new Sweden that would need to be built after the war. Brännström was undoubtedly no philosopher or strategic thinker. As chancellor, Baksi thought one had to have a broader strategic vision, particularly regarding international relations. And perhaps Brännström wasn't even interested, Baksi hoped. With Brännström's support, he would appear as the natural leader in a seamless transition of power, which would be best for Sweden's future. You cannot afford internal disputes when the country is at war, Baksi reflected a thought that crossed his mind more and more frequently.

But now he stood before his boss, accompanied by a visitor from afar, from Berlin, who did not speak Swedish.

"This gentleman has come from Berlin to meet you personally, Daniel. He claims to have information of the utmost importance, which can only be delivered to you as chancellor. He speaks fluent German and some English. Do you need an interpreter?"

Gyllenstierna stood up abruptly, shaking his head slightly to wake himself fully. His expression made it clear that he wasn't particularly pleased with the unexpected visit, especially since it was late in the evening and he had hoped, for once, to get a proper night's sleep. He eyed his uninvited guest suspiciously without saying a word. The guest, in turn, discreetly assessed Gyllenstierna from head to toe. He had heard that Gyllenstierna was somewhat run down, but the deterioration seemed worse than anticipated. He looked unkempt, which didn't suit a serious Muslim who was supposed to observe good personal hygiene and maintain order around him.

"He arrived in Simrishamn on a small civilian boat and reported himself to our military personnel, who escorted him there. He's clean. His crew of four is being held in Simrishamn until further notice."

"Okay, Alfred, I'll give him five minutes. Please leave us alone for a while."

As soon as Baksi closed the door, the visitor wasted no time.

"I have important information from the Turkish headquarters in Kreuzberg. I'm here on behalf of the general director," the voice said in Turkish.

Gyllenstierna widened his eyes in surprise at being addressed in the language of his childhood. This was a positive sign. At least no interpreter was needed.

"Aha, a Turkish brother! You're more than welcome here, then. Please, have a seat on my comfortable visitor's couch."

Gyllenstierna gestured toward the couch and placed a thermos of hot water, a small teapot, two Turkish tea glasses, small spoons, and a silver bowl filled with sugar cubes on the table. He poured the scalding water into the teapot and smiled at his guest, who carefully scanned the room, examining every detail professionally.

"It's going to be nice to enjoy some real Turkish tea," the visitor said. "But first, I must ask: Are you sure no one can listen in on us?"

"Yes. This room is a shielded security bunker that can't be remotely monitored. My friend Ali Baksi, whom you just met and who is also Turkish, has his technical experts sweep the room meticulously almost daily. There's no chance they'd miss a bug. Additionally, my top technical expert—the head of my intelligence service, NRSS—thoroughly scanned the room two days ago. You can relax."

"What? The man who received me is Turkish, too? He probably thought I was just a regular 'Fritz' because I'm fair and have blue eyes. But how is it that two Turks are leading Sweden in a war against Muslims?"

"It's just a matter of coincidence. We both made careers in the military, and it just so happened that we rose to the top. I suppose we've been quite competent. The Swedes see us as loyal citizens, so it's never been an issue."

"Are you, I mean, completely loyal? I see you have a Quran on your desk. And it looks well-used."

"Let me put it this way: Baksi has left his cultural heritage and true identity behind and is fully Swedish down to his toenails."

"And you?" the visitor asked, watching Gyllenstierna's reactions closely.

"It depends on how you look at it. My family and I owe Sweden a lot, and I fully respect the Swedes with all their strengths and weaknesses. But deep down, I will always be a Turkish Muslim. And the older I get, the more I feel it. It does feel a bit strange to be fighting against Muslims. It pains me to hear about all the dead Muslim men. Sometimes, I pinch myself and wonder if I'm on the right side."

"That's exactly how the situation was described to me. I have your entire biography right here," he said, tapping his temple with his index finger. "I know everything."

"Interesting. How did you find all that out?"

"We have excellent intelligence at our headquarters in Kreuzberg— in Berlin. There are loyal Turks everywhere in Western Europe, at all levels. Especially in Sweden, where you are an example. Just as I am a German example."

Gyllenstierna poured them a second glass of tea and sipped carefully at the hot, steaming drink.

"But why have you come to see me? It's not just to reminisce about Turkish memories, I presume. So, why?"

"Even though my official superior is at the headquarters in Kreuzberg, I truly serve the Muslim Brotherhood. It was the Brotherhood that organized the invasion of Sweden. Our goal is to conquer all of Western Europe, and as you already know, Sweden was chosen as our first target because it was the lowest-hanging fruit."

"Yes, we certainly noticed that on July 17, 2032," Gyllenstierna replied with a wry smile. "Especially me, since I was the one they intended to kill, but instead, it was my poor brother who lost his life— may he rest in peace. But now the Muslims are under pressure and seem to be losing the Swedish war."

"We hadn't accounted for the Russians. If they hadn't intervened, we would have controlled all of Sweden by now."

"That's true. Right now, I'm not sure whether to curse or thank the Russians."

"The Russians will no longer involve themselves in the Swedish war. They've already achieved what they wanted and secured the territories they desired. They have many reasons to let the Swedes fight independently, primarily because they don't want to be seen as an occupying force and risk turning the entire world against them. As it stands, they can instead parade as the liberators of Sweden."

"You're probably right," the visitor said.

"But now you've piqued my curiosity. Why have you come here?" Gyllenstierna asked with a strange expression on his face.

"My superior, General Yilmaz, wants to meet you to discuss a potential collaboration. I've brought an invitation to our headquarters in Kreuzberg."

"That's kind of him," Gyllenstierna said with a smile. "But we happen to be on opposite sides in this war," he added sharply, raising an eyebrow.

Gyllenstierna's guest rolled his eyes, acknowledging how absurd the situation must seem from Gyllenstierna's perspective. He took his time sipping the tea a few more times before finally leaning forward and responding, carefully emphasizing each word to ensure his message was unmistakable.

"That's precisely what General Yilmaz wants to change. The Muslim Brotherhood has set aside twenty-five million U.S. dollars as a testament to how highly they value your skills. The money can be deposited in an account in Dubai—or anywhere you choose—in exchange for your secret cooperation in helping your Muslim friends win the Swedish war."

Now it was Gyllenstierna's turn to roll his eyes, feigning surprise, even though he had suspected from the beginning what his visitor's true purpose was.

"That sounds interesting, but I must think through the details."

"You're only doing what you know is right. I can sense that your heart beats for the Muslim cause. With Allah's help, we will defeat the infidels and take control of all Western Europe."

"The situation for Muslims in Sweden is quite difficult right now, especially because of the Russians' involvement. What if the Swedes win?"

"General Yilmaz has significant resources that could be deployed in the Swedish war, turning the tide completely. If we launch a surprise attack from behind while you mislead the Swedes with false information, we can crush them within a few days. Once their main force is defeated, the road to Stockholm will be wide open."

"Yes, there might be a chance," Gyllenstierna replied, his thoughts seemingly already aligned with the other side.

"We will ensure that all your relatives are safely evacuated from Sweden to a location of your choice. Once we win the Swedish war, you can decide whether to retire in a peaceful Muslim country with your family or join us in Kreuzberg, where your expertise would be highly valued. You might even work alongside General Yilmaz once operations in Germany, the Netherlands, and Belgium gain momentum. Or you could become the head of the Rotterdam headquarters, which General Yilmaz mentioned as a possibility. A local commander with extensive experience in large-scale battles is needed there. The skirmishes you've seen on the continent are nothing compared to what's coming. And that's not to mention what awaits in the United Kingdom!"

Gyllenstierna's guest straightened in his chair, signaling he was ready to end the meeting.

"Consider our offer carefully. We will contact you again within a week. May I request an escort back to Simrishamn now?"

The two men embraced warmly, finishing with the traditional cheek kisses. Both knew that Gyllenstierna had already decided, even though he hadn't said it outright.

Time had flown by, and it was already past two in the morning. As the saying goes, Kreuzberg nights are long. What was supposed to be five minutes had turned into four hours, a fact noted by Baksi, who dutifully arranged for the escort back to Simrishamn. He quietly wondered what proposal the German had brought. Perhaps now Sweden could get help from the Germans to win the war against the Muslims.

A collaboration with Germany wouldn't be a bad idea, but Baksi had no clue that it was a different kind of collaboration than he had in mind.

Baksi and Gyllenstierna did not know that a certain Ken Persson had been listening to the conversation in real-time and, of course, had recorded it. The head of NRSS, as usual, sat at the top of the information pyramid and was now hurrying to have the four-hour conversation translated into Swedish.

Even without understanding a word of Turkish, except for "*kalabalik*," – uproar, used once, Ken Persson already had a vague idea of the conversation. However, he had picked up on some specific keywords.

The place names Kreuzberg and Rotterdam were mentioned repeatedly, and he wondered why. He knew that Germany's largest concentration of Turks was in Kreuzberg, Berlin, and realized it was no coincidence that the place's name came up multiple times.

Dubai and the term US dollars were mentioned several times, suggesting that the guest was trying to buy off Gyllenstierna. Was the guest attempting to lure Gyllenstierna to switch sides? He would know for sure as soon as he got the translation, but he was already pondering what to do if his suspicions were correct.

Chapter 25 – The Pizza Man from Östberga

August 28, 2033

Gyllenstierna was greeted by the same blonde secretary as before, with the same inviting smile. He noticed that her ample curves were just as impressive as his previous visit and that her outfit was even more form-fitting this time. Indeed, a prospect, thought the incorrigible womanizer Gyllenstierna to himself. A mature woman who knows her stuff. In his extensive experience, women with some extra flesh were usually the most passionate. No ring on her finger. He promised himself that he'd move when the circumstances were right. There was something special about Russian women—he had often found himself drawn into relationships with them for some reason. For now, he contented himself with gazing deeply into her eyes with an appreciative look.

"Perhaps we'll meet again. Just you and me, I mean," he said lightly, flashing his most charming smile as he held her gaze.

"You never know," she replied with that sexy Russian accent that sounded like music to Gyllenstierna's ears.

Playing hard to get was essential. It heightened the attraction though not so hard that the man would give up entirely. She took the opportunity to adjust her hair, causing her ample chest to strain against the fabric of her dress. She looked expectant. After all, it was the chancellor of Sweden flirting with her. A chancellor who was cheerful, charming, and still handsome for his age. An enticing trophy, exuding power and wealth in that confident, relaxed manner that told a woman everything she needed to know.

She began to suspect that the chancellor might offer her a thrilling ride, one she didn't want to miss. And sometimes, that ride leads to more than just a fling. A Swedish chancellor might not be so bad, even if she didn't dare hope for more than just being one of his companions.

Women find nothing sexier than power and money—except perhaps fame, which ranks even higher. The best is when all three are present, as with the man standing before her.

"My name is Olga. You know where to find me," she said with an inviting smile.

She was on board. Next time, he would book a suite and leave some free time in his schedule, he promised himself. Without further delay, he was shown into the same meeting room where he and Baksi had toasted vodka with Russia's foreign minister and Sweden's ambassador a few weeks earlier. This time, he was received only by Ambassador Iosif Vissarionovich, who greeted him with his usual stern expression. Without his superior, Larionov, in the room, the ambassador could dominate the space and play his usual hand of cards, which always seemed to consist of fifty-two joker cards. Negotiating with Larionov was much more pleasant; he naturally believed that good, functional relationships involve both give and take, unlike the ambassador, who only wanted to take.

"So, how's the war going?" Vissarionovich asked.

"It looks like it's finally going our way. We're gearing up for the major assault on Lund and Malmö."

"Let's hope it goes well without our help. The Archer systems will come in handy, I'm sure."

Gyllenstierna flinched. What Archer systems? It seemed the ambassador knew something he didn't, whatever that might mean. Gyllenstierna decided to keep his poker face. He'd need to check on this with Brännström immediately.

"When will you retake the western parts of Götaland, Halland, and Bohuslän?"

"That will have to wait until we finish operations in southern Sweden. We're choosing to concentrate our forces in the south. There's no rush since the Muslims can't bring in any reinforcements due to the no-fly zone and our naval blockade."

Vissarionovich nodded, lit a cigarette, and blew a large cloud of smoke directly toward Gyllenstierna. It was a minor power play expressing his arrogant and unpleasant personality.

"Unless the Muslims launch a major offensive and head straight for Stockholm. They know we've handed over the Russian occupation zone to you and that Sweden's resources are quite limited. But you'll have to handle the war on your own now. That's not why I asked you to come to Marieberg. Just a friendly warning, nothing more."

Now, it was Gyllenstierna's turn to nod. He waited in silence, harboring dark suspicions. He intuitively understood what was coming, and his fears were quickly confirmed.

"By the way, did you enjoy yourself in La Zagaleta?" the ambassador asked with a malicious smile.

"Yes, it was a lovely event. Very generous. Please convey our deepest thanks to the president."

"I will. If you're interested, you can have some vacation memories from La Zagaleta. There were plenty of photos and videos taken."

"Thank you, that's a kind offer, but I don't think it's necessary. I have all my memories right here," Gyllenstierna replied, tapping the side of his head with his finger.

"I believe we understand each other. Who have you planned as your successor?"

"Successor? I have no plans to step down."

"Consider it. The president believes our recently signed partnership agreement can't be ratified if a man with Muslim sympathies leads Sweden. We will lift the no-fly zone if the deal isn't ratified. There will also be no gas-powered plants and no connection to the one Nordstream pipe in operation."

"That would, of course, put us in a difficult situation. But I don't quite understand the Muslim sympathies issue. I'm completely secular."

The ambassador ignored his objection entirely.

"I discussed the matter with Larionov. We concluded that Baksi is out of the question for the same reasons. Supreme Commander Anton Brännström and perhaps your Head of NRSS, Ken Persson, might be suitable alternatives. We need a strong Swedish leader who is flexible and aligned with Moscow."

"Ken Persson? He owes everything to me. He eats out of my hand!"

"Are you sure about that?" Vissarionovich asked, locking eyes with Gyllenstierna.

Gyllenstierna sat in silence, pondering the question without answering. Had Persson betrayed him to the Russians?

"Brännström could be an exciting choice," the ambassador continued. "But the question is, how flexible is he? We've created psychological profiles for all the candidates. In Brännström, we see a stubborn bull, which could be very useful—but only if he's willing to dance the tango with Moscow. Is he?"

"Like all Swedish military professionals, Brännström harbors deep suspicion and antipathy toward Russia. Working with Moscow would be like converting to a foreign religion for him."

"And that's not easy, as you know," the ambassador teased. "I don't think we'll get any further today. To summarize, the president wants to see a strong Swedish leader who can elevate the partnership between our countries to the next level. President Putin envisions Sweden becoming Russia's ninetieth federal subject within two to three years as an autonomous district, which will bring many benefits to Sweden. You'll retain one hundred percent of your independence, except that foreign policy and defense will be managed from Moscow. As for your exports, a huge new market will open up for Sweden."

"There's certainly a lot to think about. More than I can decide on here today," Gyllenstierna replied."

"Of course. We would appreciate your reply within a week regarding your question about your successor. Since we know you've made many enemies who would love to see you fall, we also guarantee safe passage. Perhaps a comfortable retirement on the Crimean Peninsula, with its pleasant climate, might be something to consider," the ambassador concluded.

Gyllenstierna felt dizzy as he slid into the back seat while the driver gently closed the door. His thoughts raced. What just happened in there? Is this the end? Damn, La Zagaleta and all those damn whores! One misstep was all it took. Everything had been planned and rigged from the start. And why did the offer from the Turks in Kreuzberg appear at almost the same time? Did the Russians also orchestrate that? His mind spun, and despair started to settle in. He knew he had to act quickly.

The road to Bromma Airport was lined with bombed-out, sooty ruins, but at least the way was clear. Traffic was so sparse they could have easily counted every car on the road. No traffic lights were functioning, but they weren't needed anyway. The journey took them over the temporarily repaired bridge of Tranebergsbron. Only one lane was open, but that was more than enough, considering how few cars were on the road.

The old, technically outdated SK 60 plane that served as the staff's transport obediently took off and headed for Kristianstad in Skåne, where another driver would be waiting for Gyllenstierna. The Russians' pressure hastened his decision. Suddenly, it all became so obvious. He didn't trust their tempting offer of retirement in Crimea one bit.

Perhaps they'd liquidate him after he helped with the power transition? He also sensed that his position as chancellor was threatened by the Swedes themselves, regardless of the Russians. He had long harbored a vague suspicion that Brännström and Baksi were withholding vital information from him, and Vissarionovich's mention of the Archer systems only reinforced that feeling.

Sweden now had access to artillery, and he needed to inform the Muslims about it before it was too late. And that slippery intelligence officer, Ken Persson? The man who was impossible to pin down. Something was unsettling about Persson's restrained demeanor. He knew nothing about Persson. The man was like a clam, but he always wanted to know everything about everyone else. How much does he know about me? Gyllenstierna wondered. Is he planning a coup? Trust no one. Not a single soul, he thought grimly as he closed his eyes.

Gyllenstierna felt the ground burning beneath his feet. Now, it was all about escaping with his life. His next destination would be the Muslim General Staff in Kreuzberg, Berlin. General Yilmaz would welcome him with open arms. He just had to get there, and twenty-five million U.S. dollars would be his. A wonderful life in the sun, maybe in Australia or Florida. He had no intention of living in a Muslim country. He had grown accustomed to the good life in the West, with all its benefits. Living where all the beautiful women were hidden behind veils was not for him. It would be a pure desert, in every sense, like Saudi Arabia, no matter how impressive the infrastructure was. Women were meant to be seen—and sometimes more than that. It was time to seize the opportunity and flee right now. The decision was made. There was no turning back.

"I need to get to Berlin as soon as possible. Can you fly me to Berlin Tegel?"

"Berlin?" The pilot exclaimed in surprise. "No one mentioned that. The chances of getting shot down are almost certain unless we have clearance. Do we?"

"I can probably arrange that."

"OK, then, it's not a problem. But we don't have enough fuel for the trip. We'll need to land in Kristianstad to refuel. You can sort out the clearance while we're fueling up."

"Let's land first, then we'll see."

The die was cast. Once on the ground, Gyllenstierna had already begun to make strides in planning his escape. It had to happen tonight before it was too late—if it wasn't already. Vissarionovich had given him a week, but what was that worth? The Russians had decided to remove him, and they might already be executing their plan, possibly with Brännström or Ken Persson. Baksi, at least, wasn't in the loop. Gyllenstierna felt like the trap could snapshot at any moment. In the worst case, he might be arrested right at the airport. It was already 8.30 p.m. Time was running out, and Gyllenstierna's orders to the pilot were clear.

"Refuel the plane completely and stay ready for takeoff until I return. It'll probably be sometime after midnight. I'll handle the flight clearance with the Germans. Keep a low profile, so no one starts wondering what you're doing here."

"OK, I'll wait in the staff room. No one else will be there, and I can lock the door from the inside to be safe. There's a sign on the door in the departure hall. Knock three times so I'll know it's you."

"Remember, this is top secret, of the highest confidentiality. No one should know why you're here. If a superior asks, say you've been given a classified order to wait until 6 a.m. tomorrow. Do not reveal who gave you the order. Understood?"

"OK, no problem. I'll be ready for takeoff until 6 a.m. at the latest."

The pilot stepped out first and held the door open for the chancellor. Gyllenstierna stepped onto the stairs, glancing around suspiciously. As usual, the waiting car was at the terminal building, with the driver beside it. There were no signs of anything unusual. Maybe he was being unnecessarily paranoid.

As they drove through the little locality of Vittskövle, they passed two light armored vehicles. He thought they were coming to arrest him for a moment, but the cars continued northward. He felt his heart pounding at the two checkpoints where they had to stop for identification. But nothing out of the ordinary happened. It should have happened if they had decided to arrest him. He felt somewhat calmer. Everything suggested that he had at least the night, and he didn't intend to find out if he also had the morning. It would happen tonight. He would use Ken Persson's emergency escape plan for the chancellor but with a modified version that would shake off any potential surveillance and pursuers.

The journey to the general staff headquarters in the village of Sjöbo took forty-five minutes. Baksi had been briefed about Gyllenstierna's meeting with Vissarionovich and met him in the hallway. Gyllenstierna noted with relief that his old friend looked as he always did.

"I'm inquisitive about what the Russians had to say."

"Nothing dramatic. Vissarionovich just wanted to discuss a few details regarding the partnership agreement."

"Oh? Was there anything significant?"

"Not particularly. Mostly trade issues and financing the connection to the undamaged pipe of Nord Stream. And, of course, arms deliveries. I plan to cover it in tomorrow morning's meeting. Excuse me, I have quite a bit to handle right now."

"Just one last question. Did Vissarionovich mention anything about La Zagaleta?"

"No, not at all. Though I did take the opportunity to express our gratitude to President Putin."

"Glad to hear that. Hopefully, everything gets buried in the archives and forgotten. If we don't provoke the Russians unnecessarily, there's no reason to."

Gyllenstierna wasted no time. The first thing he did was contact the driver who had just taken him there via the communication radio, which was almost certainly being monitored.

"I need a ride to Simrishamn around 11 p.m. To a boat waiting in the harbor."

"OK, no problem. I'll be ready."

Gyllenstierna now understood he was being monitored by SÄPO, MUST, or Ken Persson, head of his security service, NRSS. He was sure he was under surveillance, though he wasn't sure by whom. Perhaps all the security services were watching him, he thought grimly. Now they had something to think about. If they concluded that he was about to flee the country, they would likely follow and arrest him before he could board the boat in Simrishamn.

Just before 11 p.m., the driver opened the car door for the chancellor, who took his place in the back seat.

"Simrishamn Harbor, right? We can make it in about forty-five minutes if we take National Highway 11."

The Chancellor nodded in response without saying anything. As the car pulled away, a black BMW started up and followed from a distance, its lights off. They knew where the vehicle was headed and didn't need to reveal their presence by staying too close. Inside the BMW were two SÄPO agents sent out by their boss, Bianca Popovic.

Gyllenstierna stood in his darkened room, watching through the window as the cars drove off. In the first car sat his double, a man whose existence was known only to him and Ken Persson. It was Ken Persson who had selected the man because of his striking resemblance to Gyllenstierna. With the uniform and cap on and the familiar briefcase in hand, it would take a sharp eye to notice it wasn't the real chancellor. In the darkness, it was nearly impossible. And now, Ken Persson would discover that the double could be used against him.

Gyllenstierna had managed to shake off his watchers, except perhaps for Ken Persson. Now, it remained to be seen if the trick had worked fully. For Gyllenstierna, this was a matter of life and death. What happened that night would determine his future. If something went wrong, he could be executed or imprisoned for years. But if everything went according to his plan, a bright future awaited. The next few hours would decide everything.

Had Gyllenstierna known who was standing at a window upstairs, watching the black BMW drive away, he wouldn't have had to think about who was monitoring him. There stood Ken Persson, satisfied to see that SÄPO, as usual, was a step behind NRSS. "That fool Popovic," he thought. "I'll deal with her when the time is right. How was she ever appointed head of SÄPO? She doesn't even realize NRSS bugs her and prattles on cluelessly about things she shouldn't even be discussing." That was something Ken Persson couldn't stand—such unprofessional behavior—a loser.

The SÄPO agents tailing Gyllenstierna's double to Simrishamn apprehended him on the quay. However, they quickly began to suspect that he was an impostor, as he didn't quite match the photos of Gyllenstierna they had with them. Back at headquarters, Persson and Popovic could dismiss the man as a double within seconds, mainly since Persson had recruited him. The man was a floor guy from Landskrona with roots in Bulgaria. After a brief interrogation, they released him, as he was doing the job he had been hired for—by Persson, no less. They knew he had no valuable information. Now, he suddenly found himself unemployed.

At 11.08 p.m., two NRSS agents outside the general staff building noticed the front door open, and Gyllenstierna stepped into the parking lot alone. Gyllenstierna cautiously looked around in the darkness before reaching into his coat pocket, pulling out an electronic device, and pressing a button that caused a car to blink in the distance. He glanced around again before opening the door and climbing into the military-painted Volvo XC 100, apparently planning to drive himself. The battery-powered car glided away silently, save for the crunch of gravel beneath its tires, as it left the parking lot and onto the street where the NRSS agents waited in their civilian Tesla. Once the Volvo had traveled about five hundred feet, the Tesla discreetly pulled out from its parking spot and began to follow.

The journey took them north along National Highway 13 toward the smaller town of Hörby and then to Höör, where the Volvo turned right onto National Highway 23, continuing north.

The Tesla followed steadily, keeping a safe distance while easily tracking the Volvo's taillights in the darkness. Every town and house they passed lay in darkness, with the power supply out for over a year. Naturally, there was no street lighting either. The Tesla was equipped with IR headlights instead of standard high beams.

The two agents wore night-vision goggles with image intensifiers, allowing them to see the road bathed in a greenish light, utterly invisible to the human eye without technology.

They could follow Gyllenstierna from just one hundred and fifty feet behind without him having any chance of detecting them, while they could see the Volvo almost as clearly as in daylight.

The drive proceeded at an average speed, which now meant about twenty to thirty miles per hour faster than the posted speed limits—signs that no one paid attention to anymore. The police had more pressing matters and never engaged with military vehicles, no matter how they behaved.

The NRSS agents had orders from their boss, Ken Persson, to follow Gyllenstierna to determine his plans and whether he intended to meet anyone. Once he reached his destination, he was to be apprehended, and if that wasn't possible due to the company he kept, he was to be shot dead with the AK5 rifles that the agents had beside them. Under no circumstances was Gyllenstierna to escape.

It was a long journey on the darkened roads. Only after more than three hours, near Mjölby, did Gyllenstierna pull into a darkened roadside diner, stopping the car from the entrance to a farmer's store. He urgently needed to relieve himself, so he stood beside the car with his legs spread wide, unzipping his fly while absentmindedly reading the sign on the door, which declared that only locally grown, ecologic vegetarian products were sold.

'We'll take him while he's pissing! We can't risk anything now. Who knows who's inside?'

The Tesla screeched around the corner, tires squealing, and stopped before the Volvo, blocking it just as Gyllenstierna had begun to wet the asphalt. The agents leaped out of the car and rushed toward Gyllenstierna with their assault rifles aimed at him. Gyllenstierna stood frozen, a shocked expression on his face, still holding his dick in his right hand.

"Hands up, you're under arrest!"

Before Gyllenstierna could even get his hands in the air, one of the agents barreled into him with a violent tackle at waist height, slamming him onto the asphalt. The second agent immediately pounced as well, and together, they wrenched his arms behind his back and cuffed his wrists. Wasting no time, they pulled Gyllenstierna to his feet as they stood up.

"Damn, right in the middle of the piss," one of the agents muttered in disgust, pointing at the puddle that now covered at least a square foot.

"Yeah, no kidding," the other replied, futilely trying to brush away the damp spots on his uniform with the palm of his hand. "How does someone piss like a damn camel?"

"Let's hope the chancellor's piss smells better than the piss of us mere mortals," he added with a smirk.

Gyllenstierna stared straight ahead, tight-lipped, refusing to acknowledge the conversation.

"We'll take his car back. It's much nicer," one of them said.

They opened the Volvo's back door and shoved Gyllenstierna into the backseat, one of the agents sliding in beside him. Gyllenstierna looked pale, but he said absolutely nothing. The scuffle knocked off his cap, but the agent beside him replaced it on his head. Despite its dark navy color, the wet, stained fabric was prominent, though it would dry soon enough.

Over the radio, they contacted NRSS Chief Ken Persson, who was anxiously waiting in Sjöbo.

"We've got him. He's unharmed. We should be back at headquarters around six."

"Nicely done. I knew I could count on you."

"Who was he meeting?"

"We don't know. We caught him outside a darkened roadside shop where he stopped. We thought someone might be waiting inside, but the place was empty when we checked. He probably just stopped to take a piss."

"Alright, we'll get it out of him soon enough. Handle him carefully."

The return trip to Sjöbo felt long and tedious. The agents were groggy, a natural reaction to the long drive up and the intensity of the arrest. Gyllenstierna leaned his head back and closed his eyes for the entire ride. His handcuffs had now moved to the front so he could rest his cuffed hands on his knees.

At the General Staff headquarters, Ken Persson and SÄPO Chief Bianca Popovic waited impatiently in Gyllenstierna's office, ready to conduct the initial interrogation. Afterward, Gyllenstierna would be handed over to professional interrogators who would scrutinize every detail until no questions remained. Alfred Baksi joined them after a while, clearly uncomfortable with the situation. He was about to interrogate his old friend, who was now in deep trouble. Baksi decided to stay in the background and let the others lead the questioning.

They saw the staff's Volvo XC 100 finally drive into the courtyard through the window. The real Gyllenstierna was helped out of the car, his hands cuffed in front of him, and he seemed stiff from the uncomfortable position he had been in. He shuffled the first few steps across the parking lot until his legs loosened. One of the NRSS agents held Gyllenstierna firmly by the arm as they led him to his old office, where his former subordinates—Ken Persson, Bianca Popovic, and Alfred Baksi—eagerly waited to begin the interrogation. They watched him intently as he was seated in a chair in the middle of the room. He looked exhausted, with a new and defeated expression in his eyes that they hadn't seen before.

Baksi avoided staring at Gyllenstierna, feeling deeply uncomfortable about being in this situation with his perhaps closest friend and respected leader. He could imagine how Judas must have felt after betraying his master for thirty pieces of silver.

"Welcome back," Persson said as he poured a cup of coffee from a thermos. "You gave it a good try; I'll give you that. Want a cup?"

For the first time since his arrest, Gyllenstierna spoke. "I'm sorry to disappoint you, but I'm not Gyllenstierna."

The shock in the room was palpable. For a few seconds, silence reigned as everyone's thoughts raced uncontrollably. They immediately noticed that the voice wasn't Gyllenstierna's—the tone and phrasing lacked his characteristic nasal elegance. Persson was the first to react, taking a few determined steps forward and yanking the cap off the seated man's head. Baksi and Popovic quickly followed suit, examining the man closely. It took several long seconds of scrutinizing his face before they could confirm with certainty that this was yet another doppelgänger—a far more convincing than the first.

"Well, I'll be damn," Persson shouted in frustration. "Another double, or should I say triple? So, where the hell is the real Gyllenstierna?"

"I have no idea," the man responded calmly. "I don't know anything that would interest you. My job is to protect Sweden's chancellor by impersonating him. That's all I know. I haven't done anything wrong."

"Whether you've done anything wrong is something we'll decide later," Popovic said. "But who are you?"

It turned out that the man they had apprehended was a close relative of Gyllenstierna. He hails from the same remote and isolated mountain village on Turkey's high plateau where Gyllenstierna's parents had once married and celebrated their wedding by the light of oil lamps—the only illumination available. Determining how close a relative this man was proved difficult, as cousin marriages were the norm in the region. Visitors to the village often noted how strikingly similar many villagers looked, which had a natural explanation.

The man, who claimed his name was Ertuğrul Öztürk, said that before the war broke out, he had worked for twenty years as a pizza baker at Östberga Pizzeria in Djursholm.

"Djursholm?" Baksi responded, surprised. "For twenty years, you say?" He paused, thinking for a moment. "I know someone who might be able to verify that. Bring in Max. He grew up in Djursholm; if anyone's heard of Östberga Pizzeria, it'll be him."

After twenty more minutes of fruitless questioning, the door opened, and Max entered the room with his usual unflustered demeanor. As a man with an upper-class background, he was never fazed by titles or positions. Moreover, he knew that everyone on the staff was highly impressed and grateful for his work as a special forces soldier.

"Hey there, Max," said the man sitting in the chair, dressed in the chancellor's uniform.

Max stopped in his tracks, mouth agape. He was utterly confused. The chancellor was sitting there, speaking in a familiar voice that didn't match the situation. His brain struggled to connect the dots.

"It's me, Ertuğrul, from Östberga Pizzeria. I've been making pizzas for you and your family since your childhood. Don't you recognize me?"

"Ertu? Is that you? I can't believe it!" Max exclaimed, clearly pleased, as he hugged the still-handcuffed man. "Sorry to ask, but what on earth are you doing here? I've always thought you looked a lot like the chancellor."

"The former chancellor," Baksi interjected, a note of finality in his voice.

Max looked at Baksi, shocked. This was a monumental piece of news, and a heavy silence settled over the room. The situation was clear now: Gyllenstierna had outsmarted them all right when everything was on the line. It was unsettling to realize that Gyllenstierna had proven himself more intelligent than all his intelligence chiefs, who were supposed to be the sharpest minds in such situations. As for the man on the chair—the "triple"—it was best to unlock his handcuffs and let him go. Like the double before him, he had done his job to protect Sweden's head of government. Who could blame him for that? His only mistake was stopping in Mjölby due to urgent circumstances instead of driving straight to Stockholm and parking the car at the royal palace as instructed.

"While you're here," Max said hopefully, his face taking on a pleading expression, "I've been craving a Pizza Acapulco with tenderloin and béarnaise sauce for ages. Could you make one for me?"

"You never get tired of those, do you?" Ertuğrul responded with a smile. "You've probably had hundreds by now. But sure, I can make one for you, no problem." The pizza man from Östberga Pizzeria suddenly found himself with new duties, much to the delight of the General Staff. Ken Persson opted for a Calzone, feeling its folded form and hidden contents aptly symbolized the day's events.

No one had the slightest idea where Gyllenstierna was. The investigation was stumbling in the dark despite being given significant resources. Every house was thoroughly searched, but there were no results. Gyllenstierna had vanished without a trace, as if swallowed by a big hole. No one had seen the chancellor or any high-ranking official in uniform on the night in question. This could be explained by the fact that Gyllenstierna had shaved his head, donned a pair of metal-framed glasses, and attached a thick, light-blond fake mustache to his usually clean-shaven upper lip. Before leaving the general staff headquarters, he had changed into jeans and a sweater, with his uniform tucked away in a bag —just in case he needed it later. He completed his disguise with a dark blue, logo-free baseball cap atop his newly bald head.

Despite efforts to keep Gyllenstierna's betrayal and successful escape under wraps, it took only two days for the headlines and TV reports to focus exclusively on this story. No one knew if there had been a leak or if they were under surveillance. Military and political leaders were bombarded with questions and phone calls they didn't know how to handle. Brännström eventually lost his patience and snapped at a journalist from the country's biggest newspaper, who had repeatedly asked who was now in charge: "I'm the one in charge, damn it! Don't you get that?" he snarled, ending the call with his face flushed with anger.

Brännström's unguarded comment led to headlines claiming that he had secretly been appointed chancellor, causing confusion and concern among everyone involved, including Brännström himself. After nearly a week of fruitless searching, one of MUST's agents noticed something odd in the staff's SK60 aircraft logbook. The logbook had already been reviewed a couple of hours after it was revealed that the man they had captured was not the real Gyllenstierna. The idea that Gyllenstierna might have used the staff's plane was logical, but the aircraft had returned, and the logbook showed nothing unusual. The last recorded flight was Gyllenstierna's transport from Stockholm. But when the MUST agent compared the logbook with the engine's automatic time log—a meter on the instrument panel that records the total hours of operation—he discovered that the plane had been in the air for four hours without any entry in the logbook, on the very night Gyllenstierna disappeared. It was too much of a coincidence to ignore.

It took another full day to track down the pilot who had flown the chancellor to Stockholm and back on the day in question. The pilot denied everything for hours before finally caving under the pressure from Persson and Baksi. He insisted that he was only following the orders of secrecy given to him by the chancellor himself. He believed he was helping and protecting the chancellor and had done nothing wrong. Of course, he had been a bit puzzled when the chancellor showed up looking like a completely different person than the one he had flown the day before. But the chancellor had presented his ID and uniform, and how could anyone else have known what they had agreed upon earlier? Indeed, it had to be the chancellor as his passenger, and it wasn't his place as a pilot to question why the man might be in disguise.

Persson and Baksi exchanged glances and sighed in frustration. No one had technically done anything wrong that night, yet everyone had inadvertently aided Gyllenstierna's escape. The feeling was maddening.

Daniel Gyllenstierna had ceased to exist, just like the extinguished noble family that had carried his name hundreds of years ago. But a week earlier, Deniz Öztürk had reemerged. As he had anticipated, Deniz Öztürk was welcomed with open arms by his new superior, General Yilmaz, and now worked alongside him daily. Öztürk was already settling into his role at the Muslim General Staff in Kreuzberg, dressed in traditional Muslim attire with a crocheted topi on his head. Turkish was the staff's language, which posed no problem for him. However, it would still be many months before his beard could rival the impressive facial hair of his new boss.

Yet, Öztürk felt he outshone his superior in one significant way. After all, Öztürk had been Sweden's chancellor and head of government, whereas Yilmaz was merely a general, not even the commander-in-chief. In the long run, Öztürk hoped their positions in the hierarchy might eventually reverse, but that was a matter for the future.

Chapter 26 – Rescue Plans

September 10, 2033

King Carl Philip VII was deeply involved in the liberation war. His brief radio addresses every two weeks were essential in maintaining the will to fight and national unity among the Swedish people. The king's passionate voice and carefully chosen words provided comfort and hope to the Swedes, who were quietly suffering from hunger, cold, and a lack of money, medicine, and fuel for their vehicles. More than half of the population had been without electricity since the power grids collapsed following the destruction of the fifteen power plants along the Lule River a year earlier.

Hundreds of destroyed switch gears and signal boxes nationwide couldn't be repaired without the necessary spare parts. Even if some power stations and switch gears were still operational, dozens of miles of high-voltage cables lay on the ground after explosions or heavy vehicles brought down their supporting poles.

Everyone understood that restoring the power distribution network would take many years, so they had no choice but to get used to a life without electricity. Although the summer had been more manageable than feared, winter was approaching again. No one had forgotten the cold and darkness of the previous winter, and no one looked forward to enduring the same again, but they knew they had to tough it out and keep fighting.

Since Gyllenstierna's betrayal and flight into exile, King Carl Philip had become the leader with whom most Swedes identified. Those in the know knew that it was Commander-in-Chief Anton Brännström, appointed as acting chancellor by the National Council just days after Gyllenstierna's escape, who was Sweden's true leader. Many referred to Brännström as the strongman of Sweden, often comparing him to historical figures like Churchill, Franco, and Stalin, who had become national heroes through their unwavering commitment to their nations' causes.

Despite this, Brännström maintained a low profile and focused entirely on the war. The only visible change following his elevation to acting chancellor was the removal of thousands of portraits of Gyllenstierna, with no new ones replacing them.

Did Brännström have political ambitions? No one knew what was going on in his mind behind his strictly military façade. Some wondered if Brännström knew whether he wanted to play a more leading societal role after the war. The war consumed Brännström's attention, and he rarely wanted to discuss what might come after that. Most people interpreted his reluctance to discuss the future as lacking a plan. But they would eventually discover that they were mistaken.

King Carl Philip's commitment to the war was evident not only in his radio addresses. Since his first speech on September 9 the previous year, he had kept his promise always to wear the Army Field Uniform 2022, utterly devoid of rank insignia. The king, a naval officer, would typically have worn the Naval Combat Uniform 2026, but this was a war on the ground, not a naval one. As king, he represented all branches of the armed forces, regardless of his attire.

The king loved spending time at the front, showing his presence by walking around, shaking hands with the fighting soldiers, and offering encouraging words. This was greatly appreciated by the troops, officers, and staff alike.

"Give all what you got – guys and gals! Sweden's future is in your hands. I have faith in you!" King Carl Philip would often say as he shook hands or responded to a determined high-five from the troops.

Whenever the king delivered a brief speech at the military camps, he would always end with his royal motto: "For Sweden, to the last drop of blood!"

The cheers and applause would often reach a fever pitch, with the audience standing and shouting the king's motto, sometimes substituting "Sweden" with "Skåne," much to the king's tolerant amusement. He would stand there, smiling stoically, like a rock star orchestrating his fans, letting them repeat the chorus repeatedly.

Yet something troubled King Carl Philip. He wasn't particularly fond of the role that had turned him into a revered rock star. The adulation meant nothing to him; he found it somewhat distasteful. He continued his efforts because he knew his presence rallied the soldiers around him, motivating them to risk their lives for Sweden.

But rather than being seen as a rock star—he wanted to truly "rock." He sought to fight on the battlefield like the kings of old, like his great-great-great-grandfather, Jean Baptiste Bernadotte, who was crowned King of Sweden under the name Carl XIV Johan. Bernadotte had led the decisive attack on Kråköia near Fredrikstad, liberating Norway from Denmark and forcing it into a union with Sweden that lasted ninety years.

Carl XIV Johan was the last reigning Swedish monarch to engage in battle, though not with a weapon. As one of Napoleon's most successful generals, it was natural that the king would lead Sweden's military operations. And he did—though he commanded the war from the warmth and comfort of his headquarters.

King Carl Philip, however, yearned for more than the safety of a command post. He wanted to fight with a weapon in hand, like the legendary warrior Kings like Gustav II Adolf and Karl XII. They rode, shot, and fought with their soldiers, bleeding alongside them, ultimately paying the ultimate price. Why should only Brännström be immortalized in the history books and not him? After all, he was the King of Sweden, not Brännström.

But every time Carl Philip broached the subject with Sweden's Commander-in-Chief, Brännström would steer the conversation away.

"We can't risk anything happening to you. Without your radio addresses, Sweden would fall apart. The people hold the king in the highest regard, and in times of turmoil, it's the king they turn to, as they always have. The National Council respectfully but firmly asks you to refrain. You are essential to keeping this nation together."

King Carl Philip wasn't one to be soothed by flattery. He wanted to fight—this was his one chance in life. Each time they met, he would bring the issue up again until finally, Brännström spoke bluntly, dropping all pretense of diplomacy. After all, Brännström was from northern Sweden, and he didn't mince words.

"Come on, Carl, let's be serious. This won't work. If you're going to lead troops in war, you need the required competence and training. Otherwise, you could be endangered to your soldiers, and I know that's the last thing you'd want. You're a naval officer, and that's completely different from the army."

"I never said I wanted a leadership role. I want to fight alongside everyone else as a regular foot soldier. Or, I mean, infantryman. Rifleman."

"That would be putting the nation at unnecessary risk. If you weigh what you could accomplish as an infantry soldier against the damage to our country if something were to happen to you, you'd come to the same conclusion I have.

"Maybe, but this is personal for me. I want to do my duty for Sweden by fighting! And by the way, I've earned a gold medal in marksmanship with an automatic rifle. What results have you shot?"

"I'll bring it up again at the next council meeting, and we'll see," Brännström mumbled unconvincingly. "It's been a while since I've been to the range, but I think the best I did was silver. I don't remember exactly."

"I have the navy's version of the medal, which is smaller but means the same thing. It's enameled."

"Oh, I thought that was only for serious shooting enthusiasts. If I remember correctly, you've shot gold for at least fifteen years."

"That's right. But I'm not bragging, just letting you know I can be a good soldier."

King Carl Philip realized Brännström was unlikely to discuss the issue with The National Council. He understood Brännström was hiding behind the council because he found it awkward to say no to the king of Sweden. Brännström would likely return with the predictable response that The National Council advised against the king fighting.

There was no point in waiting for a negative answer anyway. Instead, the king decided to pursue a different angle involving Maximilian Adlerswärd. Max had become the most highly regarded special forces soldier in the Swedish military since his heroic actions during the "Kebab War" in Botkyrka the previous year. Max was versatile and invaluable, thanks to his extensive training as a coastal ranger. The fact that he was also the world's top triathlete only added to his mystique. Max had taken on a legendary status and had the freedom to operate as he pleased as long as he was available for the specialized missions that few others could handle.

Max attended staff meetings without restrictions or the need to explain himself to anyone. Max's name was often first suggested when the most challenging assignments arose.

It might have seemed strange that a soldier without an officer's rank had full access to the chiefs of all the military branches, the commander-in-chief, and even the chancellor, but no one questioned it. Those in the highest positions considered it an honor to be in the presence of a living war hero and future legend like Max. Many saw Max as destined for greatness, almost godlike.

And since Max's father was a count, Max held the title too, even though his father was still alive, as the Adlerswärd family had been elevated to count status before the restrictions that came with the Bernadotte dynasty. Strictly speaking, Max should have been addressed as "The Most Noble Mr. Maximilian Adlerswärd," according to noble etiquette, but such formality was not for Max. Raised from childhood in his aristocratic status, he was utterly uninterested in such things. To Max, it didn't matter whether a person was a garbage collector or a count. What he valued were entirely different qualities.

Nevertheless, Max was, of course, acquainted with King Carl Philip. If one were to be precise, it could be argued that the Adlerswärd family was of a higher pedigree than the Bernadotte family. After all, Jean Baptiste Bernadotte came from relatively humble beginnings, much like his former commander, Napoleon Bonaparte.

Napoleon had made meritocracy the new norm in France, breaking away from the traditional hierarchy based on inherited titles. This revolutionary shift allowed the most capable men, like Jean Baptiste Bernadotte, to rise in social rank. Bernadotte carried this meritocratic ideal to Sweden as well. However, when it comes to matters of aristocratic pedigree, tradition and time hold more weight, and the Adlerswärd family had been ennobled a couple of centuries before Jean Baptiste Bernadotte was even born.

Neither Max nor Carl Philip spent much energy worrying about aristocratic status. While they were naturally connected through class and heritage, their age difference meant that they had only exchanged brief greetings at various gatherings over the years—of which there had been many.

Now, though, Max was a grown man, and Carl Philip genuinely enjoyed his company. Max's unpretentious and perhaps slightly naive manner won the king's approval. Max was not impressed by titles, not even the title of king, and he spoke to Carl Philip as casually as he would to anyone else. The two noblemen were similar in spirit—both carried a certain refinement, but neither was particularly interested in it. They had much in common and enjoyed each other's company. However, there was one noticeable difference: while Max was Nordic blond, Carl Philip had the appearance of a southern European. The king wore the Army's 2022 Field Uniform, while Max was dressed in the 2026 ADYK uniform— ADYK standing for "Attack Diver." Like Max, Carl Philip wore no rank insignia on his uniform.

Carl Philip knew that Max essentially planned his operations, meaning he requested—and always received—the material and personnel resources he deemed necessary. Max personally selected the special forces soldiers he wanted for his missions, which sparked an idea in Carl Philip's mind. If Brännström didn't want him on the front lines, maybe Max could use him. A concrete opportunity had arisen in the form of a rescue operation suddenly becoming urgent due to an unfortunate event earlier that morning.

The rescue mission was scheduled for the following day, involving only three people on the ground, plus a helicopter pilot. Max had chosen Carl Philip and the highly regarded coastal ranger Ina Sjöström, with whom he had conducted several successful missions. Sjöström was the army's most skilled sniper, or "*snajper*," as the term was now commonly used in the Swedish military.

The mission was to rescue Colonel Rasmus Wikland, who had the misfortune of being captured by a pair of Muslim sabotage soldiers after they infiltrated the Swedish zone. Wikland had been driving a civilian car on National Highway 21 near the small town of Åstorp when he was stopped. Dressed in uniform with a crown and four stars on his shoulders —signifying his rank as a colonel of the first grade—the Muslim soldiers quickly realized they had captured a high-value target. They managed to transport Colonel Wikland to the Muslim-controlled zone, where he was now being held captive in a building known as Nyvång Mining Museum, a few miles west of Åstorp.

As a local expert in the General Staff, Colonel Wikland possessed critical knowledge about Sweden's strategies, troop positions, weapon stockpiles, and attack plans. If the enemy were to extract this information from him, it would be disastrous. It would force a complete overhaul of the entire war plan, potentially delaying the liberation of Sweden by several months. These delays could cost thousands of Swedish lives and further destroy cultural landmarks.

Although the colonel had been trained to withstand hostile interrogations, it was understood that even the most vital individuals could be broken within a few days. Therefore, it was imperative to rescue him as quickly as possible.

If the interrogators were skilled in chemical interrogation techniques, they might drug him and extract all the necessary information within hours. However, it was unlikely that the Muslims had both the expertise and the essential drugs on hand at that moment.

The hope was that Colonel Wikland was still only undergoing preliminary questioning by the local military command, who might avoid using torture out of fear of reprimand from professional interrogators.

Interrogation experts typically start gently, trying to gain the trust of their subjects and promising rewards in exchange for cooperation. Most subjects begin to talk during this initial phase. However, they often try to withhold the most crucial information—a tactic the interrogators know well—so the pressure gradually increases. The damage could be contained if they could extract the colonel by the following morning, as Max planned.

The entire incident had been captured by Swedish high-altitude drones constantly surveilling the area. Within a few hours of the colonel's capture, Max had been asked whether he could mount a rescue operation on such short notice.

Max's first thought was that the extraction had to be done by helicopter. Once the alarm was raised, it would be impossible to escape by land with the colonel, who might be injured or drugged, especially given the presence of a sizeable Muslim garrison of a few hundred soldiers and some armored vehicles stationed at the strategically important intersection of the European Highway 4 and National Highway 107, just half a mile from Nyvångs Mining Museum. The entire area would be swarming with elite soldiers and jihadists within minutes of the alarm being sounded.

Now, a problem arose. The only helicopter available was an expropriated civilian, Bell 47, owned by an entrepreneur in Hässlehclm. He used it primarily to impress his prospective lovers, often picking them up outside their homes for a shopping trip in Copenhagen.

"What woman says no to a man with a helicopter?" the entrepreneur would boast. "It's expensive to fly but worth every penny!"

A couple of weeks earlier, Max had looked at the helicopter, grinning as he did so. He regarded it almost as a toy, hardly suitable for military use. The Bell 47, aside from unmanned drones, was one of the most miniature helicopters ever made and could carry only one passenger plus the pilot. The occupants were completely exposed under a transparent, thin plexiglass shell. To make matters worse, the helicopter was sixty-five years old and much slower than modern helicopters, with a speed of just a hundred miles per hour. But it flew and could land on the asphalt before the museum entrance.

The catch was that a single enemy combatant with an assault rifle could quickly shoot the helicopter down multiple times over, both during landing and takeoff. It was, therefore, crucial that no enemies were nearby —but how could they ensure that, with soldiers guarding the prisoner inside the building and possibly soldiers on the outside as well?

For once, Max was at a loss. But then he remembered that a couple of the *Snapphane* guerilla fighters had mentioned growing up on farms in the area, and he recalled that one of them had spoken specifically about a place called Nyvång. He had mentioned an old coal mine in the region, which Max figured must be related to the mining museum.

Soon, Max had established radio contact with the man who had mentioned Nyvång, and the conversation immediately sparked an idea. Not only was it the correct mining museum, but it turned out that this *Snapphane* soldier had once worked as the museum's curator and knew almost everything about the building, which had once been the mine's pump house. The pump house had been constructed directly above the mine's first and largest main shaft, which opened the possibility of reaching the site via underground tunnels—and escaping the same way.

Of course, it was theoretically possible to use the mine's tunnels, given that the main shaft was inside the building. The coal mine, which had operated for fifty-five years and produced seven million tons of coal, had left behind thirty miles of tunnels, reaching depths of about five hundred feet. However, only a tiny portion of the tunnels had been mapped, with ninety-five percent remaining uncharted, branching off in a labyrinthine manner in three dimensions.

Nyvång had underground connections with shafts extending nearly six miles to the village of Bjuv. Large sections of these tunnels were perfectly straight, carved out along four relatively thin but mostly linear coal seams. The seam closest to the surface, known as Seam A, had adjoining tunnels that might still be accessible.

Some tunnels were likely not fully flooded near the surface, and there might even be dry sections. However, no one could say for sure, as more than fifty years had passed since the mine's closure. There was a logical reason why the pump house had been the most significant building of the mine. Most of the land above the mine's winding tunnels was unusually clayey and damp farmland, making it difficult for farmers to work. Rainwater would seep into the tunnels, often only a few meters below the surface, causing the pump station to operate at total capacity most of the time.

Seam A's tunnels ran so close to the surface in some places that the ground occasionally subsided, forming small, typically round craters in the landscape. However, the tunnels near the main shaft had been mapped, and the former museum curator had personally explored parts of them. He explained that at least one passage connected to a water-filled hole, which everyone believed was an old marl pit.

Farmers had dug up marl from these pits for centuries to use as a soil conditioner. But this water-filled hole, located in the middle of a field one mile from the mining museum, wasn't a marl pit. It resulted from a forgotten ground collapse seventy years earlier, which the farm's previous owner had understandably kept secret when selling the property to its current owners.

Knowing that Max was a combat diver, the curator suggested using diving gear to access the mining museum from this underwater tunnel. As far as he could recall, this tunnel ran straight from the hole in the field, under the ruins of Västra Broby Church, which had recently been blown up, directly into the main shaft inside the museum. It was like an underground highway.

He believed that a diver with a headlamp would have no trouble finding the target. If Max couldn't locate the main shaft, he could turn back and abort the mission. It was worth a try.

Max was immediately excited by the idea and received a detailed map marking the hole in the field. The hole was almost perfectly circular, measuring a width of about a hundred feet. All Max had to do was dive into the center of the hole, and he would find himself in the tunnel. Everything suggested that he could reach the mining museum and ascend the staircase in the main shaft, leading to a door in one corner of the building.

The staircase was occasionally used by museum visitors who would descend into the shaft to view the fossilized footprints of a dinosaur preserved in coal for seventy million years. Once at the top of the stairs, Max planned to throw in a stun grenade before rushing into the room to neutralize the stunned guards.

So far, the plan seemed straightforward, though the prospect of a one-mile underwater swim commanded a certain respect. He would still need to make the return trip, but he was confident that he had more than enough stamina and would ensure a generous safety margin regarding his oxygen supply.

After eliminating the enemies inside the building, Max would secure the area before the entrance while the helicopter could land and take off with the Colonel. Max himself would then return through the mine tunnel to the starting point without the risk of being pursued. He could swim back calmly, knowing the enemy would not know where he had come from.

However, the plan had one critical flaw. If guards were stationed outside the building, the stun grenade would alert them, allowing them to take down both Max and the helicopter instantly. But Max had solutions to this issue as well. Hidden atop the two hundred feet-high slag heap, just six hundred feet from the museum building, the army's most reliable sniper, Ina Sjöstrand, would cover them from a perfect vantage point.

When the stun grenade detonated, any guards stationed outside would rush toward the entrance, and Sjöstrand would take them out with a few quick shots. At six hundred feet, with support, this would be child's play for a top sniper, and the guards wouldn't have time to realize where the shots were coming from until it was too late.

The remaining challenge was figuring out how he would reach the water-filled hole in the field, carrying the relatively heavy burden of diving gear, grenades, and other necessary equipment. He also needed to consider how Ina Sjöstrand would reach her position atop the slag heap without either of them being detected.

Max scouted the area around the mining museum by approaching it via trails between the fields around Gunnarlunda on a silent, battery-powered, off-road Yamaha bike. He covered the last stretch west of Hyllinge, which was under Muslim control, on foot. There was no clear front line except for the European Highway 4, controlled by the Muslims. Neither the Swedes nor the Muslims paid much attention to the fields between the roads, as the road network was strategically important. Naturally, there was a risk of encountering Muslim patrols in the fields where Max was moving, but it would take a lot for him to be spotted as he cautiously advanced, dressed in black with a hidden face. He was confident he would notice the enemy long before they noticed him.

Soon, he reached the Vege River. Max planned to follow the river, hidden in the dense brush, crossing under the bridge to the other side of the European Highway 4.

Max followed the river under the European Highway 4 without encountering any issues. As expected, he spotted the waterhole about five hundred feet away in the field. It was eerily quiet, as the usual hum of traffic on the European Highway 4 had disappeared with the near-complete absence of vehicles due to the fuel shortage.

A dense brush and small trees surrounded the waterhole, obscuring it from view. One problem, however, was that Max was on the wrong side of the Vege River. The museum curator had mentioned that the river could be waded across, but it turned out to be larger than Max anticipated. After sneaking seven hundred feet upstream, he realized the river was too deep to wade. Swimming across wasn't an option either, given the heavy equipment he needed to transport.

Max understood that he needed a companion to help get the gear across the river. After that, he could manage independently, as he planned to discard the equipment in the waterhole on the way back.

The companion he needed had to be a precise shooter with steady nerves. This person would ride on the back of his motorcycle and could handle any threats if someone tried to stop them, as Max would be focused on driving. Additionally, the shooter could cover him during the short, exposed journey from the river to the waterhole.

The rescue operation was planned in record time and involved only four people: Max, the helicopter pilot; Ina, the sniper stationed on the slag heap; and Max's companion, who had to be quick and effective in unexpected situations.

Max brought along Carl Philip, who had been eager to participate in an operation. Max had complete confidence in Carl Philip's abilities, having observed him during fallow deer hunts on estates in Skåne. Max was impressed by what he had seen. When a herd of fallow deer charges by, it requires quick reflexes and sound judgment to make the right shot. Hunting deer on the run is akin to shooting at a flock of ducks but with the added challenge of using a single bullet instead of a spray of pellets— a pursuit for only the most skilled sharpshooters.

Carl Philip had been trained as a hunter from a young age and even earned his enamel shooting medal. There was hardly anyone Max could trust more, he thought. However, given Carl Philip's accounts of his unsuccessful discussions with Brännström, Max decided to keep the plan a secret. There was no need to mention the involvement of a companion. They could assume that just three people executed the mission.

According to the astronomical calendar, sunrise in Nyvång was scheduled for 6.59 a.m. that day. Given the lack of electric lighting, the helicopter pilot required daylight to navigate and land safely before the museum's entrance. Max estimated he would need thirty to forty minutes for the one-mile dive through the mine tunnel. Once he reached his destination, he could wait in the shaft beneath the museum until it was time, so there was no need to cut the timing too close.

Max decided that the helicopter pilot would begin the short approach at precisely 7.30 a.m. and would only land after receiving a clear signal from Ina Sjöstrand, who would be close enough to hear the stun grenades and observe the situation outside the building. If anything went wrong on the ground, Ina would signal the mission to be aborted before the helicopter attempted to land.

The plan was set. Now, it was time to execute.

Chapter 27 – A Gift from Above

September 10, 2033

Two weeks had passed since Gyllenstierna's escape. By now, Anton Brännström, like the others, knew that Gyllenstierna had managed to reach Berlin with the help of the staff's SK60 aircraft. The conclusion was that Gyllenstierna's Muslim background had led him to despise his war against the Muslims, and his doubts had finally driven him to defect to the enemy.

There are few instances in world history where the highest leader has turned out to be a traitor conspiring with the enemy. Still, curiously enough, the few examples that exist are found in Sweden, Brännström mused. Was there something about Sweden that seemed to attract traitors? This thought led Brännström down a path of reflection.

Thanks to his deep interest in Swedish history, he knew of Queen Christina's conversion and defection to Catholicism in 1654. One didn't need to be a history buff to know about the two most recent traitors, as their betrayals had occurred in modern times.

The former Social Democratic Prime Minister, Stefan Löfven, had been exposed for his secret double dealings with the Muslims, a fact now well-documented and widely known. Together with his wife, the prime minister had done everything in his power to hand his country over to an enemy determined to conquer Sweden and eradicate those Swedes who refused to submit and convert to Islam. What kind of people were these, Brännström wondered? In the cases of Gyllenstierna and Queen Christina, religious doubts had led to their treason, and the dangers of religious contemplation spiraling out of control were well-documented. Some began to believe they were in direct contact with God and saw themselves as His prophets.

Many examples, particularly among clergy who brazenly considered themselves God's representatives on earth. The Church of Sweden had long been working in favor of the Muslims, something Brännström found inexplicable. Perhaps the church's betrayal was also rooted in religious doubts. But as far as Brännström knew, no other Christian church in any other country had converted to Islam, so why Sweden? What made Sweden so unique?

Brännström could only conclude that the indoctrination starting in daycare at the age of one, followed by a lifetime of continued indoctrination through schools and then by state television and the lies of globalist media, left only those with strong personal integrity able to resist in the long run. The masses were easily manipulated into believing almost anything—from witch hunts and fabricated climate theories to the illusion of multiculturalism, all used to steer them in the desired direction.

But the former Social Democratic Prime Minister Stefan Löfven was secular and far too simple-minded to contemplate seriously. Was it some unknown form of mental illness? Or perhaps poisoning with an unknown substance that allowed others to take over the brain? No matter how much Brännström pondered the prime minister's motives, he couldn't understand it. After all, he couldn't possibly be so mind-bogglingly stupid as not to understand the consequences of his actions. Or could he?

Recent events in the war had occupied entirely Brännström's attention. He hadn't had much time to consider how the country should be governed now that the highest position, the chancellor, was vacant. He realized that he should have taken some action. Two weeks is a long time during the critical period when new power must establish itself after a dictator's fall. Perhaps it was already too late, Brännström thought. He might be in for an unpleasant surprise at the next National Council meeting. Could he even face a coup and be removed from power? He knew he should go into the meeting with a plan, but he had no such plan. It would have to be an open discussion. At least he felt secure knowing the military was on his side. But even he wasn't entirely sure what he wanted.

As the visit was expected, a knock on the door opened without his permission. His secretary ushered in the guest, the head of the NRSS, the National Council's Special Security Service.

Gyllenstierna had created the NRSS as his personal security service and bodyguard unit. Gyllenstierna had handpicked the head of the NRSS, but information about who had been given the role had yet to be provided. The NRSS was an open security service because its existence wasn't secret. Still, no official information had been communicated, and

Brännström hadn't paid much attention, trusting that Gyllenstierna and the NRSS had been working for Sweden's best interests. But had that been the case?

Brännström extended his hand and greeted the somewhat slender, suit-clad man standing before him, who introduced himself as Ken Persson—a name that meant nothing to Brännström. He had expected that he would have at least heard the name mentioned before.

They sat down around a small, round table with compact leather armchairs. There's something particular about the expression in his eyes, thought Brännström. Wide-open eyes that seemed to lead directly into a rather brilliant mind capable of processing information at incredible speeds.

"Welcome to my humble abode," Brännström began politely. "We probably should have met long ago, but the war consumes all my time. Besides, I didn't even know who was in charge of the NRSS."

"Thank you. I felt it was time to establish a relationship now that Gyllenstierna had suddenly and unexpectedly fled. As you can see, I'm the head of the NRSS, and I would very much like to continue in that role, but as it is now, the NRSS lacks a clear directive."

"We can certainly address that, provided the NRSS serves an important and necessary function. After all, we already have three other security services that could potentially take over its duties. Can you explain, as thoroughly as possible, your background and how your collaboration with Gyllenstierna was conducted? Then, I want to know everything about what the NRSS does daily and who is part of its organization. But first, I'd like some personal references since I haven't heard of you before."

"Bertil Wiklund and Rudolf Enbom can vouch for me."

Brännström was visibly startled, and Persson could see the surprise in his wide eyes.

"Yes, those are quite the references. Two members of the National Council! I assume Alfred Baksi must also know you, considering both Wiklund and Enbom report to him as heads of MUST and FRA, respectively."

"No, not at all. We've deliberately kept him out of the loop to avoid unnecessarily spreading information about my existence. But Wiklund and Enbom have known me since my time in the military. They're largely responsible for shaping who I am today."

"What about Bianca Popovic? Does she know who you are?"

"I don't believe so, and honestly, I have serious doubts about Popovic in general. She's not up to the task. I think she should be removed. She makes too many mistakes. Look at the blunder when she sent her agents after Gyllenstierna's double. Only Popovic went into that trap. We can't afford mistakes like that."

Brännström was taken aback by the audacity of this seemingly mild-mannered man. Still, he couldn't help being impressed by Persson's candid opinions about the inner workings of the National Council. Persson didn't mention that he had orchestrated the scenario, ensuring that SÄPO agents would follow Gyllenstierna's double.

"So, who should take over SÄPO if Popovic is out?"

"Naturally, I would," Persson replied bluntly, startling Brännström. "I know more about SÄPO's operations than anyone else, including Popovic."

"One thing I've been wondering about is who the security services are monitoring. Was anyone watching Gyllenstierna? Were you?"

"A sacred rule in all intelligence work is that you never, under any circumstances, monitor your employer. Anyone caught doing that is in serious trouble. So, the answer is no," Persson lied.

"So, you wouldn't monitor me if we were to collaborate?"

"No. It's not even a consideration."

Ken Persson was surprisingly eloquent and talkative, which caught Brännström off guard. Intelligence officers traditionally pride themselves on saying only what's necessary, but that rule didn't apply to Persson. Persson was charming and forthcoming, unlike the usual stiff and somewhat dull intelligence chiefs.

Persson provided a mix of broad information and intriguing details about various individuals. Brännström quickly realized that Persson's knowledge of everyone in critical positions in Sweden was invaluable. He soon decided that not only would the NRSS continue to operate, but it would also receive increased resources, with Brännström serving as its direct supervisor.

"What about Baksi? He's the head of both MUST and what's left of FRA after the reorganization the Russians forced on us. What's your take on that?"

"If you ask me, I'm not entirely comfortable with a Muslim, or possibly a former Muslim, holding that position. The situation with Gyllenstierna should have taught us something. I consider Baksi loyal, but he could challenge you for power in the right situation. Do you want to empower someone who could potentially threaten you?"

"That's something to think about," Brännström replied thoughtfully. "I've been entirely focused on the war, assuming that Gyllenstierna—that traitor—was handling everything else. But I suppose I need to rethink that now."

"Yes, you do, if you don't want to be outmaneuvered as changes happen. Don't forget, Baksi was Gyllenstierna's right-hand man. They were old friends. Where do Baksi's loyalties lie now?"

"Ken," Brännström said quietly, leaning forward over the table to prevent anyone from overhearing despite the empty room. "I have to say, you're a godsend. I need your insights and knowledge. I want us to form a pact and keep control so things don't spiral out of hand."

Ken Persson looked pleased. Brännström had taken the bait, just as expected. The two men spent the next three hours laying out Brännström's strategy for the following day's National Council meeting.

Brännström felt thoroughly satisfied with the day's progress. He was well-prepared for the upcoming meeting. The only thing that nagged at him slightly was the realization, after Persson had left, that he still didn't know much about him. Despite Persson's long-winded discussion, even about himself, he had skillfully avoided any personal questions. In truth, Brännström still didn't know who Ken Persson was, but that would sort itself out in time. One thing was clear: Persson was one of the most intelligent people Brännström had ever met, and together, they would be a force no one could reckon with.

Everything went exactly as planned at the National Council meeting the next day. Brännström surprised everyone by immediately taking command in a way that left no room for dissent. Everyone knew what had happened to those who had challenged Gyllenstierna, and they sensed it was safest to maneuver carefully and follow the man who had the entire military behind him: Anton Brännström.

The meeting concluded with a decisive resolution: effective immediately, Brännström was appointed chancellor indefinitely while retaining his position as supreme commander. He also assumed direct control over the NRSS. To underscore the significance of these changes, it was decided that the NRSS would be renamed the Systemic Security Service, abbreviated as the SS.

Three individuals were cast out into the cold. Rudolf Enbom was deemed too closely associated with the old FRA and, not least in the eyes of the Russians, unsuitable for rebuilding the new, Russia-friendly FRA, now renamed RA—short for Radio Agency. The new RA would operate under Brännström's jurisdiction.

It was also decided that Naval Chief Fridolf Palmquist would leave the National Council, justified by the new policy that heads of individual military branches should not hold seats on the council. Palmquist, a war hero highly esteemed by the public, would continue his duties as Naval Chief. His departure from the council was attributed solely to new strategic guidelines and had nothing to do with his performance—or so it was said.

Responsibility for SÄPO was transferred to Brännström, resulting in Bianca Popovic's dismissal. Both Popovic and Enbom were placed under indefinite house arrest. While neither had committed any misconduct, it was deemed necessary to incapacitate them until the passage of time diminished their influence.

When a prominent and influential figure exits the stage, new alliances and configurations quickly replace the old ones. So-called bonds of friendship often prove worthless once the change occurs and the old friend can no longer advance one's career.

Björn Väster, tasked with overseeing the neutralization of Popovic and Enbom, estimated that six months under house arrest would suffice to render them obsolete. Afterward, SÄPO would watch them, with monthly check-ins typically enough to deter any state-hostile plans. Given their years of loyal public service, they might be offered positions within civilian agencies or government departments. Unlike Gyllenstierna,

Brännström was keen on avoiding creating unnecessary enemies—especially mortal ones.

The National Council had now shrunk to four members: Anton Brännström, Alfred Baksi, Bertil Wiklund, and Björn Väster. In the longer term, Brännström and Persson planned to maintain a core group of three, including Wiklund and Väster, whose loyalty was beyond doubt, while gradually sidelining Baksi.

Alfred Baksi's position had been weakened by his loss of control over the FRA. Due to his close association with Gyllenstierna, the plan was to push Baksi out within six months slowly. Gaining control over MUST was imperative, but for now, Baksi's position was too strong to challenge directly; he could potentially mobilize enough military force to attempt a coup, a risk they weren't willing to take.

Soon, Sweden would be governed by a triumvirate wielding complete control over the military, intelligence services, and police. Those who could read the signs realized the country was moving toward an outright dictatorship under the autocratic rule of Anton Brännström.

But lurking in the shadows was a superior, computer-like mind processing thoughts at lightning speed. That mind belonged to Brännström's secret advisor, Ken Persson, who subtly pulled the strings. The real question was: who honestly governed the country?

For now, Brännström and Persson were satisfied with the situation—except for Baksi's remaining presence on the National Council. But that, too, could change at the right moment, a moment that Ken Persson would determine.

Chapter 28 – Operation Exemption

September 11, 2033

At 4 a.m., Max flipped the switch to the driving mode. Once Carl Philip was securely seated, Max twisted the throttle of the Yamaha off-road bike, sending the royal and noble duo silently into motion, thanks to the quiet electric motor. Their gear was tightly packed in black plastic on either side of the bike, and both men were dressed entirely in black with their faces blackened. Even the motorcycle had been sprayed black down to the spokes. Max carried his AK5 slung over his shoulder with the stock folded while Carl Philip held his AK5 ready in his hands.

In the dense darkness, they were nearly impossible to spot. It's as if the nights in Skåne are darker than anywhere else, a phenomenon due to the thick fog that often blankets the fields at night. Visibility was reduced to just a few feet, and dense fog combined with darkness placed high demands on Max's navigation skills. If they were discovered, they hoped that whoever found them would ask questions before shooting, a reasonable expectation since they could just as easily be mistaken for Muslim fighters as Swedish operatives.

They rode slowly and steadily, rarely exceeding ten miles per hour on the trails and only about five miles per hour when cutting across the fields. If needed, the bike could accelerate to a hundred miles per hour in seconds. It was crucial to avoid hitting any cultivated fields, where they would instantly get bogged down in the mud, but the stubble-covered ground was firm and flat, perfect for travel. Max had memorized the entire route and felt confident he could find the way. A wrong turn could jeopardize the whole operation.

Everything proceeded according to plan, and they almost enjoyed the ride, even though they were on high alert. But as they neared their destination west of the village Hyllinge, Max spotted a couple of vehicles with headlights parked on the bridge that crossed European Highway 4, which they were supposed to pass under. What were they doing there in the middle of the night? Max stopped and thought for a few seconds, pointing out the vehicles on the bridge.

"Damned, what are they doing there?" Max whispered. "Right up on the bridge, we're supposed to go under."

Max decided to stick to the plan. Unless the Muslims had dogs, which they rarely did, they should be able to sneak under the bridge through the vegetation without any issues. Crossing the Vege River should be doable without being detected, given the darkness and the dense vegetation extending over the river from both sides. The visible water surface was only two to three meters wide. But it might be best to cross the river several hundred feet upstream from the original plan. Max cautiously accelerated to cross the small Ådals Road between two farms. He knew ditches were on both sides of the road, so he crept forward, standing on the foot pegs to maintain balance. Just as they came onto the road, a voice suddenly roared out of the darkness, only a few feet away.

"Stop, or I'll shoot to kill!"

Max brought the bike to a halt in the middle of the road, facing the voice that had cut through the darkness with a thick, guttural accent from Malmö's public housing projects.

"Stay where you are and put your hands over your head!"

In the pitch-black night, it was impossible to tell that two people were on the bike. Max leaned forward just as the sentry switched on a flashlight. Carl Philip fired a short burst, and the two shadowy figures on the road collapsed. They could only hope that the men they shot were enemy soldiers.

Max gunned the engine, speeding north along Ådalsvägen to get out of firing range in case of more enemies. At the same time, he saw the two vehicles on the bridge start moving toward the spot where the shots had been fired, but they couldn't descend from European Highway 4 due to guardrails and deep ditches. The vehicles crept along the highway's edge, scanning the fields with powerful searchlights. Max continued until they reached the river, where they concealed the bike as best they could in a thicket.

The dead bodies on Ådalsvägen would be discovered soon, and a thorough search along the river was likely the next step. It was almost sure the bike would be found by daylight, which meant the planned retreat was no longer an option. They'd have to improvise.

With the bridge now clear, they moved swiftly along the river, hidden within the dense undergrowth, and soon reached the opposite side of the European Highway 4 by the riverbank. The only concern was that they startled some ducks and pheasants, which could have drawn the enemy's attention, but it seemed no one was left on the bridge.

Max handed Carl Philip the end of the cable with the carabiner and waded into the river, slipping smoothly into the water. The cold was barely noticeable, thanks to the dry suit he wore under his clothes. He reached the other side with a few solid strokes and climbed onto the opposite bank, beginning to reel in the cable attached to his belt. The package of equipment obediently followed at his feet within seconds. He unhooked the carabiner and tossed it back across the river, where Carl Philip was ready with the second package. Max slung the two packages over his shoulders, scrambled up the slope, and began jogging across the field, covering the five hundred feet toward the waterhole. The wheat stubble still stood on the unplowed field, making his progress easier.

As he approached the waterhole, he noticed some activity, likely caused by the animals that always sought refuge in the small biotopes around the fields. A deer bolted across the other side of the waterhole, but he could only see it as a fleeting shadow once it had moved further out onto the field. He heard the rustling of pheasants scurrying through the bushes and the rapid wingbeats of a flock of partridges taking flight. It struck him how much noise such small birds could make, a thought he'd had many times during his bird-hunting expeditions, where he'd bagged countless partridges and even more pheasants.

He shoved his AK5 deep into a dense bush, along with the meal pack that would give him energy when he returned. For now, he'd have to rely on his short-barreled Smith & Wesson M&P Shield, which, thanks to its partially composite plastic frame, weighed hardly half a pound when fully loaded with a round in the chamber and seven in the magazine. The pistol was popular among those who carried a concealed weapon daily, tucked in a shoulder holster under a jacket. It was sometimes jokingly referred to as a "lady's pistol" because its size and weight made it ideal for a handbag.

Max thought that the nine-millimeter pistol might not be much in a military firefight, but it was certainly better than nothing. He tightened the straps, securing the holster to his right calf. If everything went according to plan, the toy-like firearm would be more than sufficient. He had eight rounds at his disposal, as he had opted to forego extra ammo due to weight concerns.

In a waterproof pouch strapped to his back, just below the compact oxygen tank, he carried two flashbang grenades, officially known as M84s. The M84 contained a magnesium-based explosive encased in a thin layer of aluminum housed in a perforated steel shell designed to prevent deadly shrapnel. The detonation was a deflagration, a slower explosion meant to minimize the impact of the blast wave. Those caught in the blast would be temporarily paralyzed but without suffering severe or permanent injuries.

When an M84 detonates, it produces a blinding flash and an ear-splitting bang. The flash activates all the photoreceptor cells in the eyes, causing a brief "freeze-frame" effect that temporarily blinds the target. The loud bang can cause ear injuries and disrupt the fluid in the inner ear, affecting the target's balance and creating a sensation of vertigo, where they feel like they're spinning uncontrollably.

As Max donned his swim fins on his hands and feet, he noticed a flock of mallards, which had been huddled in the small lagoon, take flight. Meanwhile, a few hares and a rabbit darted across the field. It felt like a zoo, but he had learned that the lush agricultural landscape of Skåne, a veritable cornucopia, was always teeming with wildlife. He heard an owl hooting above him, possibly about to snatch a panicked rabbit for breakfast, but the sky was still too dark to spot it.

Max thought that an alert sentry on the highway couldn't miss the commotion on the field. Even a city dweller would sense that something unusual was happening, but Muslims weren't exactly known for being nature enthusiasts, so he guessed he was still undetected.

Just then, he heard a short burst of gunfire from the direction of the river. All he could do was hope the shots came from Carl Philip's AK5. Max knew Carl Philip might be in trouble but had to focus on his mission. Still, he couldn't shake the thought of what Brännström would say if Carl Philip didn't return.

Chapter 29 – The Finspång Trials

2033

At the very first meeting of the National Council on January 2, 2033, in the Council Chamber at the Stockholm Town Hall, Alfred Baksi was assigned the critical task of drafting a legal package addressing various degrees of treason. Baksi quickly established a special national legislative council composed of six top legal experts, with Baksi as chairman. In March, the National Council adopted the Legislative Council's proposal. The sixty-page document began with a summary, which was the only part read by the other members of the National Council, although a few claimed to have read the entire legal text:

· First Degree Treason: Punishment: Execution by firing squad.

· Second-Degree Treason: Punishment: 10 years in prison, revocation of citizenship, and lifetime expulsion after serving a sentence.

· Collaboration with Muslim organizations and promotion of Islam: Punishment: 4 years in prison, revocation of citizenship, and lifetime expulsion after serving a sentence.

· Collusion: Punishment: Revocation of citizenship and lifetime expulsion.

· Dissemination of grossly anti-Swedish Information: Punishment: Revocation of citizenship and lifetime expulsion.

· Dissemination of anti-Swedish Information: Punishment: Two years in prison.

· Anti-Swedish Activities in a position of trust or general promotion of Islam: Punishment: Two years in prison.

The new laws were retroactive for ten years. The statute of limitations for future violations was set at ten years, except for crimes involving treason, which would never be subject to a statute of limitations. The legal package, popularly known as the "Treason Laws," applied only to Swedes. Muslim residents in Sweden were not affected by the treason laws but were dealt with through the so-called "Procession for Oath of Allegiance" carried out by Björn Väster.

The Legislative Council estimated that the new laws would affect approximately eighty thousand Swedes in the liberated areas, with about fifty thousand concerning the two laws with the lowest penalties. According to the Legislative Council's preliminary calculations, around five thousand Swedes would be executed for first-degree treason, and about twenty-five thousand would be sentenced under laws that included lifetime expulsion from the kingdom. It later turned out that the number of executions was almost twice as high as expected, while the other figures matched the estimates reasonably well.

Most of those to be scrutinized were politicians and employees within the state, municipalities, and county councils, particularly those in leadership positions. Many in the business sector were also scrutinized and risked being brought to trial, usually those in leading roles such as CEOs and communication directors.

In terms of violations of the law on the dissemination of anti-Swedish information, those affected were naturally individuals who, in their professional capacity, created and spread information: journalists, editors, public relations officers, teachers, priests, PR consultants, authors, film directors, and various cultural workers.

Many older, love-starved women on the left, commonly referred to as "batik witches" in popular language, were believed to have promoted illegal immigration and kept young Muslim immigrants as their taxpayer-funded lovers. They were subject to a particular clause in the collaborator law, which stripped them of their citizenship and imposed a sentence of lifetime expulsion.

Similar to the so-called "German girls" in Norway, who had relationships with German soldiers during the occupation 1940-1945, these women were so despised that they were forced to flee their hometowns in panic. Those who didn't escape in time were severely beaten by enterprising locals or lynched to death by enraged mobs.

The investigations were carried out by SÄPO, which received significantly increased resources for this purpose. Arrests and temporary detention in holding camps, however, were handled by the Police and, when necessary, by the National Task Force, both of which were under Björn Väster's command.

In addition to creating the legal framework and structure, Alfred Baksi's assignment was to oversee the practical execution of the treason trials. This required a large operation employing 650 staff, including 240 lawyers and a security force of 50 soldiers, with the remainder being administrators and support personnel.

The first step was to find a suitable location for the so-called people's tribunal where the traitors would be tried and sentenced. The choice fell on the town of Finspång. The trials, which would last nearly three years, were soon called the "Finspång Trials."

In Finspång, Baksi's criteria for the tribunal's location were met. The geographic area was well-balanced, considering the thousands of people transported to the tribunal from the north and the south. The Muslim occupation zone was west of the Grand Lake of Vättern.

Baksi's instructions from the National Council specified that the chosen site should have old, historical significance, which was seen as an important symbolic issue. The location also needed to have avoided destruction by the war, which ruled out many alternatives.

Finspång is situated at the short connection between the elongated lakes Skutbosjön and Bönnern, where a footbridge over the narrow stream between the lakes has facilitated passage since ancient times. A bridge has likely existed over this water obstacle along this natural route for as long as people have lived there, which means many thousands of years—the earliest texts mentioning the bridge date back to the thirteenth century. The prefix "Fin-," pronounced "Finn," is believed to derive from the Swedish word "finna" – meaning "find," suggesting that it might have been a challenge for travelers unfamiliar with the area to find the small bridge. Although foreigners built and developed the city, the town's old industrial setting provided the perfect, authentic atmosphere. In Finspång, the Flemish immigrant Louis De Geer, sometimes called the father of the Swedish industry, developed the metal industry with the help of skilled blacksmiths recruited from Wallonia, the French-speaking part of present-day Belgium. Appropriately, the mass production of rifle bullets had been one of the town's specialties.

Baksi couldn't help but notice that Finspång, once built by immigrants, made him reflect on why the nation of Sweden had essentially committed voluntary suicide by allowing incompetent and hostile people to immigrate into the country. Nothing could accelerate development in the right direction more quickly than immigration, and it was thoroughly proven that nothing could destroy a well-functioning society as rapidly as the wrong kind of immigration.

Finspång Castle, situated on a small, oval-shaped island resembling an elongated horse racing track, was ideal for the tribunal's activities. The island's picturesque and historic surroundings provided the exact sense of solemnity and timelessness that the National Council sought. The council members were very enthusiastic about Baksi's choice.

With its imposing round tower at the center of the front facade, the stunning castle served excellently as a prison, holding a couple of hundred prisoners at a time while they awaited trial. The guard force and service personnel were housed in the guest wing. At the same time, the organization's leadership and locally present judges and prosecutors resided in the town at the Hotel De Geer, conveniently within walking distance from the castle. This entire setup ensured efficient and swift proceedings, which was necessary given the large number of defendants who needed to be tried, sentenced, and have their sentences executed.

Most trials were conducted in various meeting rooms in the small town. These trials typically involved eight to ten people, including the prosecutor, defense attorney, and judge. The remaining participants were the defendants, who were often sentenced when the charges were the same and always behind closed doors. The National Council's stance was that there was no purpose in making these trials public. The priority was speed, both in delivering verdicts and in executing sentences. Acquittals were rare but did occur daily. The rulings of the people's tribunal could not be appealed.

However, the National Council's approach was the opposite regarding treason cases. These trials were held in the Pentecostal Church on the road called De Besche-vägen, which had ample seating for the state-controlled media, relatives, and the public and were often well-attended. Trying traitors in an open court was to set an example for the Swedish people. Many defendants were well-known figures who had held high positions and attracted significant public interest.

Opposite the castle, on the other side of the oval lawn, a hundred-foot-long sand barrier was erected to catch the bullets during executions by firing squad. The fact that prisoners in the castle could hear the gunshots and, from their cells, witness the executions with their own eyes was considered an extra punishment. They could sweat it out while they awaited their verdicts.

A concrete slab was poured before the sand barrier, with floor drains spaced every ten feet. The fire hoses used after each execution produced large amounts of water channeled into the river through a well-insulated drainage pipe that lay exposed on the ground. The pipe ended in a shallow, two-foot-deep basin, about three square feet in size, near the riverbank before the water eventually flowed into the river. A fine mesh screen covered the entrance to the final section of the pipe to catch body fragments, preventing river contamination. The bottom of the small basin was lined with a sieve, which was cranked up daily and cleared of body fragments, mainly consisting of bits of flesh and small bone pieces. These fragments were buried alongside the bodies of the deceased.

Ten slim iron posts were fastened to the concrete slab two feet before the sand barrier. The steel posts were only waist-high, with a metal ring welded at the top, to which the condemned were shackled, hands bound behind their backs, as they awaited the gunshots. Since the shots were aimed at chest height, there was no risk of ricochets. The entire setup was designed with industrial efficiency and modern environmental considerations. There could be no bottlenecks with the need to execute thousands of traitors.

Although the execution site was designed to handle up to ten simultaneous executions, it proved more practical to carry out the shootings one by one. Those sentenced to death were taken to the island immediately after their sentence was handed down at the Pentecostal Church, with little reason to delay the execution beyond the brief fifteen minutes allotted for a personal conversation with the priest in the chapel.

However, on rare occasions, such as when all employees of a department or in a newspaper received death sentences, group executions were carried out. Images of a row of shackled victims, both before and after execution, were used for propaganda purposes to deter potential opposition figures contemplating coups.

Initially, the executions were carried out by six sharpshooters, firing at eighty feet, with one of the rifles, in keeping with historical tradition, loaded with blank ammunition. But after a month, for practical reasons, the process was streamlined: three marksmen fired three live rounds each from only fifteen feet away, using automatic fire aimed at the victim's chest.

Nine bullets from AK5 rifles would turn the chest into a bloody mess, resulting in instantaneous death. The nine almost simultaneous impacts would occasionally cause the torso to explode from the immense kinetic energy, creating violent pressure waves within the body. In some instances, the chest cavity was blown open so forcefully that the entire heart-lung package was expelled, left dangling by the trachea and aorta outside the body, continuing to pump out cascades of blood from the still-beating heart for several seconds. Such rare and spectacular hits were referred to as "fountain orgasms" and often provoked a great deal of grim humor. Not a single one of the 9,553 executions carried out failed.

To spare the executioners from the condemned's final stares, thick black nylon hoods were always placed over the victims' heads before they were led to the execution site, known simply as the "firing range" by the staff. The thick hood also shielded the shooters from hearing the last words of the condemned, which could be accusations, pleas, curses, prayers, sobs, wails, or religious and political songs.

The firing squads were rotated daily to avoid putting too much strain on the shooters' psyches. After each execution, the shooters were responsible for removing the deceased's body and hosing down the concrete slab with fire hoses. This task was also handled with practical efficiency. Since the victims were shackled to the iron posts with their hands behind their backs, their bodies remained standing after the execution.

After the execution, the shooters placed a low cart in front of the body, with a platform only about four inches above the ground. The body would fall naturally onto the cart when the shackles were released. Often, no additional handling was required before the cart was wheeled down a slightly sloped asphalt path, ultimately dumping the body onto a truck parked on a connecting road below. Everything was meticulously planned, efficient, and functional.

At 6 p.m. every day, the truck carrying the executed bodies drove to the minefield Storgruvefältet in the village of Doverstorp, four miles south of Finspång, where the bodies were dumped into the former mine Krokgruvan. This five-hundred-foot-deep open pit had been used for extracting magnetite and hematite for five hundred years before mining operations ceased in the mid-eighteen hundreds. The bodies were layered with debris, pushed down by loaders from the massive spoil heaps left over from the mining. The location was well-chosen, as the three hundred feet-long pit was more than sufficient, and if needed, the nearby mines Storgruvan and Kettilgruvan pits could also be used. When the people's tribunal in Finspång finally closed, the bodies would be covered with a thirty-foot-thick layer of debris, rendering them forever inaccessible to animals and humans.

On average, nearly ten executions were carried out daily at the firing range at Finspång's Castle. The entire procedure, including shackling, execution by firing squad, unshackling, hosing down, and removing the body, took less than ten minutes. The daily pay for the shooters was five times higher than the standard rate, which led many soldiers to request more extended service as executioners, enticed by the income potential and the fact that the actual work only lasted just over an hour each day. The rest of the time, they could relax and do as they pleased as long as they remained on the island. However, the maximum length of service was limited to ten days due to the risk of lasting psychological damage.

The vast and elaborate castle chapel, which in terms of size could almost be called a church, was well-suited to the task. Executions were generally preceded by the condemned—if they wished—having the opportunity to listen to the priest's comforting words about God's forgiveness, regardless of the evil deeds they had committed.

The large altarpiece depicting the seven angels carrying the cross of redemption for fallen humanity often inspired deep existential reflection among those condemned, who knew their lives would soon end. Shots were typically fired within five minutes after the conversation with the priest.

However, not all traitors to the nation were given the dubious mercy of a quick and painless death by firing squad. In the utmost secrecy, a militant group of Sweden supporters within the extremist right-wing movement had compiled a so-called blacklist containing the names of particularly despised enemies of the people. This list, which received approval from Björn Väster without him even wanting to see it, included a few hundred individuals, including twenty ministers, two of whom were former prime ministers. Most of the names on the list were at least somewhat known to the public.

Björn Väster, who was reluctant to involve himself with such a sensitive matter, arranged for the person responsible for the list to meet with Ernst Höök, the leader of the National Guard, commonly known as the Yellow Vests. Those on the blacklist were not apprehended by Björn Väster's police force, unlike other traitors. Instead, they were captured by the special task force of the National Guard, which acted as Höök's secret police, operating under the radar and without their usual yellow vests. The arrests were carried out as discreetly as possible, either at the individuals' homes or on the street, where they were quickly bound and thrown into a white van with fake license plates.

Those captured from the blacklist were not imprisoned in Finspång's Castle with the other traitors. Instead, they were taken, without any formal detention, directly to the ancient execution site in Rökstorps Mo, eight miles south of Finspång, where a people's tribunal—better described as a frenzied mob—awaited to judge them. Rökstorps Mo, an isolated forest clearing by a low cliff, was one of three hundred execution sites in Sweden in the seventeen hundreds.

The first sight that usually greeted the captive was the remains of a previously executed and mutilated body, often left to rot as a warning. This gruesome scene was meant to instill terror in the prisoner.

The so-called trial was nothing more than a prolonged reading of the prisoner's crimes against the Swedish people, delivered in the form of screaming tirades and crude insults—often in front of a cheering, hate-filled mob—using vivid descriptions like louse, rat, snake, cockroach, or parasite. The prisoner was given no opportunity to defend or explain themselves. The death sentence was a foregone conclusion.

As the death sentence was pronounced, the condemned would often turn pale or, in some cases, faint from the fear of what was to come. To maximize the terror, the execution method was described in detail, following ancient Swedish practices.

For men, the first step in the execution was the breaking of their bodies. The condemned would be strapped to a frame, and the executioner would then crush their bones with violent blows using a thick club. An axe or iron bar was used earlier, but the club was easier to handle for the modern-day executioners, who often lacked experience with such tools. On the occasions when the former heavyweight boxer Ernst Höök was present, he usually chose to act as the executioner himself. He would don a pair of thin boxing gloves, typically used for training on a speed bag, and unleash a series of vicious blows on the victim's body. His powerful punches usually caused internal organs like the liver and spleen to rupture. Afterward, he would take up a heavy club to complete the execution by breaking the shoulders, forearms, elbows, hips, knees, ankles, shins, and thigh bones.

Höök made sure to be on hand, acting as a ruthless and ferocious executioner when the two former prime ministers were to be executed. At these two executions, the gathered mob numbered over five hundred people, who gleefully and laughingly enjoyed the spectacle, which was also filmed. At the same time, insults and spit rained down on the unfortunate victims.

A particularly hated and despised figure brought to Rökstorps Mo was the so-called Media Inspector, Öberg, a self-appointed opinion police funded by the Ministry of Culture, who for many years hunted down people expressing anti-regime or nationalist views on social media. The far-left and pro-Islam organization Expo also contributed to funding this obscure enforcer of opinions.

Those caught with the wrong opinions were reported to the police by the Media Inspector for Incitement to Racial Hatred, resulting in thousands of excellent and law-abiding Swedish taxpayers being summoned for police questioning and having their DNA swabbed. Some of them were even fined.

The Media Inspector Öberg, who himself had been convicted of animal cruelty, fraud, and possession of child pornography, also took the opportunity to sue his victims for defamation in cases where they had commented on his despicable behavior. Sweden's politically charged judicial system and media eagerly supported Öberg, making him somewhat wealthy from the damages awarded to him. However, he made the most money through secret support from various Muslim organizations.

In Rökstorps Mo, time finally caught up with the Media Inspector, as he paid the price for his private war against the Swedish people with an especially gruesome execution ritual. The ritual began with removing his ears, nose tip, and tongue. His eyes were then burned out with heated iron rods before an exceptionally prolonged execution by breaking began, followed by dismemberment with a chainsaw and culminating in quartering. Only fifteen enemies of the people were hated enough to be sentenced to execution through this particularly cruel and painful ritual. The most well-known was TV personality Robert Schwansberg, also chairman of the Swedish Publicist Association. Schwansberg had made himself rich and famous by persecuting and harassing good Swedes who dared to protest against the Islamization of their country.

The condemned needed to remain conscious when they were finally beheaded, so no blows were directed at the head or chest. After the head was severed from the body, which often required more than one swing of the broad executioner's axe, the body was quartered, meaning it was cut lengthwise and crosswise using the axe and a large bow saw, initially designed for cutting logs. After a few weeks, they switched to using chainsaws to divide the bodies, which was much more accessible. However, when the fuel shortage became too severe, the bow saw was brought back into use. Each of the four severed body parts had a limb protruding.

Finally, the four body parts were impaled on sharp stakes fixed in the ground. The head was placed on a stake fitted with a specially designed iron hook. The unfortunate women who were brought to the execution site in Rökstorps Mo fared slightly better, as they were traditionally burned alive at the stake without having to endure execution by breaking their bodies. Perhaps the word "rök" (smoke) in the place named Rökstorps Mo originated from the blazing pyres of these women.

The remains of the human bodies were eventually dumped, along with all the other bodies from the firing range at Finspång's Castle, into the nearby mine Krokgruvan.

Chapter 30 – Sniping

September 11, 2033

Ina Sjöstedt entered the Muslim-occupied zone on foot, under the cover of darkness. Like her fellow operatives, she had carefully studied the map and meticulously planned her much shorter route across the fields. Dressed in black and with a balaclava pulled over her face, she moved stealthily through the night, making it highly unlikely that she would be detected.

Along the way, she spotted two Muslim outposts, which she easily bypassed. The posted soldiers gave themselves away from a distance. Cigarettes were being smoked, their scent carrying far in the almost windless night, and their glowing cigarettes shone like beacons in the darkness. There was loud laughter, and it was so unprofessional and arrogant. The soldiers did not fear any enemy attacks in the area. Ina's ears, nose, and eyes picked up on their presence from at least three hundred feet away.

She was tempted to punish the overconfident soldiers with a surprise attack, but she had a more important mission to complete. They wouldn't have stood a chance against her, and she knew it.

The slag heap was taller than she had anticipated, but a narrow path was winding up to the top, where some vegetation provided cover. At one point, she accidentally nudged a stone that rolled away, which could also be caused by a badger or some other nocturnal animal. The sound in the otherwise silent night didn't elicit any reaction from anywhere.

Just after 4 a.m., she reached the top of the slag heap and prepared to wait until something started happening down at the mining museum, which she still couldn't see. It was nearly three and a half hours until the helicopter was scheduled to take off. She unfolded the rifle's bipod and set it beside her.

By 6.20 a.m., it had lightened enough for her to make out the outline of the building six hundred feet away. She could feel her body slipping into that particular state she relished—where everything was on the line.

Before the war, she had gotten her adrenaline kicks from free climbing in the Alps. She preferred solo climbs, especially at night when alone on the rock faces. It forced her to rely on herself in every detail and every situation. If she fell to die, there would be no point in blaming the circumstances. It was all about maintaining control and never letting up for a second. Everything depended on her, and that's how she liked it. Let others blame external factors; she had no interest in that.

Automatic weapons are far too imprecise for sniping. When it comes to precision shooting, it's all about single shots with a bolt-action rifle. Among the world's top snipers, there are many different preferred weapons, and Ina had test-fired most of them, except for the Russian and Chinese models, which were harder to come by. Ina favored the Swedish Army's Precision Sniper Rifle 19, commonly known as the PSG 19.

The PSG 19 is a bolt-action rifle with a rotating bolt mechanism, capable of holding nine rounds in its magazine. The special under-caliber sniper ammunition provides a high muzzle velocity, resulting in a flatter trajectory and less sensitivity to wind. The bolt movement required to chamber a new round is concise, ensuring the shooter's position isn't disturbed before the next shot. Although the PSG 19 is built on an aluminum frame, making it unusually lightweight for a sniper rifle, it still weighs over thirteen pounds. The barrel is free-floating stainless steel, and the stock is composed of composite plastic, ensuring it isn't affected by moisture or temperature like wooden stocks.

Ina's preference for the PSG 19 also stemmed from the fact that the weapon is optimized for winter conditions and remains effective in temperatures as low as minus forty degrees Fahrenheit. She wanted a rifle that could be used in all conceivable Swedish environments so she wouldn't have to master more than one weapon. The rifle's mechanism is designed to resist ice formation, and it can be operated with thick gloves except when pulling the trigger. For that, one can wear a glove with a finger hole. The PSG 19 is one hundred percent functional in summer and winter.

Ina always used the PSG 19 B variant, which features a foldable stock, making it easier to carry on her back, especially for smaller individuals who a longer weapon might hinder. While many snipers prefer a fixed-magnification scope, Ina favored a variable-magnification scope with a 3-12x50 range, providing greater flexibility.

At six hundred feet —the distance to the mining museum—she could hit a snuff box 39 times out of 40, and a human torso is many times larger. She could almost always deliver a fatal shot at distances up to two thousand feet, provided there wasn't too much wind. Beyond that range, it became a gamble, but she had still managed to land lethal shots at distances of up to half a mile.

Shortly after 7.30 a.m., the first flashbang went off, and Ina noted it satisfactorily. It was a powerful blast. Max had reached the mining museum, and everything seemed to go according to plan—at least so far. Then came the boom of the second flashbang, its intense flash visible through the windows that shattered from the blast wave. Following that, three sharp but smaller explosions echoed clearly up the hill, thanks to the blown-out windows. Ina knew precisely what those final sounds meant: the execution of enemies paralyzed by the flashbangs.

She was fully absorbed in what was happening inside the building, and now it was her turn to act. Two guards stationed at the entrance, previously invisible to Ina, came running toward the entrance. They were taken out with two quick shots—no more was needed. Ina kept her finger on the trigger, ready for more action, but nothing else happened except for Max opening the door and beckoned to her. Things looked good!

From her vantage point on the hilltop, Ina scanned the surroundings while catching a glimpse of the helicopter approaching. She heard the rhythmic *flap-flap-flap* of the rotor blades as she focused on a new target that appeared on the road of Månstorpsvägen across the railway. She couldn't resist the temptation, though she probably should have. Three medium tanks were moving slowly, each with an enemy head sticking out of the hatch. They were only a thousand feet away. She aimed for the head on the last tank first, then the middle, and finally the one at the front of the line. Three shots, three hits. She was in good form, she thought with a bit of self-satisfaction.

Ina resumed scanning the area and spotted enemy fighters blocking the European Highway 4 highway. She measured the distance with her laser—just over sixteen hundred feet. More than a quarter of a mile—a challenging distance. She couldn't resist the challenge. She took her time aiming carefully and squeezed the trigger gently. One fighter dropped, mortally wounded. The second shot claimed another. Now, the remaining fighters realized what was happening and dove into the ditches on either side of the road. Time to leave!

Ina dropped her PSG 19 B on the ground, leaving it behind. She had already removed her balaclava, boots, and black coveralls an hour earlier. She donned a white baseball cap adorned with the text "Rögle Hockey" and the bold eagle emblem of the local hockey club. Her neatly tied ponytail was secured in the cap's back hole. Now, she was dressed in light blue pants, a lightweight sports jacket, white socks, and white Adidas sneakers. It looked like she had just stepped out of the shower and put on freshly pressed clothes. Ina swiftly descended the slag heap, her feet quick and light. She heard explosions from the mining museum as she jumped onto the woman's bike she had stolen on an abandoned street in Nyvång at night. She counted three explosions as she picked up speed. Those final explosions weren't part of the plan, and she deeply worried for Max. Nothing could happen to him—not now when they had become one, something she had never believed could happen to her. She, who had thought she could not feel genuinely, had fallen head over heels in love like a teenager. It was for Max that she lived now, and she knew he lived for her. After the war, they would spend the rest of their lives together, in peace, as they had promised each other.

She pedaled as fast as she could away from the slag heap, heading down Nygårdavägen road. Then she turned left onto National Highway 107, where she was stopped by a group of *God's Warriors* who had been hastily dispatched due to the events at the mining museum.

"Where are you headed, and where are you coming from?" one demanded.

"I'm on my way to work in Ingelstorp," Ina replied, drawing out the last syllable and adding a heavy roll to the "r," trying her best to sound like a native of Skåne. She wasn't precisely a linguistic expert, but she had heard the dialect enough times to give it a shot. She thought she did a decent job.

"Have you heard any gunfire?" the soldier asked.

"Nah, nothing at all."

"Ah, leave her alone. She's not the one we're looking for," said another of the *God's Warriors*, who appeared to be the group leader based on his logo.

"But shouldn't we have a little fun with her since she's here?" one of them suggested, grinning.

"Knock it off! We have a job to focus on. Use the binoculars and scan the fields!" the group leader ordered, waving Ina through. The petite, sweet-looking girl with her neatly tied ponytail was spared further attention.

"You can go on. Have a good day," the leader added.

"Thanks, same to you. Maybe we'll meet again sometime," Ina replied with a grateful smile as she pedaled away.

"What was with that weird accent of hers?" one asked as she disappeared. "Sounded like she had a speech impediment. That wasn't Skåne dialect."

"But she was a fine little thing, wasn't she? Did you hear her say we might meet again? Ha, ha. She meant me, of course. I wouldn't mind that at all."

Besides the helicopter pilot, Ina rode undisturbed to the Swedish base, arriving first among the three on the operations team. Knowing the others hadn't arrived yet, she didn't ask any questions. She wasn't even tired. The adrenaline was still pumping through her veins, and she couldn't relax. Instead, she spent the afternoon selecting and zeroing in on a new PSG 19 B.

Chapter 31 – Royal Encounter

September 11, 2033

After seeing Max successfully haul the second package across the Vege River, Carl Philip set off briskly along the riverbank. His original plan had been to cover Max as he made his way to the waterhole out on the field, but the tall vegetation along the river made it impossible to see what was happening on the other side. The priority was to get away from the area as quickly as possible, especially since the earlier gunfire had alerted the enemy, who were now searching the terrain for them. He noticed more vehicles arriving, some stopping on the bridge they had just passed under. It was still dark, which increased his chances of escaping. He hoped they didn't have dogs, or he'd be in serious trouble.

When Carl Philip looked back, he saw the beams of a few flashlights moving down the slope from the European Highway 4, right by the bridge. He had only covered a thousand feet in the challenging vegetation along the riverbank, staying hidden from the enemy while moving as quickly as possible. But now, those flashlights were closing in on him alarmingly fast. The pursuing soldiers were driving along the edge of the field, covering the ground rapidly. He realized they would catch up with him soon, so he lay down, preparing to take them by surprise.

When they were about five hundred feet from his position, Carl Philip disengaged the safety of his AK5 rifle. The pursuers were shining their flashlights into the vegetation along the river as they continued along the edge of the field. Carl Philip waited until they were just a hundred feet away before taking them down with a short burst of gunfire.

His position was now compromised, and he knew he had to move quickly before other pursuers arrived. He left the vegetation cover and started jogging as fast as he could, still following the river but now along the edge of the field where the path was clear. He was now executing escape plan B, which he had prepared with Max. If retreating the way they had come was no longer an option, they would head east towards the ridge of Söderåsen, just a few miles away. The Free Rangers controlled the northern part of Söderåsen, at least north of the village Vrams

Gunnarstorp, and if Carl Philip could reach the ridge, he might find safety.

Carl Philip ran as fast as he could. Although he kept himself in good physical shape, he was over fifty years old and knew that younger pursuers could easily catch up with him. The darkness still hid him, but not for long. He could already see the first light of dawn breaking on the horizon ahead.

One concern was National Highway 107, which he would soon need to cross. The 107 lay within the Muslim-controlled zone, and he had to assume it was under surveillance. When he cautiously peeked over the embankment, he saw vehicles parked with their lights on, both to the left and right. He had to get across the National Highway 107 before dawn. Otherwise, he'd be trapped in the triangle formed by the significant roads European Highway 4, National Highway 110, and 107, all controlled by the Muslims. That triangle would undoubtedly be scoured with dogs. It was now or never. He sprinted, hunched low, across the asphalt as fast as he could and dove into the ditch on the other side. There were no signs that he had been spotted, so he continued as fast as his legs could carry him.

After five hundred feet, Carl Philip found himself on the outskirts of the little town of Bjuv. The entire town was completely dark, but the dawn light was beginning to brighten, meaning he would soon be visible from a distance. He noticed a few civilians moving about, who also saw him, but none seemed eager to confront a soldier holding an automatic rifle. They couldn't tell if he was a Swedish or a Muslim soldier. Given his appearance, they would likely assume he was on the Muslim side, which worked to his advantage since Bjuv was within the Muslim-controlled zone. No Swedish civilian would start a conversation with a *God's Warrior* unless necessary.

He kept low for the last stretch through the town, moving through the vegetation by the river. He planned to cross to the northern side of the Vege River via the bridge on a road called Bjuvsvägen. He doubted his pursuers would search the north side; they were more likely to focus on the triangle between the major roads. If the bridge was guarded, plan C was to force his way into a house, where he could lay low for a few days until the search subsided. He hoped to avoid taking hostages but wouldn't hesitate if it came to that. Moving in broad daylight was not an option.

Luckily, the bridge wasn't guarded, so he managed to slip across without any trouble.

Once across, he veered right, heading east toward the looming Söderåsen, whose outlines were now visible. He was only about a thousand feet from the base of the ridge.

Carl Philip jogged across the fields, making his way toward the ridge. When he paused to catch his breath, he saw a vehicle stop on the bridge at Bjuvsvägen, which he had just crossed, but by then, their target had already slipped away.

Finally, he reached the shelter of the beech forest and began climbing the steep incline. It looked like he might make it after all.

Somewhere in the distance, he heard the faint sound of a few gunshots—perhaps it was Ina firing from the slag heap. If so, the helicopter should be arriving now. He paused in a clearing, trying to glimpse the village of Nyvång, but the distance was too great. Then he faintly heard more shots in the distance and hoped nothing had gone wrong for Max and Ina. It was not a good sign if a firefight was taking place around the mining museum.

Carl Philip continued his ascent. He had studied the map of Söderåsen briefly and knew that if he followed the ridge southeast, he would eventually reach Höjehall, where the Free Rangers had their base. There was no need to rush now; he was safe from the Muslim search parties.

After jogging nearly six miles with the heavy weight of the bullets in his pockets and his AK5 slung across his back, he was utterly exhausted. He thought the physical effort he had just exerted seemed more suited for someone half his age. Perhaps the exhaustion was heightened by the release of tension now that the immediate danger had passed. His body had been in a constant state of alert, with adrenaline coursing through his veins. From the moment of that first firefight on the motorcycle, he had felt like a machine, totally absorbed in his mission and acting almost on autopilot.

But he had done everything right, giving him a deep satisfaction. He had fulfilled his part in the rescue operation, and now he could only hope everything was going smoothly for Max and Ina back at the mining museum. Perhaps the colonel was already safe, flown out by the helicopter. He sat down and leaned back against a small hill. At that moment, he would have given half a kingdom for a cup of coffee and a cinnamon bun, but he had to make do without. It was only two or three miles to the Free Rangers base at Höjehall, and he expected to be there within a couple of hours. The sun was pleasantly warm, and soon, he drifted into a deep sleep.

Carl Philip awoke to a light nudge at his side. Opening his eyes, he saw a young woman in camouflage fatigues gently nudging him with her boot. Beside her stood a younger man in the same uniform, holding Carl Philip's AK5.

"Who are you, and what are you doing here?" the woman asked sharply.

"I'm Swedish and here on a mission from the Supreme Commander of the Swedish Armed Forces."

"Swedish, huh?" the male soldier said to his colleague. "His face is completely black. Check out that beard. But then again, you never know these days."

"You're on the Free Rangers territory, and we're very curious why you've entered without informing us—if you are indeed Swedish, as you claim. But you'll soon explain yourself before our commander, Jeppe Hofman-Bang. Get up, we're leaving."

They walked single file with Carl Philip in the middle, the younger man taking the rear, still holding Carl Philip's AK5. After a good hour of walking steadily along the trails on the ridge, they arrived at the base in Höjehall. Carl Philip asked if he could wash the black paint off his face and have something to eat and drink before meeting the commander, which was granted. Finally, he got the coffee he longed for and a batch of freshly baked, still-warm Skåne buns.

Jeppe Hofman-Bang leaned back in his throne-like armchair, carefully observing the man sitting across from him on a simple wooden chair. His expression was disapproving, but the piercing and scrutinizing look in his eyes revealed a curiosity about his guest.

"So why did you enter our territory without asking for permission?"

"Perhaps I should start by introducing myself. I'm Carl Philip Bernadotte, which might be a bit of a surprise in this situation."

"Oh really? So, the so-called king himself honors me with his presence," Hofman-Bang replied sourly.

Carl Philip noted that Hofman-Bang didn't seem surprised that the King of Sweden had suddenly dropped into his headquarters on the ridge.

"I understand it might seem unbelievable, given the circumstances, but it is indeed I—the King of Sweden—sitting here."

"So-called king or not, it took me a second to recognize you as Carl Philip."

Carl Philip felt confused. It was clear that Hofman-Bang didn't believe he was sitting across from the King of Sweden, yet at the same time, he claimed to recognize him as Carl Philip Bernadotte. It didn't add up. Perhaps the man was a complete lunatic, Carl Philip thought. Or maybe he was one of those who questioned the coronation's legality, which had occurred in Zone 1 a year earlier. Carl Philip knew there was a slight movement questioning his right to the throne.

"Regardless of who I truly am, I participated in a rescue operation for a captured Swedish colonel. Now, I request transport to the Swedish base. Can you assist with that? They can also verify my identity once we get there."

"Oh, you mean the fool who let himself get captured without a fight. We had also planned to rescue him, but you beat us to it. So, how did it go? I heard reports that a helicopter flew in and picked him up."

"Then you know more than I do, but that sounds promising. That's how it was supposed to happen. We can get exact details once we get to the Swedish base."

"The so-called base of your so-called country, you mean. Sure, we'll take you there, no problem. Carl Philip, it was a pleasure meeting you," Hofman-Bang said, smiling as kindly as he could while standing up and extending his right hand. "Now, I have more important things to attend to, but I'll arrange your transport first."

Carl Philip chose not to comment on Hofman-Bang's rudeness. When he arrived at the base, his first questions were whether the rescue operation had been successful and whether Max and Ina had returned. He was told that the colonel was at the hospital in Kristianstad receiving medical care and that Ina Sjöstedt had returned four hours before Carl Philip without a scratch. They were all deeply concerned about Max.

Ina had heard a couple of explosions inside the mining museum as she was leaving, so it seemed something unexpected had occurred. But they hoped that Max had made it back to the waterhole in the field, where, according to his plan, he would lay low and sneak back under the cover of darkness in the middle of the night.

Chapter 32 – In the Hall of the Mountain King

September 11, 2033

Max slid into the water and swam out to the center of the waterhole before diving down. Within moments, he found himself in the water-filled mining tunnel. He realized the tunnel was about ten feet below the surface. Above him, the farmer Ove Persson, who owned the farm, had driven back and forth thousands of times with his red agricultural machines, utterly unaware of what lay beneath him.

Max turned his head, floating comfortably in the water, and let the headlamp beam play across the walls. They were pitch black, as expected. The water was clear. Below him, he could see the narrow rails where tens of thousands of coal carts had been hauled toward the main shaft. This was indeed a highway, just as the curator had said. All he had to do was follow the tracks to his destination. It couldn't be simpler.

Before setting off, he marked the spot by tying a piece of white rope to the rail, even though it was probably an unnecessary precaution since daylight should be visible in the tunnel once the sun rose. He had no desire to risk missing the only exit he knew of.

He started moving forward with calm and steady kicks, propelling himself like a torpedo, occasionally adjusting his course with his hands. It was pure bliss. He couldn't imagine a more peaceful or better place than where he was now. He felt like he wanted to stay there forever. It was in moments like this that he felt genuinely happy.

He thought of the cenotes he had explored on the Yucatán Peninsula. There were thousands of them, and he had dived into unexplored passages three hundred feet deep, almost getting lost. He knew that the cenotes had formed from the immense energy of the meteorite that struck the earth off Yucatán sixty-five million years ago, giving life on Earth a new direction by wiping out the dinosaurs. He also knew that the cenotes had formed from the heat, much like the bubbles in boiling porridge, and had remained since the limestone solidified. He wouldn't exist without that meteorite, and he certainly wouldn't have explored any cenotes, he mused as he continued to dream while his steady kicks propelled him forward.

Life, as it existed on earth, was a strange product of coincidences, but it was what it was, and all he could do was try to enjoy the good moments. In moments like this, he felt truly alive, here and now, in this very moment—and that life was as fantastic as the thought of it ending was repulsive.

The tunnel underground, through which he now steadily swam, had been created by human hands, and it was much easier to navigate than the cenotes. Otherwise, it felt the same, for even though the cenotes had white walls, these water passages also turned pitch black as soon as you swam a bit away from the hole at the surface.

About halfway through, he noticed that the water level was dropping and that he was swimming just three feet above the tracks. Soon, it became so shallow that he was partly swimming above the water's surface, and eventually, he had to stand up and walk, which was much more difficult with the bulky swim fins. For some reason, the water receded in this section. He guessed the tunnel followed the ground upward over some hill despite the otherwise flat landscape. He thought he was directly beneath the ruins of Västra Broby Church. It seemed likely. He knew churches were always built on hills, and the mine tunnel passed right under the church.

Max removed the mouthpiece and turned off the oxygen supply to conserve it. He noticed that the ceiling height in the mine tunnel was about ten feet, and he waded forward as quickly as he could. Fortunately, after about two hundred feet, the water deepened again, allowing him to resume his comfortable underwater swimming. He was getting close to his destination.

As he approached the main shaft, the water became shallow once more, and as expected, he had to walk the last stretch. The floor of the tunnel was smooth and even. Max removed his swim fins and walked the final distance in his protective socks until he reached dry land. He knew he was now directly beneath the railway, built specifically to transport millions of tons of coal from the mine.

The narrow-gauge rails in the tunnel were still intact, and he let his headlamp linger on a couple of the tiny carts used. They appeared intact but were entirely coated in rust. He was standing at a railway crossing, and there was only a difference in elevation of a couple of feet between the tracks. "Skåne's first subway," he thought, smiling despite himself. Hundred and fifty feet ahead was the door to the shaft, with the staircase leading up into the mining museum.

Max checked his dive watch and loosened the straps holding the oxygen tank and the waterproof bag on his back. The knife strapped to his left calf stayed in its sheath, as did the pistol holstered on his right calf. He had over an hour before he would launch his surprise attack. He carefully arranged his gear to quickly put it back on and move out, if necessary, though it was unlikely anyone would follow him. He unpacked the two flashbang grenades and placed them beside the oxygen tank. He had no shoes on his feet. The attack would be carried out in his socks, with the dry suit as his uniform. He was ready. It was just a matter of waiting until the time was right.

The curator enthusiastically encouraged Max to check out the unique dinosaur tracks, preserved for seventy million years and forever frozen in the coal. They were supposed to be right near the door to the shaft. But Max couldn't find them. The floor near the door was hacked apart, and he could see the marks of an ax. All that remained of the famous and eternally preserved dinosaur tracks were scattered black splinters and coal dust. The ax used by the vandal was carelessly discarded against the wall.

Max was a professional warrior to the core and didn't usually harbor personal grudges against the enemy—on the contrary, they were to be respected. But now, he felt the adrenaline surge, warming his cheeks and ears. This systematic destruction—why? This wasn't just about war and genocide against the Swedes. It was worse. It was about erasing all traces of an entire culture. The Swedish culture was to be wiped out forever, forgotten, and replaced by Muslim culture.

At 7.30 a.m., Max knew the helicopter was lifting off from its starting point. He also knew that Ina should be positioned atop the slag heap, ready to signal the helicopter pilot to land when she saw Max wave outside the museum entrance. And to eliminate any enemies around the building. Max hoped nothing had gone wrong on Ina's journey through enemy territory. If she weren't up there, the chances of a catastrophic outcome would be high.

Max ascended the stairs silently, with a grenade in each hand. His night-vision goggles, equipped with an IR lamp, were in place, casting everything in a greenish hue. He placed one of the grenades on the top step, with his pistol beside it, and listened for twenty seconds before opening the door, but he heard nothing. With a decisive motion, he pulled out the rather stiff safety pin. Still, he kept the lever firmly pressed under his fingers as he opened the door and lobbed the first flashbang grenade into the center of the room, quickly shutting the door and crouching down, pressing his index fingers into his ears.

The powerful explosion echoed through the room just two seconds later, and Max knew that if anyone had been inside, they were now paralyzed, blinded by the flash. With his pistol at the ready, he swiftly moved through the room and opened the door to the main exhibition hall, where the colonel and his interrogators were likely to be. The second grenade exploded just as the first had, with Max crouched safely behind the door, fingers pressed into his ears.

Only now did he have a moment to glance around the first room—no one there. But in the exhibition hall, there were four people, all incapacitated, two lying on the floor and two slumped in chairs. The uniform on one of the seated figures left no doubt—it was the colonel. The three enemies had begun to stir slightly, groaning faintly. Max put a bullet in each of their foreheads, just above the bridge of the nose. Now, he had only five bullets left.

Just as Max was about to push down the handle on the entrance door, he heard two rapid gunshots from outside. He cautiously opened the door and saw two lifeless enemy soldiers lying on the asphalt right in front of the entrance. Ina was doing her job. He stepped out and waved both arms broadly toward the slag heap, though he couldn't see Ina—not that he expected to. Then he heard the helicopter's rhythmic thumping in the quiet dawn and soon saw the small craft descending for a landing. Max heard three more gunshots from the slag heap, spaced about a second apart, but he couldn't see what they were aimed at. Ina was active up there, and he had to trust her judgment.

Max grabbed the colonel under the arms and dragged him backward through the room and out onto the asphalt. The colonel was starting to regain consciousness, groaning faintly with half-open eyes, utterly unaware of what was happening. The pilot jumped out of the helicopter, and together, they hoisted the colonel into the passenger seat and strapped him in. Max stood ready with his pistol, watching as the helicopter lifted off and flew away.

He heard two more shots from the slag heap before he headed down the stairs into the shaft. What exactly is going on up there? He wondered as he strapped the AK to his back and slipped on his swim fins. Is Ina okay? And what about Carl Philip?

Max quickly descended the stairs into the shaft. He discarded his night-vision goggles, secured his headlamp, and turned it on as he waded into the water with his fins on. Suddenly, he heard loud voices and footsteps in the stairwell, prompting him to hurry as much as he could in the cumbersome swim fins. Just as he dove forward, he heard automatic gunfire aimed at the light from his headlamp. Bullets whizzed past above him as he finally submerged. Now, it was all about getting away, deep into the mining tunnel, as fast as possible. If his pursuers threw grenades into the water, the pressure wave could be the last thing he ever felt.

Max kicked his fins as hard as he could, using his hands to propel himself forward. He hadn't had time to put on his hand paddles, but even his bare hands helped. He swam frantically forward at top speed, starting to feel somewhat safe, when the first pressure wave hit, spinning him around and making him lose all sense of direction. Desperately, he resumed swimming as the second, and then quickly, a third pressure wave tossed him around again. He wasn't injured, just thoroughly shaken. When the fourth pressure wave hit, he was far enough away that it only felt like a slight shove.

Now, he could slow down. He knew they would never figure out where he was headed, but he had to assume that enemy soldiers would be searching for him all over the fields, and it was now full daylight. But that would be a problem for later.

He continued swimming calmly, about three feet above the tracks, feeling his pulse slow down again. But he was still dazed and found it challenging to think clearly. That was a close call, he thought.

The colonel was saved, and Max hoped his two comrades had escaped alone. He felt confident now that he could make it back unharmed. He planned to emerge from the waterhole in the field, concealed by the dense vegetation surrounding it. There, he would change into dry clothes and boots, which he had left in the plastic bag next to his

AK5, and wait until nightfall. Under the cover of darkness, it shouldn't be too difficult to sneak back across the fields to the base. There were plenty of ditches and bushes to hide in if necessary.

Max paddled steadily with his legs, but suddenly, a creeping unease began to take hold. Shouldn't he have reached the exit by now? It felt like he had been swimming much longer than when he headed to the main shaft. But he was sure he couldn't have missed the white rope he had tied to the track, which he had followed just three feet above. He glanced at his dive watch. Yes, it seemed like he had been swimming for several minutes longer than before.

Should he turn back? He fought off the growing panic and stopped swimming to think clearly. Then, like a flash of lightning, it hit him: When he swam to the main shaft, he had passed a short stretch where the water was so shallow that he had to wade. He hadn't done any wading on the return journey. Although still not fully clear-headed, he realized his situation was catastrophic—he was in the wrong tunnel! The curator had mentioned that three main tunnels converged at the main shaft, and now he understood that he had swum into the wrong tunnel when the grenade blasts threw him around. They all looked the same.

Max checked the gauge on his rebreather. The rebreather's filter absorbed the toxic carbon dioxide, so the exhaled air could be reused with minimal oxygen input from the highly compressed nitrox mixture in his steel dive tank. The rebreather allowed for a significantly longer time underwater. The gauge showed that just over a third of the oxygen remained. He had a maximum of forty minutes before it ran out.

It was touch-and-go whether he could make it back to the main shaft. If the oxygen didn't last until then, it would all be over. He certainly wouldn't be able to reach the waterhole in the field where he had started the dive, and what would await him if he surfaced in the main shaft? His small-caliber pistol wasn't much to rely on, with only five rounds left. The most likely outcome was that he would be killed in a firefight against a superior enemy.

Surrendering and allowing himself to be captured was not an option for Max. He remembered the curator mentioning several sealed-off shafts that might be breached and potential exits created by collapses. Max decided to take his chances and continue forward.

He swam more slowly now, conserving oxygen. It was crucial to keep his breathing as shallow as possible. He couldn't afford to let his nerves take over and cause his heart to race, but the situation was undeniably frightening.

Well, they say drowning is the most peaceful way to go, Max thought as he followed the track, minutes ticking away one by one. He just had to keep breathing while the nitrox mixture in the tank provided ever-dwindling oxygen. Eventually, his inhaled air would consist mainly of nitrogen, with too little oxygen, causing him to drift off into unconsciousness slowly.

Death would come without pain, but the thought that his body might never be found left Max feeling desolate. Perhaps his final resting place would be next to a dinosaur skeleton encased in coal. Death is timeless and eternal for humans as well as for dinosaurs. He didn't believe in any paradise. Religion had never been a part of his life, and now it was likely too late to call upon God.

He probably had about twenty minutes left to live. Max paddled with steady kicks when suddenly the tracks split into two directions. Which path should he take? They looked the same. He chose the right tunnel and pressed on at a calm pace.

A few minutes later, he realized the tunnel was sloping downward. Wrong choice. He knew there would be no exit deep underground. He turned back, painfully aware that he had wasted precious minutes. The law of misfortune, as they say. If there's a fifty-fifty chance, luck rarely favors you, but Max had usually considered himself lucky—just not this time.

A few minutes later, he was back where the tracks had split, and this time he took the left tunnel. He glanced at the gauge and saw he might have ten- or twelve minutes left. It was hard to tell when he might lose consciousness, but he planned to keep going until the very last second. Perhaps miracles still happened, though he knew his odds of surviving this were minuscule.

He had lived a rich life—albeit only for thirty-one years—and had done and experienced most of what he had dreamed of. Maybe the quality of life was more important than its length, he mused. If anything mattered at all, one day, humanity would be as extinct as the dinosaurs.

Even the solar system wouldn't last, and in the grand scheme of things, it was utterly insignificant, leaving no trace in the vast expanse of the universe. There was some comfort in knowing that his death would be equally unimportant. Perhaps, deep down, he had been seeking death all along—why else would he have taken such risks time and again?

His legs continued to paddle automatically but slower and slower as Max sank deeper into his thoughts. In a moment of clarity, he no longer felt fear but noted that he was slipping into a lower state of consciousness.

Soon, his life would flicker out for good, and his legs would stop paddling. It didn't matter much, but he wanted Ina to be his last thought, so he focused on seeing her beautiful face with that wise, calm, and slightly melancholy gaze that seemed to have seen everything.

He could almost feel her embrace, holding him tightly as he lay on the bed in her arms, gently stroking her cheek and simply enjoying being alive. This was where he wanted to stay forever, drifting off to sleep. It wasn't a dream. He was there, on the bed with Ina, for real. Everything was perfect.

Suddenly, he realized he was alone, floating in the water. He kicked as hard as possible to move forward, but it wasn't going anywhere. He kicked desperately with his fins and moved a few inches before getting stuck again. It felt as though an invisible hand was holding him back. He began thrashing his arms to break free and realized his hands were breaking the water's surface, splashing around. He lifted his head.

In his dazed state, he had swum into shallow water without realizing it and had almost drowned in just a foot of water. Summoning the last of his willpower, he managed to sit up, finding himself seated in the shallow water, gasping for breath as he ripped out the mouthpiece.

After a few minutes, Max's mind began to clear as oxygen flowed back into his brain. He was lucid enough to assess his situation: he was in a mine shaft with about a foot of water at an unknown depth below the surface. The fact that there was breathable air containing oxygen could only mean one thing—somewhere, air was flowing in; there had to be an opening to the surface. The question was, could he find it? And if he did, would it be large enough for him to escape?

With considerable effort, Max stood up, noting that the water didn't even reach his knees. He loosened the straps and abandoned his air tank containing a toxic gas mixture. It was useless to him now. He kept his diving mask on in case he needed to dive again but noticed that his headlamp's beam was dimming, edging into the red zone—a sign that the battery was almost dead.

Beside his pistol, he had a small flashlight, about the size of a finger, as a backup for his headlamp. He figured he had about two hours of light left.

Max remembered the energy bar he had stashed in the same waterproof bag as his pistol holster. It was the only food he had with him. He retrieved the bar and began chewing on it while scooping water with his cupped hand. The water tasted slightly metallic, but he hoped it wasn't toxic. It was likely high in nitrates from the over-fertilized fields above him. He had already received an almost lethal dose of nitrogen, but this time, it was harmless since it wasn't in gas form.

He felt his strength returning as the quick sugars hit his bloodstream. Taking the fins in his hand, he began to wade forward. He walked along the center of the tracks, feeling the ties underfoot. The ground was even, making it easy to walk. After seven hundred feet, the water began to shallow, soon only a few inches deep. The tracks split again, and the tunnels looked identical, just as they had before. The left path had been the right choice last time, so he chose it again.

After about a mile, the water began to deepen again. When it reached his waist, Max hesitated. His headlamp was growing dimmer, and he strained to see what lay ahead. Turning back seemed pointless; he hadn't seen any daylight anywhere. He decided to press on, hoping the water would shallow out again, but soon it was up to his neck. He was trapped in the mine.

Then, about a mile back, he remembered the last spot where the tracks had split. He decided to retrace his steps and try the other tunnel.

Exhausted, Max finally reached the junction where the tracks had diverged. After sitting down and resting for a few minutes with the headlamp turned off, he stood up and entered the right-hand tunnel. Walking was easy, but the tunnel split again after a quarter of a mile.

He took the right path but soon felt it sloping downward, with the water rising again. When the water reached his chest, he gave up and turned back. He was trapped in this damn coal mine, which seemed to have no exits.

Max was so tired that he staggered as he walked but decided to make one final attempt. He returned to shallower water and reached where the tunnels had last split. Taking the left tunnel, he stumbled forward as best he could, for what he estimated was a couple of miles. At least it was relatively dry and easy to walk. But then, the headlamp finally died. He was enveloped in total darkness and sat down, slipping into a half-conscious state of exhaustion. His thoughts wandered. Would there be a gravestone for someone who just disappeared? Would there be a funeral?

The last thought that crossed his mind before he drifted off was whether he should take those pills that would end his suffering. They were in the same pouch as his pistol. Ina had taught him always to carry a small "pharmacy" of painkillers, strong enough to put him to sleep permanently if he took them all at once.

He didn't know how long he had slept, but when he awoke, he felt so weak that the idea of standing up didn't even cross his mind. It was all over—he might as well take those pills and put an end to the misery.

He pulled out the blister pack, focusing on Ina's face as he pressed all six tablets into his palm. He opened his mouth wide, but he just sat there with his mouth open, unable to bring himself to swallow the deadly pills.

Suddenly, he felt a draft against his tongue. The air was moving—quite strongly, in fact—but where was it coming from? There had to be a connection to the outside somewhere. He turned his head, straining to see in the pitch black, and now he noticed what seemed like a faint light at the end of the tunnel he was in.

The light from his headlamp had prevented him from seeing it before, but now, he could make it out with his eyes fully adjusted to the darkness. A tiny, tiny ray of sunlight was piercing the darkness of the mine, perhaps only two hundred feet away from him. There was a hole!

The adrenaline rush from this last glimmer of hope gave him the strength to get back on his feet. He dropped the pills and groped his way forward, one hand against the rough wall, and soon, he was standing directly in that small beam of sunlight. He could see the light filtering through a tiny hole in the ceiling, about eight feet above his head. The hole was just a few square inches wide but could be enlarged. But how? The rough wall was impossible to climb.

He remembered seeing some leftover mining equipment during his long swim, which might be helpful, but he needed to find out where it was.

Max opened the pouch with his pistol holster again and pulled out the small flashlight he had packed as a backup. He shined it ahead into the tunnel and saw a cart beside the tracks just a hundred feet away.

If he could only move the cart those hundred feet, he could reach the hole with his hands. He pulled and pushed at the heavy cart, but it didn't budge an inch. When he shined the light on the wheels, he saw they were completely rusted. There was no way he could drag over two hundred pounds. Another dead end—what had happened to his legendary luck?

As he swept the area with the flashlight, he noticed something resembling a pole lying against the wall. It was a nearly six-foot-long iron rod used for scaling and prying loose stones from the ceiling to prevent cave-ins. Without thinking about what the rod had been used for, Max began working on the tiny hole in the roof, holding the flashlight in his mouth to get better light.

The small hole was covered by a web of roots and fine root threads, which were annoyingly tricky. When he finally poked aside a clump of roots, he saw they were tangled around a grate, probably made of cast iron. He realized that the hole above him must be one of many ventilation shafts, which meant it was likely large enough for him to squeeze through —if only he could remove the grate. His immediate task was to focus on enlarging the hole; how he would climb up would be a problem for later.

Max drove the iron rod into the ground with all the strength he could muster, finally breaking through to the surface. Several larger holes now allowed enough light to filter in so he could put away his flashlight. The cast iron grate, rusted to the point of being brittle like a cracker, gave way under the rod, creating a large square opening for him to escape.

But he was utterly exhausted and couldn't fathom how he'd climb up to the hole to cut away the remaining roots that were still blocking his escape.

For a moment, he considered firing a few shots through the hole to signal for help, but he had no idea where he was. If he was in enemy territory, that could be disastrous. He also realized that the sound of gunfire would likely be absorbed and muffled, barely audible a few feet from the hole. He saved this last desperate move when all other options were exhausted.

Or should he aim the gun at his temple when all hope was lost? He decided to save the very last bullet for himself.

With some effort, Max managed to rig the rod at a thirty-degree angle against the wall, with the tip braced against the rail for support. Luckily, the rough wall offered a few protruding stones he could grip onto, allowing him to plant his right foot on top of the rod. Holding onto the tough roots with his right hand, he balanced himself while pulling out the knife strapped to his left calf. After a few minutes, he cut through the roots, revealing a round hole about the size of a maintenance hole cover —large enough to squeeze through if he could only reach it.

Max tugged at the remaining roots, testing their strength. They seemed to be firmly anchored. He sheathed his knife, took a deep breath, gripped the roots with both hands on either side of the hole, and jumped as high as he could with his right leg, pushing off from his only support.

He hoisted his shoulders above the ground and pulled himself up in one swift motion. He was free!

Max took a deep breath, gazing up at the sky for nearly a minute before assessing his surroundings.

As he looked around, he realized he was in the middle of a thicket on a small hill in the middle of a field. The location couldn't have been better, even if he was still in enemy territory. Now, he just had to wait for nightfall and then sneak eastward toward Swedish territory—assuming he wasn't already there.

The adrenaline rush had made him feel invincible, but soon, the cold set in, making him shiver despite the mild late-summer temperature. He noticed several cuts on his hands, but none seemed severe. A couple of trickles of blood ran down his face, scraped by the rugged, severed roots when he had pulled himself out of the hole.

His protective socks were in tatters, and he realized he would need shoes. He removed the remnants of the socks. He might be able to shuffle across the fields barefoot, but his feet were already sore and tender. It was far from certain he could make it back to the base.

After a few hours, hunger started to gnaw at Max, prompting him to stealthily approach the edge of the field in search of something edible. The local "kitchen" offered a cabbage head, pesticide-laden, which Max eagerly mashed on like a desperate rabbit. It wasn't exactly gourmet fare, but it filled his stomach and provided the vital energy he needed.

As dusk settled, Max tried to gather his strength and focus on his mission. His feet throbbed painfully, swollen to the point where he could feel his pulse. He cursed himself for losing the painkillers that he now so desperately needed.

While he lay hidden in the bushes, Max noticed a man walking along a path at the edge of the field, heading toward the thicket where Max was hiding. Max quietly jogged across the field toward him when the man was about hundred and fifty feet away. The man, oblivious to the dim light, was caught off guard.

"Stop! You have to help me. I'm Swedish," Max said, grabbing the man's shoulder.

The man turned around, eyes wide with fear, as if he had seen a ghost. The sight of Max, with his blackened and bloodied face, made the man tremble with terror. Suddenly, the man turned and bolted. Max, drained of energy, couldn't muster the strength to give chase. When the man was about a hundred feet away, Max pulled out his small pistol and fired a shot that missed, passing between the man's legs. The second shot hit the man in the right thigh, just above the knee. The man collapsed to the ground, silent.

Max, now beyond self-control, felt a surge of anger. "I told you to help me, you damn fool," he shouted, slapping the man with the back of his hand. "You've only got yourself to blame." This was far from the usual polite and refined countenance of the count from Djursholm.

Max pulled off the man's rubber boots and put them on, along with his jacket and a cap emblazoned with "Farmers Association." Without looking back, Max walked away, though he did spare a thought for the man. He would survive, even if he had to spend the night where he lay. Someone would miss him and find him on the path, or he might manage to crawl to the nearest house.

When Max slipped his hands into the jacket pockets, he found a wallet, which prompted him to turn around and toss it back toward the man on the ground. Max wasn't a thief, after all. But he kept the nearly full bag of candy in the other pocket. Stuffing his mouth with the candy, he savored the sweetness that gave him the extra energy he desperately needed.

Four hours later, an utterly exhausted Max finally made it back to the base, where he was given emergency care and an IV drip. Lying on the infirmary bed, his first question was about Ina and Carl Philip. Had they returned safely? Upon receiving a positive answer, it took only a couple of minutes before he drifted into a deep sleep, aided by high doses of painkillers and muscle relaxants. When he awoke, he felt Ina's gentle hand caressing his cheek. His eyes welled up with tears as he managed a small smile at her. Ina said nothing, simply continuing to stroke his cheek.

Max had narrowly escaped death once again. Perhaps he had used up the last of his luck. Should he continue these life-threatening missions now that he has been given one last chance? There might be a beautiful life waiting for him after the war. Unbeknownst to him, Ina was having the very same thoughts. Their lives had taken on a new dimension.

Chapter 33 – The Missing Artillery

September 28, 2033

Late one evening, as Sweden's Chancellor and Supreme Commander Anton Brännström reviewed the war situation with the Army Chief, Major General Gunhild Svartenbrandt, something strange occurred that would significantly impact the war's outcome. They had just been discussing the destruction of Ystad town by the Muslims using heavy artillery and were brainstorming ways to prevent other towns and cities from suffering the same fate. However, neutralizing the enemy's artillery seemed impossible without an air force or artillery. As they turned the situation over in their minds, Svartenbrandt suddenly had an idea, almost as if it had been handed to her from above, as her brain desperately searched for solutions.

"What happened to those twenty-four Archer artillery pieces that Norway ordered from Bofors a while back but then canceled after they had already been produced?"

Norway's order for the Archer system was placed in 2014, and its cancellation in 2018 was a significant scandal that no one interested in military affairs could have missed. It was yet another example of Norway's capriciousness and unreliability sabotaged defense cooperation between the two countries. This time, the Norwegians managed to get the Swedes in a bind because Bofors had not met the delivery deadline, which, according to the contract, allowed Norway to cancel the agreement at no cost. To everyone's surprise, they suddenly exercised this right when the artillery pieces were already finished and about to be delivered.

The Norwegians also calculated that the airplane JAS Gripen E would be twice as expensive as the Lockheed Martin F-35 when the opposite was true. This had severely damaged the trust on the Swedish side. The Norwegians seemed willing to do anything to punish the Swedes. But now, perhaps Norway's unreliability could work to their advantage.

"That was quite a while ago," Brännström said thoughtfully, scratching his chin as he pondered deeply. "From what I remember, the Swedish military bought twelve at a bargain price—it must have been in

2021. I remember it well because I had just been asked if I wanted to become the army chief, and I was thrilled at the prospect of reinforcing our artillery. But the question is, what happened to the remaining twelve pieces?"

"Yes, that's the key question. They haven't been exported; we would know if they had been. We also know that we haven't purchased them. The government didn't think Sweden needed any artillery at all, remember? Logically, those twelve pieces must still be here in Sweden, but where?"

"Unless they were dismantled and used for spare parts. But it seems unlikely that fully produced artillery pieces worth billions of kronor would meet that fate."

"If Bofors acted logically, they would have mothballed those artillery pieces, hoping for new orders. Then, over time, they were probably just forgotten," Svartenbrandt speculated.

"That must be it! But where would they be stored if that's the case?"

"Bofors doesn't have many storage locations outside of Karlskoga. We've both been there countless times. As you know, vast warehouses and factory buildings have plenty of space, plus large fenced-off areas. They practically own the entire area."

"This is interesting!" Brännström said enthusiastically. "It's worth a shot. I'm assigning you the task of going to Karlskoga as soon as possible to dig up whatever you can. But this must remain top secret—just between the two of us. And you know why."

Svartenbrandt nodded several times, letting out a deep sigh. "I know why. Gyllenstierna. I'll head to Karlskoga first thing tomorrow morning."

Svartenbrandt's discreet and patient investigation eventually led her to a large storage hangar within the Bofors industrial complex in Karlskoga. All twelve Archer artillery pieces were neatly parked and mothballed, waiting for the Norwegians to change their minds or for other orders that never came.

The artillery pieces had long since been written off and removed from Bofors' balance sheet, giving them a formal value of zero kronor. As a result, no one in Bofors' management had taken an interest in them for years. The leadership had changed several times since the Norwegians canceled their order.

The Archer artillery pieces had been forgotten, mentally relegated to the history of failed export attempts. Military procurement is unpredictable because politicians can suddenly change their minds, especially when budget issues arise. And Saab-Bofors had so many successful export deals to focus on instead. There was no reason to undermine their market by trying to sell material that could be perceived as outdated or even substandard. It was better to sell newly produced equipment, resulting in better profits and better for Bofors' image.

Nevertheless, the artillery pieces had been stored in a dehumidified environment, regularly inspected, function-tested, and, when necessary, serviced by a meticulous service engineer nearing retirement. The artillery pieces were essentially in brand-new condition. Most importantly, the Archer system was the best artillery system in the world. The Swedish military was ecstatic about its unique performance, reliability, and the system's unmatched speed and mobility. And the best part: at A9 in Boden, personnel were trained and proficient in operating the Archer system, which had been the backbone of Sweden's artillery for many years. All the necessary expertise was available there—operators, service technicians, and support staff. Everything was ready to go.

The newly discovered Archer pieces were function-tested and calibrated at Saab-Bofors' firing range outside Karlskoga. Everything went perfectly. The artillery was in mint condition, aside from some light oxidation on metal parts and minor components on the circuit boards, but this had no impact on functionality.

The artillery pieces had been stored in a controlled environment with constant temperature and humidity for fifteen years, coated in grease and covered with tarps. The outer layer of the rubber on the six-wheeled vehicles' tires had dried and become brittle despite being greased, but the thick, rugged tires were so durable that it didn't matter. It was just a thin surface layer, a few millimeters thick, that had been slightly affected by time.

After fifteen years of using the Archer system, the extensive knowledge at A9 Regiment in Boden ensured everything went smoothly and routinely. Everything was the same as on the Swedish artillery pieces, except that the labels, instrument displays, manuals, and service handbooks were in Norwegian.

The Swedish army now had artillery to deploy in the war against the Muslims, which was desperately needed as large-scale battles were brewing in the Lund and Malmö areas, still controlled by Muslim forces. With effective field artillery, the infantry's prospects were entirely transformed. Launching a major infantry assault without artillery or air support is impossible, as the losses would be uncontrollable, and the chances of success would be nonexistent.

Large-scale assaults without artillery support haven't been attempted since the nineteenth century. The introduction of machine guns changed everything. Attacking machine gun nests is suicide and hasn't been practiced since the early days of World War I when millions of young men were senselessly sacrificed by officers who hadn't adapted to modern warfare and were still trying to wage war as Napoleon did.

For now, this remained a secret between Brännström and Svartenbrandt. They wanted to ensure that the Muslims would be in for a significant surprise when the day came to deploy the artillery.

Chapter 34: Attack Plans

November 13, 2033

It was well known that all of Sweden's artillery had been stationed at Regiment A9 in Boden in northern Sweden when the large power plant dams along the Lule River were blown up a year earlier. As a result, the entire A9 base ended up submerged under forty feet of water. Everyone knew the artillery had been rendered unusable due to the destruction of all electronic equipment. While the gun barrels weren't damaged by being underwater, the electronics were destroyed.

The cannons were unusable without GPS navigation, laser-based targeting systems, computer-controlled elevation angles, and communication with other Swedish units. The artillery pieces couldn't even be fired without functional electronics. The damage was so extensive that it would be cheaper to produce entirely new pieces than to attempt a total renovation, which would take years, considering the lack of spare parts.

Without fear of what might happen with the information leaked to Gyllenstierna, who had defected to the enemy in Kreuzberg, Supreme Commander and Chancellor Brännström and Army Chief Major General Svartenbrandt could now openly discuss the military secret they had kept for several months. Sweden was no longer without artillery.

They had discovered the twelve missing Archer systems at the weapon manufacturer Bofors plant in Karlskoga and prepared them under the highest secrecy. It was a significant and very positive surprise for the rest of the staff to learn that the Swedish army had access to a highly effective artillery system in the form of twelve fully operational Archer units. Everyone was well aware of the power and unmatched speed of the Archer systems, as they were the standard artillery system of the Swedish army.

The availability of artillery completely changed the dynamics. It had recently seemed hopeless to cross the wide Kävlinge River in Skåne and breach the Muslim defense line. The Muslim troops were well entrenched and dug into trenches and fortifications on the southern side of the river. All bridges over the Kävlinge River had long since been destroyed. The idea of infantry crossing the river in boats under heavy fire was a fantasy, as was the notion that engineer troops could construct bridges for heavy vehicles under such conditions.

The Kävlinge River—called Lödde River in Löddeköpinge and further west—forms a five-mile-long arc from its source at Lake Vomb. It flows through the wet meadows of Vomb, called Vombsänkan, past the villages and small towns of Revinghed, Flyinge, Gårdstånga, Håstad, Kävlinge, and Löddeköpinge, before emptying into the Lomma Bay at Löddesnäs, north of Bjärred. The river mouth is only three miles south of the two decommissioned nuclear reactors in Barsebäck.

"The rivers in Skåne aren't exactly known for being Mississippis," said Brännström, a native of northern Sweden, with a sarcastic smile. "But the Kävlinge River is still around a hundred and thirty feet wide, with an average depth of a couple of feet, and flows well. I didn't think there were such substantial rivers down here in the deep south," he continued, with a sarcastic tone and extra emphasis on the last word.

The Kävlinge River presented a challenging obstacle that had to be crossed to approach Lund and Malmö from the north, which seemed to be the only viable option since the Muslim defensive positions east of Lund and Malmö were exceptionally strong. It was clear that the Muslims expected the Kävlinge River, along with eight thousand well-entrenched Muslim soldiers, to be such a problematic barrier that the main attack would have to come from the east.

"We've named the attack Operation Dekanus. My plan is to begin with two feint attacks from the east, right where the Muslims expect the main assault to come, which we can confirm from their troop concentrations east of Malmö and Lund," said Major General Svartenbrandt as she swept her pen across the map projected on the screen. "We'll deploy enough resources to make it look like the main attack."

"What do you mean by two feint attacks?" asked Baksi. "And what resources are you planning to commit?"

"We'll conduct slow advances along the European Highway 65 and National Highway 11, each with approximately six thousand infantrymen and several hundred of our lighter Russian armored vehicles. I haven't finalized all the details yet," said Svartenbrandt.

"So, the main assault will be across the Kävlinge River, but where exactly?" asked Jöns Möller, the leader of the *Snapphane* guerilla fighters, who Svartenbrandt had invited to participate in the planning of the attack. Möller commanded significant military resources in the form of fiercely determined Skåne patriots, who had now grown to a force of six hundred and forty, all with an intimate knowledge of the local terrain, as nearly all his guerilla fighters were native to Skåne.

Möller's years as a battalion commander at regiment P7 in Revingehed positioned him as a critical figure in war planning. Like the other officers on the staff, Möller was trained at the Swedish National Defense College in Karlberg, and most of his practical military knowledge came from his time in the Swedish Army. This made him fully compatible with the other officers on the staff despite leading the *Snapphane* guerilla fighters, who were regarded as a free militia.

Many of Möller's Skåne warriors were also fully integrated with the Swedish Army, having previously served as conscripts or professional soldiers under Möller's command at P7. The junior officers and some non-commissioned officers were also trained at Karlberg. The high motivation and willingness to sacrifice among the *Snapphane* guerilla fighters made them a unit feared by the enemy despite lacking heavier weapons.

The *Snapphane* guerilla fighters closely resembled a Swedish Ranger unit, with their physically fit soldiers who moved swiftly through the terrain on foot and acted with flexibility and adaptability, often taking the initiative without waiting for orders from above. A platoon of twelve *Snapphane* guerilla fighters could typically hold off significantly larger enemy forces in firefights due to their superior marksmanship and faster magazine changes and reloads. They always carried far more loaded magazines and considerably more ammunition than the enemy soldiers.

On one occasion, six *Snapphane* guerilla fighters held their ground for hours against hundreds of *Holy Warriors*, who failed to advance even a single foot under the precise and relentless barrage from the well-trained *Snapphane* guerilla fighters while waiting for reinforcements.

"We'll execute two main assaults simultaneously, both at locations where the enemy might expect an attack—which goes against most of what we were taught at Karlberg," Svartenbrandt replied, turning to Möller.

Svartenbrandt took a few steps toward the table and sipped from a mug of cold coffee while the fourteen officers pondered the plan and studied the map.

"Why would we launch the assault exactly where the enemy expects it?" Möller asked. "And where is that?"

Svartenbrandt pointed to the map with her pen again.

"The easiest way to cross the river is where it's shallowest and where there's a road network capable of supporting our heavy vehicles, which ideally should move at full speed to avoid becoming easy targets for enemy anti-tank weapons positioned on the opposite bank. These two criteria are met in the two largest towns along the river—Kävlinge and Löddeköpinge."

"That makes sense," Möller acknowledged. "There's a reason these towns developed where they are; they formed around the best fording points along the river. You're also right about needing solid roads. The fields near the river are so muddy that even tracked vehicles can get bogged down. During winter, vehicles weighing tens of tons could easily sink three feet deep near the river."

"That's exactly where the Muslims have concentrated their largest forces," Brännström pointed out. "But I assume you've already considered that."

"Yes, of course," Svartenbrandt replied. "The availability of the Archer systems changes everything. The Muslims have no idea that we can obliterate their positions in minutes, so the attack will still come as a surprise. After that, we'll send a smaller force to paddle across the river in inflatable boats within seconds and establish a bridgehead on the other side."

"The river can indeed be forded both at Kävlinge and Löddeköpinge," Möller added, leveraging his extensive local knowledge.

"But naturally, where it's shallowest, the river is also at its widest. The water depth at the ford is about thirty inches now in winter, and it takes time to wade across. It's not possible to run through it. We estimate it might take up to a minute, and then they'll have to climb the muddy and slippery bank, which could be challenging with full combat gear."

"We need proper coverage to prevent a massacre if our troops get stuck there," Svartenbrandt stressed. "We plan to have around ten thousand soldiers each ford the river at Kävlinge and Löddeköpinge. The exact numbers will be determined shortly."

"In both cases, the fording points are a thousand feet downstream from the destroyed bridges," Möller noted. "As a former tank major, I believe it might be possible for our Leopard tanks to drive straight across at the fords. The water depth isn't an issue, but there's a significant risk that the tanks won't be able to climb the bank if they sink too deeply into the mud. My recommendation is to wait until the engineering units have laid the bridges. We could test it with one Leopard to see how it goes before sending more."

"If we wait, we'll be without armor for several hours," Brännström cautioned. "But I believe a hundred soldiers with anti-tank weapons could first cross in the inflatable boats. They would then receive reinforcement from those wading across. They should be able to hold the position while our engineers lay beams and build bridges on the remnants of the destroyed bridges and lay pontoon bridges where needed. We could have functioning bridges supporting tanks within four to five hours. With the help of our artillery, we'll fend off any large-scale counterattacks. The enemy won't stand a chance of getting close to Kävlinge or Löddeköpinge."

"How many infantrymen are available, considering those allocated for the feints?" Brännström inquired.

"We should be able to deploy at least twenty thousand troops, which will undoubtedly catch the Muslims off guard. Most of them are stationed in Eslöv and Teckomatorp. We'll keep a reserve force of five thousand in Röstånga," Svartenbrandt replied.

"OK, I think we've got something workable here," Brännström acknowledged. "Continue refining the details and come back with comprehensive lists of volumes and the heavier weaponry we can deploy. I want exact numbers of vehicles, artillery pieces, and ammunition broken down by type. Additionally, I want a detailed operation schedule with maps, movement arrows, and precise timing for advances. I'll personally review and consider every detail before giving my approval. Can you have that ready by tomorrow?"

"We're already far enough along, so that shouldn't be a problem. We have the night to finalize everything," Svartenbrandt answered with a slight smile.

"I also want a more thorough analysis than we currently have on the enemy's available forces," Brännström continued, turning to Bertil Wiklund, head of MUST.

"I'll see what additional information we can gather beyond what you've already received," Wiklund responded.

"By the way, what's the set date for the attack?" Brännström asked.

"Preliminary, it's scheduled for the fifth," Svartenbrandt replied.

"The attack will occur on December fourth," Brännström stated firmly. "I'm particular about that date. It marks 357 years since we decisively defeated the Danes when they tried to reclaim Skåne. And now, we'll defeat the Muslims on the same battlefield."

"Damn, I had no idea," said Baksi. "So, now it's our turn to make history."

"You can bet your life on that," Brännström affirmed. "Everyone sitting here has the chance to become historical heroes, and we're going to seize it. Let's hope it's a little less bloody than in 1676, at least on our side. Back then, the losses were seventy percent on both sides."

"Did the Swedes cross the Kävlinge River back then too?" Jöns Möller asked.

"The Swedes, you say, as if it's a foreign people—ha-ha," Brännström joked. "The real question is, which side was your family on back then—ha-ha."

Möller looked less than amused, his expression icy as he stared at Brännström without the slightest hint of a smile. Yet another stiff upper-north Swede questioned his and all the Skåne people's loyalty. Brännström, oblivious to the sensitive territory he had stumbled into, continued his speech with amusement.

"Yes, we did cross the river—but actually in the other direction, over the frozen Kävlinge River, in an attempt to surprise the Danes by storming their headquarters. That effort failed. However, the primary battle took place on the southern side of the Kävlinge River, just as it will this time. We had fourteen thousand men, of whom about ten thousand were cavalry. The Danes had a few thousand more but used outdated and ineffective tactics. They rode forward in rows, firing their flintlock pistols, often from too far a distance with little impact. Then, another row would follow while the first reloaded. We—the Swedes—used cavalry charges in tight wedge formations, breaking right into the Danish ranks after firing our pistols and slashing away with our swords like madmen.

The formations were so tight that the horses' bodies touched each other. The riders had to crouch with their legs tucked under them to avoid getting crushed between the horses."

"Wow, you know your stuff," Baksi remarked, impressed.

"Top marks in Swedish military history at Karlberg," Brännström said with a satisfied smile.

"Every course. And I'm probably Sweden's biggest military history nerd. By the way, do you know the colonel's name who led the central foot guard so effectively that the king rewarded him? A bottle of Cognac to anyone who knows!"

"No idea. Torstensson, maybe?" Wiklund guessed.

"No, now you're thinking of Gustav II Adolf about fifty years earlier. The colonel's name was... Gyllenstierna."

"No way, that can't be true! And now our damn Gyllenstierna is fighting on the enemy side."

"But our so-called Gyllenstierna is a fake who traded his way into a fancy, historic name. Daniel Gyllenstierna's real name is Deniz Öztürk, as you probably already know. From now on, let's call him nothing but 'The Öztürk,' OK?"

"The great traitor, the Muslim, and that Turkish bastard, Deniz Öztürk!" Wiklund blurted out, without thinking. Baksi looked anything but pleased, glaring hard at Wiklund.

"I'm also Turkish—a Swedish Turk," Baksi said, continuing to stare at Wiklund, who raised his hands in a gesture of apology. "And Kurdish. I'm secular, but my relatives in Turkey are Muslims, and they're good people."

"Sorry, sorry, you shouldn't take that personally," Wiklund said, blushing and clearly on the defensive. "I get that. I know they can be great people."

Brännström pretended not to notice the tension between Wiklund and Baksi and moved on as if nothing had happened.

270

"Or maybe he's just returned to the side where he truly belongs—the side of the entrenched Swedish haters. Gyllenstierna is a Swedish adaptation of *Gyldenstierne*, originally from a Danish noble family. Someone from the *Gyldenstierne* family acquired an estate in East Denmark—which Skåne was called at the time—in the fourteenth hundreds. After the Swedish occupation, the name was likely changed to Gyllenstierna to avoid appearing provocatively Danish. Most Danes lost their estates, but not the Gyllenstiernas, and several later served in the Swedish government."

"This is getting a bit confusing," Baksi remarked. "It seems like there are tensions and conflicts everywhere. Still, it's nothing compared to the chaos where my parents come from, in the Kurdish region of Turkey. There are so many sides, shades, and loyalties that it makes your head spin—ethnic, religious, geographic, and never forget—which clan you belong to. Sometimes, I wonder if anyone understands the whole situation."

"It's truly horrifying that our clueless politicians voluntarily destabilized and 'Balkanized' Sweden, which was one of the most homogeneous countries in the world," Wiklund said. "It's like they wanted to start a war in Sweden, and eventually, they succeeded."

"Those idiots never realized that globalists were subtly and cleverly manipulating them," Baksi added. "Our intelligence services are fully aware of this, with hundreds of documents and recorded conversations to prove it."

"My view is that the media pushed the politicians to make those fateful decisions that ultimately led to the war," Brännström said. "But that's something for future historians to unravel. Our only focus is winning this war—everything else can wait."

Brännström stood up and poured himself another cup of coffee. The coffee wasn't just invigorating; it was therapeutic, too—a calming, distinctly Swedish ritual.

It's been 375 years since Skåne became part of Sweden through the Treaty of Roskilde, but the wrongdoings of the Swedish occupiers are far from forgiven. The fact that the farmers of Skåne were freed from Danish serfdom doesn't seem to have left much of an impression on the consciousness of the Scanians."

"Just one last question," Baksi said. "What about the Barsebäck nuclear power plant? It's been quite a few years since the reactors were shut down, but the radioactivity lingers for decades. What happens if the Muslims blow it up?"

"We've thoroughly reviewed the situation," Svartenbrandt replied. "The reactors were dismantled long ago. The spent fuel rods have been transported to Oskarshamn on the east coast for storage. Other highly radioactive components, like the reactor cores, were cut into pieces and stored in Oskarshamn, so it shouldn't pose a problem."

"What remains on-site is an interim storage facility for intermediate and low-level radioactive waste," Brännström noted. "The storage building has forty-inch-thick concrete walls that effectively block radiation. We assess that even if the Muslims were to blow up the building, which would require significant effort, the spread of radioactivity would be minimal and only affect the immediate area."

"The cut-up reactor parts are stored in steel tanks with four-inch-thick walls. Even if the building were destroyed, releasing any dangerous levels of radioactivity would still take a lot of work."

"We won't allocate resources to Barsebäck," Brännström concluded.

"Thanks, I just wanted to make sure," Baksi replied.

The meeting adjourned, and most participants quickly left for other meetings. There were hundreds of details to finalize before Operation Dekanus, which was set to be the most significant battle the Swedish military had engaged in since Karl XII's Russian campaign more than 305 years ago.

Chapter 35 – The Will of Allah

November 24, 2033

"Time flies," muttered General Mahmoud Khalil to himself, resting his chin on his knuckles with his elbow propped on the armrest. It was hard for him to believe that it had been a year and a half since he and Ahmed Ben Barka, with Mahmoud as Ahmed's right hand, launched the invasion of the infidels' land. The land that the infidels called Sweden—but which all true believers now referred to as *Alzuwid*.

This cold and barren country, close to the North Pole, has strange and silent people who seem devoid of emotion, more frigid than the corpses in the graveyards back home in Cairo.

A sparsely populated wasteland, devoid of culture, where the sun rarely shines, especially now at the end of November, Mahmoud thought as he gazed into the darkness from his fourth-floor office in the headquarters. He saw nothing outside, as the entire city was blacked out, but he could hear the rain lashing against the window in the strong gusts of wind.

But it rains constantly, he thought grimly. The Swedes claimed that it only rained like this on the West Coast, and of course, that's where he had the misfortune to be stationed. Yet, he suspected it was just as miserable everywhere. Everything was gray—in the land of *Alzuwid*, the colors of the rainbow had been reduced to shades of gray. As impoverished as their history and culture. There weren't even leaves on the trees. Just ugly, barren branches, looking as dead as he felt inside.

Sure, the Swedes had built a high material standard, and their homes were modern and well-kept compared to the houses in Cairo. But still. He could never live here. He felt tired, listless, and drained of energy. Everything felt pointless. It was a new and foreign feeling. Was this what it felt like to be depressed? He had heard of people who fell into depression, and he wondered if he was in that state now. Maybe it was the weather. Or the war. Or both.

Often, he questioned what good Muslims were doing in this remote corner of the world. Perhaps it would have been better to let the blond, blue-eyed bastards keep their country to themselves. If they stayed here, at least they wouldn't pollute his land.

Egypt had been plagued for centuries, if not millennia, by tourists who came to admire the masterpieces the Egyptians had created long ago when *Alzuwid* was still in the Stone Age. Ever since he was a child, Mahmoud had despised the foolish tourists, especially the Western ones —crowds of Christian, pale, fat idiots with ruddy faces viewing the pyramids through their camera lenses.

Then they hurried on, eager to photograph the next monument, which they didn't understand either. They lacked spirituality. And dignity. Did they feel anything? Did they see anything? Did they even perceive smells and tastes?

Their vacations merely expressed consumerism and their constant pursuit of status. They traveled just to have something expensive to flaunt in front of their neighbors. They were so rushed that they seemed to lose themselves somewhere.

Mahmoud thought, trying to snap out of his gloom, that a Muslim rule under Sharia law might be what they needed. If they converted to the true faith, they could be purified from their sins. Allah forgives those who honor His signs.

One day, the Swedes would be grateful to those who brought the light to *Alzuwid*. They would be thankful to Mahmoud and all his *God's Warriors* and *Holy Warriors* who had attacked them. But first, many of them had to die.

Another person who needed to die was his superior, Ahmed Ben Barka, and that would happen soon. Allah had decreed it when Mahmoud sought guidance in his prayers.

What Ahmed secretly indulged in was *haram*. It wasn't just that he habitually sneaked away to meet with young boys whenever the opportunity arose—something Allah might overlook, even though it wasn't desirable.

What was worse was that Ahmed lived like a Westerner, even though he tried to hide it. He drank whiskey from small crystal glasses when he worked alone in his room, all while listening to the music of polytheists. He smoked at least half a pack of cigarettes a day. Violating the prohibitions on alcohol and tobacco was a severe offense—no devout Muslim lived like that.

Ahmed's wardrobe was filled with Western brands. Exclusive garments with names and symbols that Mahmoud had seen in the most expensive shops of the infidels in Dubai during his vacations. Even his underwear was from high-end, luxurious brands that were unfit for a true Muslim, who was supposed to be above the vain temptations of life.

It was no coincidence that the Prophet had decreed that mosques should not be adorned with artworks and beautiful things—in contrast to the infidels' churches. Worshippers should not be blinded by superficial decorations that only obscure the essence of the teachings and hold no real value, like everything else on earth. The short time people spent on earth was not meant for pleasure. On the contrary, life was full of duties and obligations, a mere preparation before meeting Allah, who decided who would enter paradise.

Only those who lived as the Prophet had commanded would be allowed in, and Ahmed would not be one of them. Ahmed was a depraved hedonist who would soon be on his knees before Allah, trembling with fear. He would regret it, but it would be too late to ask for mercy by then.

Mahmoud felt proud and honored to have been given this mission. He was chosen, and he knew that Allah would remember this when the time came for his judgment.

Sometimes, Mahmoud replayed the events of that day when they recruited new suicide bombers shortly after the invasion last summer. It was in the park called Brunnsparken in Gothenburg where Ahmed recruited young Moroccan boys, and he didn't just recruit them to carry bombs in their backpacks or hide under their clothes.

Mahmoud's informants had filmed Ahmed at the famous Europa Hotel, where he went with two boys, lighting a cigarette nonchalantly and offering one to each young boy. And there were more films that Mahmoud didn't even want to watch—footage from hotel rooms and apartments where Ahmed met with these young boys.

Once Ahmed was out of the way, Mahmoud would show the films to the rest of the command staff and reveal Ahmed's Western habits. Then, they would understand why Allah had forsaken them in the Swedish war and why their fortunes had turned. Everyone knew they needed Allah's help to win the war. Mahmoud knew the entire command would rally behind him once they knew the truth.

One morning, as Mahmoud was walking down the corridor on his way to the daily staff meeting, he happened to overhear Ahmed's loyal adjutant and master chef, Hassan, informing Ahmed that the presidential suite had been reserved at the Radisson Blu on Östergatan, in the Old Town of Malmö.

Mahmoud instantly understood that this was a message from Allah, signaling that the day had come—the day when Allah's will would be fulfilled, the day when Mahmoud would carry out the duty he had been chosen for, the day Mahmoud would make history.

Mahmoud noticed that Hassan looked worried when he realized Mahmoud was within earshot as Ahmed received the information about the suite reservation. The carpet muffled Mahmoud's footsteps as he approached Hassan from behind, inadvertently causing Hassan to breach his duty against his highly admired superior. Perhaps it was the first time Hassan had ever failed his chief, which deeply troubled the perfectionist within him.

Ahmed immediately sensed the situation with his unfailing intuition and placed his right hand on Hassan's shoulder.

"It's alright, Hassan, *Habibi*, everything is as it should be. Thank you for being so helpful."

Mahmoud was familiar with the Radisson Blu in the town's Caroli district. He also knew what was supposed to happen in the presidential suite. But today, Ahmed's disgraceful acts would not be completed.

After the staff meeting, Mahmoud went straight to his office and drew his little companion, the Yarygin, from the holster he wore on his right side, even though he was left-handed. Like Wild Bill Hickok, the famous gunslinger of the Wild West, he wore the weapon on the front of his hip, almost on his stomach, with the grip facing the wrong way so he could draw it quickly. But Mahmoud had never heard of Hickok, as he, unlike his superior, never watched Western movies.

Mahmoud had a special bond with his Yarygin 6P35 from the Izhevsk Mechanical Plant. Like thousands of other weapon enthusiasts, he had visited the factory in Izhevsk, the capital of the lesser-known Udmurt Republic, east of the Ural Mountains.

No foreigner would ever visit the modest industrial city by the Iz River if it weren't for the fact that it was hallowed ground, where iconic weapons like the Kalashnikov AK-47 assault rifle—modernized and renamed the Kalashnikov AK-74 in 1974—and the Soviet PM pistol was first created. The Soviet PM is known as the Makarov Pistol after its designer. The Yarygin 6P35, which replaced the Makarov, quickly succeeded, achieving iconic status within just a few years. The Yarygin 6P35 is a 9mm caliber pistol, like the Makarov, but thanks to modern specialized ammunition, it has significantly more impact.

Mahmoud loved his Yarygin 6P35, even though it had more accessible competitors to carry. Fully loaded with eighteen rounds, it weighed well over two pounds. But the weight gave it a steady feel in his hand. As the specifications promised, the weapon was effective at a shooting distance of up to one hundred and fifty feet—double that of the Makarov Pistol, which still serves as the standard sidearm in about forty armies worldwide. However, in countries with better economies, the Makarov Pistol has often been replaced by the Yarygin 6P35.

Today, Mahmoud's little companion, the Yarygin, would prove its worth. Mahmoud opened his desk drawer and placed a box of ammunition on the desk. He loaded round after round until the magazine was full, allowing him eighteen shots. In everyday situations, he usually settled for six rounds in the magazine to keep the weight down, but today was no ordinary day. Today, Mahmoud would carry out Allah's command and couldn't afford to fail.

Just after five o'clock, Mahmoud heard the lock click as he swiped his key card against the electronic door lock. The door opened almost silently, and Mahmoud heard soft footsteps on the carpet coming from at least two pairs of feet. The door closed with a muted thud, and he heard Ahmed's voice, "*Yumkinuk shunq huna. 'Aetaqid 'anana nabda bishambaniaa saghiratin.*"

It felt a bit strange to hear Arabic. Mahmoud had expected a Swede since his informants had noted that Ahmed seemed to have developed a preference for increasingly younger, blonde boys, especially recently. The other person giggled loudly. It appeared Ahmed had settled for just one boy today. They were going to start by drinking champagne.

"*Ladayi alqlyl min aldukhkhan 'aydana.*"

The boy wanted to smoke some hash or possibly brown sugar, and Ahmed was not one to refuse, enhancing the experience another notch. Mahmoud had a strong feeling that they knew each other well. The tone was relaxed, but it was clear that Ahmed was in control, which wasn't surprising given the age difference and Ahmed's status.

"*Mathal dhlk, baed alshambanya. 'Anah yueaziz alshueur.*" As Ahmed decided, smoking would follow the champagne, and now Mahmoud felt it was enough. He didn't want to hear more.

Mahmoud stepped into the suite's living room with his Yarygin in his left hand. Ahmed and the boy, still fully clothed, sat close together on a sofa, each holding a glass of champagne. They stared in shock at Mahmoud, who aimed the pistol at Ahmed's chest from a mere ten feet away. It was impossible to miss from that distance. Ahmed, mesmerized by the weapon, didn't say a word.

"I'm sorry, but I have to do this. Allah came to me in my prayers. I've received a divine command."

"Wait, Mahmoud, my friend, *Habibi*—just let me say something. Haven't I been a good friend you could trust for many years? I made you what you are—have you forgotten that? What has gotten into you? Why do you want to harm me?"

"It's not me who wants to harm you. It's Allah's will."

"Please, Mahmod, I can arrange for you to have ten million US dollars in an account anywhere you want. Just give me a chance!"

"Allah's will cannot be bought."

Mahmoud aimed at Ahmed's heart.

The gunshot echoed through the room, and Mahmoud collapsed instantly, struck between the shoulders and right in the spine. He died on the spot.

"I apologize for intruding on your private matters," said Ahmed's adjutant, Hassan, quietly from the doorway, the same one Mahmoud had just walked through. "But I felt I had to overstep my bounds today, and I hope you can forgive me."

Ahmed and the boy remained shocked, still holding their glasses aloft for the toast that never happened.

"Enjoy your evening," Hassan said to the stunned pair on the sofa as he opened the door to the corridor. Before closing it, he poked his head back in.

"I'll arrange for someone to come and take care of Mahmoud's body. For dinner, your favorite course, Moroccan Tagine with seafood, will be served."

Chapter 36 – Operation Dekanus

December 4, 2033

The Battle of Lund was scheduled to commence with an artillery bombardment on December 4 at 7.50 a.m., precisely twenty-two minutes before sunrise. The attack would co-occur in the towns of Kävlinge and Löddeköpinge, where the road networks and crossing points offered opportunities to cross the river on a larger scale.

The plan was for the Archer artillery systems to decimate the Muslim positions along the riverbank on the opposite side of the Kävlinge River with an intense barrage, supported by fire from the four Model 90 grenade launcher carriages, that had survived the floods at A9, which had destroyed Sweden's artillery a year earlier.

As dawn broke and daylight made visibility possible, even for a few feet, the barrage would shift a thousand feet forward to prevent Muslim troops from advancing toward the river. At the same time, Pioneer units would cross to the other side in rubber boats before there was enough light for shooting in case any Muslim soldiers had survived the bombardment. Once the pioneering soldiers had established bridgeheads on the opposite side, thousands of armored foot soldiers would begin crossing the river, hopefully without facing enemy fire.

Other pioneering soldiers would cross the river in rubber boats around thousand feet upstream, where the remnants of the destroyed bridges were located, in both Kävlinge and Löddeköpinge. Once these soldiers had established bridgeheads, heavy trucks, and cranes would be brought in to build bridges capable of supporting the heavily armored vehicles within a few hours.

It was a meticulously crafted plan that required detailed analyses by the army's logistics experts. Hundreds of heavy vehicles and even more light vehicles would be set in motion.

The nightmare scenario that had to be avoided at all costs was the narrow access roads becoming clogged. A single vehicle breakdown in the wrong place could cause traffic jams, leading to hours-long delays, potentially derailing the entire operation, and giving the enemy the time and warning they needed.

In the shadow of the infantry's large-scale advances, two companies of seventy-eight men each from Jöns Möller's *Snapphane* guerilla fighters would be deployed to strike the enemy from behind and exacerbate the confusion and disorder that the surprise artillery bombardment was intended to create.

One company, led by Möller himself, would be landed in small motorboats from the sea at Bjärred. The other company would cross the Kävlinge River in rubber boats at Västra Hoby, a couple of miles upstream from Kävlinge.

The *Snapphane* guerilla fighters spread out in the terrain, moving on foot in groups of six soldiers. Each group leader was given a preliminary route to avoid collisions with other groups. The route was then improvised depending on the conditions encountered. The advantage of moving on foot is that maneuvers can often be done without detection. Hostile roadblocks and troop concentrations can be discreetly bypassed if engaging the enemy is not deemed necessary.

The distances were short enough that the movements involved only a few miles, depending on the situation. The downside of moving on foot is that only light weapons could be carried, mainly since the *Snapphane* guerilla fighters always carried more loaded magazines and significant amounts of ammunition than usual. Just the M/86 anti-tank weapon weighed almost fifteen pounds and, with its length of forty inches, was somewhat cumbersome to carry around, even for the well-trained guerilla fighters.

Each group of six men carried two M/86 anti-tank weapons. If a quick retreat became necessary, the anti-tank weapons would be dumped or, if the situation allowed, fired off so they wouldn't fall into enemy hands.

The anti-tank soldiers from the *Snapphane* guerilla fighter's unit had undergone rigorous and intensive special training. Their leaders, who were professional officers in the Swedish Army, along with Jöns Möller, made it clear to the anti-tank soldiers that their lives were considered less valuable than scoring a direct hit on an enemy armored vehicle. Anti-tank warfare was not for the faint of heart or for those who clung to life at all costs.

Although the *Snapphane* guerilla fighters were armed only with automatic rifles, hand grenades, and handheld Bofors M/86 anti-tank weapons, their combat effectiveness was significant. With twenty-six groups of these guerilla fighters in the field, the Muslims were in for some very unpleasant surprises.

The *Snapphane* guerilla fighters carried fifty-two anti-tank weapons, most of which were fired in surprise attacks on the enemy from concealed positions behind bushes by the roadside or similar cover.

The guerilla fighters' detailed local knowledge gave them a considerable advantage. Some group leaders were operating in areas where they had grown up and played as children. To say they had local knowledge is an understatement. They knew every path, bike trail, drainage ditch, marl pit, and even individual large trees and rocks. They knew exactly where the few small hills offered views over the flat, almost treeless agricultural landscape.

Whether and how Jeppe Hofman-Bang's Free Rangers would participate in the attack was not confirmed, as Hofman-Bang refused anything to do with the regular army. To avoid the risk of Swedes shooting at other Swedes, Brännström had tasked Jöns Möller with informing Hofman-Bang of the timing of the assault. For security reasons, this information was provided as late as the night before the attack, resulting in the Free Rangers not participating in the initial assault. Instead, they took it upon themselves to track down and eliminate Muslim soldiers or small groups who had escaped the battles and were hiding in the terrain or in houses they had managed to infiltrate.

The Free Rangers worked very effectively over the three days following the battle, using their dogs to track down enemy soldiers who had been spotted. They received frequent tips from the locals as they went from house to house, knocking on doors. The guerrilla fighters prided themselves on never taking prisoners.

On the night of December 4, at 2.20 a.m., the first troop transport vehicles slowly began to leave their encampments in the towns of Eslöv and Teckomatorp, heading toward nearby Kävlinge and Löddeköpinge. The reserve force of five-thousand-foot soldiers remained stationed in Röstånga.

Even though all vehicles moved with their lights off, slowly and carefully through the pitch-black night, with no streetlights to guide them, they had to assume that the enemy might somehow observe or be informed about their movements. Launching an operation of this scale without the enemy noticing was a fantasy. However, they hoped the enemy was unaware of the Swedes' access to artillery, as this information had been kept within a very tight circle. The Archer units and the Model 90 grenade launcher vehicles were stationed separately with their crews in Svalöv.

By just after 5 a.m., all the infantries had taken their positions near Kävlinge and Löddeköpinge. Now, it was just a matter of waiting. Sporadic fire from enemy grenade launchers sent a clear message: We know you're there, and we're ready. Come on, if you dare! They would have been far less confident if the enemy had known what was in store for them. Two and a half hours remained before the assault would begin.

At 5.35 a.m., the four Model 90 grenade launcher vehicles began moving from Svalöv. The era of towed artillery was long over, at least within the Swedish Armed Forces. Two tracked artillery pieces took National Highway 110 toward Löddeköpinge, while the other took National Highway 108 toward Kävlinge. Although these roads had been under Swedish control for months, they were still guarded by regularly placed sniper groups at six hundred feet intervals. The Swedes couldn't afford to let the enemy remove their limited artillery before it could be used, so no risks were taken.

Forty-five minutes later, the twelve much faster six-wheeled Archer vehicles set off, each accompanied by a support vehicle of the same basic model. These support vehicles, also part of the Archer system, were packed with ammunition, service tools, and spare parts. Six teams traveled along National Highway 108 and six along National Highway 110. The thirty-five-ton, forty-six-foot-long convoys moved at maximum speed with low beams, traveling forty miles per hour.

The Archer is an advanced version of the world-renowned Bofors Haubits 77B artillery piece. The gun's upper carriage is mounted on a heavy off-road vehicle, the Volvo A30E. The support vehicle is essentially the same Volvo A30E model. Thanks to a unique composite armor developed by Bofors, these vehicles are protected against shrapnel, small-caliber fire, and mines. The cars are also NBC-classified, meaning they are protected against nuclear, biological, and chemical weapons.

Compared to the Bofors Haubits 77B, the Archer has been upgraded for better firing performance. This is partly due to a six-foot longer barrel with a telescoping mechanism that increases range and precision. The gun is remotely controlled via a computer from the driver's cabin, so the three operators do not need to leave the cabin when the weapon is in use. The system's computer gives the operators complete control over ballistics calculations, firing, safety checks, ammunition handling, communication, combat management, navigation, operational monitoring, surveillance, observation, and fire control.

In artillery systems like the Archer, V0 measurement, which indicates the muzzle velocity of the shells, has long been a standard practice. Ensuring that all shells have the same muzzle velocity is crucial for maintaining high precision and keeping ammunition manufacturers on their toes.

Archer's excellent firing performance and short repositioning times enable a combat technique that significantly increases the system's survivability while delivering rapid and effective fire on target after receiving the fire command.

When the Archer vehicles were two miles away from their respective deployment points—Ålstorp for those targeting Löddeköpinge and Norrvidinge for those attacking the enemy at Kävlinge—they halted on the road, waiting for the go-ahead from operations command.

After a brief pause, they received confirmation that the grenade launcher vehicles were in position: two just north of Löddeköpinge and two on the outskirts of Kävlinge. All that remained was to await the marching orders from Brigadier General William Magnusson, which arrived precisely on time at 7.35 a.m., delivered in his unmistakable Värmland accent:

"All Archer units, move to your positions. Prepare for combat!"

A few minutes before schedule, all Archer units reached their pre-selected positions and deployed into their assault starting positions. The support legs automatically extended within thirty seconds while the telescopic, extra-long 155-millimeter barrels deployed.

The vehicles resembled enormous insects with the support legs extended along their sides and the barrels protruding like long antennae. The brigade artillery was ready for battle. On the operators' screens, the message "Ready for firing at pre-selected coordinates" flashed in bold red letters. Below that, another line in green letters read "Pattern: Zigzag line," followed by "Coverage: 100%."

Since the enemy was positioned along a line following the river's curves, each Archer unit was assigned to fire along a predetermined "curved" line between two selected points. Given the inherent margin of error in shell impacts, a zigzag firing pattern was chosen along the line, causing some shells to land just before the line, others just after, and some directly on the line.

"Coverage: 100%" indicated that every point along the enemy's line would be hit with deadly force. The gun's computer system automatically adjusts the barrel's aim for each shot, ensuring that shells are randomly distributed according to the zigzag pattern. Each shell lands in a different spot, leaving the enemy unable to predict where the next shell will strike.

The system's computer can launch shells in any chosen pattern. For instance, a circular area is a standard preset when targeting an area with enemy artillery within a confined space. In such cases, shells are randomly distributed over the circular area.

The system also allows for adjusting the concentration of shells in specific areas within the circle by setting percentage values. Custom patterns can be quickly drawn on the screen. For example, suppose the enemy is positioned within an irregularly shaped area resembling a banana. In that case, the operator can draw a banana shape with his finger over the area on the screen, and the system will handle the rest.

If the enemy's position is divided into groups, several small circles can be drawn on the map. The system then automatically targets these groups, so no shells are wasted in the areas between them.

The computer is linked to two trigger buttons. Both must be pressed simultaneously for the system to begin firing. Adjacent screens displayed maps and satellite photographs of the pre-programmed targets, which were the enemy positions along the southern bank of the Kävlingeån. The world's fastest artillery system was ready to engage in combat for the first time.

Finally, Brigadier General Magnusson's raspy Värmland accent crackled through the headphones.

"All units, prepare for storm fire in sixty seconds."

The seconds ticked away slowly in the ominous silence.

"Storm fire in thirty seconds."

And then, silence, only silence that seemed to stretch on forever.

"Fifteen seconds."

Breath held, hearts pounding. Unexpected thoughts surfaced from nowhere just when they were least needed.

"Ten-nine-eight-seven-six-five-four-three-two-one-FIRE!"

Precisely on time, at 7.50.00 a.m., all hell broke loose as the twelve Archer units simultaneously opened fire on their pre-programmed targets. The first three shells from each unit were automatically fired at different elevation angles so that they would impact the target simultaneously, maximizing the element of surprise. With twelve units firing, thirty-six heavy shells rained at once on an utterly unprepared enemy.

The serene calm instantly transformed into a roaring inferno, where the ground shook continuously in the enemy's lines. The only thing the soldiers in the Muslim positions could do was press themselves as close to the ground as possible, face down, and hope that the hell would end. It was a futile hope, as it turned out.

The core strategy of the Archer system is to regroup and fire three new shells from a new position even before the initial three shells have impacted the target, continuing this pattern with rapid relocations.

The computer retains the coordinates and automatically adjusts the system to the new firing position, meaning no time is lost except during the actual movement. These rapid relocations—known as "shoot-and-scoot" tactics—are necessary because a sophisticated enemy can quickly pinpoint the positions of the artillery units after the first volley and deliver counter-battery fire, potentially destroying the units.

The most common method for locating artillery positions is to track the trajectory of the enemy's shells using radar, which can then pinpoint the locations of the enemy's artillery units. Subsequently, these positions are targeted with counter-battery fire, or ABEK, short for "artillery counter-fire" in Swedish.

Additionally, fighter jets, drones, guided missiles, and target-seeking tank munitions can often locate enemy positions within minutes. This is why Bofors developed the world's fastest artillery system. Since the Archer units are already on the move before their shells hit the target, it's nearly impossible to take them out except by sheer luck.

Given the Muslim enemy's limitations in advanced ABEK technology, the commanders of the Archer units were ordered to remain in position and continue firing as rapidly as possible. Maximizing the rate of fire was prioritized over likely unnecessary safety measures. However, if the situation became too dangerous, it was up to each unit commander to decide when to relocate.

The Archers unleashed a barrage of 155-millimeter shells on the enemy, firing one round every seven seconds. With twelve units operating, nearly two shells per second detonated in the enemy's positions.

The continuous explosions blended into a thunderous roar, making it impossible to distinguish individual blasts. Every twentieth round was a smoke shell intended to create further chaos and blind the enemy.

Despite having a range of up to fifty kilometers, the Archers were as close as three miles from the enemy's positions. This proximity was due to the impending forward shift in their targeting and the fact that precision increases the closer you are to the target. Wind can sometimes cause significant drift from the intended target.

The four Model 90 grenade launcher carriages had been deployed earlier, with two stationed in Kävlinge and two in Löddeköpinge.

When the Archers began firing at 7.50 a.m., the four mortar carriers also opened fire with their 120-millimeter, short, smoothbore grenade launchers. While their range and shell size are smaller than the Archers' 155-millimeter rounds, they are still formidable weapons."

The system is a basic grenade launcher system without advanced technology, mounted on the Swedish Army's workhorse, the Combat Vehicle 90. These grenade launcher carriages, the only battalion-level artillery available to the Swedes, were commanded by Battalion Chief Colonel Karl Uusitalo from Swedish Tornedalen, close to the Finnish border up north.

Uusitalo was about to order the engineers to cross the river in inflatable boats, followed by the mechanized infantry who would wade through the water. But first, the four grenade launcher carriages were to fire two magazines of shells each, totaling 448 rounds that would explode directly in the enemy's positions.

Although the Swedes had few grenade launchers, they had ample ammunition, so there was no reason to conserve it. Missing the target was nearly impossible at less than a quarter of a mile range.

After twenty minutes of relentless, deafening bombardment, the firing suddenly ceased, and everything fell silent. Many Swedish soldiers used night vision goggles to study the remnants of the enemy's positions on the other side of the river.

A light southern breeze slowly pushed the smoke from the smoke grenades toward the Swedish side, complicating the subsequent phases of the operation. Through the smoke, no movement was visible. All that could be seen were piles of earth and scattered debris, still smoldering and smoking. The enemy's positions along the river were utterly obliterated. Not a single enemy soldier in the line had survived.

Soon after, an order came from Brigadier General William Magnusson to resume the Archer artillery barrage, this time targeting a line one thousand feet south of the river, where most of the enemy's 250 combat vehicles were stationed.

These vehicles, a mix of tanks, lighter armored cars, and other combat vehicles, had been started and were now battle-ready. They began slowly advancing toward the river while firing on the Swedes across the way. The enemy reinforcements needed to be prevented from reaching the river before the bridgeheads were firmly established.

It was equally critical to stop the enemy fire before the Swedish mechanized infantry could leave their cover to wade across the river.

During this artillery fire round, ten Archer units deployed the so-called "Bofors Bonus" base bleed shells, each containing two submunitions designed to turn off armored vehicles. As the shell neared the target area, a propellant charge ejected the two submunitions from the shell casing.

The submunitions have an asymmetrical wing, causing them to descend in a corkscrew-like motion. At an altitude of five hundred feet, the infrared seeker activates, scanning the ground for heat signatures that match those of an armored vehicle. Each submunition can scan an area of approximately ten thousand square feet during the roughly four seconds it is active.

If a target is detected, an explosively formed projectile is fired at it. If no target is found, the charge detonates when the submunition reaches the ground.

The effect was devastating, as hundreds of armored vehicles emit heat. Out of the enemy's 250 combat vehicles, the "Bofors Bonus" submunitions destroyed ninety-four of them within twenty minutes.

However, a problem that reduced the effectiveness of the bombardment was that several shells targeted the same vehicle, resulting in some armored cars being hit by two or even three submunitions. This was an inefficient use of the sophisticated shells.

Two Archer units used the XM982 Excalibur shell, of which only ninety were available—all Sweden's military budget could afford. The XM982 Excalibur is a collaboration between American Raytheon Missile Systems and BAE Systems Bofors.

This shell, which had proven highly influential during the war in Afghanistan, is precision-guided using GPS. It is fired at a high angle and then glides toward the target. Once the shell reaches its maximum altitude of twenty thousand feet, the wings deploy and begin sliding toward the target. The final descent is nearly vertical, which maximizes the blast effect, striking unsuspecting enemy vehicles like a divine thunderbolt seemingly out of nowhere.

The XM982 Excalibur took out many enemy vehicles, but to be fully effective, the firing range and maximum altitude should have been more excellent. Colonel Uusitalo's grenade launchers also began their second round, firing shells toward targets around a thousand feet beyond the river.

The twenty-three available Leopard tanks were positioned along the riverbank, evenly distributed between Kävlinge and Löddeköpinge, with one tank every thousand feet. They were ready to fire armor-piercing projectiles from their 120-millimeter smoothbore guns at any remaining enemy vehicles. However, few targets remained, as many enemy tank commanders turned their cars around in panic—perhaps out of a sense of self-preservation—and fled the battlefield in every direction possible, given that the Kävlinge River blocked any northward escape.

With the Swedish artillery barrage preventing a retreat directly south, most enemy vehicles moved along the river in the two possible directions, keeping a safe distance from the river.

Those heading southeast encountered the force of the *Snapphane* guerilla fighters, who had crossed the river upstream of Kävlinge in inflatable boats. The anti-tank weapons of the *Snapphane* guerilla fighters, fired from close range, turned vehicle after vehicle into smoking wreckage, forcing the remaining tank commanders to turn south to try and bypass the artillery barrage to the east.

The enemy vehicles heading southwest met the same fate as those heading southeast, as the guerilla fighters, who had landed from the sea, had already spread out and positioned themselves with their anti-tank weapons.

Then came Colonel Karl Uusitalo's order, delivered in his distinct, gruff voice with an unmistakable Finnish accent.

"Fourth Company, at Kävlinge: Move forward, with a leap, to the other side of the river! Spread out and take cover!"

The fifty soldiers quickly reached the river and began slowly wading to the other side without encountering enemy fire. Additional companies soon followed them.

As the dawn light grew brighter, thousands of soldiers laden with combat gear could be seen slowly wading across the river, struggling to climb the muddy embankment on the far side, which was riddled with deep craters from the artillery barrage. The wet boots made the churned-up mud as slippery as a vast banana peel, causing most soldiers to stumble and fall multiple times before reaching solid ground.

At Löddeköpinge, similar scenes unfolded, with the difference that the water depth was more significant than expected, making the crossing more difficult and slower. However, this didn't matter much since all enemy activity had ceased.

Many of the soldiers at Löddeköpinge held their AK5 rifles above their heads to avoid water damage, though this precaution was unnecessary as the weapons' reliability was unaffected by water. Weapons maintenance would be conducted regardless after each use.

While the *Snapphane* guerilla fighters and the Free Rangers continued their relentless hunt for fleeing and hiding enemy soldiers, Svartenbrandt and Brännström could already confirm, early in the morning, that Operation Dekanus was a complete success.

Brännström pointed emphatically towards the slowly rising sun.

"The sun over Austerlitz, damn it, that's the sun shining over us," he exclaimed loudly, playfully placing his right hand inside his jacket in a stiff salute, mimicking the classic Freemason pose of Napoleon as he's often depicted in the field—a pose that felt exceptionally comfortable for Anton Brännström, who was himself a Freemason of the eighth degree in Luleå's Freemason lodge.

Today, he felt like Sweden's Napoleon and intended to savor and hold onto that feeling for as long as possible. He deserved it after all the effort, and they all deserved it.

The enemy was utterly crushed. By the end of the day, the tally showed that 143 enemy vehicles had been destroyed and approximately six thousand enemy soldiers had been eliminated.

The Swedish losses amounted to two Leopard tanks along with their crews, totaling six personnel and thirty-seven fallen foot soldiers, along with twenty-four others who sustained various injuries. These were treated at the field hospital set up by the well-prepared Quartermaster. Those with minor injuries were transported by ambulance to the Central Hospital in Kristianstad, while the more seriously wounded were flown by helicopter to the Regional Hospital in Linköping, which was once again fully operational.

The following day, reports came in regarding the losses among the *Snapphane* guerilla fighters and Free Rangers, which together amounted to twenty-nine killed and twelve wounded—a significant toll considering their relatively small numbers.

The enemy losses were adjusted to 152 vehicles and nearly seven thousand soldiers. Operation Dekanus was a brutal and total victory for the Swedes, forcing the enemy to hastily abandon Lund without a fight and regroup instead in Malmö. Despite no battles being fought within the city, the destruction in Lund was extensive.

The list of demolished buildings was long, and it was clear that the enemy had focused on erasing as much of the Swedish-Danish culture and history as possible: the Lund Cathedral, AF Castle, Church of Allhelgonakyrkan, The House of Dekan, the Old Observatory, Church of Helgeandskyrkan, Grand Hotel, House of Krognos, Liberiet, Nöbbelövs Church, Stäket, Saint Peters Monestary Church, Palaestra et Odeon, The Royal House —all lay in ruins. Operation Dekanus, or the "Second Battle of Lund," as military historians later would call it, was the most remarkable success the Swedish military had ever experienced in its entire history.

The Supreme Commander, former Army Chief Anton Brännström, had secured his place in the history books. Yet, a much stricter challenge remained: Malmö. Not to mention Västra Götaland and Gothenburg, which would have to be dealt with later.

"When you're eating an elephant, the only way to do it is one bite at a time," Brännström often said, with his characteristic and descriptive logic.

Brännström was right: Many bites remained before Swedish territory would be cleared of the enemy. But today, December 4, 2033, was a day to celebrate, not to worry about future challenges. This sentiment was perfectly captured in another of Brännström's now-legendary sayings: "Don't worry about problems in advance because then you'll have to face them twice."

The others in the staff laughed heartily at Brännström's reassuring words. Tonight, they would celebrate—and do so accordingly.

Chapter 37 – German Fall

Fall 2033

The Muslim Brotherhood's invasion of Sweden in the summer of 2032 shocked Europeans across the continent. The full-scale civil war that followed served as a wake-up call, particularly for the populations in countries where the expansion of Islam had progressed the furthest: Germany, France, the Netherlands, Belgium, and the United Kingdom.

If the unthinkable could happen in Sweden—until recently, one of the most stable countries in the world—it could happen anywhere in Western Europe. There were many signs that what was occurring in Sweden was merely the beginning of something much more significant, an irreversible process that could not be stopped.

In the Muslim Brotherhood's strategy, Sweden was the catalyst intended to spark civil wars across Western Europe, and it appeared they were succeeding.

The situation was alarming throughout Western Europe. Muslims, emboldened, openly brandished their Kalashnikovs in and around the thousands of Muslim enclaves.

Armed Muslim mobs roamed the central parts of cities, vandalizing banks, department stores, and war and democracy monuments and assaulting ordinary people who happened to cross their path, terrifying the native populations. Paralyzed politicians had no idea how to respond. Confronting the aggressive Muslims militarily seemed like a bad idea, as it would almost certainly lead to an open civil war.

The situation was worse in Germany. The explosive growth of Germany's Muslim population signaled a demographic shift of epic proportions, permanently altering the country. Nothing seemed capable of stopping the tidal wave of Muslim immigrants, whose birth rates were three to four times higher than those of Germans. The Muslim population now exceeded ten million, and the rate of increase indicated that Germans were on their way to becoming a minority in their own country. It was as if being German and being Muslim were two distinct races.

The question increasingly being asked by Germans was whether there would be any place for them in Germany in the long term. The signs were not promising. When Muslims successfully bombed the European Central Bank tower in Frankfurt on Germany's national day, October 3, 2033, many saw it as the final proof that war was inevitable. The destruction of the EU's economic heart was a symbolic act of enormous significance, resonating across the shattered remnants of the EU and echoing worldwide.

In Berlin, Hamburg, Frankfurt/Offenbach, Cologne, and Munich, outright street battles were being fought between Muslims and the German riot police. The police's intimidating rolling fortresses—developed by Bozena in Slovakia—proved invaluable.

Protected behind the vehicles' large, deployed shields, thirty-six riot police could advance despite being fired upon while water cannons blasted and tear gas grenades were launched. The rolling fortress also carried a grenade launcher, primarily intended for tear gas grenades, but which could also be loaded with military explosive grenades. However, these had not yet been used.

Through a loudspeaker system and a large display behind bulletproof glass, appropriate messages were communicated, almost always in Turkish, to the opposing forces before the riot police launched their attack, shielded behind their handheld shields.

"Bu yasadışı bir gösteri. Katılımcılar hapis cezası riski altın- dadır. Defol git buradan! – This is an illegal demonstration. Participants risk imprisonment. Leave now!"

The situation was significantly worse in Germany's most populous state, North Rhine-Westphalia. The Ruhr area was mainly under the control of Muslim jihadists. The elliptical area formed by connecting the cities of Duisburg, Essen, Bochum, Dortmund, and Wuppertal was effectively a Muslim zone governed by Sharia law.

Germans had been leaving the area in large numbers for months, now counted in the millions, encouraged by aggressive jihadists who offered them free bus transportation out of their territory. In the East German cities like Leipzig, Dresden, and Nuremberg, as well as in most small towns across Germany, the Germans owned the streets, marching with flags bearing nationalist symbols. Many of these symbols were easily recognizable and associated with what the left-liberal press called the far right or right-wing populism. The Celtic cross, sun wheel, Odal rune, and Týr rune were standard, as was the Iron Cross. Some flags even bore the swastika.

It was in the former East Germany, where there was little acceptance of Islam—and — significantly fewer immigrants – that the resistance and will to fight were most intense. Torchlight processions quickly followed one another, and the well-known songs from another era, a hundred years earlier, echoed once again between the buildings.

Some of the marchers, often in uniform, carried placards with portraits of Adolf Hitler.

They fervently wished for a new charismatic leader who would save Germany in the struggle against Islam, but so far, this new Adolf was nowhere to be found.

It was only after the Salman Rushdie affair in 1989 that Europe's Turks, Bosnians, Pakistanis, Moroccans, Tunisians, Egyptians, and Algerians began to be seen as Muslims in the public consciousness. Rushdie's publication of the novel "The Satanic Verses" immediately sparked outrage in the Muslim world, where the book was considered to give an incorrect portrayal of the Prophet Muhammad. The book was quickly banned in Muslim countries. On February 14, 1989, a *fatwa* was issued by Iran's religious and political leader, Ayatollah Ruhollah Khomeini, via Radio Tehran, declaring that Rushdie must be executed for blasphemy against Islam. A reward was offered to anyone who killed Rushdie. A political consequence of this was that the United Kingdom broke diplomatic relations with Iran on March 7, 1989.

Meanwhile, unrest erupted worldwide, with firebombs targeting bookstores and publishers associated with the book. Muslim groups held competitions to see who could burn the most copies of "The Satanic Verses." Many people involved in translating and publishing the book were subjected to death threats and harassment, with some being murdered and others seriously injured.

Despite numerous promises from Tehran that the *fatwa* against Rushdie would be lifted, this never happened. In 2012, the leader of an Iranian religious organization announced that the reward had been increased to two million U.S. dollars.

On August 12, Faith caught up with Salman Rushdie when he lectured at the Chautauqua Institute, south of Buffalo, in New York. A black-clad man named Hadi Matar assaulted Rushdie on stage, who was severely injured by the fifteen stab wounds that the assailant managed to inflict. Rushdie miraculously survived but with permanent disabilities. The Rushdie affair made some Europeans aware for the first time that Islam could indeed be a potential threat to European societies and democracy itself. However, the issue was dismissed by the media and politicians, who instead began to speak of the multicultural society in dreamy and lyrical terms.

As Muslim immigration increased throughout Western Europe, the government propaganda machine continued to soften the souls of Europeans. Criticism of Islam was labeled as religious persecution, and critics were branded as Islamophobes, implying that they suffered from psychological issues, so-called phobias.

It was all deemed to be a mere delusion, and many critics were sentenced to prison for violating laws against hate speech. Criticism of Islam led to social ostracism and the loss of both jobs and friends. All critics were seen as racists and Nazis. Resistance was forced underground.

Occasionally, events occurred that exposed cracks in the multicultural facade. The most attention was drawn to the murders of several well-known critics of Islam, which led many other critics to fall silent permanently out of concern for their own and their families' safety.

Around the turn of the millennium, all these different nationalities of Muslims that had immigrated to Western Europe in large numbers began to appear as a single, homogeneous group. Muslims demanded special treatment and exemption from national laws concerning things like polygamy, pedophilia, child mutilation, ritual slaughter, and violence against women—and their demands were willingly met by the bought-off politicians. At this point, the people—the voters—should have awakened and reacted against the Islamization of their countries, but the propaganda and repression against critics of Islam were too strong.

Instead, Islamization gained further momentum as it was solidified through agreements between authorities and Muslim organizations, guaranteeing the protection of Muslim community properties, approval for the construction of mosques, halal food in schools, prisons, and hospitals, the introduction of Muslim holidays, Muslim representation in state institutions, and a long list of other rights and privileges.

In many German cities, starting with Wuppertal, the streets were patrolled by bearded Muslims who appointed themselves as "Sharia police." These self-proclaimed moral enforcers worked to enforce Islamic law on the streets by distributing yellow flyers that explained the Islamic code of conduct.

Across Germany, radical Muslims infiltrated elementary and high schools, where they imposed Islamic norms and values on non-Muslim students and teachers, who often dared not resist these demands.

Despite nationwide laws prohibiting religious attire in public buildings, Muslim women and men were allowed to wear their clothes and symbols. All businesses were forced to set up unique prayer rooms where Muslims performed their religious duties during paid work hours. Muslim children were exempted from visits to churches and concentration camps, the latter being an otherwise mandatory part of Holocaust education.

The fact that Germany had willingly embarked on a slippery slope that allowed violations of laws against severe crimes and a general breakdown of public order disturbed the relatively few with the courage and insight to realize where the development was heading. However, the mosque constructions most disturbed the broad and unsuspecting public, which were soon followed by the irritating calls to prayer at maximum volume five times a day. If the Germans had understood that these calls to prayer, spoken in Turkish or Arabic, proclaimed that Muslims would conquer Germany and that Germans would be eradicated and driven from their land, perhaps their instinct for self-preservation would have been awakened, but the Germans continued to sleep. Those who were awake rarely dared to do anything but close their eyes.

Many mosques were built with tax funds. In Duisburg, in the state of North Rhine-Westphalia, the influential central mosque—Ditib Duisburg Merkez Camii—was constructed with financial support from both the state government and the EU. With the backing of other taxpayers across the EU, German taxpayers were forced to finance their demise.

However, most of the hundreds of mosque constructions were funded by Muslim countries of origin, including Turkey, Saudi Arabia,

Kuwait, and Qatar. The German foreign ministry's demands that all countries disclose donations and state subsidies to religious organizations in Germany went unheeded. No one knew the extent of the funds being pumped into Germany from these Muslim countries to accelerate Islamization.

The mosque construction in Cologne initially met with much resistance, not least because of its size, with its two 170-foot-high minarets and large dome. The cost of the building is unknown, as are its financiers. Still, it is a spectacular architectural structure in modern style, now Germany's largest mosque and one of the largest in Europe.

When Turkey's President Recep Tayyip Erdogan, standing side by side with Germany's Chancellor Angela Merkel, inaugurated the mosque in Cologne on September 29, 2018, the Germans should have been awakened by his words, which confirmed that mosques are indeed command centers for Islam's holy war, Jihad.

"Mosques are our barracks, the domes our steel helmets, the minarets our bayonets, and the faithful our soldiers."

When confronted by the media, Angela Merkel refused to comment on Erdogan's warlike message. At the inauguration of the central mosque in Cologne, many attendees, including President Erdogan, made the so-called Rabia sign by folding the thumb into the palm. At the same time, the other four fingers pointed upwards. The Rabia sign signifies loyalty to the Muslim Brotherhood, whose motto is: "Allah is our goal. The Quran is our constitution. The Prophet is our leader. Jihad is our path. Death is our wish. *Allahu Akbar!*"

It was during this time—the first three decades of the twenty-first century—that Western Europe's fate was finally sealed, but only a few noticed it, and even fewer dared to raise their voices in protest.

By making the mistake of allowing Muslims to stand above the law, there was no other path forward than the one leading to civil war. The core of the Prophet's teachings—conquest, domination, and ruthless violence against non-believers—had been effectively hidden from the public, but it would later become all too evident.

Chapter 38 – Operation Kadyrov

December 11, 2033

Since Russia invaded Chechnya in 1780, many wars have been fought in the region, located in the northern part of the Caucasus, the mountain range between the Caspian Sea and the Black Sea.

Despite a small population of just over a million, the Sunni Muslim Chechens have historically offered fierce resistance and have inflicted several humiliating defeats on the Russians. For Muslims worldwide, the example of Chechnya serves as proof that a superior enemy can be defeated if one shows enough determination and willingness to sacrifice, just as the Prophet's warriors did fifteen hundred years ago.

No jihad fighters exhibit greater fanaticism or higher morale in battle than the Chechens, making them highly sought after as leaders and motivators at all levels in Muslim armies. Chechens are highly respected, and many have held leading military positions within ISIS and al-Qaeda.

In the aftermath of the Soviet Union's dissolution, which officially occurred on December 26, 1991, Muslim separatists saw a new opportunity and declared Chechnya an independent state.

It wasn't until three years later, after the chaos surrounding the union's dissolution had subsided, that Russia could act, attempting to crush the separatists with a military invasion. The Russian army leadership made the mistake of thinking that sending tanks, supported by a thousand infantry soldiers, to the capital, Grozny, would be enough to scare the Chechens into submission. After all, rolling in tanks had been enough in Budapest in 1956 and Prague in 1968.

The Russian army, which was in decline at the time, severely underestimated the determined Chechens, whose core fighters were former Soviet army soldiers. They were well-trained, experienced soldiers with good access to Soviet weapons, while the Russian soldiers sent to Grozny were young, primarily recruits in their early twenties. The Chechens, knowing that a Russian attack was inevitable, had three years to prepare.

The Russian armored columns rolled into Grozny with minimal infantry support, meeting no immediate resistance. However, this calm was deceptive. The defenders had turned the city into a fortress, complete with a system of bunkers, tunnels, minefields, and snipers on rooftops and in apartments.

During the night, Chechen soldiers emerged from the tunnels, armed with anti-tank weapons, and began to destroy the Russian armored vehicles parked in long rows along the streets. They targeted the rear of the cars, where the armor was weakest.

Hundreds of armored vehicles, including around fifty heavy tanks, were destroyed before the unprepared and often heavily drunk Russian soldiers could organize themselves for defense.

During the day, the situation for the Russians worsened as they tried to retreat from the city. Snipers fired anti-tank missiles from apartments above the tanks, targeting the vehicles' roofs, which had little to no armor protection, with devastating results. The well-trained Chechens knew that tank cannons couldn't be aimed at the upper floors of buildings because the firing angle was too steep.

The Chechens' tactics were reminiscent of the Finnish "salami tactics" used during the Winter War of 1939–1940, when the Soviet army corps invaded Finland along narrow forest roads. They blocked the way forward by destroying the first vehicle in the columns. Then, they targeted the last car, cutting off the retreat. After that, it was like shooting fish in a barrel. The long columns were sliced thinner and thinner, just like a salami.

Just as in the Finnish Winter War, the inexperienced Russian soldiers in Grozny were terrified and highly reluctant to leave their transport vehicles, which provided them with a false sense of security. The only chance of survival in Grozny would have been to abandon the cars and engage the enemy to clear a path forward. Russia lost two hundred tanks, numerous lighter vehicles, and eight hundred soldiers in just one day. It was a massacre.

The battles in Grozny led military experts worldwide to conclude that tanks were ineffective in urban environments. Several countries decided that the era of tanks was over and eliminated them from their armies. An anti-tank missile or a drone costs a thousandth of what a tank does. Tanks are also easily targeted by aircraft and artillery. After several failed attempts to take Grozny, which cost thousands of Russian soldiers their lives, the Russians resorted to their standard method: mass fire, a tactic they had developed during World War II.

Mass fire involves the maximum and simultaneous use of all available weapons, which requires ample ammunition. Heavy artillery rains shells down on the target, and rocket artillery and grenade launchers provide continuous bombardment. Heavy bombers, attack planes, and attack helicopters carry out intense airstrikes. Tank cannons fire armor-piercing rounds and explosive shells, supported by automatic cannons, rocket launchers, and machine guns. No distinction is made between targets. The entire area where the enemy is located is ruthlessly obliterated.

After weeks of mass fire, with tens of thousands of shells and bombs, little remained of the Chechen capital, Grozny, but a smoldering pile of rubble.

The Swedish military leadership was deeply concerned about how Malmö could be liberated. Through infiltrators and by intercepting the Muslims' radio communications, the Swedes began to understand what awaited them. The Muslims' standard phrase in their defense planning was, "We will make Malmö the next Grozny," which was an ominous sign. The Swedes knew all too well what "the next Grozny" meant, as the Battle of Grozny is studied in military academies worldwide, including Karlberg in Sweden.

Using the Russian method of mass fire was out of the question, and in any case, the resources weren't there. A siege wasn't an option either, as it would lead to tens of thousands of Swedes dying from starvation.

Malmö had to be taken soon without reducing the entire city to rubble. A ground attack was not feasible; the enemy was too well entrenched in their defensive positions. Such an attack would result in enormous casualties with very little chance of success. The risk of turning Malmö into another Grozny was too significant. A ground attack was quickly ruled out.

Massively deploying paratroopers at strategic points could have provided a partial solution. Still, more resources were needed for this, as there was a shortage of planes and paratroopers. Moreover, deploying paratroopers deep into enemy territory is a hazardous endeavor. Military history is filled with disastrous airborne operations in which paratroopers were quickly surrounded and annihilated or killed before they even reached the ground.

Given the Swedes' total naval superiority, an attack from the sea had better chances of success. Landing and establishing beachheads would occur under intense fire but was still considered feasible. However, after the landing, the troops would still be drawn into the bloody and hopeless ground battles they wanted to avoid. An attack from the sea was just a more complicated way to conduct a ground assault. Nonetheless, naval superiority could still be leveraged in combination with another operation.

All the options were either impossible or, at best, inferior. Inspired by Grozny's defenders, who had successfully used underground tunnels, the Swedish staff, under the leadership of Alfred Baksi, began investigating Malmö's underground infrastructure. Baksi actively sought out anyone who might know about the tunnels, which led to an initial large meeting with representatives from Malmö City, plumbing and electrical companies, infrastructure companies like Eon and Svenska Kraftnät, construction firms, various civil engineers, consultants, demolition experts, and engineers from the Sjölunda Water Treatment Plant.

Before long, the staff had access to detailed maps of Malmö's underground network, with marked connections to the surface. Most major cities use tunnels for large-scale sewage systems, but in Malmö, pipes have always been used. However, the future for the growing metropolitan region was sewage tunnels, which had led the politicians to approve the construction of a four-mile-long sewage tunnel extending from the Turbine Treatment Plant at Malmö Technical Museum, eastward, under the harbor areas, always north of the railway tracks, continuing eastward past Malmö Central Station.

At the street of Flintrännegatan, the tunnel veered north toward the Sjölunda Treatment Plant. The tunnel was under construction, with planned commissioning in 2035. Additionally, two connection tunnels, each just about half a mile long, were being built. One connection tunnel was being constructed from the Rosendals Pump Station at the street Byggmästaregatan 21, connecting to the main tunnel under the street of Västkustvägen. The other connection led from the Spillepengen Pump Station directly to the Sjölunda Treatment Plant.

About ten cable tunnels were identified, which were too small for large operations but could be suitable for smaller sabotage groups. The staff, who were unanimous in their conclusion, quickly determined that the liberation of Malmö would begin from underground, possibly supported by an attack from the sea.

In the chaos that invariably arises during battle, they anticipated opportunities for local ground attacks by smaller infantry units here and there, driving steel wedges toward the city center, splitting, and isolating the enemy forces into smaller, more easily defeated groups.

The detailed planning, led by Baksi, Army Chief Svartenbrandt, and Navy Chief Fridolf Palmquist, the hero from the naval duel off Slite the previous fall, was extensive. It involved the navy and the army and included two main phases, with numerous sub-operations that needed to be synchronized as well as possible.

In war, plans rarely survive long once the battle begins, as the enemy's countermeasures are unpredictable. Amid the ensuing chaos, success depends heavily on improvisation, where the skill and judgment of the officers and commanders on the ground are crucial. Every unit must operate independently and to the best of its abilities. The determination and morale of the soldiers significantly influence the outcomes achieved. The operation, set to commence on November 11, was named "Operation Kadyrov" after the Moscow-backed president of Chechnya.

Drawing inspiration from the defenders of Grozny in 1999, the Swedish command decided to launch the assault with a surprise attack through the underground tunnel systems. To maintain the element of surprise, the number of troops involved had to be limited. The command decided that 120 armored infantry soldiers would enter Malmö through the tunnels, each equipped with an anti-tank weapon.

Just as in Grozny 1999, the infantry would emerge onto the streets in the dead of night to destroy as many enemy vehicles as possible. After firing their anti-tank rounds, the soldiers sought strategic positions for the upcoming battles. Although it wasn't openly stated, everyone involved understood that the losses among the infantry would be severe. Rumors whispered that it was a suicide mission.

Simultaneously with the infantry's action, Swedish warships would move towards Malmö. They should shell select targets, but in a limited scope and with strict orders not to fire near the areas where the infantry was operating. The naval attack was partly a feint, designed to convince the defenders that a landing from the sea was imminent.

As the attack on the enemy's armored vehicles began, 850 infantry troops should advance through the large sewage tunnels under construction. Then, they should emerge onto the streets from thirteen different locations.

The main force would act once the fighting had flared up across most of central Malmö and the enemy had shifted resources to prevent a supposed landing from the sea. Large infantry units would advance above ground towards Malmö's center, clearing as much territory as possible of enemy forces.

In total, twenty-three thousand soldiers and three surface ships would be involved in Operation Kadyrov: The Battle of Malmö.

The plan was complex, with many elements that needed to be synchronized, but not so complex that it couldn't work. Of course, every operation launched by general staff is believed to be foolproof, but military history is full of examples where things didn't go as planned.

Chapter 39 – War Fatigue

December 12, 2033

This time, the council meeting was held in Finspång. National Order Councilor Björn Väster hosted the event and chose Finspång Castle as the venue so the other three council members could witness the ongoing operations firsthand.

Väster had no desire to bear sole responsibility for the executions of thousands of Swedes. No one could predict what kind of regime might seek revenge on those accountable in the future, and now the other council members would no longer be able to claim they did not know what took place in Finspång.

Väster had ensured that a photographer documented the arrival of the council members at the castle. The council members were now Väster's captives, though they didn't realize it. At the very least, none of them could later accuse Väster of acting without their knowledge and approval. As the saying goes, covering all bases is essential.

The daily executions continued, albeit at a slightly reduced pace. Currently, about five people were being executed by firing squad each day at the shooting range, which was visible from the conference room Väster had booked. Väster had made sure that a total of fifteen executions would take place during the council meeting, all before 6 p.m. when the truck carrying the bodies, always punctually, would depart to dump them in the Krokstorp mine.

Brännström had politely but firmly declined Väster's offer for a brief sightseeing tour of the Krokstorp mine. He claimed to have never heard of the particular execution site in Rökstorp Mo and expressed no desire to see it.

Väster struggled to hide his disappointment. The council members wouldn't even go down to the shooting range to witness an execution up close, which Väster thought would be a fitting break to stretch their legs and get some fresh air. Watching traitors and enemies of the people, have their chests torn apart by automatic fire was, in Väster's mind, as refreshing as the chilly December air. But Brännström insisted there wasn't time. The schedule was jam-packed, with many important points to cover. Critical decisions needed to be made to determine Sweden's future, Brännström emphasized.

Väster, who had instructed the photographer to be ready at the shooting range, felt somewhat insulted by Brännström's lack of interest. He was proud of the well-oiled organization he had built, which the other council members barely acknowledged. He knew what he was doing was good, which must be enough. He was getting old enough not to need anyone's praise or validation anymore. Väster was his own man, happiest when he was his boss and making his own decisions.

But it still bothered him that he always had to take on the dirty work, and it bothered him even more that the others barely showed any interest in the projects crucial for Sweden's future.

Without Väster's efforts, there wouldn't be any future at all. He was the one tasked with the thankless job of cleaning up after the complete collapse of Swedish democracy, which had plunged the country into war. According to today's agenda, he had twenty minutes to report on the state of the Procession for Oath of Allegiance, the deportations, and the ongoing and ever-expanding de-Islamization program. Twenty minutes— what a joke! He needed three hours.

The only person of any importance who explicitly showed appreciation for his efforts was Ernst Höök, his subordinate. "Ingratitude is the world's reward," Väster thought bitterly, "but what won't a man do for his own country?"

During Brännström's opening speech, short bursts of automatic fire rang out from the shooting range twice, ten minutes apart. Väster had opened the air vent to its maximum so that the sharp sounds of the gunfire would be heard, and they echoed loudly between the room's stone walls. Brännström was momentarily thrown off, and his expression troubled as he furrowed his brow and lightly shook his head before regaining his focus. After the opening speech, it was Baksi's turn.

"Now we find ourselves in an unofficial ceasefire, likely to hold until we move into Malmö, which will happen very soon. I expect we'll have to fight for every building. The losses will be significant, but we have no other choice."

"No, we don't," Väster replied. "A prolonged siege would only mean that the Swedes starve while the Muslims consume whatever food remains."

"We can't wait with Malmö," Brännström said, "but as we prepare to liberate the city, we also need to start planning an offensive in Western Sweden."

"I completely agree," Baksi said. "But the question is, how long do we have to wait before launching an offensive in Western Sweden? The army leadership says they need at least two to three months to gather sufficient resources."

"That feels like an eternity," Bertil Wiklund objected. "The intelligence reports from MUST are extremely grim. Every hour we delay, more Swedes are being executed. MUST estimates that around fifty thousand Swedes have already been executed in the Muslim-controlled zone in Western Sweden. Our intelligence agents have intercepted plans for many more hangings. It's only going to get worse."

"And let's not forget the cultural devastation," Brännström added. "They've supposedly drilled away every single petroglyph in Tanums Hede. The fortress in Marstrand has been blown to bits. Nearly every historic building in Gothenburg and the whole occupied area is destroyed. Skara Cathedral, Våmb Church, St. Luke's Church—blown up, and I have no idea about the rest of the churches."

"I believe nearly every church in the Muslim-occupied zone is in ruins," Wiklund said. "Another sickening act is that they've sunk oil tankers and large cruise ships to block the ports of Gothenburg. No harbor is operational, which suggests they've practically given up on the battle before it's even begun."

"They know they can't break through Palmquist's naval iron barrier, so it doesn't change much for them," Brännström remarked. "But they intend to turn Gothenburg, Halmstad, Borås, and Trollhättan into new Malmö's. We can't wait. We need to attack with all available resources, and we need to do it very soon."

"It seems they're willingly giving up most of the territory to wage urban warfare in those mentioned cities," Baksi noted. "They're concentrating their forces in urban areas, using civilians as human shields, knowing they no longer have the resources to meet us on the battlefield.

Their strategy is obvious: to kill as many Swedes as possible and destroy as much as they can before they are annihilated to the last man. The *Holy Warriors* are eager to enjoy the seventy-two virgins waiting in paradise as the Prophet promised them."

Baksi stood up and began pacing the room as he continued his briefing.

"We need to make one more attempt at—" Baksi was interrupted by a short burst of gunfire that echoed so loudly he covered his ears, as did the others in the room. As he prepared to continue, he walked over to the window and looked out. Turning back to his three listeners, his face showed apparent discomfort. Väster couldn't suppress a slight smile, which Baksi noticed, glaring at him angrily.

"It seems they shot three at once this time. That's why it sounded so much louder than before."

"If three were shot, that's twenty-seven rounds in rapid fire from nine shooters. Of course, it will make a racket," Väster said. "I apologize for the disturbance. I didn't think the noise would carry this much into the conference room. Is the window even fully closed?"

Baksi glared at Väster and cleared his throat to steady his voice.

"Anyway... we need to make one last attempt with the Russians. If we can secure their support, we could launch an attack soon. I've met Ambassador Vissarionovich a few times with the traitor Gyllenstierna - Öztürk. He's a pretty dull character, but at least I've established a personal connection with him, so I suggest that Anton Baksi and I meet with him as soon as possible."

"Schedule a meeting with Vissarionovich," Brännström instructed his secretary, who was also taking minutes. "We have to end this war that's devastating our entire country. I'm so tired of this that I'm proposing we offer the Russians more territory if it means they'll help us put an end to the killing."

"I agree. Ending the war is our only goal—by any means necessary," Baksi concurred.

"Another grave issue is that we've received reports indicating they're planning to blow up the nuclear power plants at Ringhals," Wiklund said. "That could render large parts of Western Sweden uninhabitable for hundreds of years."

"We've already anticipated that. I've tasked our war hero, Max Adlerswärd, with a plan to secure Ringhals with a special force of ninety ranger soldiers and all possible support. We'll deploy them if we detect any attempts to carry out such an attack."

"Wasn't he supposed to retire after what he went through in Skåne? At least, that's what I heard," Väster asked.

"Yes, he did consider that. And I don't blame him. He and our fiercest sniper, Ina Sjöstrand from the Amphibious Corps, apparently fell head over heels in love and suddenly ran off to get married in Arild's Church. It's a beautiful, romantic place, by the way, that the Muslims never reached."

"Yeah, there aren't many churches left to choose from. Only cats have more lives than Max, and he's probably used up all of his. But if he's changed his mind, all the better."

"Max and Ina are available to recapture Western Sweden. The plan will be activated within a few hours' notice."

The meeting concluded in agreement, just before midnight, with the attendees worn out from the discussion and the war, which had been raging for a year and a half.

All military and political resources would now focus on swiftly ending the war. It was do or die. The war would be finished, and no sacred cows would be spared. No price was too high.

Chapter 40 – The Video Clip

December 14, 2033

"This film might give him the push he needs," Ken Persson said to Brännström. "Look at this!"

Brännström watched silently, focused on the tablet as the soundless film played.

"Well, that's our very own Alfred Baksi out there, enjoying himself, I see," Brännström remarked. "Looks luxurious—lobster, champagne, and all that. Where is this?"

"The film was taken on the Costa del Sol this summer, July twenty-ninth. It's at a place called Zhemchuzhina Ispanii in La Zagaleta."

"Never heard of it. The closest I've been to this is probably the Canary Islands. But why does the name sound Russian? I get bad vibes just thinking about Russians."

"Zhemchuzhina Ispanii is the name of Putin's residence. I'll give you the details later, but it doesn't matter where it is, does it?"

"What the hell was Baksi doing at Putin's residence? This doesn't feel right at all. Look, there's Gyllenstierna too! What kind of secret gathering were they at? And without even giving me a heads-up. I wasn't informed at all."

"They probably had their reasons for keeping it under wraps."

"A whole lot of fine ladies that I missed out on. Now I'm upset, ha-ha!"

"You should probably be grateful for that. Watch now!"

The cameras followed Baksi as he left the party, a young woman on each arm and a hopeful grin on his face, heading to his suite.

"Looks like this is going to be quite the party," Brännström said, a bit embarrassed. "Hell, I'm not even sure I want to see how this ends. I have a feeling it will get a bit too intimate for me. Threesomes aren't my thing. Neither are porn flicks, for that matter."

Persson said nothing as the film continued. Now, the trio was inside the suite. The young woman held one of Baksi's hands, guiding him to the bed. They began undressing him while kissing and caressing him all over. Then they undressed themselves, applied some oil to their palms, and gently started massaging Baksi, lying face down, his face buried in the mattress.

"Well, he seems to prefer them quite young and slim. How old is that Chinese girl, anyway? Is she even fourteen? This is nothing but pedophilia, for Christ's sake!"

The film rolled on, and after a few cuts, it showed a dark-haired, naked man by the bed where Baksi was lying face down.

"Ugh, that's disgusting!"

The film ended. Brännström shook his head, wearing a displeased expression, his gaze turning inward.

"By the way, where did you get this film?"

"The Russians. But they don't know I have it."

"How did you get your hands on it?"

"I hacked the Russian embassy a while ago and planted a few Trojans they won't find any time soon. I can read all the email traffic that goes through the embassy."

"Isn't it encrypted?"

"Of course, it is, but I was recruited as a top cryptographer by MUST, thanks to Bertil Wiklund. So far, I've cracked every system I've targeted. The problem is that it takes time, and the Russians are tough. Their systems have an automatic function that changes the encryption method—not just the key, but the whole methodology—every day. So, whenever I want to read something, I must start from scratch and spend a whole day on it. And even then, I can only read the system's email traffic until the encryption method changes again."

"Okay. But there must be a ton of stored information in those systems."

"Unfortunately, I haven't been able to access any databases. It seems almost impossible."

What Ken Persson told Brännström wasn't true. He didn't want to reveal that the Russians had discovered his identity. The truth was that he had been discreetly summoned to a meeting with the Russian Ambassador, Vissarionovich, where he was handed the film from La Zagaleta on a USB drive and informed that Moscow wanted Alfred Baksi removed from the National Council.

Long before this, Persson had tried to hack the Russian embassy systems occasionally but failed each time. The Russian systems were layered like an onion, with the innermost layers being impossible to penetrate—at least as far as Persson could tell. This was the first time he had admitted defeat.

Perhaps the systems could be hacked with the help of supercomputers, but he didn't have access to any. The Muslims had destroyed both the supercomputer at The Royal Institute of Technology in Stockholm and the one at Linköping University.

What bothered Persson the most wasn't that he had failed to hack the Russians. Worse, the Russians knew of his existence, which he believed was known only to Brännström, MUST Chief Bertil Wiklund, and former FRA Chief Rudolf Enbom. And, of course, Gyllenstierna—but it seemed unlikely that Gyllenstierna would have contact with the Russians after his betrayal. After all, the Russians had pulled the rug out from under Gyllenstierna.

Persson's intuition told him that it must have been the ousted Rudolf Enbom who leaked the information. In Persson's view, Enbom was released from house arrest far too early. It was impossible to imagine that Brännström or Wiklund would falter in their loyalty. It had to be Enbom; nothing else made sense.

Unless Persson had been hacked or bugged by the Russians, that couldn't be the case if they hadn't even known he existed.

It was clever of the Russians. First, they exerted pressure to have Enbom pushed out. Once Enbom was out in the cold, furious after serving his country with absolute loyalty, he was vulnerable to contact and, more importantly, without a source of income. After a lifelong career in the FRA, Enbom had access to top-secret information, which would be worth a fortune to a foreign power—most likely spelled R-U-S-S-I-A.

It was a significant blunder to oust Enbom without severance pay or continued salary. He should have been paid off to keep quiet or taken on a helicopter ride over the Baltic Sea. Persson would have preferred the helicopter option, which would have left no loose ends. A helicopter ride would have closed the matter for good.

He cursed himself for not having instructed Brännström, or better yet, handled it quietly. He had no one to blame but himself. Now, he was burned and would never again know who knew his existence.

The rules of the game had changed, and if he wanted to win, he needed to ensure that he wrote the new rules.

He felt it was time to consider what role he would play in the future seriously. Perhaps it was time to step into the light. Doing so would make his work more accessible in many ways.

Brännström let out a heavy sigh and stared intently at Persson.

"Well, that was disturbing to watch. It's good that pig Gyllenstierna is out of the picture; at least we don't have to wonder what he was doing there. But what do we do about Baksi?"

"Yes, what do we do about Baksi? For starters, it's unsettling that the Russians have leverage over him," Persson replied.

"Alfred is always talking about how important his family is and how much he loves his wife. I wonder what she would think of the film?"

"Are you suggesting we make sure she gets the film? We could do that anonymously if we wanted. But sabotaging his family life doesn't add anything."

"You're right. In that case, sending the film to him directly is better. He'd probably assume the Russians are sending a message that they have the footage, which would mean they'll be coming back with... let's say, 'requests' soon. But how could he be so stupid to fall for this?"

"He, of all people, should know everything about honey traps. He's set up a few himself during his career as intelligence chief," Persson remarked.

"Another option is to show Baksi the film and tell him we received it anonymously. He'll figure out that the Russians made the film."

"A third option is to tell him the film is everywhere and that he must resign because he's made a fool of himself. Someone on the National Council can't behave like that, especially not the intelligence chief."

"I think we're all in agreement that he needs to be removed from the National Council," Brännström concluded. "Option three is probably the best."

"That might not be enough, considering the knowledge and information he possesses. Unfortunately, Baksi probably needs to be silenced permanently. Anything less could jeopardize national security—who knows what he might do? Don't forget, he's a Muslim and best buddies with our dear traitor, Gyllenstierna Öztürk."

"The bastard! You might be right, even though I'm against that method, as you know. But regarding national security, the ends must justify the means, whatever those means are."

"So, you're saying Baksi must be eliminated. Should I handle it discreetly?"

"I'm turning a blind eye. Remember, I don't know anything about this at all."

"Of course," Persson replied, giving a warm thought to the bug he had hidden inside his jacket. The recording might come in handy someday.

"Honestly, I've been bothered by the fact that he's a Muslim ever since we first met. But it wasn't appropriate to voice those thoughts if I wanted to keep my job as army chief, and I did want to keep it. Although, that feels like a very, very long time ago."

"I never trust a Muslim. They're programmed wrong and shouldn't be allowed in positions of trust, at least not at the national level. They should be entirely barred from the military and intelligence services."

"We agree on that. Sweden needs to be de-Islamized on many levels," Brännström said thoughtfully.

"I promise to contribute to that with all my strength and energy," Persson said, smiling ingratiatingly at Brännström.

He could if Persson intended to outmaneuver Brännström, as he was confident. He couldn't just appear out of nowhere and take the helm. If he had ambitions to wield real absolute power, he needed to build a platform where he was respected within the military and at least somewhat known to the Swedish people.

Of course, he wouldn't be able to compete with Brännström's popularity, but if something happened to Brännström or if he disappeared, it wouldn't matter.

There were many ways to solve that problem without casting any suspicion on himself. Many people could be seen as motivated to eliminate Sweden's head of government. And there was certainly no shortage of methods in Ken Persson's world. Creativity had never been in short supply. There were always solutions to everything. He could handle this easily when the time was right and if he genuinely wanted to.

But for now, the priority was to remove Baksi from the board. After that, he could see what the future held. For now, his task was to keep Brännström in good spirits.

Chapter 41 – The Battle of Malmö

December 18, 2033

Jöns Möller was adamant that he and his *Snapphane* guerilla fighters should be responsible for the challenging and risky first phase of "Operation Kadyrov," where the underground tunnel system would be used for a surprise attack against the enemy's armored vehicles. And his request made sense. The *Snapphane* guerilla fighters had undergone rigorous training in anti-tank missile operations by the best and most demanding instructors in the Swedish Army.

Another significant advantage was that almost all *Snapphane* guerilla fighters were familiar with Malmö's street network. Many had grown up in the city and wouldn't need to worry about navigation when they emerged from the tunnels. The whole of Malmö was entirely blacked out, and it would only take a small mistake to get lost in the darkness and fall prey to the enemy patrols that monitored the streets around the clock.

Möller got his way. All one hundred and twenty anti-tank gunners would be *Snapphane* guerilla fighters, but that wasn't enough for him. Möller also insisted that the eight hundred and fifty infantrymen attacking via the sewer tunnels should consist solely of his guerilla fighters and the Free Rangers. Möller argued that the dangerous first phase of the operation, which resembled "Grozny," required both dedicated, self-sacrificing soldiers and local knowledge of Malmö. That was a decisive advantage. Möller's arguments made sense, and he got what he wanted; the core force in the battle of Malmö would consist of free soldiers from Skåne.

Möller didn't need to use his most potent argument: that he believed the Swedish infantry didn't have the necessary skills for the intense close-quarters combat awaiting them on Malmö's streets and that he feared the Swedes' will to sacrifice might falter at a critical moment. He had no desire to witness a Swedish retreat through the tunnels, leaving his anti-tank gunners to die.

Brännström, who appreciated symbolism, supported the plan. The people of Skåne would liberate themselves and take the heaviest losses. Now, the people of Skåne had the chance to write themselves into the history books as heroes, and Brännström liked history books, especially those about war.

It was decided that Möller would be responsible for the detailed planning, with assistance from Army Chief Svartenbrandt, Navy Chief Palmquist, and various experts, including the leader of the Free Rangers, Jeppe Hofman-Bang.

"Jöns, I hope you know what you're doing, putting so much responsibility on the Free Rangers," said Brännström, a bit concerned. "Can you trust Jeppe Hofman-Bang?"

"I know what I'm doing. Jeppe and I work together exceptionally well. His Free Rangers are elite and highly motivated for the task. I don't see any problems."

"Well, he's an intelligent and capable, damn psycho, I suppose, as long as I don't have to see that bastard. He even had the nerve to insult our King Carl Philip, and that I don't like."

"He is what he is, a bit twisted in some respects, but we've discussed that before. His force has grown to over seven hundred men, and we will use that when we liberate Malmö."

"That many? I didn't know that! That's almost as many as you have."

"I currently have 1,157 guerilla men in excellent shape, and more are eager to take up arms if we can train them. There are hundreds on the waiting list. We will deploy all the *Snapphane* guerilla fighters and Free Rangers in the battle for Malmö. Those not in the initial force of eight hundred fifty soldiers will come in as a second wave through the tunnel system. They'll improvise and exploit situations as they arise during the fighting. They'll also serve as relief forces when our troops get into tight spots. They'll operate in groups of twenty, completely independently, under strong leaders with full authority to make any necessary decisions."

"Sounds like the enemy will have plenty to think about," Brännström remarked, satisfied. "So, we have a simple and clear division: *Snapphane* guerilla fighters and Free Rangers will handle everything through the tunnels, and the Swedish Army and Navy will take care of everything else."

"The Muslims will get their 'Grozny,' but not quite the way they planned. I can hardly wait."

Möller, with his superior local knowledge, would lead the operation from the command center as best as he could once the fighting began. But when it was time for the regular Swedish troops to act, command of the remaining operation would be handed over to Major General Svartenbrandt. By then, the free soldiers from Skåne would act independently within their groups. Group leaders would decide whether to advance, retreat, or hold their positions where they were. The group leaders were, as always, equipped with radio communication, but when the fighting began, most of it would likely be jammed anyway.

According to the astronomical calendar, the sun was set to rise over Malmö at 7.39 a.m. The anti-tank gunners were to discreetly emerge from the tunnel system and begin their attack around 6.45 a.m.

At the very moment the first anti-tank shots were fired, the free soldiers of Skåne were to flood the streets at eleven different points and launch an immediate attack. Simultaneously, the Navy's mini helicopters would fire their Hellfire missiles, after which the Navy and Archer artillery would begin bombarding the harbor area. In mere moments, the peaceful night in Malmö would be transformed into a blazing inferno, designed to disorient the enemy and cripple any attempt at a counterattack —or at least, that was the plan.

The timing of each group's departure was calculated backward. The journey involved two to three miles underground on relatively easy-to-navigate concrete paths. The cable tunnels were so narrow that the soldiers would have to walk in single file, resulting in long columns of men.

The sewer tunnels were much wider but still under construction, meaning the ground varied from smooth concrete to rough surfaces that required careful footing. According to Möller's scouts, who had mapped out the entire system, there were even puddles of water several inches deep in some areas.

Several of the cable tunnels extended beyond the city area controlled by the Muslims, making it possible to descend and move toward the central parts of the city under the enemy's defensive line.

Through the cable tunnels, one could reach the main sewer tunnel and its two connection tunnels, allowing access to virtually all parts of the city.

The most extensive cable tunnels led into Malmö from the decommissioned Barsebäck nuclear power plant, with an entry point just west of Alnarp. This entrance at Alnarp was used by forty anti-tank gunners and three hundred *Snapphane* guerila fighters and Free Rangers. The rest of the forces used different entry points, leading to smaller cable tunnels, each heading toward their targets.

High-altitude drones showed that the largest concentrations of enemy vehicles were in the park Pildammsparken, at the square Nobeltorget, and in the areas around Casino Cosmopol. Consequently, half of the anti-tank gunners, sixty men, were assigned to these three primary targets.

Another significant concentration of enemy vehicles was at the square Posthusplatsen near Malmö Central Station, which served as a service hub for military vehicles. The railroad tracks had been torn inside the central station to accommodate military vehicles. Archer artillery was to target Posthusplatsen, while the central station was to be spared, if possible.

The rest of the enemy vehicles were scattered here and there, to be dealt with by smaller groups of anti-tank gunners, who would sweep the main roads and destroy every armored vehicle they could find.

It was decided that no naval or artillery bombardment would target the central parts of the city to avoid unnecessary destruction and because the Swedes were being used as human shields, with the Muslims entrenched in residential areas.

The naval attack would be carried out by HMS Luleå and two Visby-class corvettes—HMS Helsingborg and HMS Nyköping.

The Navy's role was limited by the risk that naval bombardment might affect the residents of Malmö, even though the harbor area was the primary target. Any missed projectile could continue and explode in the city.

Most of the sophisticated weaponry aboard the Navy's pride, the over three hundred feet long corvette HMS Luleå—the most modern and the only one of its class so far—as well as the two hundred feet-long Visby-class corvettes, was designed for naval combat. Torpedoes, depth charges, mines, radar, sonar, and countermeasure systems were useless for this mission. The automatic cannons, multi-purpose Bofors 57 Mk3 guns with a firing rate of nearly four rounds per second and a range of ten miles, could also only be used to a limited extent. The 57 Mk3, which equips warships worldwide, is excellent for anti-aircraft warfare and has tremendous destructive power against almost any target. Still, in this case, the city's buildings were in the background.

To avoid hitting the city's buildings, programmable ammunition of the type of FUZE 3P was decided to be used, set to airburst over the harbor area. Airbursts are effective against soft targets like troops and civilian vehicles but do minor damage to armored vehicles. A direct hit by a projectile is generally required to take out armored vehicles.

The heavy machine guns on the aft deck couldn't be used at all out of concern for the residents of Malmö. The Visby-class corvettes each carried eight RBS 15 Mk2 anti-ship missiles, with warheads weighing four hundred pounds. These missiles are ideal for taking out ships but vastly overpowered for destroying armored vehicles.

HMS Luleå carried 34 RBS 15 Mk3 anti-ship missiles, an upgraded version with more excellent range than the Mk2. HMS Luleå was also equipped with two uncrewed mini helicopters, each capable of firing four Hellfire missiles, an American missile typically used by drones. Given that the attack would be carried out in daylight, it was assumed that the remote-controlled mini helicopters would be shot down unless the enemy was surprised. Therefore, the plan was to begin the assault by firing eight Hellfire missiles from the mini helicopters. At the same time, the corvettes approached Malmö at their maximum speed of thirty-five knots, coming to an abrupt halt one mile offshore.

The Hellfire missiles were to be fired immediately at the armored vehicles on Posthusplatsen the moment the first anti-tank shots were fired, wherever they were in Malmö.

The bombardment with air-burst ammunition from the autocannons would be carried out stationary to ensure maximum accuracy. From this position, a total of three anti-ship missiles would also be launched: three aimed at the harbor Norra Frihamnskajen and three at the so-called lake Ökensjön, quarter of a mile north of Frihamnskajen, where large amounts of equipment had been stockpiled.

Simultaneously with the Navy's attack, Archer artillery would begin its bombardment from their positions in Bokskogen, north of Svedala, where the units could be deployed, hidden under the dense foliage. The bombardment of Frihamnskajen and Ökensjön would be carried out with 155-millimeter base-bleed shells, with additional charges necessary due to the distance to the target being as far as ten miles.

The Archer artillery would not target Posthusplatsen to avoid damaging the Central Station and other culturally significant buildings.

After the coordinated bombardment by the Navy and Army, nothing would likely be left in the harbor area—neither vehicles, equipment, nor troops.

After ten minutes of shelling toward the harbor area, the Archer artillery was redirected to the area south of Bunkeflostrand. Sporadic bombardment with thousands of base-bleed shells continued throughout the day or until the battle ended.

The entire coastline west of National Highways 110 and 108 was still in Muslim hands, down to Trelleborg. South of Bunkeflostrand, there were plenty of targets in the form of troops, vehicles, and other equipment. The artillery bombardment would also prevent reinforcements from reaching the area from the south during the critical first hours when the battle would be decided.

At 4 a.m., the one hundred and twenty anti-tank gunners began to move, descending into the tunnel systems at four locations. Sixty-six of them carried individual Bofors M/86 light anti-tank weapons, a recoilless weapon with a total weight of thirteen pounds, including the single projectile. Most of them had the so-called BU model, which could be fired from inside buildings without harming the gunner, thanks to an ingenious design and a slightly reduced charge.

The maximum range is fifteen hundred feet, but it should be fired at much closer distances to achieve maximum effectiveness. The three-pound heavy projectile has a shaped charge (SC), which focuses its energy as it passes through a metal cone, forming a concentrated jet that "cuts" through the armor. Despite its shaped charge, the M/86 anti-tank weapon has insufficient explosive power to completely turn off modern tanks equipped with TUSK armor or active protection systems. Still, it is powerful enough for most armored vehicles.

Fifty-four anti-tank gunners were organized into nine groups of six around the heavier and more powerful M/48 Carl Gustaf recoilless rifle, often called Grg m/48, which is highly effective. Each group consisted of a group leader, two gunners, two loaders, and an extra ammunition carrier. In addition to their primary tasks, the loaders and the ammunition carriers were responsible for protecting the gunners with their AK5 rifles.

One of the anti-tank groups was led by Kenny Alfredsson, the instructor who had trained the anti-tank gunners. His group targeted the square of Nobeltorget, which was considered the most challenging mission due to a large encampment of *Holy Warriors* near the square. The first projectiles were aimed at the encampment in hopes of quelling resistance before it could begin. Alfredsson's group was accompanied by another group of six, as it was believed that a doubled rate of fire would be necessary.

All the anti-tank groups used the m/75 tracer HEAT rounds, which had a shaped charge. Each round weighed seven pounds, making the load heavy for everyone in the group. The extra ammunition carrier had five double packs of grenades in his oversized backpack, resulting in a weight of seventy pounds. Naturally, the grenade carriers were always big and strong men. One of the gunners had the recoilless rifle, which weighed almost thirty pounds.

At 6.23 a.m., the first firefight broke out when Muslim guards detected movement at one of the exits from the main sewer tunnel. This was a setback for the Swedes, who partially lost the element of surprise. All remaining anti-tank soldiers exited the tunnels and moved as fast as possible to begin targeting the enemy's armored vehicles before they could defend them.

The first anti-tank shots were fired just three minutes after the initial firefight, and then the frequency of explosions rapidly increased.

Kenny Alfredsson's group, who approached Nobeltorget via the street of Lantmannagatan, was among the first to open fire on the soldiers' barracks on the north side of the square, at the corner of Nobelvägen and Amiralsgatan. At 6.34 a.m., Alfredsson, the group leader, gave his first order in a low voice.

"Load with a Flare."

The area around Nobeltorget was still quiet and dark. A faint glow on the eastern horizon hinted at the impending sunrise. The gunner carefully loaded his rocket launcher in the darkness and knelt into position. The tension in the air was palpable.

The shot was fired skyward at an eighty-degree angle, launching a Flare m/82. The detonation instantly transformed the dark square into a brightly lit scene as the flare slowly descended on a parachute. Now, the team had thirty seconds to identify their targets—the armored vehicles parked in long rows along the streets and clustered haphazardly in the square. They needed to avoid wasting shots on civilian cars, which in the darkness could be mistaken for military vehicles.

Thirty seconds felt like an eternity in such a tense situation. After only seven or eight seconds, everyone in the group had their targets locked. It was time to fire the first shots in the flare's light.

"Shots are coming!" the gunner shouted from his prone position.

"All clear behind!" yelled the loader, alerting the team to the backblast, lethal at close range and dangerous up to a hundred feet away. The gunner fired the first shot from five hundred feet away, sending the projectile crashing into the barracks where a large number of soldiers were stationed.

The gunner reset the mechanism and secured the weapon.

"Reload!" the gunner shouted.

"Reloading!" the loader responded, opening the breech with her left hand and flipping the latch to eject the spent cartridge. She inserted the new round, which she had ready in the crook of her right arm, into the breech with her left hand, then closed it with her right hand, just as they had drilled.

"Ready!" the loader called out, signaling the gunner was set for another shot.

The second loader crouched nearby, holding another round in his right arm.

The building quickly emptied of surviving *Holy Warriors*, who rushed out in droves, throwing themselves to the ground, crawling and scrambling for cover. But confusion reigned as they struggled to determine where the shots were coming from, and many took cover on the wrong side of walls and other obstacles. It didn't matter much, though, as the anti-tank rounds were targeting both the barracks and the vehicles.

By now, the second group, which had reached Nobeltorget via Torekovsgatan, had also started firing. The same well-practiced commands rang out repeatedly in hoarse, excited voices.

"Reload!"

"Reloading!"

"Shots coming!"

"All clear behind!"

"Bang!"

The thunderous blasts of the shots were somewhat muted by the double hearing protection everyone in the group wore, but each shot from the recoilless rifle sent powerful, hot shockwaves across their faces. Sometimes, their voices were drowned out by the roar of the other group's shots and the detonations of the Hellfire missiles fired from the mini helicopters. But the teams were so well-rehearsed that they knew exactly what to do, even without verbal communication.

All nine of Alfredsson's anti-tank teams reached their maximum rate of fire—ten shots per minute—but that was theoretical since they had to move between each shot to line up new targets. They had to make the most of their twenty-five rounds, ideally without missing a single shot.

From the sea, a continuous roar could be heard as the Navy's autocannons began spewing out air-bursting shells from the three corvettes. The twelve Archer units in Bokskogen rained down shells on the harbor area, resulting in deep explosions that shook the ground. The barrage of heavy fifty-five-millimeter shells was so intense that it caused a constant rumble, shaking the earth as the entire harbor area was pounded into rubble.

The enemy had now fully awakened, and the response from thousands of AK-47s across the city added to the chaos as they fired blindly, trying to locate the Swedish positions. The return fire from the eight hundred and fifty *Snapphane* guerilla fighters and Free Rangers was fierce as they engaged in intense firefights across the city in the pale light of the November dawn.

Alfredsson's group successfully fired seventeen of their twenty-five seven-pound shells, which had devastating effects. The first three shots had reduced large parts of the enemy's barracks to rubble, and the next fourteen had each struck an armored vehicle, causing them to explode and catch fire. The entire square of Nobeltorget, as well as the streets of Nobelvägen and Amiralsgatan, had turned into an inferno of burning cars and scattered bodies.

Alfredsson's team had taken cover behind the corner of a stone building, coming under heavy fire from several *Holy Warriors* shooting from windows on different floors. The ammunition bearer and one of the loaders, who had switched to using their AK5 rifles, returned fire. At that moment, disaster struck—four members of the group were hit by gunfire from a new shooter who had appeared in a window behind them.

Only Alfredsson and the sturdy ammunition bearer avoided being hit. They quickly dove behind a low stone wall in the square, leaving the rocket launcher lying sixty feet away along with a spare round the loader had taken from his backpack before he was killed.

"Cover me!" Alfredsson rasped, pointing at the window where the enemy shooter continued to pour long bursts of fire toward their cover.

The ammunition bearer aimed and fired his rifle at the third-floor window while Alfredsson crouched low, sprinted to retrieve the thirty-pound rocket launcher, and grabbed the spare round by its handle with his partially free right hand.

"Now he will get it!" Alfredsson screamed, his voice filled with a wild fury. He loaded the grenade into the chamber and closed the breech. "Cover me again!"

As the ammunition bearer unleashed more automatic fire at the window, Alfredsson set the rocket launcher on its bipod, lay prone, and carefully aimed at the target.

"Firing!" he shouted instinctively, squeezing the trigger. The grenade shot out, obliterating the entire apartment.

"That bastard's wallpaper now!" Alfredsson howled, his eyes wide with a berserker rage. He had transformed into a Nordic warrior, feeling invincible.

But new threats quickly emerged as a heavy machine gun on an armored vehicle opened up, sending stone chips flying from the wall they were hiding behind. The powerful, large-caliber bullets whizzed just above their heads, the armored vehicle inching closer while the machine gun continued its relentless barrage.

"Get out of here!" Alfredsson yelled at the ammunition bearer. "There's no point in both of us dying here. Go, now, fast as hell!"

The ammunition bearer followed the order, quickly crawling along the wall without looking back, while Alfredsson loaded another grenade into the chamber. Taking cover against the wall, he fearlessly exposed his entire upper body above the wall, firing a perfect shot into the front of the vehicle from almost three hundred feet away, turning it into a burning wreck.

In the corner of his eye, he spotted yet another armored vehicle approaching from behind. It was one of the feared, nearly unstoppable Abrams main battle tanks. Alfredsson knew he was in serious trouble. He quickly loaded his last available grenade into the chamber and closed the breech in one swift motion. Rising to his knees, he rested the rocket launcher on his right shoulder, determined to remove the tank before it was too late. This time, he took the moment to use the scope before pulling the trigger.

"Long live free Sweden!" Alfredsson roared as the armor-piercing grenade exploded against the tank's heavily armored front.

Alfredsson, who had long wondered whether an Abrams tank equipped with TUSK could withstand a direct hit from a Grg m/48 at close range with RSV ammunition, never got his answer. A burst of large-caliber bullets tore his body apart before he could see the result of his shot.

The second wave of *Snapphane* guerilla fighters and Free Rangers surged out of the tunnels across Malmö, rushing to aid their comrades who desperately needed reinforcement. Many of the groups were heavily pressed by the Muslims, who outnumbered them significantly.

Six anti-ship missiles were launched from HMS Luleå and the two Visby-class corvettes toward the harbor. The four hundred-pound warheads caused massive detonations that shook the ground across the city, sending large chunks of facade crumbling from nearby buildings.

Here and there, the regular army began to move toward the city center, meeting fierce resistance and having to capture buildings one by one. Their trusty old Grg m/48s often paved the way for their advance.

An unwelcome surprise for the Swedes was that entire large buildings exploded and collapsed as the Muslims detonated charges they had pre-placed in hundreds of structures. The Swedes also noticed that the Muslims were methodically using their automatic cannons to demolish buildings, at least when Swedish soldiers weren't nearby. The Muslims seemed to have no shortage of grenades but were suffering from a significant lack of ammunition for their automatic rifles.

After a couple of hours, the Swedish soldiers noticed the resistance weakening. The wild automatic gunfire, which rarely hit its targets, had become increasingly sporadic. The Muslims were relying more and more on single shots. Nearly all enemy vehicles had been destroyed by noon, leaving them without heavy machine guns or automatic cannons. Swedish regular forces closed in on the city center from all directions, occasionally meeting with groups of *Snapphane* guerilla fighters and Free Rangers, who reported that most of the resistance appeared to have been crushed.

The Muslims' ammunition shortage became more acute, and firefights grew fewer. The Swedes methodically cleared building after building, block by block, killing any enemy soldiers they encountered.

By the afternoon, more and more white sheets began to appear in windows, hung by defenseless *Holy Warriors* who preferred to remain alive rather than become martyrs. Those who surrendered were spared and gathered at Malmö Stadium, where over eight thousand prisoners were held. It took three days to eliminate the last of the snipers.

The total Swedish losses amounted to 4,653 dead, including 3,806 regular soldiers, 453 *Snapphane* guerilla fighters, and 397 Free Rangers. In addition, there were over eight thousand wounded to varying degrees. Of the one hundred and twenty anti-tank gunners who had gone through the tunnels, only thirty-four survived. The enemy's losses were never fully counted but far exceeded those of the Swedes by several thousand.

Malmö was liberated but at an enormous cost. The city was destroyed, and only a few buildings escaped severe damage. Most of the town lay in ruins, and of the buildings still standing, the majority would need to be demolished. Malmö was a ghost town and would remain for half a decade until the arduous reconstruction work could begin, aided by international assistance.

Chapter 42 – Möller's Reflection

December 23, 2033

As a final act before the inevitable advance of the Swedish army into Malmö, Ahmed Ben Barka ordered the city's destruction to level it to the ground if possible. The campaign of destruction was carried out under the banner of a fitting quote from the holy scripture, personally chosen by Ahmed. He selected verse seventy-four from Surah fifteen:

"And We turned the city upside down, and the bricks rained down upon them."

Most of the buildings were demolished by explosions, while others were reduced to rubble by artillery fire. The automatic cannons unleashed tens of thousands of deadly rounds on the buildings, indifferent to the people inside. They perished with the structures that housed them. After all, there weren't many Muslims among the landmarks, at least not enough to matter.

Ahmed viewed the destruction of Malmö as an opportunity to set an example for the battle that would eventually come for the city of Gothenburg and the Västra Götaland region. By then, it was clear that the war in Sweden was lost. The focus now was on causing maximum devastation and taking as many infidel dogs as possible down with them. Jihad forbade surrender, and Ahmed would never permit it, but in Malmö, things didn't go as he wished. When the ammunition ran out, and all resistance became futile, the outcome was inevitable.

The impressive high-rise Kronprinsen building still stood for some reason, with only a few bullet holes in the facade and some shattered windows. At three hundred feet tall, Kronprinsen had been Malmö's tallest building for years until the world-famous skyscraper Turning Torso was completed in 2005.

From his position on Kronprinsen's roof, Jöns Möller had a panoramic view of the entire city. He could zoom in on individual buildings almost one mile away through the large telescope mounted on the tripod before him.

It was a clear day with excellent visibility despite the midwinter chill. The sky was blue, the wind was still, and everything seemed frozen in a magical moment as if captured in a photo. It felt like gazing at a postcard where time had been forever suspended.

The Öresund Bridge appeared as a pencil line drawn across the horizon, stretching over the water to the unyielding neighboring country Denmark. It extended to the island of Peberholm, which, at five miles away, seemed inseparable from its larger counterpart, the isle of Saltholm. Möller had to use the telescope to see where the pencil line was broken— just beyond Limhamn, where the Muslims had blown up the bridge a year earlier.

Perhaps Kronprinsen had been the Muslims' headquarters, whose location the Swedes had never managed to uncover, Möller thought.

Maybe he should interpret it symbolically. Jöns Möller reflected that Sweden's then brave Crown Prince, Carl Philip, remained, now known as King Carl VII Philip, since his coronation on September 9 of the previous year. Carl Philip's time as Crown Prince lasted only five days between Queen Victoria's passing and his coronation.

Jöns Möller loved his hometown with all his heart, a city he now gazed upon with a deep melancholy. There wasn't much left of it. The "City of Parks," or rather what was left of it, desperately needed a new epithet. Perhaps it should be called the "City of Ruins" from now on? Or maybe the "City of Death," he thought.

In his hometown, it was here that the seeds of the well-organized, social democratic people's movement in Sweden were first sown. On November 6, 1881, the death anniversary of the warrior king Gustavus Adolf—chosen as a deliberate provocation against the bourgeoisie—the first speech on socialism in Sweden was delivered under the title, "What Do the Social Democrats Want?" The venue was the grand hall of Hotel Stockholm, located at 13 Baltzarsgatan in the Old Town of Malmö. The meeting drew more than a hundred attendees, one of whom was Jöns Möller's great-great-grandfather. After the meeting, he hosted the speaker in his cramped home. The tailor, August Palm, had no money and, like many revival preachers of that era, relied on the generosity of those who gathered.

With a deep sigh, Möller let the focus of the binoculars sweep back and forth over the ruins until he finally recognized the remnants of City Hall, located in Lugnet, near the site where his parents had moved into a small, single-story house as newlyweds. It was in City Hall that, in a fit of rage, he severed ties with his party comrades and left the movement on Walpurgis Night, nineteen years earlier.

He occasionally wondered what had happened to Mona Wahlbin, who had called to the meeting. Rumor had it that she had been brutally gang-raped and beaten to death. Could that be true? But she had disappeared. That much was certain.

Möller knew for sure, however, that Morgan Olofsson had been taken to Rökstorps Mo, outside Finspång, where he was executed under the most horrific circumstances imaginable. Möller shuddered at the thought despite being hardened by all the death and destruction he had witnessed.

Regarding his childhood friend Anders Skenström, Möller was almost sure he had been inside the Umm al-Muminin Khadijah Mosque when Zlatko Muslimovic blew it up. Mutual acquaintances had confirmed that Skenström had been invited as an honored guest and had gone to the mosque. But who could say for sure? Given the circumstances, Möller felt that all three had received exactly what they deserved. They were traitors to the nation. As for himself, he was just a fragment of his former self, but he found a small measure of satisfaction in knowing he had done everything in his power to save Sweden.

The City Hall stood at August Palm's Place—where else, thought Möller, as he pondered what his great-great-grandfather, a co-founder of the Social Democratic Workers' Party, would have said about the destruction of the society he had helped build.

In passing, Möller noticed that the beautiful old market hall was also nothing more than a memory. Everything that reminded him of culture and history had been systematically destroyed with precise efficiency. He tried to orient himself in the city he knew so well, but it wasn't easy, as all the significant buildings had been leveled. The Turning Torso, The Point, Malmö Live with its Concert Hall, Dockan, Triangeln, Kockum's House, Slagthuset—all landmarks were gone. Even the latest architectural pride, The Needle, which was to become the tallest building in Northern Europe, partially funded by the Qatari government, had been demolished before it reached half its intended height.

Sweden's flattest city, without a single natural hill, was once again almost as flat as the land had been before people took possession of it nearly eight hundred years ago to build a marketplace for herring trade.

Jöns smiled bitterly as he thought about how all the recent high-rises had English names, as if Swedish wasn't good enough for Malmö. Perhaps it was a desperate attempt to pretend the city was a cosmopolitan metropolis, a successful example of multiculturalism when, in reality, the town had been sharply divided between Swedish and Islamic areas. The big lie of multiculturalism had to be maintained until the end, he thought to himself. Why was it so important to uphold something everyone knew was a lie?

Möller's thoughts returned to the present and the harsh reality. The childhood neighborhoods around the square of Davidshallstorg were at least easy to recognize, even though most of the buildings had been reduced to ghostly, soot-stained skeletons. He hoped the movie center Filmstaden had survived, though he questioned what it mattered now.

The grand "Tailor House," Skräddarhuset at the intersection of the parade streets Regementsgatan and Fersens Väg, was still recognizable, even though it too had been bombed. It was there, at the street Regementsgatan 20, that the Social Democratic Prime Minister Göran Persson had lived in his spacious duplex before he moved into Sweden's prime ministerial residence, Sager Palace, by the Stockholm waterfront, following his divorce in 2004.

It seemed as if the circle had closed after 123 years, thought Möller. It was the irony of fate that the founder of social democracy had been a tailor from Malmö, and the very last Social Democratic leader who took responsibility for his country and his people had lived in Skräddarhuset, in Malmö. Persson's time as prime minister, after his move from Malmö, was just a two-year-long, painful stretch for the mentally exhausted Göran Persson, who had lost his energy and enthusiasm. As a resident of Malmö, Göran Persson made a decisive contribution as the leader who cleaned up the economic mess left by the former government led by Carl Bildt.

The uneducated, historically ignorant, and intellectually limited Social Democratic Prime Minister Stefan Löfven, who took office after the 2014 election, came to be the final nail in the coffin of a free and democratic Sweden. With a domineering wife whose life's work had been to promote Islam in Sweden, it could only end one way: "My Europe doesn't build walls." "Refugees, welcome!"

Möller gently touched the black, hard eye patch fastened with a strap around his head. Shrapnel from a ricocheting bullet had taken his right eye. He thought he looked like a pirate with a black patch over his eye, but several of his friends claimed he resembled Israel's armored hero from the Six-Day War, Moshe Dayan. But without the sinister smile, someone had kindly added. The comment mattered to Möller, who preferred to see himself as a good person who meant well. After all, at heart, he was a good social democrat. But not anymore. Not now.

Jöns Möller unconsciously shook his bald head as he gazed at his devastated hometown from his vantage point on the roof. What had been had been, and there was nothing to be done about it. And he couldn't imagine any future, not even one measured in hours. Möller had no idea that the next day was Christmas Eve.

All that remained was emptiness. Emptiness and more emptiness. There was the same silent and empty desolation before him, around him, and inside his head. He looked out over the ruined city one last time before it was time to say goodbye for good. He felt nothing, absolutely nothing.

Chapter 43 – A Bright Future

New Year's Eve 2033

It's incredible how quickly time passes, thought Deniz Öztürk as he sat waiting to meet the newly appointed commander overseeing all Muslim forces across Western Europe.

The secrecy had been total. Not even Öztürk's superior, General Yilmaz, the head of the General Staff in Kreuzberg, knew who their new leader would be. Deniz Öztürk was anxious and eager to know. If he could establish the right kind of relationship with the new commander, he would soon be able to address his own, far too low, rank within the organization.

Given that he had been both chancellor and supreme commander in Sweden, he believed he should be the one leading the General Staff in Kreuzberg, not Yilmaz, who, after all, was merely a military man, even if he was highly ranked. Yilmaz might be a skilled strategist, but he needed more depth. To manage an army position at that level, one needed to be as much a politician as a soldier, Öztürk mused. It had to be someone who could unite the roles of military leader and politician—someone like himself. Such talents were rare. He hoped the new commander was wise enough to recognize his qualities.

Just four months ago, Deniz Öztürk had been a Swede named Daniel Gyllenstierna, a completely different person. That was before he fully surrendered himself to Allah. Now, he was a Turkish Sunni Muslim. The time he had spent with the strictly religious Turks in Berlin over the fall had made a profound change in him. It wasn't just the beard that had grown, giving him the right look—he had grown as a person, internally, reaching a level of mental clarity he hadn't believed possible for himself.

There was an immense power in the teachings. The Prophet's message had taken hold of him and was now carrying him toward his goal, like a swimmer caught in a strong river current, swept along with no chance of turning back. There was only one direction and no return. Everything he did had a higher purpose. Every step he took on the street carried a religious significance. Every step moved him closer to the ultimate goal—Europe's final Jihad, after which Sharia law would reign forever. The weak, lost, and divided Europeans would stand no chance against the conviction and determination of the tens of millions of *Holy warriors*.

Many of the infidels would also choose to fight for the Muslims, consciously or subconsciously aware of who would emerge victorious. The number of voluntary conversions was already increasing, surprising and pleasing him.

Deniz Öztürk was convinced that all of Western Europe would be united into a single Muslim caliphate within two or three years at most. It was a bit unsettling that the war in Sweden was going in the wrong direction, but once the Muslims had seized control of Continental Europe, Sweden would be conquered again. Then, the Swedes would understand who they had defied and face the consequences of their stubborn resistance. And there would be consequences—death tolls on a scale not seen since the Muslim Mughal conquest of Pakistan and northern India.

Deniz Öztürk had a profoundly personal motive when it came to Sweden, a motive that fortunately aligned with Allah's will. Seeking revenge against the infidels who had wronged him was entirely in line with the Prophet's teachings. He would ensure that when the time came, he would return to power in Sweden—not in a military uniform this time, but in religious garb. The Swedes would face his wrath when that day arrived.

The Şehitlik Mosque, where Deniz Öztürk now waited to meet Europe's new commander, technically stood on Turkish soil, if one were to be precise. The cemetery where the mosque was built in 2005 was on land gifted to the Ottoman Empire by King Wilhelm I of Prussia in 1866. Yet, no one thought of it as anything other than the grand Şehitlik Mosque in Berlin, just a few miles south of the General Staff headquarters in Kreuzberg.

Under its vast dome, the mosque could accommodate one thousand five hundred worshippers, and it was only one of a dozen larger mosques in Berlin. Things had undeniably advanced since the early 1980s when operations started in an old potato warehouse near Oranienplatz, now known as the FHXB Museum, where "FH" stands for Friedrichshain and "XB" for Kreuzberg. Coincidentally, Berlin's heavily guarded Jewish

Museum on Lindenstrasse was just a few blocks away—a situation Öztürk mused wouldn't last much longer.

Öztürk glanced impatiently at his watch as he sank into a comfortable leather chair in the mosque's office. Occasionally, he'd rise and pace around the room, looking out through the partially obscured glass wall. It seemed the time had finally come as he spotted two men in kaftans approaching through the corridor. General Yilmaz was easy to recognize by his prancing gait. Öztürk noted with satisfaction that the slightly smaller man beside Yilmaz moved with more remarkable elegance. He looked fresh and fit, free of the big tummy that Yilmaz and most of his Turkish colleagues carried around. Öztürk appreciated men who cared for their health, smelled of cologne, and dressed smartly—much like himself.

Öztürk stood as the door opened, with Yilmaz holding it for his new superior. The new commander visibly started and couldn't conceal his utter shock when he saw the important person he was about to meet. Their schedule had been so packed that they hadn't had a moment to discuss the man they were about to encounter. The commander stared intensely at Öztürk before finally finding his voice.

"Daniel Gyllenstierna! I don't think I've ever been so surprised."

Öztürk remained standing, momentarily speechless as his mind raced to place the vaguely familiar figure before him. Then, the astonishing truth hit him.

"Ahmed Ben Barka! This is just too much! Unbelievable."

Öztürk shook his head repeatedly, showing how surreal he found the situation.

"So, you two know each other from before?" General Yilmaz tried to interject, but neither man paid him any attention.

"Yesterday, we led our forces against each other in battle—today, we fight on the same side," Ahmed said with a wry smile. "It's a small world, as they say. But I'm glad you're with us now because I know the qualities you bring to the table. They cost us victory in Sweden. Hmmm. It was smart of you to negotiate with the Russians. But now, I'm looking forward to a fruitful collaboration."

"I've reclaimed my true name, Deniz Öztürk. I've devoted myself to Allah."

"I should have made the connection; I've heard that name before. But I never could have imagined this. Of all the people in the world, you were the last person I expected to meet today."

The two men exchanged traditional cheek kisses before settling into their chairs, still wearing contemplative but amused expressions.

"We certainly have a lot to talk about," Ahmed began warmly. "But let's start with some old memories before we dive into the essentials. I'm curious about Sweden's relationship with Moscow and whether the Russians might involve themselves in the war in Western Europe."

"I'll tell you all about it. The relationship is quite complicated, so that might take some time."

"I've got all the time we need. But tomorrow, I head to Rotterdam, where we've established our command center to conquer Western Europe."

"Fascinating! This is entirely new information to me," Öztürk replied.

"We haven't released details about our upcoming offensive yet. You're the fifth person to be informed. But I can assure you, we're headed toward a bright future, given our allocated resources."

Öztürk nodded enthusiastically while General Yilmaz remained silent, observing the interaction between the two men. They mirrored each other, leaning forward in their chairs, unknowingly imitating each other's body language, and punctuating their conversation with nods, smiles, and affirming comments. Remarkably, they even resembled each other physically.

General Yilmaz was not pleased with the unexpected direction the meeting had taken.

Afterword

The problems in Sweden are so significant that it must be described as an ongoing societal collapse. The rampant crime is out of control. The queues in the healthcare system are years long. Swedes are becoming increasingly poorer due to the enormous costs of mass immigration. Yet the mindless mass immigration continues in full scale.

Swedish critics and debaters are being intimidated into silence by a left-liberal media mob that labels anyone who criticizes the mass immigration of Muslims as racist, which often leads to lost opportunities for livelihood. The method is the same as that used by the communist regimes that ruled the countries in Eastern Europe until the fall of the Berlin Wall in 1989.

The persecution of establishment critics is increasing and with new methods. A couple of months ago, I had both my private and my company accounts closed at SE-Banken, one of Sweden's largest banks, without justification. The method of excluding critics from banking services is used in several countries in the West.

This week, two more of my fellow writers are on trial. Their crime is that they criticize the establishment. Sweden has left freedom of speech and democracy behind.

Finally, I would like to extend a big thank you to my writer mentor who chooses to remain anonymous for fear of personal persecution

Djursholm, June 4, 2025